Destiny

Part 2 of the Liberty Saga

by
Rita Chapman

Strategic Book Publishing and Rights Co.

Strategic Book Publishing and Rights Co., LLC
USA | Singapore
www.sbpra.com

For information about special discounts for bulk purchases, please contact Strategic Book Publishing and Rights Co. Special Sales, at bookorder@sbpra.net.

ISBN: 978-1-946539-23-6

Prologue

Life—this existence which I am drifting precariously through—could not get any better at this moment in time, because it is as near to perfection as I could ever have believed or dreamed it could possibly be.

Without thinking too hard or dwelling on the past too much, I know exactly how far I have come from my beginnings and how far I have developed as a being of strength among those whose strength is almost unimaginable.

I know that my existence is the only one of its kind; at this point in time, my existence is a unique and unparalleled one.

I was born into a world that, on the surface, is ruled over and controlled by vampires. Their reign and rules are considered absolute; however, as I have grown within this world my eyes have been truly open—I now know that there are other beings outside of the vampire families to whom this planet and its inhabitants respond readily, though with less fear perhaps.

My memories of the now—the time from when my existence among these beings really began, when my mother and I were captured and imprisoned in an Enclosure—remain ever vivid in my waking thoughts.

I have only my dreams of the life I had before that, dreams of my father and distant family and friends.

These dreams occur regularly throughout my sleep and are all of the time before the Enclosure, and they show me images of long, velvety dark green grasses taller than my adult waist and magical in their softness.

In my dreams I see myself standing at the edges of thick, shrouded moss-veiled forests with gigantic gnarled ancient trees; there is no fear as I stand on the edge, although even in my dreams I have no wish to enter.

I dream of the warmth and freedom of sunshine, and within those dreams are warm feelings of happiness. Lastly I dream of my father, who is, and has always been, a handsome shadowy figure of strength that seems ever present in the shadowy world of my peripheral vision.

The first memory that I know for certain is true, the one of me standing with my mother, huddled with others in the dark greyness of evening, pressed tight against each other, all of us cold, frightened silent in our fear, and surrounded by guards and vampire disciples.

We waited while the Ophir, the Disciple in charge of the Enclosure, recited rules and regulations. I still cannot recall any of the words that dribbled from his mouth in a monotonous stream. My attention was only given when he ended his speech by informing us all that our lives were no longer our own and that we all, from that moment, belonged to a vampire master.

Enclosures are usually a standard collection of dull grey, dismally unhappy square buildings with no character or life, which are gathered within an enclosed or fenced-off area. These buildings are regularly and systematically patrolled and guarded by black uniformed Disciples, as if in some perverse way their content is precious; they are the holding places for the errant humans of the planet.

It was at the Enclosure that I, as well as many other children like me, were educated and prepared for the life on the outside or whatever role I would be given within my new vampire-dominant world.

Fortunately for me, my life was not as awful as that of many of my playmates, and very shortly after my arrival I became one of the more desirable children, foremost because of my much favoured blonde hair and blue eyes and then because of my intelligence and strength of nature. Although the vampires required us to be submissive, they also liked their humans to have a little of their own spirit.

It was because of these valued traits that, during my time within the Enclosure, I had a fair bit of attention from those who would see me do well, and from some of those who constantly spent time moulding me into a worthy human being. I became very much an object of their own pride, an object of achievement, almost a poster child for those humans who did not possess my looks or nature. I was held up by many of my superiors as an almost perfect example of humanity. (We were constantly made aware that there was no such thing as a perfect human.)

All the education and chances I was given were worth having, because during my Life Role Ceremony I was the one who led the others into the Arena. It was I who shone first, and it was at the ceremony that I was eventually given as a gift to David, the son of the Ruling Emperor.

Although I do not believe I was ever destined for bad things, the fact that David was given very little choice as to whether he gained possession of me or not still makes me wonder what would have happened if Rachael hadn't been as proud of me as she was, because it was a tradition which was invoked by Rachael as she tried to protect me from another vampire called Vivien that propelled me towards David and into his reluctant ownership.

Therefore, when I was just thirteen human years (the thirteenth year is the magic one, when, according to my world's tradition, I had symbolically left all that connected me with my human existence and I became mature enough to enter their world), one of the things that I had to say good-bye to included my mother.

From the moment the ceremony ended, I began a new life living in an ancient castle. To this day I haven't been able to find out exactly when it was first built. The castle stands alone, majestically tall yet foreboding and proud, with its roots firmly implanted at the centre of an ancient and sprawling Celtic Kingdom.

It is a vast and complex building with many rooms on many levels, both above- and belowground, and even now I still am not completely certain that all of those levels are safe for me to visit. There are times when I fear it as much as I love it, but I have known for a while now that the Castle and all those who dwell in it are as much a living part of me as the air that I breathe.

My new life began and continuously evolved within the castle walls. I am proud to say that I now have many friends there, vampire and otherwise, whom I love dearly and who have become my family.

I also have a secret within the castle. There is a being that very much holds my interest, a being as dark as my David is pure, yet I cannot easily walk away.

I have asked favours from him and given nothing yet in return, but I try not to think about this too often as I am afraid of the price I might have to pay.

For David and me, though, it took us a while to grow and become used to each other. We have found a way to blend, and now it seems we cannot be separated. There is an unbreakable bond between us that binds us together.

Proudly, I am now the Everlasting Life Partner to the most beautiful creature on this planet. He is tall and handsome with pure white hair and deep violet eyes. He is still a vision that continually takes my breath away.

My two closest friends, both Dwellers, also live within the castle, along with David's parents and numerous members of staff.

David was also born a Dweller. His infusion was done as part of a treaty which allowed the Dwellers to step back and the vampires to take control of our planet.

There are also on this planet beings other than humans, collectively called Earth Carers.

I remain human through my own choice. Although I am fit and healthy, I am also extremely fragile compared to the other members of my family.

My humanity remains ever important to me, although, due to a recent incident when I was poisoned and almost killed, I now have features that are more like the vampire faces that surround me than any from my human heritage.

My most striking features—and also, in my opinion, my best features—are my eyes. They were originally a clear pale blue, but since I recovered from the poisoning they now are an unusual mix of reds and blues.

Another thing that has changed are my senses. They are simply better than they used to be, and I have learned to open my mind and communicate with those with whom I wish to share my thoughts (but I do this only if the other being is willing, unlike some vampires who like to try to intrude on mine).

The only other thing I will mention is that since I was a child, I have been visited by an ancient being whose name is Sarah.

Sarah is a magical sorceress from a time many centuries ago who predicted the possible demise of this planet and the birth of a free child who will unite all the earth's Elements (races) and save the planet.

Sarah visits me in my dreams and informs me with some urgency that I am that "free child" and that I may be destined to become something much more. . . .

Chapter 1

Today the air is warm and still, and although it has been a few months since the Commitment Ceremony, in my head it still seems as though it all happened yesterday; I even have my precious dress still hanging in the room where I sleep. I keep it as a constant reminder of that perfect day and enchanted evening.

Immediately after our Commitment Ceremony, life seemed to become a blur for a while because there followed days and days of holidays, royal banquets, and special celebrations. It was exhausting since I was dutifully paraded in front of most of the population of this planet, or so it seemed.

On the day following the ceremony, as an extra gift to me, David's father, Emperor Marcarius, even decreed that the humans within the Enclosures be allowed a day of rest and to have the food of their choice, which I believed ensured my popularity among my own kind.

These days of celebration included the formal giving of gifts, especially some of the more exotic animals I still have no idea what to do with—and neither, I suspect, do the castle keepers who have been left to care for the animals as best they can. Some of the more manageable ones I have given over to Heather, and she has set them free in the expansive forests and fields that surround the castle.

The visitors and the guests who had become residents for a while within the castle eventually left and returned to their own territories, and thankfully our life within the castle settled again and became much like it had been, quieter.

I have tried very hard to adjust to my new life, but the hardest thing, which was also the most confusing, was getting used to the vampires who insisted on addressing me as 'Mistress.' There are, of course, also the vampires who refused to acknowledge me as anything other than a mere favoured human slave of the emperor's son, which is fine since I am just happy for them to know that they can't touch me—I am protected.

At first I felt that the eyes of the entire planet were on me all of the time. I felt as if I had even less freedom than I ever had; even within my home I became acutely aware of certain things I could or could not do.

Although I was allowed to move freely through the corridors of my beloved castle, it seemed too quiet at times, as if the castle itself held its breath in anticipation of what I might do next.

When I tried to speak to my friends of the way I felt, if they didn't laugh they dismissed what I said as nonsense. The only one who might have understood seemed to have gone from the castle; I never could sense him outside my door anymore as I had been able to in the past.

I also found that not all of those who observed me did so with indulgence. If there is one thing I have learned about vampires growing up among them, it is that they are bound by their own rules and traditions, many of which are outdated and overly stringent—at least, that is what I thought personally.

During our first few nights together as life partners, David and I explored each other both physically and emotionally, although I should add that on the emotional side the exploration is a little one-sided because with the introduction of essence into their bloodstream, vampires apparently lose the ability to feel. I suppose in a way David's detachment made my smallish outbursts all the more catastrophic.

I am no stranger to nudity. I had become accustomed to it even as child since it was normal to me to have no privacy, but the first time I fully removed my clothes in front of David it was different. I believed that he saw me as more than an object, and as I removed my clothes I felt myself blush with self-consciousness.

Fortunately David has always appeared to enjoy and love my humanity, especially the parts that make me blush or fluster. He often said that he found my shyness endearing and actually funny, particularly the part where, afterwards, I explained to him that I thought I was being alluring and seductive in taking my clothes off slowly.

Within the bedroom I seemed to be the one with all the pent-up emotions, and I know that on our first night together I was the more aggressive partner in the bed, acknowledging my own physical needs without knowing restraint, whereas David was methodical, tender, and thorough, his face serene as he concentrated on my body with his cool hands, until I burst with an almost primal scream; a feeling that I had never felt before tingled up and down my body.

Although David looked vaguely alarmed at my outburst, he also seemed to find it hilarious, and as I was trying to recover from his touch he started laughing. I wasn't offended since I learned very early on in our relationship that it was my clumsy ability to make him laugh that made him want to be with me, to remain at my side, and to know and understand me further. He was and still is very curious as to what makes me who I am. I smile to myself sometimes wondering if he knows how long that journey of discovery is, as I don't know myself . . . yet.

At first there were whole days when I was positive that his sole purpose was to watch me, suppressing smiles as I fumbled my way through my new daily routines, in some ways wishing that I could go back to the semi-anonymity that I had experienced before the ceremony.

Our afternoons at that time were spent doing seemingly endless interviews and having our photographs taken. Very occasionally when we managed to dodge the interested parties and castle officials, our afternoons were spent together exploring the castle grounds and taking the time to check in with each other. Most evenings I would eat and rest while David caught up on the formal paperwork required of the son of our ruler, and the future emperor.

The early mornings when the sun was at its brightest were spent inside, usually resting. I admit, during the mornings I usually slept well, the sun and warmth somehow making it easy for me to sleep deeply and dreamlessly, with no thoughts of any others. David and my friends who only rested infrequently accepted my behaviour, even encouraging it when they thought

I was irritated. It wasn't easy being human and living among beings that could last for days on end without needing to rest.

It was about a month after the ceremony when David did the sweetest thing and surprised me by packing up a few of my personal belongings. I know that Mia must have helped him because most of the things that were packed were my favourites, things I would have insisted upon myself. It turned out that he had arranged for us to spend some much needed alone time together, somewhere other than the castle or its expansive grounds.

We prepared to leave just before the Winter Solstice, which also happened to be my birthday. My birthday falls on the most celebrated day of the Vampire calendar; I was born on Halloween, which is still acknowledged as the Day of the Dead, a favoured day among the vampire beings to infuse their human subjects. Celtic tradition blurs the line between the living and the dead, claiming that the darker beings who exist in the shadows can sometimes cross the line and reach the living on that night.

We left the castle on the eve of my birthday using one of the latest hovercraft vehicles that had recently appeared on the transport markets. David loved these new travel machines and took every opportunity to tell me about the latest models. I did try to understand and look suitably interested, but they never seemed to make quite the same impression on me.

David had often offered to exchange my little car, which had been a gift from Theo, for something more befitting of a princess. I always refused because I still could not drive it. Mia could, though, and we would often go out driving together around the castle grounds (followed, of course, by my bodyguards in one of the larger castle vehicles).

The castle had acquired two of the hovercrafts shortly before my surprise journey. Theo and David had insisted that they test them personally. Although I was prone to worrying, I knew that my life partner was virtually indestructible, with only—to my knowledge—silver and fire to fear.

On some evenings I could hear the newly purchased vehicles skimming the grasses of the castle grounds as I drifted into sleep. There were times when I felt that David was happy for me to sleep so that he could do some fun male things like hovercraft racing, just as I liked it sometimes when he was busy and Mia and I went shopping.

These new modes of travel skimmed the land and the sea effortlessly; the only difficulty with them, as I understood it, was that they were too large to travel through forests or small valleys. Otherwise they could go pretty much anywhere the driver wanted them to on the planet. I am positive that if a smaller version were ever invented, I would constantly be travelling on a seat behind David, trusting him as I did every day with my life.

Although I would definitely consider the hovercrafts to be male toys, I have to admit that I was smitten by the huge one that arrived for our journey. Its interior was designed to contain everything any traveller would need. I think David had his hand in this one's design because I can only describe it as perfect, like travelling in a portable castle. When the metallic shield slid back and the floor panels opened, a glass floor gave both David and me a chance to view the beautiful green flatlands of the European Territories.

I had travelled extensively with David across the planet, but on previous journeys our usual modes of transport, fast cars and even faster jet planes, afforded us little opportunity to enjoy the scenery surrounding us.

On our journey now, even though the scenery was beautiful, the time seemed to go slowly. Although our quarters were opulent and luxurious, David seemed slightly restless, almost as if he felt trapped. In any event, the days and nights rolled on and I began to lose track of time.

I often became tired and fell asleep for brief periods of time, not always in the evening. There were times when I awoke to find myself wrapped up in David's arms. I often kept my eyes almost shut just so that I could watch him gazing out over the lands of the European Territories, the look on his face distant, his eyes bright as they scanned the horizon in front of him.

Whenever I asked David where we were going, he simply smiled and refused to tell me, explaining that he had given Mia his oath that he would not tell me our destination before we arrived.

After one particularly long sleep I emerged from our quarters and joined David at the controls. I noticed that we had left the land and were now travelling, hovering just above the water. As I approached him he told me quietly that we were almost there, wherever 'there' was.

The scenery had suddenly become much more interesting to David and me. We both felt a sense of excitement, although I am sure for different reasons. To me, the water looked deep and mysterious and filled me with a slight sense of foreboding. To David, I can only guess that it must have invoked memories held deep within him, his true heritage emerging close to the edge of his conscious mind, his eyes developing an unfathomable look as they scanned the endless ocean.

As I joined him he handed the controls back over to our driver and made room for me on the seat next to him. We remained seated in front of the large glass window at the front of the hovercraft as it continued to skim the top of the ocean waves. We saw nothing in front of us for what seemed like hours; all that was there was bright blue sky, the occasional bird, the occasional jumping fish, and darker waters.

Towards evening we could see a storm appearing off the horizon, with its black clouds rolling forward like a dark fog. The atmosphere within the craft also changed as the storm approached.

Eventually, after a tense period of waiting, the storm engulfed us, bringing with it dark atmospheric noises and bright angry streaks of light, the rain sounding thunderous, almost deafening, to my enhanced hearing. Beside me David remained sitting statue still, appearing almost transfixed as together we watched the lightning perform its wild vivid dance, the waves extending their white-tipped claws.

We passed through the storm relatively quickly, though, as the craft danced just ahead and out of reach of the rolling waves. There was very little respite, however, since another storm appeared to be approaching, but this time something else caught my attention. Running before the craft on the horizon was the most beautiful sailing vessel I had ever seen.

Chapter 2

The sailing vessel was like something from an old fairy tale. I just knew as soon as I laid eyes on it that it was as magical and mysterious as my home on dry land. Don't ask me how, but I knew from the moment I saw her that she was a she because she was far too beautiful and elegant to have been anything else.

I discovered later that the vessel was called Destiny, and she was heart-stopping, breathtakingly beautiful. She was an object you could truly feel love and loyalty for from the moment you saw her. At a glance I could tell how proud and strong she was as I watched her dancing on the rolling waves, skipping, rising, and dipping as she ran ahead of the incoming storm.

As she fast approached us she seemed to leave the storm behind her and the storm, almost as if it sensed its defeat, it appeared to dissipate and retreat as quickly as it had gathered.

Back at the castle, to fill my time I had taken to reading books on history, and though I am no expert, Destiny looked to me as though she had been modelled on sailing vessels from the early nineteenth century. She appeared to have been made during a time when boats had no engines to drive them—just masts, figureheads, and sails and propelled solely by the strength of human men.

As I studied her I found myself coming to the realisation that the vessel in front of me was no copy; she had survived for many centuries and had withstood the advancement of time as her builders intended.

Our hovercraft began to rise until we appeared level with her deck. As we were hovering steadily close to her, a section of the rails on the upper deck slid back as if we were being allowed to advance. As the edge of the hovercraft rested inches away, we prepared ourselves to board her.

There was a strong wind which carried with it the distinct smell of the ocean. I inhaled deeply before I let go of David's hand and took the hand of the sailor who stood poised and ready to receive me.

As I stepped forward onto her deck, I couldn't help but notice that it was made from the darkest polished black stained wood; there was an almost iridescent sheen on it which I knew would reflect the stars when they shone at night. I wasn't at all surprised, as I had already recognised her magic. I expected the wood to be cold, but as I bent down to touch her deck, the wood beneath my feet contained warmth as if she actually still lived. Her warmth sent a glowing chill up my spine, and I shivered slightly as I straightened at David's approach.

On top of her mast she flew the reds and golds of David's family colours and crest, but beneath it there was another flag which was black with a simple silver circle at its centre. When David saw me looking up at the flags, he whispered that the vessel was protected by Father Moon as well as by the emperor.

Once we all had disembarked we were greeted by one of the captain's men, a man of few words. He invited us to freshen ourselves and then, turning his back, proceeded to take us to our quarters.

As I walked down the corridor, I felt an urge to continue to touch her elegant surfaces and found myself running my hands along her smooth rails and panelled walls. Although there appeared to be a gentle, caring feel to her, I also knew in my heart that she belonged with the warriors who steered her. Even with my enhanced hearing there was minimal noise below the deck, and as we descended deeper into her hull she made no sound as she sliced through the vast oceans. Deeper in the spaces below my feet, I sensed she had a quietly beating heart; a rhythmic throb resonated up through the floor and into my soul.

When we finally arrived at our more than adequate quarters, our luggage was already there. David and I settled ourselves in and I had a short rest. After bathing myself I chose to wear a deep blue strapless, ankle-skimming gown. David chose to dress a little more casually. We were collected from the room by another crew member who also did not have a lot to say.

We followed as instructed. David's long, cool fingers sought my hand and interlocked our fingers gently, and for the first time I noticed the gentle sway of the vessel as she rolled gently on the waves.

The meal was a reasonably informal affair. There was some good simple food and lots of company. I would have said that the majority of the crew had joined us, and it was held in the Destiny's banquet hall. The vast room was decorated simply, strewn with garlands of pearlescent shells that were reflected in the dark, highly polished wooden panels of the walls.

I gathered that the crew consisted mainly of infused humans. They appeared muscular and well toned. The skin on their faces was almost the same colour as the vessel's interior. They all looked happy, even content. The captain who watched over them and the entire ship was a huge, surprisingly wrinkled Hiltian vampire called Anthony.

Even though I felt no malice emanating from him, I found myself greeting the old vampire shyly, almost cautiously. I did not understand why, but I felt as if I should have known him, as if he should have been important to me, as if I shared a bond with him. I tried to dismiss the feeling as my simply being a little tired, but as we walked away I could not stop myself from looking back at him. He was engrossed in a conversation with the hovercraft captain, but I knew he felt my gaze.

After that, David and I were alone on that first evening. He said he had seen the way I had looked at Anthony, but assumed that I was curious about Anthony's massively wrinkled exterior. He took it upon himself to explain that centuries of salt water and sea sun had aged Anthony's skin. I went on to ask David if he knew how old the captain was, and he explained that only his father, the Emperor Marcarius, knew Anthony's real age. He added that Anthony was another older member of Marcarius's staff and that he had looked after the royal fleet of ships for hundreds of years. He hadn't attended our Commitment Ceremony because he no longer felt comfortable on the land; he had spent too many centuries on the oceans and seas, and he found it difficult to stop the sway and stand still for any length of time when on land. He told me that Anthony's services during our journey were his ceremonial gift to us.

I sat next to David listening to his words and slowly drifted off to sleep as he went on to explain that the infused humans on board who served as the vessel's crew were individually handpicked for their more-than-human strength and their stamina. They were trained to be unobtrusive and discreet; every one of them, David said, could be trusted to maintain their guests' privacy. The crew manned the oars all day and all night, working to match the steady rhythm of the oceans, and those who were resting stayed silent and out of sight.

The next afternoon we were given a general tour, and each crew member we encountered appeared to show pride in his ability to maintain such a beautiful vessel. Many of them seemed unafraid to smile, and some even addressed Anthony in a friendly, informal manner. I was pleasantly surprised that he listened, took notice, and sometimes laughed at their freely given comments. It became apparent that Destiny was their very private world where they, as a united crew, had made their own rules.

David and I spent most of the hot, sunny days which we encountered on the southern hemisphere locked in our beautiful cabin. Out on the water the sun simply became too hot for David's skin to tolerate, and after only a short period of time his skin would begin to dry out and crack and blister if we tried to venture out on the deck.

He had tried to anticipate this and had bought some of the most effective sunscreen that our best scientists could produce, but still it was thick and needed to be smoothed liberally over the skin and was not conducive to David and me enjoying our time on deck.

Occasionally for my own vanity, when David was otherwise occupied with the papers and documents that he always seemed to carry with him, I felt compelled to find an out-of-the-way place and lie out in the sun just to give my skin a little colour and a healthy human glow that David really appeared to appreciate. I would lie on the deck of Destiny with my bare skin against her warm ebony boards, with the rhythm of her oars echoing her heartbeat.

The crew steered us to all the most picturesque places on the planet, similar to the ones that I had seen on the old-fashioned picture postcards that Mia and I had found in an old scrapbook in one of the less visited parts of the castle library. As the time passed luxuriously slowly, David and I continued to enjoy each other. We were becoming well rested and usually emerged in the early dusk refreshed and happy . . . and totally besotted with each other.

We usually then had something to eat, with David constantly trying to accommodate my human taste in food while trying to be discreet with his own liquid diet. We spent most of the nights gazing at the beautifully clear midnight blue skies and watching the bright silver moon and stars, and on the brighter nights we also took our time swimming in the warm, clear waters.

I shouldn't have been surprised that David was a phenomenal swimmer, which was another indication of his natural heritage. While we sailed on board Destiny, other than my care and happiness, swimming became his next priority, and after a few days we found our own routine: as soon as we emerged from our cabin, he would start gazing at the sea that surrounded us with an unnatural eagerness to jump in.

He was patient and kind, and at times he tried very hard not to laugh as he patiently tried on a number of occasions to teach me how to swim. And I tried very hard to understand what he was instructing me to do. I did not exactly swim. For me it was more flailing about on the surface of the water, trying not to go completely under. It wasn't necessarily unpleasant, but it wasn't something that I would gladly take up as a hobby.

But David could swim under the surface for long periods of time and went deeper than he should have been able to, even for a vampire. Often when he resurfaced he would tell me of a tingling sensation behind his ears. When I had first met David, I had noticed and questioned him about two small scars which were parallel to each other just behind each ear. He said he did not know where he had got them, although he had always had them and they had never completely disappeared. I knew enough about Dwellers who had been infused to know that the essence did not completely remove the characteristics of their heritage.

One night as David was swimming and I was resting, lying back and gazing up at the stars, the clear midnight skies timing my breathing to the rhythm of Destiny's heartbeat, I sensed a movement near me. When I lifted my head I saw Anthony lowering himself to sit beside me. "It is where he truly belongs, do you not think, Princess?" he said in a surprisingly deep and thoughtful voice.

I turned and followed Anthony's gaze; he was watching David as he swam and dived silently, hardly disturbing the flat surface of the still, black water.

"He belongs where the emperor, his father, says he belongs," I answered carefully, trying to speak with confidence and loyalty, not entirely sure of what the old vampire wanted me to say.

At my answer he smiled a friendly smile. "Of course you are right, Princess, but the pull of the water is still strong in him, don't you think?"

"Yes, I know, I also can see that," I said, not knowing what else to say. "But it does not matter. He will continue to do the bidding of his father, the emperor," I added, still unsure why the vampire was speaking with me.

He said nothing more about David; instead he turned and smiled gently at me, his smile openly reaching his eyes, making me smile back. I realised that, even though I was feeling a little unsettled by our chat, I liked this old vampire, whoever he was. "You feel her, don't you?" he asked.

I knew what he meant, so I simply replied, "Yes."

"You are rare for a human because you listen and you learn. Destiny feels you too, you know. She does not welcome everyone, and because of her choices we are honoured by your presence among us. If there is a time you have need of me, simply call me. I have a feeling that this will not be our only encounter," he said with a slight nod.

"Thank you," I said with humble sincerity, knowing that the ancient vampire was honouring me, although I had no idea why I would need him or how to call him if I ever did. The old vampire stood then. As he walked away, the fact that he had told me that I would always be welcome while he was Master of the Destiny for some reason did not surprise me. I watched as he disappeared back into the dark recesses of the vessel and then shut my eyes to let my mind drift.

Chapter 3

I continued to let my mind drift, trying to follow my thoughts, and realised I had missed something. While Anthony had been in close proximity to me, my Commitment ring had suddenly felt cold and unusually heavy; it felt loose as if it was made for another hand—as if it did not belong to me.

I reached for it, and as soon as I placed my hand over my ring, it seemed to warm itself and fit my finger again as it should. It was difficult to understand what had happened—did I imagine it? Even if it had happened, it was a mystery to me. Why had the ring reacted? I had felt no threat from the old sailor.

The thoughts unsettled me, so I sat up. I stayed where I was and watched David in the water. For my benefit he stayed just under the surface so that even when the night sky had very few stars and the water was black, I never lost sight of him. I shivered a little at the perfect sight of him. I felt a fascination watching him, knowing that he was one of the most powerful vampires on our planet and he was with me.

At first when David started these evening swims, the fish and other creatures of the oceans seemed to be afraid of him, almost as if they wanted to avoid him. As the days progressed, though, many of them simply appeared to have a look at him, their curiosity overcoming their fear. They seemed to have sensed somehow who he had once been, and although they kept their distance, they began to follow him.

I sat as still as possible, trying not to breathe so I would not disturb what was happening, mesmerised as I watched shoals of moonlit silver fish follow David's moves. David's own skin seemed to glow with an iridescence that was breathtaking. It glowed with the moon's rays and reflected deeply in his spiky pure white hair. The more David swam, the more he looked as if the ocean was where he truly belonged. There was a freedom that shone from within that was captured in David's eyes whenever he surfaced.

By the end of the first week, I would often wake up in the evening alone. When I emerged on deck, David would already be in the water surrounded by many fish; some that would have been classed as predators stayed on the outer edges of the groups. It was unusual for them not to attack their normal prey. Instead they stayed eyeing David as if his presence gave them amnesty.

It became harder to track the days as they progressed, but both David and I knew that we couldn't stay on Destiny forever. There was a real world that we, especially David, had to deal with.

I came up on deck on the second-to-last day and was stopped in my tracks. A whale large enough to consume a small boat rose up out of the water and seemed to present itself to David. I don't know how the leviathan did it, but it raised its massive body up until its head was clear of the water and then gently lowered itself until its huge eye was level with David's head.

Even though I knew most whales to be placid, this beast seemed to be almost aggressive as it stared down David. There was an imperious look in its eye that was fearful. I walked slowly forward, stepping as quietly as possible. It looked as if some type of communication was happening between them. The silence and intensity of the moment were almost palpable, and then the spell was broken and I saw David nod his head slowly; the seriousness of the look on his face told me that everything was far from all right.

"Liberty, I, no we, would like you to join us in the water. My beloved, I am asking you to trust in me as you always have. You will be safe at least for a while, and I have been given their word. I am told that there is someone who wishes to meet you, and it is someone that I would also want you to meet. Come to me and do not be afraid, my beloved." As he spoke, his eyes never left the whale in front of him.

I had goose bumps on my skin as I listened to his words. David's voice sounded calm but strange, as if he was being forced to speak those words against his will. "David, I know something is wrong. I can hear it in your voice. Are you all right?" I asked, standing still on the edge of the boat, not sure if I wanted to join him or not.

I tried to send a thought to him, attempting discreetly to see what was happening, but I couldn't. It was almost as if something was shielding him from me.

"Liberty! Do as I ask," he said with a sudden urgency in his voice, as if he were fighting something for control. "Please! Beloved, it is not polite for you to keep such a one waiting."

I trusted David and I knew that I had never met a being on this planet that could get the better of him. I had to believe I was safe, so without further hesitation I walked forward and started to climb down the rope ladder that we had unfurled earlier in the day. When I got near to the water, I sat down on one of the lowest rungs and put my feet in the water, slowly acclimatising myself. The water was cool but not cold, although I felt a chill of apprehension as I lowered my body into the water.

"That's good, my beloved, and now I want you to let go of the side and I want you to make your way over to me," he said softly, his eyes continuing to make contact with the whale in front of him.

"David, I don't know that I can," I said, feeling the first tendril of panic grasp my stomach, knowing that it was too far for me. I had only just learned to keep my head above the water for short periods of time when I was still, let alone when I was trying to swim as well. I didn't think I could do it.

"Liberty, let go of the ladder now and come to me!" David's voice told me that he wasn't coaxing me anymore; he was commanding me. So I did. I understood then that there were no more choices left open to me, or even to us.

As soon as I let go, I struggled to stay afloat. I tried to reach him, but the more I moved, the more I seemed to sink below the surface. I tried not to panic, to stay calm; I tried to think of the lessons I had had, but I couldn't. Nothing made sense to me, and suddenly I felt alone in the ocean. I felt as if I no longer had his protection and wasn't strong enough to do this on my own.

I tried to call to him, but every time I opened my mouth, it seemed to fill with salty water. I couldn't even begin to close the distance between us, and I felt my arms and legs getting heavier and heavier until I could barely move them. Eventually my whole body became too heavy to keep my head above water. I could hear David's voice pleading with me to try to reach him where he could protect me, but as I sank below the surface even his voice left me.

As I slowly began to sink, my eyes stayed open and I could see David, his beautiful body, his shoulders, his waist, and eventually his slowly kicking legs in the distance. He looked tiny next to the body of the whale.

Sinking farther down, I couldn't hold my breath any longer and the cool water suddenly seemed to be in my chest; I could feel it begin to fill me from within. At first I panicked again and tried my hardest to get back up for just one more breath, one more gasp of air, but even though I could still clearly see the stars, I knew that the surface was receding and just too far to hope for.

In a moment of pure clarity I understood that I was probably going to die, and all I could think was that after everything that had happened to me, they were all wrong; those who thought I had a destiny were wrong, and I felt sadness at the realisation.

I began to get sleepy—ready, I guess, to receive death—when I realised that it was actually quite beautiful down there, and that underneath the water the stars created sparkles that danced just below the surface. Once I spotted them, they were all I could see. They were mesmerising.

I didn't want to die with my eyes open because I wanted my face to register the peace I felt as I sank ever lower. Mentally I had already said good-bye to those whom I loved, wondering if my thoughts would reach them. With hardly any effort I closed my eyes as the sparkles began to fade and the darkness of the depths reached up to take me.

I had stopped living; I knew that because my heartbeat seemed to have stopped. My mind, though, was still registering what hovered around in in this watery abyss, and what would soon be my grave. I was no longer cold or frightened—I simply was, floating through my new silent world. I was just coming to terms with the fact that I no longer existed in the world above when I felt something—a push from real hands, hands pushing me upwards. It wasn't a gentle push; there was force behind it. Strange as it may seem, I found the fact that someone was disturbing my dying thoughts to be irritating.

I ignored the push, did nothing to help—at least I tried to until I felt another one. I heard a voice that I didn't recognise in my head say, "Get up!"

"If you are who they say you are, then prove it! It is said you have a task to do that will affect us all. Now go up! You who are supposed to love him beyond all others, you who are his chosen!" the voice almost shrieked at me, its high pitch slicing through my thoughts.

"What!" I responded suddenly, thinking clearly again. Already beginning to struggle to stop my descent, I responded, "I am dying, so how do I not give up?"

"You must return to him because it is he who is in danger now. The guardian will not wait forever. It is he who is being tested"

I knew that I loved David more than life itself, and if I needed to come back from the death that awaited me because he was in danger, then that was what I would do. The helpful hands pushed me again upwards.

It was so hard to wake myself, to connect my mind with my body, especially since I knew I couldn't take a breath. Yet my heart began to beat again, waiting impatiently for more oxygen to give it strength.

I concentrated on the movement of my body first. I willed my legs to work to push me upwards. Each of my arms mirrored the movement of the other one as I reached and pulled, reached and pulled, bringing myself upwards.

Eventually the darkness gave way to the real sparkles again and I could open my eyes. I was startled to see I was not alone. Watching me intently was a female Ocean Dweller. Her silvery white hair was long and fanned out around her in the water, creating a stunning white aura. The sparkles seemed to bounce off her iridescent skin. Her eyes were large and bright, the violet vivid with no trace of the black that David's eyes held. Her body was covered by a clinging material that followed the contours of her body like a second skin.

Although she stayed with me she offered me no further help. She simply watched as I made my way to him in my struggles. Eventually I could see the tail of the whale. I could follow the line of its body, until I saw him—or at least his legs. With a final effort I broke the surface of the water.

I didn't breathe immediately, so I couldn't speak, but I was frightened and suddenly so angry that our perfect time together, David's and mine, had been ruined. I sent a thought to the whale, simply telling it to stop. In response I felt only resistance, an almost impenetrable barrier.

If David was going to die, then I would have to die too, and I wasn't ready. Although I could only hope, I was doubtful of my ability to communicate with this monstrous animal, but I felt the whale hesitate. It was then that I felt the Ocean Dweller break the surface and tread water at my side, again not interfering but simply observing. I forcefully sent my thoughts out again to the whale—"Stop!"—and waited to see if my command could penetrate its thick rubbery exterior and break down its defences.

Soon it became clear that the whale was backing off and away from David. As the whale slowly retreated, whatever spell David had been under seemed to lift and I saw him become aware of his surroundings and the immediate danger he was in. David then spoke softly, with a gentleness that wrapped itself around me and lifted me. He said one word. He said the only word that would have brought me back to him and my world above. He simply said, "Liberty."

At the sound of my name, I realised that if I wanted to survive above the surface I had to breathe. I wasn't prepared, though, for the pain and the confusion that my body felt when I told it to take that first breath. As I breathed in, the air felt like fire as it travelled to my lungs. I suddenly felt extremely tired, as if I had been in the water for days, and not minutes.

The heat that travelled down through my chest as it did what it was supposed to do made me gasp again to breathe in some cool air, to cool the searing of the breath before. Soon my heart started to beat with strong regular rhythms, and I knew I would live.

David still remained dangerously close to the whale in front of him, no more than an arm's length away, but this time his posture was different; it was David who was facing off against the whale. And then something strange happened: a streak of silver flashed past me and came to a stop between the whale and David. The Ocean Dweller broke the surface of the water again, and David saw her clearly for the first time. "Mazu," David said in surprise, "is it really you?"

"David is the name you have, so I will address you as such, but you are still Makai to us," the Ocean Dweller answered.

It was strange hearing her speak; her voice was soft and melodious yet full of power. As I watched the pair of them, they seemed to be studying each other's faces as if they were trying to invoke a distant memory. Then, with the very last bit of my strength, I made my way to the rope ladder and managed to pull myself up on its lowest rung.

"Did you send this guardian to me, to us? Are you still representative of the Royal Argyra? Is the house well?" David asked quietly, his eyes still holding hers.

"You need not worry. All is well within the house," she answered with a gentle, subtle smile.

"Mazu, was it only you who sent the guardian?" David asked again.

"Perhaps," she answered softly.

David looked confused and asked why.

"I wanted to—no, I needed to—see if what your parents told me about your chosen path was true," Mazu answered.

"And is it?" he asked softly.

"I remain uncertain. I acknowledge she is more than she should be for a human, but she is still weak. I have to respect that I have just witnessed her pulling life back into herself when she thought you were in danger, and because of that I will accept her for now." At that moment they briefly broke eye contact as she quickly glanced in my direction, and the tenderness that I saw in her face when she spoke to David soon vanished. She said something softly to me. It was a single word; I couldn't quite make it out, but I suddenly felt a stab of heat behind my left ear. When I put my hand there to investigate, it felt as if I had been scratched. There was a thin line etched into my skin.

Before I could react, I saw Mazu reach forward and gently place her hand on David's cheek. She moved her body as close

19

to David as she could without actually touching him. "Be well, Makai. The oceans appear much larger without you. You are and will always be missed by us all."

"Be well, Mazu. It has been good to see you. Although I am surrounded by new friends in the lands above, I realise that I miss the tranquillity of my ocean home and the cherished ones I have left behind."

"And you, human, you also be well, for it is not simply your own destiny that you have a part in." With those words Mazu turned and gently placed her hand on the side of the whale. After a moment of silent communication, she touched the flat grey skin on the side of the whale's face and turned to me, bowing her head slightly.

"Come," she said softly to the whale. David and I stayed perfectly still as she disappeared underwater again, barely causing a ripple on the surface, and the whale, with its large black eyes never leaving David's face, followed her down into the depths of the ocean.

Chapter 4

D avid and I stayed where we were for a while, not moving, watching the silent water remove all trace of Mazu and the whale. After a few seconds there was no trace of them at all, nothing to show that anything had happened.

When the magical moment had passed, he turned to face me. For just a moment he was even more beautiful, if that was at all possible, than he had ever been. He had a smile on his face that reflected his joy at what had just taken place.

For me, when the moment passed I felt very cold and tired, and as I began to weaken and slip back into the water, David was at my side holding me gently to support me. He continued to hold me while he moved confidently up the ladder, supporting both of us. He held me tightly as he lifted us both onto the deck. On board once again, I started to shake with cold and exhaustion. As we stepped onto the deck, a line of crew members silently watched us. Their faces were difficult to read.

David seemed to know what was happening to me, because as he carried me he did it awkwardly, trying not to hold me too close, knowing that he could not offer me any warmth from his own body. He hurried through the corridors to our room, pushed open the door, and told me to stay on my feet while he began to remove my wet bathing suit. When it was removed, he sat me down and wrapped me in the thick, warm covers from our bed, but it wasn't enough; the chill was bone deep, and suddenly my whole body was trembling uncontrollably and my teeth chattered together so much they began to hurt. Alarmed, David called out to Anthony, who appeared immediately. David explained the situation and Anthony then disappeared quickly, only to return with a small glass filled with a golden liquid.

"Make her drink this. There will be no sipping—only one good mouthful and she will be okay. Its heat is instant," said Anthony, smiling at me.

David took the glass, and I opened my mouth to let him pour the liquid in. I swallowed the mouthful of fiery liquid quickly. I had never tasted anything like it, and I don't think I ever want to again. While it was tolerable in my mouth, it burned like fire when I swallowed. Its heat seemed to start within my abdomen and spread outwards, following its own path and reaching every part of my body. Within moments I had to push myself away, even from David's arms. Not caring about anything else, leaving the covers in a pile on the floor, I didn't care that Anthony was still standing in the door observing what was happening. I got up and I started to walk, to pace the floor backwards and forwards, gasping for air as the fire burned through my bones and perspiration drenched my body.

"My Prince, you might want to think about placing some warm clothes on her while she is still hot. The liquid I have given her is very effective, but it is short-lived and we don't want to give her another shot. That is something I have never had to do, not even for a member of my crew, so I do not know what effect it would have on her," Anthony said quietly.

He was right. I could feel that I was getting cooler but had no desire to try another shot of Anthony's fiery liquid. I quickly dressed myself in a soft top and matching casual trousers, and then I sat down and tried to relax a little. My core temperature finally began to right itself, and then Anthony merely gave David a nod of approval and discreetly left us, rightly knowing that I needed to have some questions answered by David.

The first question I asked him was who Mazu was. He appeared reluctant and started to speak hesitantly at first. He told me of her position as a royal bodyguard. With a little more persistent questioning, he finally started to tell me about the obvious bond that still existed between them.

He told me, with sadness in his voice, of their relationship before he was infused. As I listened I felt only love and compassion for him. He spoke of her softly, although because of the essence that flowed through his veins, I knew that whatever feelings he had for her in the past were no longer there. I knew he was lost to her.

As the morning sun rose fully in the sky, I lay exhausted in his arms and listened to his words. Occasionally I couldn't help but touch the scar that had begun to itch slightly, reminding me of its presence. When David saw what I was doing, he moved my hair aside and gently removed my hand. As he looked at the scratch, he told me softly that I was to leave it to heal, and then he said he was proud of me, proud of what I had done. But then his face took on a more serious look. He said he feared that this test (if that was what it had been) might only be the first and explained that the Dwellers from his past were hard to please.

I asked him to tell me more about them, the Ocean Dwellers. I knew that this would be a rare moment, that he had memories and knew what his real heritage was, but he had never been willing to discuss this with me before. This time was different because we both knew that I had experienced a small part of it.

He smiled and continued with his narration. I felt my eyes begin to close. Feeling warm and comfortable, I drifted off to sleep and began to dream of a warm, magical silent world beneath the ocean waves, with beautiful female mermaids like guards of silvery palaces. I dreamed of sparkles of light and caressing waves, of silver fish and ancient Dwellers of the deep, long forgotten by those that dwelled above.

When I finally opened my eyes again, David was still at my side, lying beside me and watching over me as I slept. There was still so much I didn't know, so feeling refreshed after my nap, I began to question him again, but not without telling him of the vivid images that had flashed through my consciousness when I was asleep. After a few minutes of thought, as if he was searching for the right words, he explained that the mark I was given behind my ear allowed me a glimpse into their world. My curiosity was piqued and I wanted to know more, much more, but the shrill ring of his phone broke through the mood and I knew when he turned away and answered his phone that the subject had just become closed.

I waited until he stopped speaking before I asked him who it was. He started to laugh slightly as he turned to face me. "You had better make yourself presentable. It appears we are going to get some visitors very soon."

"Who! What visitors?" I asked, getting up and making my way quickly towards the bathroom.

"Well, it appears it will be everyone," he said, still smiling.

I knew by the way he was looking at me that I would get no further information out of him, so I did as he asked and hurriedly set about the task of making myself presentable.

Chapter 5

By the time I emerged from my shower, David had already left our cabin and I could hear him up on deck chatting with someone. His voice sounded relaxed and happy, even excited, at the prospect of visitors.

I put on a warm jumper and soft comfortable trousers, leaving my hair loose and wet and my feet bare, and went up to join him. His smile got wider when he saw me, and he opened his arms in welcome. We stood together, side by side as close as we could be, on the deck to await our visitors.

The evening sky was beautiful and the sea was calm. The world felt good in that moment, and I felt suddenly blessed. We waited for a short while, watching the sparkles of the stars and the moon on the gently expanding ripples extending out from Destiny until there was a shout from one of the ship's crew who had climbed to the top of one of the main masts. David turned his head slightly, looking out at the horizon, his face relaxed and his eyes scanning the distance, and then he smiled.

I turned and tried to follow his line of sight, my own eyes straining to see what he was looking at. I could see nothing; everything still looked completely clear even to my enhanced vision. I continued to stare until my eyes hurt—and then I registered a tiny black smudge on the horizon. I was surprised to see how swiftly the smudge grew. Within moments it had grown until I could just make out the small shape of a sailing vessel. A few minutes later the vessel was close enough for me to see the castle emblem on its side. A few moments more and the side of the vessel was all we could see, since the castle warship dwarfed the dainty vessel Destiny.

It was sleek and imposing, looking every bit a boat of combat with none of the beauty or romantic lines of Destiny. As with all of the castle's vehicles, it was completely black and had no soul. The front of it was streamlined to an imposing point; it had holes in its side which resembled deadened eyes, a testimony to the aggression that the vessel had probably been witness to. I knew the holes hid weapons.

Even though Destiny was tiny compared to the other vessel, I still felt the strength of her underneath my bare feet. At the vessel's arrival, Anthony came forward and stood with us. "It appears that your sister has brought an unnecessarily large army with her. You know that very few are welcome by Destiny," he said, looking at David seriously, no hint of a smile on his face.

"My apologies, Anthony, but Mia can become very excitable when it comes to the safety of my beloved," he said, equally serious as he tightened his arm around my shoulder, pulling me closer.

"I understand. We all care for her safety. She does invoke a very strong need to protect, doesn't she? But it remains Destiny's decision," Anthony said, looking at me and smiling secretively.

I suspected then that David remained unaware that Anthony had had a conversation with me, and I understood that was probably the way it should remain. "I shall be below should you require me," Anthony added as he gave the black ship, which was now close beside us, one last disapproving look.

"Too many visitors make him nervous," David said by way of explanation as we both watched him go below.

Moments later a walkway appeared to reach out to Destiny, drawing us nearer until we were connected. Then they were there. The first ones to emerge from the warship were two castle guards, both of them looking apprehensive as they boarded Destiny. They were followed closely by Mia and Theo, who moved swiftly down the walkway towards David and me.

As soon as they reached us, Theo had me up in his arms and Mia was firing questions at David, although she knew I was well protected. Apparently, Mia had become a little worried when they could not sense me under the water. It took a lot of fast talking and a little while for both David and me to calm them both and assure them that I hadn't been damaged in any way. I reluctantly showed them the small scar that had appeared behind my ear, knowing that they would have discovered it anyway. That earned me and David some more questions.

By the time Rachael, my voice of reason, had arrived and had removed me from Theo's arms and placed me back on the deck, David and I had practically given a moment-by-moment explanation of what had happened, from both of our points of view. Eventually we stopped speaking and I laughed nervously as I noticed that the deck of the Destiny was becoming a little crowded, knowing how Anthony felt about strangers on his home ground.

Unnerved by all the noise and commotion, Anthony re-emerged from his rooms below and came forward. Amid the exclamations of surprise in response to my newly acquired scar, he stood facing me, ignoring the others, and gently tilted his head so that he could reveal to me the two scars behind his left ear. He pointed out that I was now qualified to be a member of the Destiny's crew, as they had all been tested and had survived by those who dwelled in the planet's oceans.

It was Rachael who interrupted Anthony. She bowed to him as a mark of respect and asked that we be allowed to share a meal on board his vessel. Anthony smiled at her, apparently appreciating the formality of her request, and after a moment's hesitation he agreed; however, he did not agree to all of our friends spending their rest time on his ship.

While some of the others returned to the castle vessel to get ready for dinner, the night's activities began. I felt a slight sense of sadness as I overheard Anthony instruct his cook to prepare us a final meal, explaining that it would be our last meal on board the Destiny. He commanded some of his crew to aid with the preparation of the formal dining room below the deck and then he left us again.

I had not really ventured too far beyond the cabin that David and I shared, so it was with curiosity and excitement that I got myself ready for the meal that night. I had always known that, like the castle, Destiny had its own lower levels, and I couldn't help but wonder what secrets they held.

Mia and Rachael had chosen some suitable attire for both me and David. They had chosen a sumptuous royal blue gown, which had various jewels sewed into the full skirt, for me; they had also chosen formal gowns for themselves.

Once we were all gathered and partnered appropriately, a few crew members appeared and escorted us down onto the lower level. We were led down a long sloping corridor which was dark and poorly lit, and the sound of the oars' rhythmic strokes grew louder. On the lower decks Destiny's heartbeat appeared stronger.

I couldn't sense other beings among the shadows as I could in the lower levels of the castle, and I admit that I was a little bit disappointed. It didn't take long for us to reach our destination, and as we approached, a huge double-fronted door opened inwards to reveal the dining room.

The dining room was magnificent, so long that I guessed it probably ran the whole length of the ship. Like the corridors outside, it was wood. In theory it should have been dark, but it wasn't, even though it had no windows. It was panelled from floor to ceiling with pale wooden panels, giving off an ethereal glow that warmed and sufficiently lit the large room. The air as we entered appeared to shimmer with warmth and light; it was almost as if the warmth and light came from within the wood itself. Down the centre of the floor was a huge dark wooden table made from the same ebony wood as the decks. On it were goblets and plates of crystal glass, which again appeared to reflect the inner glow of the wall.

Even though I was keenly aware of the crew's discomfort with so many strangers in one place, it was good to see all of my friends again.

Shortly after our arrival we were seated and served by members of the ship's crew. Anthony briefly joined David and me at the head of the table but was conveniently called away shortly after the first course had been cleared.

The food, as it had been throughout the week, was exceptional; no fish were served out of respect for both the ocean and for David, but there were plenty of breads, cheeses, and meats. For those who dined on liquids alone, large golden decanters were constantly offered by selected crew members who had been ordered to serve us as we dined.

We had an enjoyable meal together, full of animated conversation and laughter, and at the end Mia tried to convince me to spend my last hours on the warship with her. I refused, explaining that I wanted one more night alone with David on Destiny.

After the meal, the table was cleared and moved. Those crew members who could play an instrument or sing did so for our entertainment, and everyone appeared happy and relaxed. Anthony rejoined us for the festivities, sitting with Rachael and Theo, and often deep in conversation with the pair of them. I understood how Anthony would know Theo, but I was a little curious about his relationship with Rachael; they seemed to be very comfortable in each other's company, which made me wonder whether this was the first time they had met.

We all enjoyed the evening and stayed until well after the midnight hour, until I had to admit to David that I had had enough and needed to rest. Now that they were certain that I was safe, Rachael, with a nod from Anthony, insisted that everyone leave the Destiny, and David and I were once again on our own.

However, with the arrival of those who would protect me, the moments of peace that we had wished for were finally gone, and David and I spent our last moments together packing and tidying up. Both of us understood the need to leave the cabin we shared on Destiny exactly as we had found it.

In the early hours of that predawn morning, David had his final swim while I rested. When I woke I went to find Anthony, and together we sat and watched as David swam effortlessly with the usual ocean visitors who had visited regularly and had become David's swimming companions during our time on the ship. There was sadness in his eyes when he eventually left the water to join Anthony and me on board. With a final gesture, he stood and saluted both the ocean and its inhabitants.

Before we left, David formally thanked each member of the crew, and of course Anthony, for their hospitality. Even though I was a little in awe of Anthony, when it came to saying good-bye I felt safe enough to hug him even though he gingerly held out his hand to shake mine. Although he did not hug me back (David laughed at his slight discomfort), Anthony did not push me away and patted me gently between my shoulder blades.

The following afternoon we boarded the castle's warship and began the long journey back to the castle. The return journey was very different from the one that had brought us because we travelled extremely fast and were unable to see anything other than blurs of blues and finally the greens of the land. As we travelled back towards the castle, I regretted that I had slept so much during the journey there.

Chapter 6

After our return to the castle, our lives within it settled down again, too quickly for my liking. Again our time was not our own since we had to attend to things that were now formally expected from us. For me this mainly consisted of spending a lot of time parted from David. Sometimes I would not see him for days. Thank goodness for my friends and loved ones, because otherwise the princess life would have been a very lonely one for me.

Upon our return, David found he had a lot of work to do with his father, the Emperor Marcarius, especially in regard to his taking over the ruling of the planet within the relatively short span of ten years. All new rulers come with ideas of their own, wishing the planet to benefit from their guidance, and David was no exception. He had many ideas and modern changes that he knew would be met with resistance from the older, more traditional vampire families. One of the changes that was going to be made almost immediately, one that David announced shortly after our return, was that we were working towards free citizenship and equality for all Dwellers.

To start that process, David decreed that law-abiding Dwellers were no longer to be hunted, and their domains — the mountains, oceans, and forests — were to be respected. He proclaimed during a public announcement that they were to be treated with respect as the carers for the planet. This revolutionary edict was met with enthusiasm by most, especially those willing to improve the present strained relationships, but it was also met with strong resistance from some of the traditionalists. The idea behind it all was that the Dwellers were to be allowed the freedom to care for the planet in the hopes that they could repair some of the more damaged areas. David knew without a doubt that the planet was now suffering at the hands of those who had supposedly rescued it from human beings.

David also found it disturbing that since the departure of Samuel, George, and Miranda, we had discovered they were not alone in their obsolete views, that there were many others who, like them, had no regard for the planet or its present human or Dweller inhabitants; they just wanted to take or use up, never considering the idea that they needed to give something back. We also discovered that there were networks of small, almost unnoticeable groups spread throughout the territories who seemed to be following their own agenda and who appeared not to care.

I was so proud of him for the giant step forward he was taking, and for the way he made his proposals appeal to the majority of his subjects. It wasn't very often, but occasionally he asked me to accompany him and stand by his side, which I did proudly, as if I were the first example of the changes to come.

It was during one such long and drawn-out update meeting with the castle's researchers, when the various officials of the World Council were discussing the agenda, that I first heard of the possible existence of another set of scripts. In fact, there was the probability of more than one set, and although the comments were fleeting and perhaps a little dismissive, my mind snapped back from the daydream I was having.

Of course, I would not have dreamt of interrupting the meeting to inquire, but by the time it was finished I was wide awake and eager for more information. I knew my peers well enough to know that I would probably have to find out further information myself. I decided to give myself a little project at that point, and it was also a way for me to pass the time waiting for David.

The more I thought about it, the more it made sense. In our ancient history there were many groups of beings that had dwelled on the planet. Some beings were no longer in existence, but it was not inconceivable that there were other destinies that had survived; it would be narrow-minded of me to think that mine was the only one. From what I had overheard and understood, these other scripts described a different parallel destiny for the planet and its inhabitants, a destiny that was rumoured to follow the 'dark ways,' whatever they were. I had found a reason to get up early and to occupy myself without pining for David.

The next morning I got up with a sense of purpose; I found the possibility of the existence of other scripts and destinies fascinating. I couldn't help wondering as I went through the motions of getting dressed if there was another human child like me who was being nurtured and educated as part of the planet's destiny, and what these 'dark ways' were and what they meant for the survival of the planet.

I was frustrated but not surprised to find very little information in the research library. There was nothing at all about other beings. It was almost as if the large, ancient library with its vast history section was intentionally incomplete. I had to remember, though, that there were still places within the library that were closed even to me, the princess. I knew, for example, that Emperor Marcarius had his own vault in the lower levels that David would only be able to gain access to upon his ascension to his father's throne when it was time.

No one else seemed to be interested in even trying to find out if the stories about alternate destinies were true; the only one who did not dismiss me straight away was Rachael. I was grateful for that, and not surprised. As a teacher, she was open to the idea, but she could only speculate in the same way that I could; at least she listened as she always had.

Though David indulged me by listening, he was also dismissive as the others had been at the meeting. He simply wanted to believe that we could all unite and live with each other, and in doing that we could all learn to love and show respect for our planet again. To him the words 'dark ways' spoke for themselves, and they were obviously something to stay away from. David also seemed leery of my taking an active role in looking into the affairs of Sarah, scripts of any kind, and the hunt for Molly. He simply wanted me to enjoy my new role as a royal princess, which as far as I could make out meant a lot of shopping and telling others to do things for me that I was perfectly capable of doing myself. I also felt watched constantly, no matter where I went. I knew that it was his way of protecting me, so I just had to smile and pretend that it was fun and that I didn't mind. I did find, however, that he also wanted me to mix less with those who oversaw my well-being and spend more time with those who held a similar station to mine. When I questioned his reasoning, he pointed out to me that although I was surrounded by those I loved and who loved me, all of them were subservient to me now that I was his Life Partner.

I tried very hard to do as he wished, and I even organised some of the other royal princesses to spend time with me. I tried to be enthusiastic, but in truth it was awful. I simply felt like walking food when I was around them; I could almost see their nostrils twitching. Most of them had no respect for me when David was not around and made no effort to disguise what they really thought of me. Out of desperation and endless boredom, I asked for Mia to arrange for me to have extra tutoring with Tutor Vincent, Rachael, and Miss Davinia on anything, just to occupy some of my time and appease David, since I was doing things he approved of.

The visits to Miss Davinia helped me to gain a sense of the being I was, not as a princess but as me. Miss Davinia used to tell me constantly, when she thought she could sense me focusing on my humanity or on my insecurities, that all of the queens that presently sat beside their ruling partners were once human girls and that very few of them had come from any form of ancient bloodline. In fact, she showed me a sense of humour that I did not previously know she had by often laughing with me as she pointed out the mistakes of the other princesses. I had not seen her laugh since the death of her daughter Alyssa, whose death was also at the hands of the twins.

She told me when I looked doubtful that all of the present kings had taken centuries to find a mate that they would infuse. Some of them had chosen wrongly at first and had simply destroyed their chosen partners when they became bored with them; she laughed when I told her that those tales made me feel even less secure. Mia also laughed when I asked her about what Miss Davinia had said. She told me through her laughter that if ever David got bored with me, she would protect me against her brother. Although all the queens had agreed to be infused before the commitment ceremonies, historically I was unique because I was the only one who wanted to remain human. The other queens were breathtakingly beautiful, and I knew that I would have a beauty to match theirs if I had essence flowing through my veins, but it was one of the decisions that David said was mine to make. I wasn't in any hurry to become one of them. I liked being me, and this seemed to make me even more precious to my friends. Even at the beginning I knew that I needed to remain that way to each and every one of them.

During my time with Tutor Vincent, he was often accompanied by the young Prince Christiaan and Master Giles. I rarely got to see Master Giles, so it was always a pleasure to see him, and on the days I was with him, Rachael often joined us for some light refreshment served with his preferred china tea set.

Prince Christiaan was the younger and almost forgotten brother of the Samuel and George twins who had previously ruled the British territories and who had tried to have me killed. Master Giles had been appointed by David to chaperone and mentor the young prince until such time as Christiaan was ready to rule and control his domain. It was not going to be the easiest of territories to rule since Samuel and George had many supporters.

Christiaan resembled his brothers, and at first I didn't really want to be anywhere near to him, but after a while I found that he was the exact opposite of his twin brothers; he was charming and had nothing at all in common with his older siblings that I could see. He was polite and funny, with a wicked sense of humour and an infectious smile. He sometimes joined us in our lessons where Tutor Vincent explained the divisions of the planet. It was easy to understand why the twins had considered him insignificant and refused to give him any formal education. Christiaan shared the same views as David; he wanted change that would bring about the unity of the beings that dwelled on the planet.

Tutor Vincent tried to teach us the names and positions of all the twelve ruling families, where their domains began and ended, which family was next in line to succeed the throne, and so on. I tried hard to keep up with the quicker mind of Christiaan but often failed miserably.

Mia, to help me with my confidence, also sorted out some minor public appearances and more fun photo shoots for the world's media. Some of the minor duties I did with my friends, some I did with David, but most of them I did by myself. At first it was exciting seeing pictures of me everywhere. At any given time I appeared on more than a few plasma channels. I was seen on various entertainment magazines, and with the empress's encouragement I became the poster girl for human children, the 'look-who-you-could-become' girl.

Some of the pictures were taken inside special studios; some were within the banquet rooms of the castle. (These were my personal favourites because I was dressed in traditional vampire gowns.) I was draped with luxurious clothing and was given a dramatic hairstyle and makeup, and definitely looked the part of one of their princesses. Some of the more dramatic ones David had enlarged and framed, and he allowed me to hang them in our apartment. One or two of the photographs were taken at strategic shops, with me surrounded by my personal bodyguards, promoting certain premises as favours for beings that served David well in some way.

Janet and her staff had a full-time job just dressing Mia and me for our frequent public appearances. Janet taught me how to breathe, walk, and look relaxed in some of the more elaborate and restrictive of the costumes I wore. The more I was seen, the more I seemed to become popular with both the humans and the Nedas and Adwar vampires who dwelled and worked within the Inner Districts and their cities. In some of the reports, some beings still associated me with the old human story of a young girl called Cinderella. I read the story, and I must admit I liked the comparison. My days were once again filled and David could relax as he continued his own education.

David's next big project was to change the Enclosures, especially the way the humans within them were treated. He visited many of them with his researchers and then brought back what he had learned to the castle, where he formed another subcommittee within the Youth Council. To these beings he set the task of looking at and reforming the whole structure of the way they were being run. A lot of his Hiltian colleagues were beginning to understand and were coming around to the idea that closing their Enclosures and reintroducing more humans into the Inner Districts to live and work would be beneficial to everyone. We knew that these changes would take time, but we were happy with the general reaction to his new proposals.

Every spare moment that we were allowed to be together I spent wrapped in David's arms, as he discussed things that troubled me or asked questions as to what I might not understand. During those busiest early days I often also visited the Temple of Thought, and sometimes I would just go there to be on my own, just for a little peace. The temple did not accept everyone, and if Mia was otherwise occupied my guards would have to stay outside. Sometimes I encountered and welcomed Sarah and other times I refused to acknowledge her. At the times when I was completely on my own, I found myself walking around the temple touching its walls and surfaces and gently feeling it welcoming me.

The temple had its own powerful magic, another treasured piece of the planet which convinced me of its precious life. Although there was very little written about the temple, there were various stories of how it had appeared in the centre of the castle. Even though it was supposed to be as old as the castle, I sometimes felt that the magic within was as old as the planet itself. My personal theory was that the temple had appeared when it needed to, when we needed reminding of the life of the planet.

Sarah still persisted in her urgency for me to find more information about the missing Element and scripts. The Element was a Sky Dweller, a being who was previously believed to be extinct, and the whereabouts of ancient scripts that foretell the coming of a human child of freedom—which many believed to be me. I understood the importance of Sarah's words, but it was hard sometimes to convince her that there were a number of castle staff whose only job was to find the information for us and that nothing more could be done to make things happen any faster.

At times she was more impatient and dismissive, as if all of our resources never seemed to be enough for her. However, when I asked her for clues to the scripts' whereabouts, she had no information to offer; she simply implied that in order for us to do what was laid down in the scripts, we would have to find the scripts ourselves.

Chapter 7

On one of my 'free' afternoons I was given the job of selecting my own personal bodyguards. It was made clear that I had to select them from among the royal or castle guard, as it was traditional to do so. Even though I had heard of such a tradition, I had foolishly thought that with all the protection from my friends I would not have to choose the guards, but it was one tradition that David insisted upon. He offered very little help and refused to influence my choices. He would only tell me that I had to trust whoever they were and 'know' them on sight. If I was still unsure after I had spoken to all the candidates, he said he would give me encouragement but not advice. The reasoning behind this was that royal guards were all well-known to each other; there was a code among them that bound them to protect the royal families. Each individual guard had his or her own network of friends and associates and could probably find information on impending attack within any of the royal castles quicker than David's own spies could.

After a fair amount of resistance, I agreed to make a choice, and eventually with Theo's help I spent an entire afternoon and evening interviewing various guards that Theo thought might be suitable. At first it was easier, since I instinctively knew whom I did not want, but the selection process became increasingly difficult. Eventually, after what seemed like days of interviews, I acquired the customary two royal bodyguards, Alex and James.

It was an odd choice in a way. I chose them because they did not appear to want the position as readily as some of the others.

There was something about the way they behaved in front of me that drew my attention to them; they did not appear to have a lot of respect for me, even when they knew who I was and why they had been called to see me. They intrigued me, and the fact that my friends picked up on their attitude and warned me against them added to my intrigue. I made my choice. It took a little persuading on all sides, but with an explanation supported by Theo my decision was accepted as final and both Theo and I set about gaining a little of their respect and changing their surly attitude towards me and my friends.

To prepare me and help me to deal with my new bodyguards, Theo gave me a brief history lesson on the royal guards. He explained that they lived by their own rules and that they were the absolute law within the castle for all of those who worked there because they were handpicked and trusted by the royal families. They had their own laws, courts, and punishments. At first, even though I could have forced their allegiance because of what Theo had told me, I didn't; instead I gave them time and choices where they should have had none, and eventually they began to soften and trust me a little, and even started to suggest ways in which I would be better protected within the castle.

Although it was a group effort, with Mia particularly keen, it took much longer for us to make them appear to like who they were supposed to be. Mia had a vision on how she wanted us to look as a group in public. For the first few days, they had the annoying habit of seeming to stare blankly over the top of my head, with their faces displaying their inner disinterest. After a while, things began to improve and I grew to think they were the perfect accompaniment to our group in every way.

Alex was tall and blond with a perfect physique. He was charming and talkative, and he always seemed to know the right thing to say in any given situation. His whole demeanour was one of peaceful control; he was every inch the handsome royal guard, and he usually got a smile from any female who ventured near him. He knew his own charisma and quite often used it to his advantage. From Theo I learned that he had a reputation as a charmer among the females who dwelled both outside and within the castle—not a bad thing because he was a good source of gossip when he put his mind and special talents to it.

James was almost the exact opposite of Alex. His hair was dark and he was of average height, but in his own way he also had a perfect physique. But that was where the similarity ended. There was a fire within him that threatened to erupt at any given moment, bubbling just beneath the surface of his pale skin. Whereas Alex was smoothly talkative, James was a being of very few words. He constantly appeared to be on edge; it was almost as if he was afraid to speak because whatever he was going to say would be threatening or unpleasant. It was this dark broodiness about him that seemed to attract almost as many females as Alex's charm did. There was a definite attraction to his dangerous side. Yet of the two of them, it was James's smile that could light a room and melt the coldest of hearts. He rarely smiled, but when he did it was incredibly genuine. Of the two, James attracted and intrigued me more.

At the beginning they both remained aloof. At first it did bother me; in fact, it bothered me quite a bit, but I soon got used to them remaining on the fringes of my vision, doing exactly what was expected, and I decided it was enough for me just to know that they were there. David did not appear concerned by their behaviour, so neither did I. Unusual though for vampires, they were extremely close in mind and blood and they often behaved as if they were twins. Very soon it became obvious to many of us that they shared some type of telepathic link.

I couldn't be sure until I discovered it accidentally one evening. We had just returned to the royal apartments after I had been at one of my tutorials with Miss Davinia, and I was relaxing to ease some of the tension I felt; I found it hard sometimes to suppress my own darkness. Then I felt pressure from an unknown trying to enter my defences. It wasn't enough to alarm me or make me uncomfortable, so I simply stopped what I was doing and held on to the pressure. I turned to face them both, knowing that there was no other being near enough for it to be anyone else. "Which one of you do I have a hold on?" I asked, smiling sweetly. I did not apply any pressure, showing them that to hold their thoughts and minds was almost effortless for me. I watched and waited patiently as they made eye contact with each other before some type of decision was made between the two. It was Alex who nodded, though he seemed as relaxed as I was with the situation.

"We had heard that you had certain abilities, and we were simply curious and perhaps looking for confirmation," he said quietly. James stood still, staring at me, and I suddenly felt another mind wishing to enter—perhaps to protect his friend. Again it took very little effort for me to gather and hold the pressure I felt from him also.

"Are you both satisfied now, or do you want to test me further? Not that you have seen anything of the real me. If rumours are to be believed, I have almost unnatural abilities even for a vampire." I was still smiling at them as I spoke. I released the tendrils of their curiosity totally unafraid and continued to smile. I even managed a little laugh with a sense of relief, because for the first time since they had agreed to protect me, they were also genuinely smiling. I knew that finally I had surprised them with something they could respect. I had found the link to them that would eventually bind their allegiance to me.

"Can we press deeper? For a human you have a very remarkable mind," said an abrupt James.

"Of course, but not here in the corridor," I answered, laughing loudly. Then I made a little invitation: "Let's have a little getting-to-know-you period when we get back inside the apartment, since it will be empty and everyone has their own duties at this time. I believe that there will not be anyone there until much later."

When we got back to the apartment I was right we were alone. I poured myself a glass of orange juice, which was still my favourite drink, and joined them at the dining table, where they were waiting patiently for me. We sat facing each other, none of us saying a word. I looked at them both until Alex again tried to enter my head. I sent back the thought: *That is both rude and annoying. I will not deny you, but just ask before you enter and I will not stop you. I learned long ago that this is a safe way for me and those whom I consider friends and family to communicate and to keep me from doing silly things.*

How can you do what you are doing? That ability is not usual for a human. It is a raw talent, but your ability is stronger than most of even my kind possesses, Alex continued to question me silently.

I honestly don't know, but I could do it before I was poisoned. Maybe I could always do it, but I believe this ability grew stronger once I was threatened and needed to protect myself, I explained.

41

"Can I join in?" James intruded. "What have I missed?" he asked, looking at Alex. I sat back as I listened to Alex repeat what I had just 'told' him. James was curious about the other members of my group, but Alex did not have an answer for him. Out loud I said, "Most of the group, my close friends, know, and those who want to communicate with me in this way do. As I have already told Alex, this ability has saved me from embarrassing myself on more than one occasion. I do not try to listen when they communicate with each other, even when they are communicating in my presence. I can usually tell when those around me are communicating, but they all know what they are capable of and, although we try not to keep secrets from each other, it is up to you whether you want to reveal your abilities. It is not my place to reveal such a secret. It is for you to reveal."

After looking at each other and conferring silently for a few moments, James said simply, "We would rather not reveal ourselves just yet, like you. Our ability has saved us from embarrassing ourselves, and though we know all of our kind has the ability to influence, in some it does not extend to thought reading."

"Right, we will say nothing more, but please, I would ask you both to respect the thoughts of my friends and not to intrude without an invitation," I said to conclude the topic. After that, nothing more was said. I went for a bath while they chose to stand guard at their usual positions just inside the doors. All three of us knew that our relationship had changed; it was better and, in some ways, deeper.

Even though their link with me was also strong, they were true to their words and did not intrude on my thoughts, which was a good thing considering some of those thoughts I had when I was near David. After a while, when our trust began to build and they seemed to lower any last residual barriers they may have had towards me, they simply became part of us, and a very necessary part of our group since their contacts within the castle surpassed even Cassius's and Theo's.

Staffing levels surrounding me increased and I finally found myself setting boundaries, which I felt I needed, since vampires appeared not to feel the need for privacy as I did. It is hard to explain even now, but sometimes the fact that I was continuously watched enraged me and I could, and still can, become very difficult.

It took a while for the feelings of resentment to build, but I recognised what was happening; my control was beginning to slip. I was less patient with trivial things. I could feel the darkness seething and coiling around my insides, but before I did something silly I picked an evening and gathered every one of them in the apartments, where we relaxed and shared some food, and I spoke to them gently as a group.

It took a lot of self-control, but I managed to gently persuade all of them to respect my space and privacy, especially when I wanted some alone time. I explained that if it meant that much to them, they could keep an eye on me from a distance, a very long distance. I promised them as a compromise that I would never go anywhere that I shouldn't, or anywhere that I felt was dangerous, nor would I leave the castle or its grounds. I also would not hesitate to call if I sensed any trouble. That understood, my restlessness began to subside.

A few days later I also added to my personal entourage a photographer called Nick whom I had met a few times. I liked him because he could take a picture of me, and no matter how I felt or looked, he always managed to make me look stunning, which was becoming a necessity for me now. I also added a reporter, Lisa. I asked her to work for me directly since she was an acquaintance of Janet. She was also another talented human who was dating a Nedas vampire. She was a good reporter, one who would rather wait to speak to me than print something that might be untrue.

Chapter 8

As time went on I noticed Mia and Patrick, her handsome prince from the Irish Territories, had begun to spend a lot more time exclusively together. I realised that with all the changes that had taken place, it had been such a long time since Patrick had asked her to become his Everlasting Life Partner. He nudged her about the ceremony since it was getting nearer and none of us had given it much thought. Although she made time to see me every day, Mia suddenly seemed to have a million and one other jobs to do, which were constantly on her mind and filling her days and nights with worry. Of course, she rejected all offers of help. When we did manage to spend some time together, we would often talk about what she imagined her dream Commitment Ceremony would be like.

On those days when Mia's visits were shorter and when I had enough of being by myself, I usually went to join Rachael in the research libraries, always accompanied by Alex and James to please David. At first I was wary because David had expressed a wish that I detach myself from the research being carried out by Rachael and her team, but then after a while I relaxed, stopped thinking of David's misgivings, and tried to find more evidence or mention of the other script. For quite a while David didn't seem to know, or at least he didn't mention my visits to the research library, but I should have known better. After a particularly bad and long day for the pair of us, I had my first real argument with him when he made the mistake of trying to forbid me to enter the library.

At the onset of the argument, it was just irritability that came to the surface, but after many words a solution still seemed out of reach, so knowing that it would escalate, we went into our bedroom and he shut the door behind us. As I took my jumper off and sat on the bed with my back to him, I heard him tell the others not to enter until he had given his permission. At that point I knew something was very, very wrong. When he turned to me there was none of the softness in his features that he had when he spoke to me. What I saw made me feel cold. As he stood in front of me, all I saw was a Master looking back at nothing but an inferior being. I could feel the power within him bristling with anger. It had been so long since I had been looked at by him in such a way, and my heart began to beat with fear.

David's eyes were black and cold, with none of the vibrant violet that usually shone through when he looked at me. "Where were you?" he snapped at me through gritted teeth, his expression seething with anger. "I have been trying to reach you throughout this day. I do not have time to worry about you, and do you not think I have enough to be concerned with, without trying to locate my human Life Partner? This transition of power is not an easy one, and you should know and at least respect that."

"I have been nowhere of concern because I was here for all of the morning, and then once noon had passed I went to see Rachael," I said quietly, trying to show him respect, knowing that the situation with him was becoming a little dangerous. At the same time I tried not to drop my gaze as he glared at me. And even though I answered him quietly, it was difficult not to answer him in the same tone of voice that he was using. I had become stronger since coming to the castle, and with all that had happened to me since arriving as a child, I knew I should behave as a lesser being, but the darkness within me was already stirring, its protective anger beginning to awaken, and I knew it did not know the constraints of rank; it only knew the preservation of me.

I realised that before that moment I had hardly ever been afraid of David or the darkness within, but I could see the power and anger behind his eyes build and I could feel my own rise up, ready to meet it with perhaps equal power. I still did not know. However, a voice—a soothing, tranquil, calming voice, a voice of sanity—told me that it was not the time for my own strength to be revealed. I accepted the voice's reasoning. I had to calm myself quickly, knowing without a doubt that if I called upon my inner darkness in a fight against David at that time, I would be destroyed and so would our relationship.

"If you were where you were supposed to be, then why did you not respond to me when you knew I was searching?" he asked, pronouncing each word precisely and with slow deliberation as he stepped forward towards me, lowering his face until it was level with and very close to mine.

"I didn't know and I didn't bring my phone because I am aware that they are not allowed in the research areas. I could not sense you. David, I had nothing to do because all my needs are catered for and you are away almost all the time lately. We used to take time to be with each other, but since our return from Destiny there has been so little time for us," I said, rising and taking a slow, careful step away from him. I did not want to sound like a spoilt, petulant child, but even to my own ears that was exactly what I sounded like.

"Liberty, you have committed yourself to me, yet I feel that you do not behave as you should. I need you to support me, to understand. I have already asked you not to attend the libraries, but it seems that asking is not enough for you to obey me. You know you are in constant danger both from the fanatics of my kind and from those who would cause me pain through damaging you. Therefore, I will tell you again that I do not want you to attend the research facilities. If you wish to see Rachael I will have her visit you here, and if you wish to read she will bring books to you, do you understand? I forbid you from going to the library and will instruct the guards to prevent you from going there without my immediate permission. If you choose to attempt to disobey me further, there will be a consequence. Is that clear?"

I didn't understand at all, but as he took another step towards me, I felt the power he held within begin to descend on me, trickling over my senses and dulling them. It felt like a weight descending on me, wrapping itself round me, and becoming almost too heavy for me to remain on my feet. I closed my mouth and bowed my head to him, and even though I am certain that he would not have willingly hurt me, I also knew that he was still very angry.

He stood over me for a while. I didn't look at him in his face, but it wasn't out of fear that I would not meet his gaze. I didn't look at him because I admit I was again becoming angry myself. Once I had myself under control, I looked back up into his face and said simply, trying to keep my voice neutral, "It is clear, my Master. I am only here to obey your wishes, is that not so?"

I tried to smile to soften the moment, but the darkness still seethed and I just wanted to defuse the situation. It worked. In just a few moments the tension started leaving him and his body visibly relaxed. I continued to look down, however, not wanting him to see how he had made me feel. I still did not move when he placed his hands on my shoulders, and it took a moment longer for him to lift my chin so I could again look into his face. I closed my eyes and tried to look suitably sorry, biting my lip and making my chin tremble, looking as vulnerable as possible so that he would not be able to recognise the anger I still felt towards him.

After a few seconds, when I was certain I had my inner feelings under control, I opened my eyes and looked into his. There was nothing there to suggest the anger I had seen a few seconds earlier. What I saw was only the look of love that I recognised, but I knew it wasn't enough, not this time, and that it would take me a long time to forget what had happened just a few moments earlier.

David then reached for me and held me against him. "You must understand it is only for your own protection. I cannot even begin to describe how precious you are to me," he murmured softly into my hair, his breath sending the usual goose bumps down my spine. I felt myself shudder and relax as my own anger began to leave me. I took a long, deep breath in and gently returned his embrace. We stood there for quite a while, him with his arms wrapped tightly around me and his head gently resting on mine.

Inside I felt confused and raw at what had happened, and as he held me I felt tears beginning to burn in the corners of my eyes. I knew that there was nothing now that could change what had passed between us.

Eventually we broke apart and David opened the door of our bedroom, revealing my friends, who, comically, all appeared to be preoccupied with random things, as if they had no interest in what had passed between me and David.

Nothing more was said at that time—nothing more was needed—but I knew that I had some things to think about. I realised it was the look and not the words that worried me; it was the look that had caused all of my hurt. I had become used to being an equal among them, and David had never made me feel like anything less than that until that moment, at least not since I was a small child.

Later when we were alone, I spoke softly to him, apologising for worrying him, and he held me close and told me he may have overreacted and was surprised himself at the anger that had come forth. Eventually we came to a compromise and decided that I could only go to the library when there were more than one of my bodyguards available to watch me and when there was nothing else for me to do—no duties for me to perform, no tutorials, and no friends available to occupy me. I had my suspicions that David would ensure that such moments would be very rare indeed. We then locked ourselves in our room for a very different reason as we reconnected with each other.

Chapter 9

For the first time in what felt like a very long time, it was I who lay with my eyes open while David rested beside me. I was suddenly uncertain how I felt about him, about everything. I knew that I loved him deeply and would love him eternally, but I felt as if that love had actually stopped me from understanding what and who the being beside me was.

I gazed down on him while he rested; he was beautiful, I couldn't deny that. His pale skin was blemish-free, but as I looked at him that night I saw in him a vampire just as he had seen the human in me. The inequality of us as beings, on every level, had begun to threaten the love I felt for him. I could not rest that night, and I found myself looking for shadows as I had when I was younger; yet once again there were none. I could not stop the tears that night, and for the first time in a very long time, I cried until I was exhausted enough to go to sleep.

Thankfully, once that particular day was over, nothing more about it was said between us and life carried on. Eventually I managed to put the incident out of my mind. I tried very hard to do as David said, I really did, but less than a week later I became restless again, and stubbornly I felt as if the research library was the only place, other than the Temple of Thought, where I could find any peace. Maybe because it was forbidden, I simply felt drawn to it; I don't know. Anyway, I prepared my argument well, leaving no excuse for David to prevent me from going.

I rang him. I knew that particular afternoon and evening was a very busy period of time for him. Visitors had arrived the previous evening, and I knew it was packed with various appointments and meetings. I chose my time very carefully, deliberately, knowing when he was at his busiest and therefore distracted. After a short discussion, and many promises of good behaviour on my part, he agreed that I could go. He was pleased that I had called to ask his permission and inform him of my plans. Apparently, for some unknown reason, that phone call had made all the difference.

Alex and James were both available after they had performed their morning rounds with Theo, so after I had eaten a light breakfast, I had a shower, got dressed, and waited for them to join me. I felt so happy about going, and as the sun rose to its highest point in the sky and the windows of the castle were being shuttered, we made our way to the library.

Because the libraries were so extensive and on many levels, Rachael had to ask permission from the empress to section off a part for our use alone. This meant that Rachael could maintain at least a small amount of privacy. Also with the empress's blessing, Rachael had handpicked the researchers from among the libraries' caretakers, and only those she wanted to work with were allowed to enter the area she had chosen.

At the beginning there was a team of six researchers just working for us, but as the search grew so did their number. Rachael had them concentrating on finding anything they could on ancient scripts or the extinct Sky Dweller, whether it was large or small. We had no real starting points, so first we looked into anything we could find about the scripts and the missing Element. At the research library I really tried to catch up on any progress made without getting in the researchers' way. Although I tried not to make too much of a nuisance of myself, Rachael often seemed a little impatient when she saw me. She could still give me that look and make me feel like a small, errant child getting in her way. After entering and greeting Rachael, I went about my business in the library, with Alex and James following behind me discreetly. I didn't mind them; even with my enhanced senses, they still managed to appear more aware of my surroundings than I was, and with our unique way of communicating, we barely spoke to each other out loud. They generally kept me out of trouble and from hurting myself.

I would assign myself topics to research such as the Earth Carers and the various known histories of the Dwellers. I would try to read as much as possible with every visit; that is all I did. I sat and I read, and after a short while Alex and James appeared to relax. After a while, feeling that I was safe, they wandered off to find Rachael and left me alone to wander.

It felt good to be alone again, even if I knew that my protectors were just an aisle away, and I found myself following a little maze that seemed to take me farther into the heart of the research section. While I was looking around, I found a book that looked particularly interesting and perhaps a little out of place. At first I walked past it, but after wandering about for a short while longer, I found myself standing in front of it again. I felt drawn to it. It was as if it held something I should know. The sensation was strange; it felt like I was being guided. I realised that I had to read the book. I have to say that when I first saw the book, I knew I needed to read it.

I wasn't afraid because I had felt similar urges before; in fact, I felt like I had been guided like that all my life in one way or another. Before I could question or stop myself, I took down the book, opened it, and began flicking through the pages without really looking at it. The book was very old looking; the cover of it was plain black with just a few faded marks on it. I could not even make the marks out to be letters; they looked as if they had been rubbed many times, almost as if they had been worn away deliberately. I realised they may have been runes or something else, but I just could not tell. I was surprised when I opened the book because I was expecting the inside to be as old as the outside, but it wasn't; inside the pages were clean and bright, the type precise and clear. It became clear to me that the book told of a very different time, of another 'pure blood' that was also an ancient bloodline formed during an earlier time in history than that of Marcarius Alaunus.

As soon as I opened to the first page, I was intrigued and felt my heart beat faster with excitement. Maybe the book held the answers to some of my unanswered questions. After I had turned a few pages more, the book caught my undivided attention because I recognised the face that was pictured within. I stared at the picture and then felt a familiar thrill in the pit of my stomach as I realised that the book was written about Elathan and perhaps his predecessors.

He was there in all his glory, handsome and dangerous as always. When I saw the picture, I realised how much I missed him. I still thought of him as my dark knight. Many months had passed since I had seen him, and suddenly my world felt lonely without him. It was as if he added a balance to my life. He balanced me against all my friends and loved ones who were constantly guiding me. Besides, he was the only one who saw the other side of me, my own dark side. I felt that he knew and accepted the true inner me.

Under the picture it stated his original, oldest, and truest title: he was the Celtic Lord of Darkness, the Overlord of the Shadowlands. The second title made me smile because it seemed to fit him so well. Of course he was the Overlord of the Shadowlands, and I knew with certainty that this castle was probably his original home and not the home of Emperor Marcarius. I already knew from Tutor Vincent that the castle was situated at the centre of the ancient Celtic Kingdom, a magical anchor for the European Territories.

I shut the book when I knew instinctively that the time had come for me to go back to my rooms, even though I was totally engrossed and wanted to read more. I heard Rachael calling my name, her voice approaching quickly, but instead of placing the book back on the shelf I tucked it under my arm. I knew that I needed to read more to find out more. I couldn't put it back, not just yet.

"Interesting, is it?" Rachael said from directly behind me. When she spoke she was close enough that she managed to make me jump, and even though I had no real reason to, I could feel myself blush slightly. But she did not seem to notice my nervousness, and even if she did, she just chose to ignore it. Yet still I became slightly defensive.

"I just wanted to read something different, you know, maybe a different history. It just caught my eye and I am interested. Do you want me to put it back?" I asked, trying not to appear too bothered or to look too guilty, but knowing that the words were tumbling too fast from my mouth.

"No, child, of course not. Any reading or learning should only be encouraged, but just be careful with it and please return it to its rightful place when you have finished. The last thing we want to do is upset the librarians," she said with a smile.

I noticed that she smiled a lot lately and wondered if it had anything to do with Theo. I smiled back at her and walked out of the research area and back towards the royal apartments, the book tucked tightly and discreetly under my arm. On the way, I stopped at the kitchens to order myself some food because I did not know when I was going to see David or if I was going to see him at all that night. I didn't think I was, so I decided that I would curl up on the sofa and do a little bit of research for myself.

As I arrived back at the royal apartment, I met with Cassius and Theo. Thankfully, neither of them appeared interested in the book I was carrying, although it was becoming difficult to carry because it appeared that the nearer I got to the apartment I shared with David, the heavier the book became.

I was becoming uncomfortable about having it in my possession, as if it was suddenly not such a good thing I was doing in wanting to read it. I didn't understand where the thoughts were coming from, so mentally I tried to calm myself; it was difficult as I felt the discomfort rising, well aware that I was being influenced again but not knowing who disapproved of the book. No one near me showed any interest in what I was doing. I wondered sometimes if the poison had done more damage to me than good because I seemed to have so many states of consciousness—each, it seemed, with its own voice.

We all entered the apartments together and were joined by Alex and James, who gave Theo a thorough account of what I had been up to. While they were speaking I prepared to eat some of the food, which had arrived promptly from the kitchen, and then I told them that I was really tired and that I was going to sleep until David returned.

I took my food and the book and entered the bedroom, closing the door while they made themselves comfortable in front of the plasma device. Soon the conversation outside fell to a low murmur while the volume of the plasma device suddenly sounded a little louder. I knew then that they were settled and watching some kind of ball game between two teams of local Forest Dwellers.

When I entered my rooms, I had a quick hot bath, put on my casual clothes, ate my food, and lay down on my bed to read. Soon nothing else mattered but the contents of the book.

Chapter 10

At first while trying to keep myself from becoming too excited, I simply skimmed through the book, only stopping at the parts that I thought I would be interested in. For instance, I only paused at the pictures that I recognised, especially ones of the castle and its surrounding lands.

The castle was every bit as beautiful and imposing during the time of Elathan as it was now. The lands were still as expansive, reaching out towards the distant forests. I stopped simply scanning the pages and began to take a real interest in what I was reading. I felt a strange and exhilarating thrill of excitement at the knowledge that I was now living in a castle that had been the centre of another ancient world, and that it had existed during a time that predated vampires.

The castle was my home now, and the more I read about it, the more I realised I loved living within its ancient walls. It almost had the same feeling that the vessel Destiny had: I felt protected within its walls, and even though there were places where even I would not venture, I did not fear them. I knew somehow that the castle would never allow me to go down to those dangerous depths. I felt that it knew me and was aware of my limitations.

There were slight differences that I noticed. The grounds around the castle were less groomed, a little wilder. The flags that hung from the turrets of the castle in the picture were not red and gold as they were now; they were black and gold and designed to look like fire, Elathan's fire. I just knew it!

My heart raced as I stared at the picture. As I carried on reading, I realised that up until then I had always believed that the castle had been built around the Temple of Thought. As I continued turning the pages of the book, it struck me that it was possible that the temple may well have been formed later inside the existing castle. There were so many questions that were forming in my head that eventually I had to put the book down for a while, just to gather my thoughts and to prevent myself getting a headache.

I could not refrain long from picking up the book once again. I soon learned that I knew very little about the heritage of the beings surrounding me, and that I definitely wanted (or needed) to know a lot more. I found a pen and some paper and started making some notes as I continued to find more clues as to the castle's origin. If the castle was as old as the book stated it was, perhaps Sarah may have known Elathan. I wondered then if there had ever been a time when they shared the castle, maybe even knew each other. I now had doubts too about how old the Temple of Thought was and wondered whether it was Sarah or another powerful sorcerer or sorceress who had been allowed to will the temple into existence. I questioned whether Sarah knew where Elathan was now, or if it had been Marcarius who had nurtured the tree and allowed the temple to develop around it. The book seemed to question most of the history that I had been taught about up until that moment.

I wrote some questions specifically for Sarah. I reasoned that I would have to see her soon to determine if she could answer any of my questions. I carried on reading as the sky changed from the grey of dusk to the deep velvet blue of the midnight and into the lightening starless blue predawn. I was engrossed, knowing that I would not be disturbed, until I came to the section of the book dedicated purely to Elathan and the beings that he ruled over.

I knew that I should shut the book because I knew that Elathan was a secret I kept from David; it wasn't the only one, but it was the one that would hurt him the most. Deep down I knew it was wrong, but I couldn't tell him, not yet, because I had to know more about Elathan and his origins for myself before I shared him with the others.

It was a fact: Elathan had already been in existence when Marcarius had arrived with his armies of vampires. The book said that the Celtic Lord had fought Marcarius in a war for many centuries, willing to share neither the land nor the castle, almost as if whoever ruled the castle ruled the planet. The war continued until the land surrounding the castle began to suffer and until both had met under a flag of truce. An ancient test was taken by both of them, which Marcarius apparently won, and that was how he really became the Master of the castle and ruler of the planet. The book also stated that both Marcarius and Elathan were following their own destinies and that neither of them had been fulfilled. I knew from my history lessons that it took many centuries more for Marcarius and his army of followers to invade and take over the dying planet completely.

As I read further I could visualise the contents of the book as clearly as if I had been standing there watching the great battles take place; I became almost breathless as the events unfolded. I found myself wanting to absorb every word written of the battle, my enhanced vision allowing me never to miss a word. After the chapters of the battle I felt tired, so I shut the book again for a while and lay back, closing my eyes. My mind drifted, wondering what the test would have been and how Marcarius had eventually won.

I must have fallen asleep for at least a short while because I woke with a start; for the first time since my arrival, I dreamt of Marcarius as being a dark presence, the enemy descending on the castle, the thoughts of the castle being my rightful home, mine to defend, running through my dreams. After my short but deep sleep I felt better and reopened the book. This time I turned the pages more selectively and came across a page that held a picture of a beautiful black rose with a living section within its centre.

I read that the rose was actually a 'remembrance gift' often given by Lord Elathan to those whom he wanted to remember. It was written that once the centre of the rose had been given life, there would always be a link and that a twin flower was fashioned at exactly the same time, which Elathan himself kept safe and close. The second rose also had life given to it when the other received a drop of blood; it created a strong, almost unbreakable bond between the giver and the receiver. I had a feeling I should have been worried, but I wasn't. Instead, in the privacy of my room, I took the rose from my private drawer and laid it on the bed beside me, watching the bright red centre pulsing slowly, full of life from the drop of my blood, seeing its beauty and feeling only love.

I knew that the need to see him came from within me and that he did not have to manipulate me. Even though the Lord of Darkness himself gave the gift, it was also stated in the book that gifts like the black rose were given rarely, and they were given usually as a gesture of friendship and of rare feeling.

However, it wasn't the only gift I had been given. I carried on reading until I finally came to the page I was looking for; it contained a large picture of a black cobalt chain with an equally black heart pendant at its middle. As I read, as if it was becoming a ritual, I carefully removed the necklace from its resting place and again laid it on the bed between me and my living rose.

As I read about the heart, I finally began to understand why Elathan had prevented me from wearing it on that night. The heart, it appeared, was a little more binding. I read that once the heart is worn, it calls to him and a connection is made. Each time the heart is worn, that connection becomes stronger and the bonds created are eventually unbreakable, bringing whoever wears it to Elathan's side for eternity. It was also documented that the Lord of Darkness would often use the necklace to ensnare royal women. The heart was a pure temptation, as he was, because with him there was still a dark, secretive mystery. The more I read, the more appealing that mystery became.

Very near the end of the book I found a small section that spoke of Elathan's most trusted advisers. The book named them as his lieutenants and stated that they were diabolical twins. They looked to be no older than me.

Accompanying the text, there was a picture of a young boy and a girl. It was the girl who interested me more. Her name was Lillith, and apparently her prolonged touch meant death. Although she did not come directly from Elathan's bloodline, she was described in the book as the Princess of the World Beneath, the Lady of the Shadowlands.

The story in the book told how she was once a human who had been mistreated by her first love. It was said that his touch meant only pain to her, and while she was still only a young girl she was slowly tortured and poisoned by him. Eventually when he took no more joy from her pain, he threw her away and she was left in a wasteland to die.

While she was barely clinging to life she was discovered by Elathan and was taught to use the poison that had stayed within her blood. He taught her to control its malignancy by directing it away from her inner self; her anger gave her strength. Elathan helped her to channel the years of pain, fear, and resentment, and it was now her touch that became pain and death to others. As I read about her, goose pimples rose on my skin and the hairs on my neck bristled, leaving me cold. I could feel my anger awakening as I read her story. I realised that she and I shared a similar experience, only she was nursed back to health by the Celtic Lord of Darkness and I had been nursed back to health by those who surrounded me and loved me now.

I reread some of the paragraphs about her and realised that she could have been human. There was no mention of her being any type of vampire or demon. I wasn't even sure that she was a demon. Could she have been their child of freedom? Did she follow some type of preordained destiny? Questions and thoughts raced through my head.

I continued to read and discovered that shortly afterwards her brother was also found dying in the wasteland. He had been beaten half to death and had some of the same marks and scars that his sister had. He was barely conscious when he was found by his sister. They were twins, and she had felt some of his pain and sensed she was losing him. As his life ebbed away, she cradled him in her arms as he tried to mumble an apology to her, saying that he had tried to find her but he had been too late. He murmured with his last few breaths that he had tried to exact his revenge but had failed and fallen prey himself.

He recognised the changes in her and had begged his sister to come back with him, to return to the world above, to the real world of the living, but Lillith explained to him that she couldn't, that she had found her place, a place where she was not a victim, and that she no longer wanted any part of that world above where the real monsters lived.

He could have lived above on the planet. His wounds could have been cured—they were not fatal—but once he heard her decision he did not wish to live without her at his side. With his permission it was Lillith who took the rest of his life away. He became her first true victim.

At her hand and her guidance, her lessons from Elathan learned well, although he did not have the pain his sister had, they still managed to use his pain, anger, and hatred to give him strength while he learned to poison his touch.

At first he could only cause a mild discomfort with his touch until he discovered how much pain his sister endured. He became angrier and angrier until his touch became enough to cause people endless hours of misery. I knew with certainty that their power came from the darkness within them, and that thought frightened me. I felt as if I could be as strong, perhaps even stronger, than Lillith if I allowed my darkness its freedom.

I had to read a number of passages to finally realise that Elathan's realm reached into the depths of our planet, that there was no place on this planet that it didn't reach. I sat up for the final chapters, shaking off all the fatigue I felt. My heart began to pound with excitement, knowing that finally there may be actual proof of another destiny. The very last pages of the book referred to a destiny that had been written in a time before Elathan. It spoke of a being that would rise from the World Beneath to escape the restraints of the World Above and rule the planet.

I finally became too tired to continue reading and put the book away. With it I placed my most secret and precious gifts back in their private place. For the first time in a long time, I dreamt of Elathan and, as always, I felt myself running and resisting, but this time it was different because I did not know whom I was actually running from. My sleep was restless and disturbed until I felt the coolness of David as he settled himself by my side, and then the dreams stopped.

Chapter 11

I must have slept right through because I awoke the next morning just before noon, content and extremely happy to be lying safe within David's strong, cool arms again.

The dreams that had disturbed me during the early part of the previous night remained on my mind, but in the early daylight they seemed a little less threatening and perhaps just a little less intriguing. I felt more settled.

The need, however, to see Elathan was just as strong and exciting, but that morning when I woke up I also knew I could afford to be patient and wait a little while longer. There was time for Elathan and there always would be. I was conscious of the book, and although I knew it was hidden in a safe place, I also knew that it was important to return it to its place in the library as soon as possible. I knew that David would not pry into what he considered to be my private things, but I was slightly worried that he might find the book accidentally. After reading its contents, I knew that he would not approve, nor would he understand. I was afraid that it would bring up all his feelings of resentment towards the research again, especially as he had begun to relax and enquire about my whereabouts less.

That morning, feeling a little shameful about my deception and feeling as if I needed to reassert my bond with him, I asked him softly and very sweetly if he could spend the day with me. I also guessed he would be going on a trip in a short while; it was part of our 'plan of change,' and I knew that he had been studying the laws of the African Territories. I also found some documents on the table next to our bed the previous night and sneaked a quick look.

Even though the Vampire Laws were universal, every territory had its own small customs and each royal family had its own way of implementing those universal laws. These laws generally had not been reviewed or changed in any way for nearly three thousand years. The World Council continuously worked to ensure their laws were obeyed by other vampires and, in turn, human beings. However, David had begun a campaign for change. This meant he was on a mission to visit each of the royal families in their own territories. He was planning to observe and put forward some of the new proposals and changes he wanted to see happen at the beginning of his rule. He also wanted to understand his subjects and the various politics of the other royal families, and what they would want for their territories. David felt that although his father was loved and very well respected, he had ruled from the Throne Room within the castle. He felt his father had felt uncomfortable leaving the heart of his domain and, as a result, had to some extent lost connection with the other royal families. David believed that had his father stayed in touch more with Prince George and Prince Samuel and their followers, my kidnapping and subsequent poisoning might have been prevented.

David simply wanted to know whether the other families could adapt the existing laws and accept the proposed changes, I knew he was trying to give them a choice, but they all knew that David's word and rule would be absolute when Marcarius stepped down from his throne. Among the papers I had also seen an invitation from the World Council for David to join them when they held their next conference. It was a routine meeting, but older vampire rulers felt that David needed the experience.

Of course, because of its location, the hosts of the council were going to be King Bello and Queen Abiba, the ebony-skinned rulers of the African Territories. I had met them once before and knew that they were both very charming. I would have loved to accompany David, but I wasn't invited.

There was no need for any of the members of the Council to sleep; therefore the entire two days were going to be taken up with the Universal Laws, with a vampire-style banquet given on the final night.

However, on that day, while he was still with me in my bed, I won David over and rang his personal assistant to cancel his duties and scheduled meetings. We took our time and lay together, deciding how best to fill our day. We eventually decided that we should contact and gather everyone from our group so that we could have a little fun; there hadn't been too much of that lately.

It was no surprise that there was no resistance from anyone; in fact, everyone seemed quite pleased when they were excused from their formal duties to join us. After a few more moments of pleasure and alone time with David, I got up, had a shower, and got myself dressed. By the time I was ready, most of our friends had already arrived and were sitting in the entertainment area of our apartment. After a lot of friendly arguments, some decisions were made as to what we would be doing. This period of indecision was almost my favourite part of us coming together because when the likes of Mia and David started to make decisions, they were almost as comical to watch as most brothers and sisters usually are. Of course, Mia won all the arguments; she was far more stubborn and wilful than David, and she always appeared to have the sense to use me and my education as a persuasive argument. Therefore, after about an hour of friendly debate, it was decided we should go to one of the new restaurants that, with David's approval, had started to be built within the Inner Districts.

I dressed for the weather because it was dry but not yet warm; I chose comfy old jeans and an elegant, fashionable but warm jumper. I chose this because it was almost standard casual dress for me. Over my trousers I pulled on my favourite new pair of soft brown boots that reached high above my knees and placed my hair in a ponytail.

Theo, Alex, and James wore uniforms of black jeans, black T-shirts, black boots, and long black leather coats. I laughed when I saw them because Theo had become rather obsessed with films shown in the late twentieth century, the ones where most of the heroes and villains seemed to have a leather coat in their wardrobes. I giggled even more when Rachael appeared in a similar uniform, accompanied by a diamond-studded black satin eye patch. Mia and Patrick were wearing similar warm outfits that fit in with what the rest of us were wearing.

As soon as Theo saw her enter the room, his whole demeanour changed. He softened slightly and even smiled a little, especially when Rachael casually nodded and winked at him. I wasn't the only one who noticed, and there were a few additional smiles from others who were already seated.

While the rest of them were getting ready, David put on dark blue jeans, black knee-high boots, and a short leather jacket as I sat and watched the latest world news on the plasma device.

There was nothing new on to see, just yet another debate between those who felt that David was being too quick with his decisions to give the Dwellers their freedom, the council members being very careful to agree with David's choices but expressing the need for him to be cautious.

Bored with that, I turned the device off and sat back, content to listen to the gentle discussions of the beings I loved. While she was waiting Mia had phoned Heather, Janet, and Sebastian, who were all expected to join us at the new restaurant. When I asked David about Mia's enthusiasm, he explained quietly that Mia was excited because the restaurant where we were headed was new and unique to the planet, the first of its kind. Another call was also made to both Lisa and Nick; both of them were invited, but unfortunately theirs would be a working lunch since they were offered an exclusive photo opportunity and interview session following our meal.

Eventually we were ready to go and left the apartment. Whenever we moved as a group, a naturally protective circle formed around me. When everyone was happy with the positioning, we would all move as one. David always maintained physical contact with me, usually just by holding my hand and walking a small step ahead of me. Surrounding us both were my personal bodyguards, a group which also seemed to include Rachael.

Of course, Cassius was also among that inner circle of protection because just as Theo would give up his soul and end his life to protect me above all others, Cassius would gladly do the same for David. I was fine with that. Cassius and I were still very close, and I understood and even approved of his choices and where his loyalty was placed. He had to make the choice when we were both a lot younger and were already growing close. We were almost ready to appear among our friends as a couple and then David appeared and began to show an interest in me. As David's friend, Cassius chose David's feelings over his own.

Following them were Mia and Patrick. Although they did not hold hands, something unheard of for these cold-blooded, detached people, they walked very close together, practically shoulder to shoulder and in perfect unison. I smiled to myself, knowing my good influence was rubbing off on them. The chemistry and bond between them was almost tangible, as if an aura cloaked the pair of them. It was obvious, even to those who did not know them as we all did.

Once we emerged from the castle we were bombarded with the usual but select few flashing lightbulbs. There were a few beings, mainly vampires and variety of Dwellers, that would call out for us to turn to face them. They were demanding yet always remained polite, their calls never frenzied and their voices hardly ever raised. It was all very controlled in case they angered their prince and lost their privileged place. As expected, there was the occasional hint of someone trying to discover secrets or influence me, but I had learned to brush such intrusions aside and ignore them.

As we walked towards our transport, David moved ahead and spoke softly to Theo, asking him to clear the grounds of the photographers as soon as we returned. There wasn't a problem, but every now and again David had them all removed when he felt there were too many to be comfortable with. This, of course, began the games where each magazine and media company would try its hardest to compliment David's choice of partner and ideas, all the while saying that they really did respect our need for privacy.

We didn't stop walking until we reached the cars, which were waiting for us with their engines already running. The first vehicle was an extremely large Jeep, which had been especially built to accommodate Theo easily. It was one of the very first things that I bought him when I made him my head of security, and it was one of Theo's most prized possessions. The Jeep was the size of a large people carrier, but as far as I was concerned it was the least I could do for him. It also was big enough to accommodate all of my bodyguards as well as David and me. Mia and Patrick opted to travel in a smaller car of their own.

The journey to the Inner City was a relatively short but enjoyable one. The afternoon was warm, reasonably bright, and not too cold. Heather was waiting at the edge of the forest outside the gates of the Inner District, so we stopped and waited while she got in our vehicle with us. It was always such a pleasure to see her again.

Heather continued to be every inch a representative of all Forest Dwellers. Her red hair hung below her waist in coppery waves of fiery yellows, oranges, and reds. Her bright, pale jade green eyes lit up as soon as she saw us. There was warmth in them that added radiance to her; she seemed to glow from within. She was dressed in soft suede trousers which she had tucked into thick fur-lined utility boots. On her top half she wore an emerald green blouse with a dark green wrap covering her shoulders to keep out the chill of the afternoon.

I realised that I missed Heather and that it had been too long since I had seen her. She had been busy travelling constantly with their cousin Thomas since David had chosen them to be representative ambassadors for their people, a role that they took very seriously, although they were often met with resistance. Their temperament was mild, and they were patient enough to be able to speak for those among their kind who still had a deep mistrust of vampires and often brought David valid arguments against his proposals. It appeared that vampires were not the only ones against any form of change or cooperation. Heather and Thomas travelled the forests dispelling as many myths and half-truths as they could, on behalf of both David and vampires and the myths of their own kind. They had the full protection of the emperor, with the punishment of instant death to any who harmed them in any way; they had been given their own group of bodyguards and protectors both from the Forest Dwellers and from the castle.

When Heather was seated in the vehicle, I left David and my own seat and practically sat on top of her, wanting her to tell me of everything that had happened since I had last seen her. I found the stories she had to tell mesmerising. As we chatted I found myself closing my eyes, letting her words carry my mind through vast forests, imagining the people within, trying to understand their mistrust of vampires, knowing that I was still very cocooned and protected within my little world. At parts I sat upright, suddenly keenly interested as she described the development of protected areas within the ancient forests where newly planted saplings were being cared for by younger, newly educated members of the Forest Dwelling communities.

She told me of the younger generations who were now being educated with modern ideas as well as following the handed-down traditional teachings of their elders. A new generation of Dwellers for a new generation of Forests—I could feel my happiness and excitement rising as she spoke. Perhaps there was hope yet for this planet.

Heather was on her own on that occasion because Thomas, even though he loved us all dearly and was reasonably comfortable among us, generally shied away from groups of people, often preferring to keep his own company. As long as I saw Thomas occasionally and I knew he was well, I was satisfied.

As she spoke, I couldn't help notice how beautiful Heather was. I thought that she looked both strong and confident, almost like a warrior for her people, and it was obvious that the role of Ambassador suited her.

Eventually David came over and sat with us. His questions were far more concise and less romantic, and in his unintentional way he broke the spell that her words had been weaving over me. Heather sat more upright when David joined us. With her eyes closed, concentrating, she told us of the progress that she and Thomas had made and also where she thought David would meet the most resistance against his plan of social integration.

She told us that sadly, like the vampires, the Forest Dwellers did not believe that any concessions should be made towards human beings, that they were still the biggest threat to the planet. She gripped my hand as she told David of the last piece of news, assuring me that change takes time, and went on to add that Thomas sent his love. As she said this she kissed the top of my head, and I knew it was passed on from Thomas. She also added that Marta had told her to punch me in the eye, but she had obviously refused and that made everyone laugh for a while. We all sat that close together until we reached our destination and the vehicle finally stopped. I opened my eyes.

Chapter 12

When I opened my eyes I felt content, as if Heather's words had reassured me that everything was moving along as it should be. As soon as the vehicles stopped, Mia was at the door of our vehicle, and as Heather stepped onto the ground, Mia reached for her. For a few moments they stood facing each other silently, studying each other as if memorising any changes. They looked very similar, but Mia, when she had been infused, had lost some of the vibrancy that her pure Forest Dweller sister still had. They quickly embraced each other and then stepped apart as we all gathered once again ready to enter the restaurant, David reaching for my hand.

I didn't really recognise the place where we had stopped; I had seen no advertisement for it on the plasma screens. The restaurant where we had decided to eat was called Free Food. The name referred to the fact that humans could earn the right to eat there alongside their vampire masters. Once there, the humans were allowed to pick freely from the menu. There was a strict 'no harm, no hierarchy' rule, which meant that whoever dined there could speak freely and as equals.

The restaurant was a tall thin building situated on its own; the buildings on either side were a discreet distance away. The outside of the restaurant was simply designed with white painted walls and pictures of the food sold inside on its windows and doors.

The inside was larger than expected, with many small tables decorated with clean white cloths. The restaurant appeared to be deserted at first, but as we went to sit at one of the many tables, a female vampire came out to greet us. She introduced herself and told us to call for her when we were ready to order our food; then, as quickly as she had appeared, she left us.

I sat between Mia and David and listened as Mia excitedly explained why the restaurant was so special. She explained that the restaurant promised safety and neutrality to all those inside its doors; it was the only place on the planet where human beings could sit among vampires and Dwellers with no risk to themselves.

It was the brainchild of one of David's researchers, a female Hiltian called Charlotte, a relatively new vampire who understood and approved of what David wanted to achieve. She worked tirelessly on David's new projects, and she, like David, believed that the planet would benefit from the unity of all its inhabitants. The restaurant was probably built as more of an experiment at first, but it was working surprisingly well, and although it was still the only one of its kind, David had now put the Hiltian Charlotte in charge of promoting and developing the option of further restaurants throughout the other territories.

When I asked Mia why we were the only ones there if it was so successful, she laughed and told me that the restaurant was usually a little busier, but this was the first time the royal party had visited them and the restaurant had been cleared. I was impressed, even more so because the restaurant claimed to provide all its patrons, no matter who they were and whatever their taste, the freshest food. They assured us that the meat they served came only from animals that were well treated and free to roam the acres of land owned by the restaurant. None of the meat was infused with anything; in fact, there was nothing artificial in any of the food.

The restaurants also owned many fisheries, which David personally found appalling; out of respect for his feelings, I would never have ordered fish in front of him, even though fish is something I would have liked to have tried.

Although David still absolutely adored the emperor and empress who were his adoptive parents, things had changed slightly with the gift of the shell, which he listened to almost constantly when he wanted peace. It was given to him as a gift after I had become his Life Partner. He had put it away for a while when he became engrossed in his new duties, but after his encounter with Mazu he appeared to need it more again.

Since our little holiday, in the little spare time he managed to get, David had begun to study more of his original heritage, gathering literature from the libraries and placing the information that he had found particularly interesting in his personal vault so that he could study it further at his own leisure. Even though I was a little curious, I did not ask him about his newfound interest. I assumed he would share his heritage with me in time, if I was patient. For me, the only thing I had to remind me of my encounter with Mazu was the tiny scar behind my left ear, and that didn't bother me much. Once we returned to the castle after it happened, the memory faded quickly. Although I tried very hard to hold on to those memories of our stay on Destiny, after a few days I could not even remember how or why it had happened, and those around me had stopped asking.

Humans who did not eat meat were offered only fruits and vegetables, which were also pure or free of chemicals and had not been made into the cream mush that was still served within the Enclosures. Vampire masters were given a choice of bloods, which had been given freely and freshly the same day. The blood was given freely because the humans who donated were usually well paid and well cared for by the restaurant staff; some would even argue that it was given out of choice.

The humans who donated their blood to the restaurant were all housed together in the same building within the city, but their building was fashioned on the old apartment buildings that were spread throughout the cities in the centuries before. The more money they earned, the more comfort they could buy for themselves.

We all had an array of delicious food and drink, and the atmosphere was relaxed and happy, with all of us treating the day as a wonderful escape. The service we received was wonderful. Our waitress was swift and courteous, always knowing when to appear and when to retreat. It was a happy time, and as I ate I looked around the large table at my friends and felt an almost overwhelming sense of belonging, the feeling of that place at that time being so right.

After we had eaten, we stayed there for a while, just chatting, all of us unwilling to leave that place of peace. Although they sat at another table, Nick managed to get some really good photos of us enjoying ourselves and Lisa asked the occasional question that would be relevant to the collection of photos that, between them, they intended to publish.

Eventually we did have go back and resume whatever duties we had left behind, so as the afternoon turned into evening we finally made our way back to the castle. We went the same way we had come, and even though news of our meal had obviously reached the ears of the local media, they kept a respectful distance. Heather chose to travel all the way back with Mia and Patrick, her obvious approval of him making Mia glow with beauty and pride.

When we arrived back at the castle, with a little bit of pressure from us, Heather agreed that her duties could wait until the following day and she agreed to stay with us in the royal apartments, just for a short while.

She seemed happy and relaxed chatting to Cassius, something that did not go unnoticed among us. I saw that Mia didn't look particularly happy, but she was too preoccupied with Patrick to really do anything about it. Once we were within the safety of the royal apartment, away from the eyes of others, they freely made and maintained physical contact. We spent the night talking and laughing, knowing that all our duties would be there for us the next day.

I stayed curled up in David's arms, occasionally falling asleep but also trying very hard to stay awake, to be with my friends and not to miss a thing; it seemed important. One of the things we all discussed during the early hours of that morning was the soon to happen Commitment Ceremony of Mia and Patrick. Mia had already spent a lot of time planning most of the details for the ceremony, and David, like her, really wanted their ceremony to be a huge public affair. He wanted to give his much less recognised sister the ceremony she had been dreaming of and planning since she had met Patrick. Because of the attitude of others outside of the castle towards Mia, I knew that for one day David wanted her to be treated like the princess she really was.

After a while silence fell, and then Patrick stood up slowly and took Mia's hand to pull her up to her feet. He then turned to

David, bowed formally, and said that he would have an answer to some of David's questions about further arrangements for the ceremony later that day, or at least before David would have to be away from us with the World Council.

With that they both left us, Patrick trying to look solemn and serious but not really succeeding, and Mia following him, smiling gratefully at David as if he had given Patrick the push she thought he needed to make the final arrangements. All in all, the day that I had persuaded David to stay with me could not have been more perfect, for all of us.

Chapter 13

Once Patrick and Mia had left, the others seemed to just drift away, and I was happy to see that it was mainly as couples. Theo offered to escort Rachael back to her quarters and she graciously accepted, winking at me when she saw me smiling. Although she had nursed me back to health and returned me to David, she initially wanted to stay at the Enclosure where she had spent decades teaching human children how to survive in the vampire world, but we wore her down. It took a little bit of persuading, but when she was asked to look into the prophesy, Rachael decided it would be better for her if she moved nearer to the castle's research library. I was so grateful that she had because she was almost a mother to me and knew me better than anyone else.

Cassius also got up at the same time as Heather, and though neither of them spoke, the look that passed between them gave me the feeling that he would see her safely back to the outskirts of her forest, at the very least. Of course James and Alex stayed, since they always stayed just a room away from me.

As the last of our friends finally left, I drifted off to sleep, and I felt David pick me up gently and cradle me in his arms as he carried me into our bedroom. I felt him lay me down softly and begin to kiss my neck gently. Even though I was exhausted, I reached for him and he responded. We disrobed and I enclosed us both in our own pleasurable personal intimacy, the coolness of his pale, smooth skin a perfect match for my own warmth. For a while, I don't know how long, I lost myself in him, but when we had finished, I lay in his cool arms and drifted off into a deep sleep. I am not sure how long I stayed asleep, but I know that David stayed with me that night, just holding me, although I knew he did not need any rest. I woke when the room was already growing a little lighter and I heard a loud knocking at the outer door.

I could hear voices. As the sleep cleared from my head, I heard that it was Mia arguing with someone; the other voice was James's. I listened until I realised she was telling him to let her pass. David looked at me, a question already forming on his lips. But before he could ask the question I just smiled a little and shook my head, placing a finger over his lips to stop him from asking it, mainly because I wanted to listen to what was being said. I had forgotten to inform him of a new arrangement I had agreed upon with my royal guards.

I could hear Mia's voice slowly rising as she questioned James about whose authority was stopping her from entering our bedroom. I felt my face growing warmer and I blushed, just a little, when I heard my name being mentioned more than once in the conversation. David had raised himself on one elbow and was looking at me with a strange but intensely interested look on his face. I whispered to him that I wanted this room to be just ours; I finally had a place that I wanted to be private. I knew that Mia meant more to me than almost anyone, but if I was going to make this work, we had to have the same rules for everyone. I told him that I knew she would not like it at first, but since she had agreed to become Patrick's Everlasting Life Partner, I thought that perhaps she would understand better the need for others to ask before entering. I must have looked determined because David kissed the top of my head gently. Holding back a laugh, he phoned James to find out what all the noise outside our room was.

When Mia had moved to open our door again, I knew that James had moved to stop her. David sensed that she was almost at a point of no return and asked James to hand his phone to her. David then went on to calmly explain to Mia that we had requested that James and Alex give us prior notice of anyone who wished to enter our room. Of course we trusted her, but it was really to save any embarrassment just in case we were caught in a compromising position. At his last comment I had to bite my pillow to stop myself from laughing out loud because even though he was holding back the laughter himself, to her, at least, he must have sounded sincere and calm. I did not want her to believe that we were not serious; I loved David so much in that moment for supporting me and not dismissing my request for privacy.

His words obviously worked because her voice got quieter; I couldn't hear what she was saying anymore because she was no longer shouting. I should have known she would try something else, but I was slightly surprised when her voice whispered the word *open* through my mind, which irritated me immediately. So much for respect and equality. Instead of answering her, I simply got up and covered myself as I heard David tell her to give us a few more minutes. He asked her to show some patience and we would soon be out. I went to take a shower, still managing to smile.

I can't answer why the urge for privacy was so strong within at that time; I just felt I had to put some of my own rules in place and that it was important they be obeyed. After our argument a couple of days earlier, I needed to feel like an equal being among them again since David's reaction to me then had left me feeling vulnerable and upset.

As I was getting dressed, David came to kiss me and have one final embrace, and to tell me that he would be with his father finalising the details of his upcoming visit to the African Territories. He promised that he would do everything possible in order to see me later that evening.

I heard Mia try to question him as he passed her in the hall, and I heard him inform her that I would call James to admit her when I was ready, the impatient tone of his voice finally silencing her for a few moments. When I had finally finished dressing, I picked up my phone, called James, and formally told him to allow her entry. I tried to look relaxed, although I knew she was seething at me; I could sense her anger before she even came into view.

I was standing by the window with my back to the door and took a few moments to turn and face her. When I did, I saw the look on her face as she walked towards me; I realized it was the same as the one I had seen on David's face when he became angry with me because of my visits to the library.

I felt the room go a little colder and my heart grow heavier as I realised that Mia was thinking of me as a human and not as an equal. The look she gave me was one of intense displeasure. For a split second my resolve faltered and I almost apologised, but I knew that I couldn't. I stared right back at her, determined not to lower my gaze as I had with David, knowing that there was no reason to feel inferior. After all, in the world they had created, I was the Life Partner of the future emperor and that made me superior to all of them. Strange, but I felt my inner strength beginning to build again. I was beginning to think of it as less of a darkness and more of a necessity. I realised that I needed what it could give me. I understood then as I stood facing her that this was meant to happen and that whatever happened in that room, I could not concede to her. I had a will of my own that could match hers and was no longer a child. Neither was I merely an indulgence in their world. I had become a royal being who was now known in their world, a world that was fast becoming my world in which I had a real place.

I turned away from her again. She had gone into statue mode and didn't even appear to see me anymore. I stood silently, waiting for the questions, to be scolded, but it didn't happen. She said my name once, in a voice that was both detached and cold. Again I faced her and watched her as she thawed, as she switched back to seeing me again, her expression softening. Eventually she began to relax and I could sense the anger leave her, and again she was the Mia who had helped me to grow and had always been there for me.

Neither of us said anything, and I didn't move from where I was because for the first time since I had met her, I didn't want to go to her. I didn't want to forgive her or please her. I felt that I was the one who had nothing to be sorry for. After a couple of seconds, she came to me and actually hugged me. After a moment's hesitation, I hugged her back, equally as hard, a small smile twitching at the corners of my mouth as my inner strength subsided. Both of us knew that she was forgiven, but both of us knew that what had happened had changed us and our relationship, probably only slightly, but changed nevertheless.

After a moment of silence together, she pulled away, bowed her head, and said, "Sorry." The word melted my heart. I was myself again, full of remorse and love and just relieved that the mood was broken.

"It's just because I am getting older and I want someplace where I can be alone. I have been surrounded by others all my life, and finally I am at a place where I can request some privacy and others have to do as I say," I said, looking at her face as I explained how I felt.

"Mia," I continued gently, "there is no going back on this for me or you. I would, however, say this. If ever I was on my own and I did not respond to your call, either within my mind or by the more conventional phone, you, and only you, have my full permission to enter my room uninvited. I will let Alex and James know right away." A little of her unhappiness seemed to leave her as she pushed my phone towards me. I picked it up, and in front of her I spoke quietly to James, explaining what I had just promised. I spoke with an authority that had been lacking in my voice before; I felt as if I had suddenly grown, perhaps even aged.

Chapter 14

After I had finished talking to James, Mia and I sat together on my bed. I listened quietly while she spoke constantly about Patrick. She was sad at times, she told me, and she was lonely that day because apparently he had gone to visit his aunt, Queen Sinead, in the Irish Territories. He promised her that he would be back later that day, hopefully with the queen's royal seal of approval.

I tried to listen and be sympathetic, but at the back of my mind I also knew I needed to return the book to the library; the thought nagged at me. I knew it needed to be done quickly and discreetly, and I was very aware that I still had it and was certain that I didn't want Mia to find it or to ask too many questions. That inner voice again warned me that she would probably be even less understanding than David if she knew I had that book.

At my first opportunity to interrupt her, I told Mia that I wanted us to visit the Temple of Thought a bit later that day. She looked a little surprised at my suggestion since I hadn't shown any interest in going there for a while. To explain my request I made the very valid point of suggesting to her that time would go quicker if we were kept busy. Eventually, and a little reluctantly, with Mia saying she had nothing better to do, she agreed to come with me. When Mia left me briefly to attend to some chores of her own, I quickly retrieved the book and placed it in my bag with some other of my private belongings. I grabbed something off the table to eat on the way, and when she returned we left the apartment.

We went to the library first, where I successfully I played down the significance of the book when Mia finally noticed me placing it back on the shelf from which I believed I had originally taken it. To distract her from thinking anymore about the book, when we walked away I started talking to her about the more mundane but widely known history of the castle. I left out anything that would probably have interested her until she seemed to become more than a little bored and did not pursue the questions further. While we were there we had a brief catch-up conversation with Rachael and then continued walking on the upper levels of the castle to the Temple of Thought.

As always, as I entered the temple I felt the peace of the planet at rest wash over me. Sarah was, as she always is, present; I could sense her immediately and knew that she had been waiting to speak with me. Not wanting to keep her waiting any longer than necessary, I closed my eyes and relaxed as I felt the modern version of the temple melt away and the ancient temple where Sarah waited patiently for me came into focus.

"Hello, child, are you well?" she said as she came into view from the usual small black corridor in the deep, recessed shadows of the cave. It was good to see her. She wore, as she always does, a simple white gown and her blonde hair was flowing loosely around her shoulders. Her appearance remained young and childlike to me, even though since my vision had become enhanced I often caught glimpses of the much older, extremely powerful sorceress behind the image.

"I am well, Sarah," I responded politely.

"And you are making progress, I hope? Have they made more discoveries with regard to my script?" Her voice was gentle as she continued, "It is strange, since I have not existed physically on the planet for more than an age now. I like that fact, that I am not yet forgotten. It is still nice to hear that I am remembered," she said, smiling.

"Yes, I am sure it is," I said with a smile. I had no intention of telling Sarah that she was only known by a few at that time and that my questioning had actually reawakened interest in her and the scripts. The darkness within felt a little restless. I smiled wider, although a little uncomfortable in her presence, because I knew with certainty that she thought the only thing that we did was look for the missing scripts and Elements. There was nothing more important to her.

"The progress is slow, but I believe that we come a little closer to what we need to know each day," I said, trying to sound confident and positive.

After pausing for a few moments of thought, Sarah spoke a little more slowly and deliberately, as if she wanted me to really concentrate on her next few words. I sat up and looked at her as she spoke. "I also believe that you are near the truth with your comments. I feel less restless being here of late. Perhaps I feel that another part of your destiny will be revealed to you in the near future. Although it is probably not necessary to remind you, you must be aware there will be trials along the way. But know this: you must succeed in order to survive your ordeal."

"As always, I will do my very best," I said in response, not knowing what else to say, I had heard similar words of warning from her before. I started to make preparations to leave when I turned to face her again. "Sarah, do you know of a being that apparently still resides within the castle and has been here since before the reign of Marcarius?" I asked casually.

"I know of no such being, child," she said abruptly, suddenly turning away. "Now do not distract yourself from the tasks that lie before you. Haven't I told you of their importance?"

"Are you sure his name is Elathan? I found a book and read about him. It says that he was here before Marcarius. Were you here during that time?" I asked.

"As I told you, I know of no such being. Now why do you insist on questioning me?" she said, turning to face me.

I could sense her disapproval, and as always when she felt challenged, her youthful image began to slip and I could see a much older, more intense being beneath it, a being that was no less beautiful but ancient, with pale blue eyes and an intensely wise face. I did not sense any malice from her, and I thought that maybe in the future I would be ready to ask to see her in her true form.

I sighed, as instinctively I knew she was not speaking the truth to me about Elathan, but before I could ask her another question she began to fade slightly, as did the walls of her temple.

As I began to leave her temple and enter mine, I stopped worrying about the things she had said to me since I knew that my fate had apparently already been decided for me. I knew that I would do whatever I had to do to fulfil my destiny.

When I returned to the older temple, it took the usual few moments for me to gather myself. I could hear a high-pitched ringing and could sense movement near to me. As my senses returned to the present, I realised that it must have been Mia's mobile phone because when I opened my eyes I was alone in the temple. Although there was urgency to the ringing, I wasn't in a hurry, so I stayed long enough to light some candles and gently rearrange some fresh flowers at the base of the tree. I said a silent prayer for my parents, wishing each of them peace wherever they rested, and then I left.

When I got outside of the temple, Mia was waiting for me with a worried smile on her face. She told me that Patrick had called her from an airport within the Irish Territories. It seemed that his cousin Queen Sinead had insisted on coming back with him to help with all the arrangements for the traditional banquets and to be present at the formal public announcement of their commitment. Mia started to pace back and forth in front of me as she added that they would be arriving at the castle at some point the next morning.

I laughed gently when I saw the panic that was starting to show on her face. I knew that she was thinking nothing had been arranged, and I knew that she hadn't really expected much from her intended Life Partner. I sought to help her, and after answering a few questions I made some quick—and what I hoped sounded confident and commanding—phone calls. By the time we arrived back at the royal apartments, we had already arranged suitable accommodations for the queen and her entourage.

I had spoken with Miss Davinia, and she had assured me that she knew Queen Sinead very well and that the rooms she had chosen would be well stocked with her favourite vials. When Mia had stopped in the corridor with a horrified look on her face, stating that she had nothing at all to wear, I contacted Janet and made arrangements for us to view her latest designs later that day. When Mia was satisfied with our progress and accepted that there was nothing else to be done, she accompanied me back to my apartments.

I waited for Alex to catch up and told him to locate James and Theo. I said that I would need a castle vehicle ready at the entrance in a short while. Although his face told me he was curious, thankfully he said nothing and simply nodded. When he left I shut the door and went to the dining table, where various foods had been laid out for my midday meal. I realised I hadn't eaten much of a breakfast, so I ate the food and went to sit down in front of the plasma device.

I sat there flicking from one channel to another, not really sure what I was looking for and nothing really holding my interest. Eventually Mia came over and sat with me. I got the impression that she wanted to speak about what had happened between us earlier, but I did not want to. As far as I was concerned nothing more needed to be said, so I continued doing what I was doing and not meeting her gaze.

Still not looking at her, I asked her, "What do you want to do with the queen while she is here? Do you even know how long she is going to stay?"

"No," she said in a voice that told me she knew what I was doing. I smiled at her and she smiled back. There was a space between us that I knew she desperately wanted to fill as much as I did. "No, I don't even know why she is coming," she groaned.

"I think we may have a very busy afternoon and evening on our hands, then," I told her with a giggle. "And Mia, nothing happened this morning that changes anything," I said with finality, knowing that I wasn't exactly speaking the truth but hoping that she would take my words at face value.

"Okay, if that is how you feel, then I am satisfied. Let's do this," she said, watching me finish my meal and switching off the plasma device. We both grabbed our coats and went to meet Alex, James, and Theo, who were waiting for us outside of the castle entrance. There were the usual cameras and media who wanted to question us, but we didn't have time, so with Theo partially blocking their view of us, we hurried into the waiting cars without even acknowledging them. As David had spoken to Theo about their removal, and Theo spoke to some of the castle guards that accompanied us. He asked them to ensure that the grounds were cleared on our return.

The car we were in moved rapidly away, and in the quiet darkness of the interior we passed the time by trying to guess what the media would write about our serious-looking departure. During the journey, for some strange reason, I decided that I had not felt the security of Theo's massive arms for a long time, and I was suddenly feeling tired and irritable.

I managed to make eye contact with him, and he must have sensed there was something wrong because he casually opened his arms to me and gestured for me to go to him. I know that I wasn't a child anymore, but sometimes I needed the absolute security of this being; Theo was, among other things, my true protector who had given me his oath.

The journey was a reasonably short one, so it wasn't long before we got to the Inner District. We instructed the driver to take us straight to Janet's design studio, which was above her first shop. When we got out there the media presence was sparse. This wasn't a staged visit or publicity event, so they obviously had no prior knowledge of our arrival.

Janet was there to greet us and so was her Everlasting Life Partner, Sebastian, the Nedas of the Inner District. It was good to see them, and I greeted them both with a kiss on the cheek and a hug. They were both dear friends; I had also known them since I was very young. I did giggle when Sebastian held me long enough to gently smell the line of the veins in my neck. It tickled, but I knew that he would never hurt me, even though I knew that he was one of the vampires who did not understand my reluctance to be infused. He had jokingly said on many occasions that he would gladly offer the 'first bite,' earning himself a growl from Janet, who was a much younger vampire than he was and far less controlled.

Janet used to be human but had opted to be infused for her lover. She was a genius and created many inspiring pieces, and since I was a child, I could not resist her designs, nor could Mia. We all tended to like the same type of designs; Mia tended to pick the greens and browns, which were the colours of autumn to match her beautiful jade green eyes and chestnut hair, and I tended to choose the dark blues and violets of the summer evenings to match my oddly coloured eyes. Janet, on the other hand, often dressed herself in blacks and silvers with clean, crisp lines.

After we had purchased what we thought we needed and Mia was feeling a little more sated and a great deal calmer, we called for the driver and made our way back to the castle. Theo needed to oversee the details of the increased security that would be needed for visiting royalty, and Alex went with him, leaving James with me and Mia. There was not much more to be done, so we just spent the afternoon and evening sitting together chatting while trying on our new outfits. It was easy to forget problems when playing dress-up with one's best friend.

The afternoon flew by and the room grew darker as the shadows grew longer with the approach of evening. I must have fallen asleep at some point without even realising it because the next time I heard Mia speak, it was to David. Soon I felt him lift me gently and carry me into our private bedroom.

As we entered the bedroom, I heard him agree to delay his visit to the African Territories until Mia had done what she needed to do.

Chapter 15

T he next morning I woke up in David's arms again and was glad that he had delayed his visit to the African Territories. I knew the delay was only temporary, but at least I knew he would be with us for a short while.

I emerged from a deep, dreamless sleep when I heard his voice whispering through my head. This time he was telling me to keep quiet, indicating that he was the one who was trying to listen. He explained quietly that Mia had just entered our apartment. We both listened intently as we heard her approach our door. We waited as we heard her speaking quietly to Alex, who was in position outside our door; there was no shouting this time, just a civilised request. Again David made a phone call to Alex, and Mia was placed on the phone straight away. All David managed to say was "Come," and she was there at the side of the bed, in person, ready to carry out whatever task she had placed at the top of the to-do list in her head.

Obviously we were trying to be a little more patient, knowing how anxious she was feeling about the coming days. Gently, before I knew it, she held in her hand my bathrobe. Beyond her, through the open door, I could see she had placed my breakfast on the table in the next room.

"Come on, Liberty. You have to get up now because they are arriving shortly and there is much to arrange still," she said as she started to pace up and down the bedroom, muttering to herself, occasionally frowning or shaking her head at her own decisions.

"Mia, you have to calm yourself," I said as I got up, obediently took the robe, and put it on.

"I have spoken to Mother, and she has suggested an announcement banquet in our honour tonight," Mia said, pacing even quicker. My eyes could barely follow her as she rushed about the room picking up my clothes and placing them in the basket.

"Mia, stop it! Why are you behaving like this? There is no one I know on this entire planet who is better at organising things than you are," I said, trying to figure out what had gotten her so nervous.

"Yes, but the things I organise are not really for me, are they?" she said, looking slightly irritated. I understood, then, from the impatient, withered look she was directing at me that it was going to be a long day.

I sighed as I went to get my breakfast from the next room. I brought a plate of lightly toasted bread over to the bed and sat down next to David. "All right, let us get organised, then, but I think we are going to need more help," I said as I reached for my phone.

I arranged an emergency meeting with Heather, Thomas, Rachael, Miss Davinia, and Sally. I wasn't sure what I was doing, so I invited all the people I thought that Mia would invite if the roles were reversed. Secretly, on the inside, with each phone call I got more and more nervous; I had no idea how to proceed. The last time I had arranged phone calls for Mia, everything was done by other people and I didn't really have to do anything. As each minute passed, more and more things occurred to me, so I asked David to arrange a time when we could see and speak to the emperor and empress to ask them if it would be possible for me to borrow one of their personal assistants.

I also sent Alex to find Janet and Georgina with a message to meet me urgently at the castle. When all that was done, I slowly and calmly began to eat my toast. Mia, who I know had been watching me closely, suddenly burst out laughing and hugged me to her.

"Are you calmer now?" I asked, smiling without looking at her as she sat down beside me.

"Are you?" she responded, giggling.

"Look, I am just a little nervous about doing all of this. I know how you all think of me and believe in me, but please understand that this is the first time I have tried to arrange something and I want it to be perfect for both you and Patrick," I said.

When Mia went to speak, I put my hand up and continued, "I also know you won't let me do this all on my own, but please try to relax and trust the people we talk to. You must let them do what is asked of them because, you said it yourself, this is all for you. I am asking you to be nice. I forbid you from making any other being nervous or reducing any of them to tears . . . otherwise I am not going to do it," I added, smiling.

My phone started ringing almost before I had managed to finish getting myself dressed. The first call I got was to say that Janet and Georgina had been found and were on their way to the castle.

At the same time the empress's personal assistant arrived, and between us things really started to get organised. The word 'multitasking' didn't quite cover how fast she accomplished the tasks that were set; I was in awe of her. Although I had met her many times, I still didn't know her name. She smiled at me when she saw me, but it was a strange smile; it was as if she knew something I didn't and perhaps should have known. Sometimes Rachael smiled at me the same way, but Rachael's smile never made me uncomfortable. The assistant told me her name was Emma, but there was something about her that did not fit the name; she did not look like an Emma. I was about to question her a little more when a hush seemed to go through my mind and I suddenly felt questioning her was perhaps not the right thing to do at the time. My misgivings about Emma faded quickly as she turned out to be an absolute miracle worker; within a very short period of time, she appeared to be able to anticipate my questions and needs before I even understood them myself. Emma remained distant from the others who surrounded me, and she seemed able to coordinate her time with me so we were mostly alone; the other helpers were out doing errands. We made a lot of satisfactory progress during the morning, but in the middle of the first set of meetings Mia received a telephone call from Patrick, and just after noon Mia had to leave.

Heather went with Cassius and Mia to greet the Irish queen at the airport. They took with them a suitably sized escort selected from the more handsome royal guards, knowing that the queen had a taste for the younger males. For me the rest of the day was filled with visits and arrangements. I honestly don't know what I would have done if I had not had such an experienced team of castle beings at my disposal. It helped that Emma appeared to be well respected among the employees of the castle. Oddly, though, at times I thought some of them looked almost afraid of her. I found their fear interesting; the darkness within made me observant yet detached.

I didn't see much of Mia for the rest of the day. She was obviously spending time with Patrick and his cousin. As the day turned to evening, I finally sat down with Rachael and dismissed all the other helpers. Emma was one of the last to go. She seemed reluctant to leave at first, but I reassured her that we would use her again and gave her a hug. In our brief embrace, she whispered softly that she was here to help, and the look she gave me, again, said that should mean something to me, which made me pause after she left. In a hurry, though, and after Rachael left, I called David. When he arrived we got ready together to play our part in the announcement.

Chapter 16

Over the rest of that day and into the evening, the castle became alive with various activities. Thankfully, everything we had organised earlier that day went according to plan. David and I both wore formal costumes; he chose to wear his usual black trousers, knee-high boots, black high-necked shirt, and a floor-length cape embroidered with his family crest and colours. I chose to wear a floor-length crimson dress; crimson was the colour favoured by vampire women, and it was considered a traditional colour among vampires in general. The dress was corseted at my waist, and its satin-material skirt clung to my legs. It had no sleeves, so my tattoo of the Alaunus family crest was clearly visible. I had chosen to wear black velvet slippers on my feet since I had learned from experience that a vampire banquet could last a long time and I wanted to be as comfortable as possible for this one.

I wore the usual very dark, dramatic makeup. Mia had commissioned someone to do it for me. Again, this was all part of the perfect vision she wanted the queen to see. However, as David preferred my hair loose, I did it by myself and let it fall softly around my shoulders, but kept back from my face by an elegant and delicate black diamond tiara. Theo and the rest of our usual escort wore black shirts and trousers. Each of them looked groomed but brooding. When they stood together their clothing resembled a uniform.

Mia and Patrick joined us in the Throne Room just before we were about to make our entrance onto the balcony. Mia looked stunning. She was wearing an emerald green dress that followed the lines of her body. Its neckline plunged almost to her belly button and the waist was pulled in with a wide golden belt. The dress was floor length and trailed slightly behind her. On her feet she had chosen to wear golden sandals with straps that fastened above her ankles. Her hair was left loose and flowing, with a gold tiara made from entwined bands of the precious metal. She had used diamond dust eye shadow in browns and golds to brighten the green of her eyes. For this occasion Mia definitely looked more Forest Dweller than vampire. Her smile, though, was radiant yet tinged with nerves. My heart melted at her insecurity, so I gave her a brief hug, making sure not to put so much as a hair out of place.

We walked carefully through the empty Throne Room, past the ornate columns to the far wall. We stopped behind the podium, which held the thrones, and for the first time I noticed that one of the royal portraits had been pulled aside. Without knowing why, I shivered slightly, but I couldn't tell you whether it was from anticipation of the cool passageway ahead or from excitement as I realised that the passageway revealed a set of stone steps. I had never been up that way before. I realised I might do a little more exploring at some future time when the castle was quieter, with fewer guests. Since reading the book, I found myself looking more closely into the shadows and recesses of my home. I knew with certainty that Alex and James would not mind if I did so, nor would they share my adventures with anyone if I asked them not to. They were my guards and their loyalties were with me. In that moment I was glad I still hadn't shared their secret of telepathy with any of our group, not even David or Theo.

The narrow stone corridor was dark, and as I stepped forward I got the feeling that the steps were not used very often anymore. I felt a thrill as I heard my feet on those stone steps. There was an ancient echo of austerity about them, and they did not invite any speech or noise, so we moved upwards in silence.

The passage itself was completely dark when the portrait was repositioned behind us, and the corridor was narrow enough so I could steady my ascent by resting my hand on the wall. The stone was smooth beneath the flat of my hand and had warmth within that surprised me. I found myself smiling, again perfectly happy within the confines of darkness. I wondered whether Elathan had ever walked the same stone steps many centuries before. I wondered if he missed having access to his home and his kingdom.

At the top of the steps, we walked through an open door onto a huge stone balcony that looked out over the southern grounds of the castle. The night was clear and the air was cool. There was an almost tangible air of excitement as we took our allotted places. David and I were seated to the right of the thrones of the emperor and empress in our equally ornate but smaller thrones. Queen Sinead was seated at the left-hand side of their thrones and next to her were seats for Patrick and Mia.

Below us I could see that within the grounds of the castle stood what appeared to be most of the Forest Dwellers population from the surrounding forests and also most of the world's media representatives. We had decided to broadcast the announcement at the same time the emperor and empresses gave the couple their formal blessing and issued their seal of approval for the commitment.

Queen Sinead looked radiant; she had chosen to wear a full-skirted crimson dress with a tightly laced bodice. It reached to the floor and swirled around her feet. Her dark hair was piled elegantly on top of her head and secured with emerald hairpins that matched her emerald eyes. I could see the resemblance between her and her cousin and realised for the first time they might actually have been related by more than the essence that flowed through their veins.

Queen Sinead was the first to rise and speak, her voice loud and clear. She spoke with confidence in a voice full of love and pride, tinged with a lilting accent that easily carried over to the crowds below. She told of how much she loved Mia, how quickly her love and respect for her had grown, and how she relished the thought of Mia becoming part of another royal family, and her family within the Irish Territories.

The next to speak was Emperor Marcarius. Although he spoke to the world, as he always had through his Life Partner, Constantina, he also began by telling the planet of his pride in his other adopted child, his daughter Mia. The way he announced his feelings for her surprised all of us, I think, because Mia had never been publicly acknowledged as anything more than the empress's gift. The speeches went on for a while, all of them warm and welcoming. By the end, both Patrick and Mia looked joyously happy and proud.

When it came to Patrick's turn for a speech, he turned and faced Mia, lowered himself down onto one knee in front the planet, and formally asked Mia to become his Everlasting Life Partner. Patrick knew that he did not need to ask her in such an old-fashioned way, but he knew she revered the way such traditional rituals had been carried out in the centuries before vampires, in all their detachment, had become the rulers of the planet. He then presented her with a betrothal ring that he had especially designed; it was a thin golden band of tiny, intricately perfect leaves overlapping to form the eternal circle.

Of course, Mia said yes and everyone below the balcony started cheering and clapping. Many of the Forest Dwellers threw petals and leaves into the air, creating a cloud of floating colour. The mood on the balcony was ecstatic.

As soon as all the speeches were over, out of respect we allowed the emperor and empress to leave the balcony first and then we all made our way back down the stone stairs of the narrow corridor. Once at the bottom and away from the cameras and the eyes of the beings who had attended, I first hugged the Irish queen, who laughed and hugged me back with equal affection. It was so good to see her again, and even though we had met only a couple of times before, I had liked her from the first.

Of course, I also hugged Patrick fiercely, infecting him with my laughter and happiness, and then it was Mia's turn. I simply held her close to me and she responded with equal emotion and affection. There was lots of laughter, and eventually even the male beings among us embraced each other, albeit briefly and less emotionally. It was clear, though, this was a memorable moment for all of us, and to an outsider probably a bit comical to watch.

The only one who had tears to accompany the laughter was me, as usual, but everyone knew that they were not tears of sadness but joy, and that led to more laughter, with Mia trying to stop the tears from running my eye makeup. Unfortunately, there was not much time for more than initial congratulations since we had to walk the short distance to the banquet room nearest the Throne Room, where a celebration had been planned for the happy couple.

Mia looked so happy she positively glowed. She had a very tight grip on Patrick's hand during the walk even though they were both speaking to different individuals who approached them. I couldn't help noticing that the Irish queen frowned slightly as she noticed their physical closeness, but I did not think it was a problem for her. I did know that it took some of the other beings a while to understand and get used to the way we all behaved towards each other.

As we watched them I felt David's hand find mine, and at his touch I could feel my own betrothal ring glowing snugly and warmly between our fingers. I felt so much love for David—for us and for the future. We walked together smiling, watching and relishing the joy and happiness of two of our favourite people. As we got near to the hall, Mia and Patrick took up their positions in front of us all with Queen Sinead directly behind them. David and I stood behind her and, of course, Theo, Cassius, Alex, and James stood behind us as the royal guard.

The others in our group—Rachael, Heather, Thomas, and the others, those we regarded as our friends and who had been given VIB invitations—began formally joining up in pairs to bring up the rear of our little procession. The doors were swung open and we slowly entered to the sound of a haunting, traditional local melody played by a group of well-known and popular Forest Dwellers.

One of the emperor's personal assistants stood off to the left-hand side of the door and announced each of us as we entered. Emma, Marcarius's personal assistant, appeared, on hand to guide the guests to their allotted places. Even though there was a loud murmuring of voices as we approached the hall, at the sound of the first announcement every being that had joined us for the meal rose to their feet and stood silently, watching us as we made our way to our tables.

The hall was decorated with the reds and golds of our family crest, but entwined within those colours were the vibrant golds and greens of the Irish royal family. Our family crests hung side by side behind the head table.

We all took our places at the head table especially reserved for us and shared nourishment together. The rest of the hall was packed with visiting dignitaries and, of course, representatives of all our local Forest Dwellers. After we had been nourished we sat quietly and listened to various speeches of friends and acquaintances. Heather was allowed to speak first.

I observed that some of our subjects seemed to disapprove slightly of the Forest Dweller having been invited to speak in front of the emperor. She did not seem to notice as she spoke of her joy at the impending union of Patrick and her sister. As she continued I began to let my mind wander a little; I was beginning to tire as the evening moved slowly into night.

I couldn't help but look for Emma among the guests. I don't know why, but I felt as if I was drawn to her. Eventually I found her seated at one of the back tables. As soon as I saw her, she turned and looked straight back at me, her smile indulgent but unreadable.

My mind snapped back into the present when I heard Queen Sinead announce that her cousin and his intended betrothed would be accompanying her back to the Irish Territories, where the Ceremony of Commitment would take place in exactly one month's time. As the queen made the announcement, I looked at Mia and heard her thoughts cut softly through my own: *I am sorry. It has not long been decided, and though I wanted time to tell you, it was not given. But this is for me and mine. It will be fine. I promise we will speak about it all later.*

Of course I understood, so I smiled at her and raised the customary miniature vial I always insisted on and made a special salute to my friend. She took a sip in a return salute, and I put my vial to my lips and took a sip of the warm blood inside. I didn't particularly like it; I wanted to spit it out almost immediately. The liquid in my mouth was thick and slightly salty, but I swallowed it and managed to maintain my smile, working hard at not looking too disgusted. David looked at me with curiosity but said nothing.

After all the speeches had finished, there were a few dances. Even though not everyone seemed to want to join in, no one left the banqueting hall until the emperor and empress departed. Once an appropriate amount of time had elapsed after their departure, we all made the decision to leave together. As a group we all retired to the privacy of the royal apartments.

Once there, I sat with Mia because apparently she would be leaving within the next two days, and I felt at a loss almost immediately. I really wanted to go with Mia, and I do not doubt that David would not have stopped me, but something—a feeling—told me that I should stay, that it was important for me to remain where I was.

Patrick appeared to understand our need to be together before they left and drifted away, saying he had matters of his own to attend to. Mia seemed keen for me to stay at the moment, but I think her departure for the Irish Territories was decided upon because she needed to concentrate on the arrangements for her Commitment Ceremony and not be distracted while she became acquainted with the customs of her new family.

I would miss her incredibly, and I was saddened that I would not be there to help her organise one of the most important days of her life, but I knew that I would be with her and Patrick to celebrate it. We held hands and pretty much didn't let go of each other for the next two days. I even let her stay with me during the night until it was time for her the leave. David and Patrick kept a discreet distance from us, both of them understanding that we needed the time together since it would have to last us until they returned. The night before she had to leave, she lay beside me but I wasn't able to sleep much. When I did my dreams were confusing. On the one hand, I felt an extreme amount of loss; on the other, I felt as if an invisible restriction which had been placed on me had suddenly gone, disappeared.

I told her on our last night that I couldn't go with her beyond the walls of the castle and that I couldn't bear to see her leave anywhere other than my apartment. So the morning of her departure I ate my breakfast as I watched her get ready to go, and then she leaned over me and hugged me gently. Neither of us said a word because there was nothing left for us to say. She closed the door quietly on her way out and I cried.

I didn't have a lot of time to miss her at first because she sent a message at every stage of her journey until I eventually told her to stop, that I was okay and that one message a day would be enough. Even David had to laugh. He knew that I needed him, though, so for the entire day after her departure he stayed at my side, most of the time passing me tissues and listening to me babble about how great it would be for Mia and how much I was looking forward to standing with her at the ceremony.

Chapter 17

T he next couple of days were miserable—or, at least, I was miserable. I didn't want to do anything much. I missed Mia so much. I hadn't realised how much I did with her and exactly how much of my day she filled with her presence, and even if she wasn't physically with me, she was always speaking to me on the telephone or communicating with me in some way.

Eventually I could sense that even David was becoming a little exasperated with my moping about. He had again delayed his trip at my request, placating me after yet another emotional outburst. It was after a particularly miserable day when he walked out of the apartment in frustration. After that, I made a bit more of an effort to function in some type of normal way. To the relief of everyone else, I started venturing out of our apartments more, going for walks and spending time at the temple.

I found a type of contented peace there inside the castle again. It was good to wander and explore once more, and to take my mind off Mia. Rachael took some time away from her research and arranged for us to go shopping, and although it was fun, it wasn't the same as it had been with Mia. Rachael tended to be a little more intimidating and we had less attention from the shop assistants, who appeared more than willing to stay at a discreet distance. And her choices of clothes were sometimes a little too revealing even for my liberal tastes.

After that initial uncomfortable shopping trip, I found that if I looked hard enough there really was plenty to do within the castle and again, with Rachael's help, we persuaded David that it was a good and dutiful thing for a princess to study occasionally. Poor David was no match for Rachael. He was already at a disadvantage worrying about my state of mind, and when he started to put his foot down and protest, she firmly pointed out to him that I did not have the luxury of a history being passed down to me and it would good if I had at least some knowledge before I mingled with royalty at Mia's ceremony.

David couldn't disagree; there was a way that Rachael had about her when she thought that someone was going to attempt to disagree with her. I had felt in fear of her as a child, and I suspected David, who had not known her for very long, also felt it with her as an adult, especially when she felt he was not being very cooperative. I stood very still watching; the whole scenario made me smile. When they had discussed and eventually agreed on topics that would not hurt me, I was allowed to travel to the library with David's final blessing.

During my first few visits I tried to stick to my allotted topics and began to study more about David's ancestry and the time before the vampires, even though the records seemed scarce. I tried to pinpoint when exactly the vampires had taken total control of the planet and memorised as much as I could, knowing that there was every chance that David would be asking me questions. Another subject that I had decided to study properly was the history of Forest Dwellers. When I discussed this second choice of topic with David, I told him it was because of his sister and the fact that we were surrounded by them. As time went on, I found the topic very compelling. I even decided to spend some time with Thomas and Heather to try to see for myself how they existed within the forests.

David again was a little resistant to the idea of my leaving the castle without Alex and James. It was common knowledge that vampires were still not very welcome within the domains of the Forest Dwellers, and he was obviously worried that I would come to harm. Although vampires were the strongest of the beings that inhabited the planet, there were reports that some Forest Dwellers had begun to use the magic of their forests to strengthen or enchant their borders. These enchantments were rumoured to expel or cause the disappearance of unwanted visitors. Of course, it was just rumours. No one had come forward with any real evidence, and most of the time such claims were dismissed by vampires, who had a tendency to believe they were indestructible. As far as the Forest Dwellers were concerned, vampires were not welcome in their domains because for thousands of years all vampires had done was destroy the land and those who tried to care for it.

While there was an uneasy truce due to the ancient Treaty of Deliverance, vampires typically had never shown any remorse or respect when they had entered the forests since. Although both Theo and David were both born as Dwellers, they seemed to have forgotten how powerful these beings were within their own domains and believed that as Heather's honoured guest I would be protected. At first they were too stubborn and unwilling to listen. Time and again it took the intervention of Rachael on my behalf for them to listen to my arguments. To drive home my point I invited Thomas to the castle. I knew David liked and respected him and his seriousness, and I was so grateful to Thomas because his calm assurance led David to agree to allow me to walk through the forests near the castle with some Dwellers as escorts. Thomas, in other words, was able to convince David how safe I would be out there without all my castle guards.

I was so excited I could hardly sleep the night before. I got up early and made sure I ate well. I dressed sensibly for the day, knowing that it would probably be quite a difficult one and because I had a good idea that we were going to play some games, with me as the prize. I dressed myself in a warm tight-fitting jumper and tight hard-wearing trousers, which I tucked in my soft low-heeled boots. I tied my long hair tightly behind my head in a practical ponytail and didn't bother applying makeup. It wasn't that type of visit.

I joined Alex, James, Theo, and even David, who had elected to be my bodyguards in the forest. Theo could have stayed behind, but I knew he wouldn't (and so did David and everyone else, including Rachael). The apartment was quiet and a little tense when the knock on the door came. My protectors were obviously concentrating on ways to protect me. There were lots of long, meaningful looks; they had obviously devised a plan to prove their point.

When the knock did come, they all rose as one and stood slightly behind me. As I went to open the door, I stopped; I was suddenly a little worried and felt uneasy. Already I could feel the tension emanating from them. I realised then that they intended to prove to me that they needed to protect me, that they alone could protect me no matter what the cost. Before I opened the door completely, I looked at them all and said, "You will behave, all of you." I said this quietly, looking at each of them and showing them that I was becoming irritated. "Or perhaps I won't be as cooperative as you might want me to be. Is that clear?"

It took them a moment, but the look on my face must have shown them that I meant business, and I thought it seemed to settle them at least a little, even David. I knew that they all wanted to smile, but to their credit they didn't. They were superior in every way to me, but I had organised this meeting and decided whoever was going to be with me would obey me during that day.

"I mean it," I said, once again trying to make eye contact with each of them. It was Theo who held my gaze the longest until eventually even he gave me a surly, unhappy look and nodded in agreement.

When I opened the door, standing directly in front of me was Thomas. He had brought with him Marta and another Forest Dweller that I had only ever seen once before, and that was only because he was one of the Forest Dwellers that had attended our Commitment Ceremony. For some reason I couldn't recall having seen him at Mia's announcement.

I hugged Thomas warmly as soon as I saw him; it really was good to see him in person again. Beside him, inevitably, was Marta, the oldest Forest Dweller I had ever met. I knew her well. She had helped to save me once, but I only nodded briefly at her since she really didn't care much for pleasantries. Although Marta appeared to dislike humans immensely, I think that she had a little bit of a soft spot for me because she actually nodded back at me. That was enough, and actually a huge improvement from the first time I had met her, when she had punched me in my face and blackened my eye.

The Forest Dweller behind Thomas was the tallest being I had ever seen. I barely reached his chest. He wasn't as broad-shouldered and tall as Theo, but he was definitely broader and taller than David. I waited for Thomas to introduce him before I acknowledged him; I suspected that the tall being in front of me would be the one who would be demonstrating their own brand of protection. Thomas informed us all that his name was Adair. Apparently he was the local headman, which meant that he tried to maintain more than one forest in an area. He would visit, listen, and judge to try to unite the Forest Dwellers whenever there was a problem to be disputed or solved.

I took his hand when he offered it to me and bowed slightly in greeting. I never took my eyes from his face, which showed nothing, not even curiosity. There was no warmth or recognition, and I had a feeling that he was as much a traditionalist as some of the vampires that were opposed to me. I also got the impression from him that he had been around for a very long time. After his cool and detached handshake, my senses went into overdrive, every one of them jingling, telling me to be wary of him. He was not my friend.

As I went to pull my hand away, he wrapped his hands a little tighter around mine, and suddenly his large hands were smothering mine. They were large and both rough and warm to the touch, indicating that there was also an intense inner strength to him. He had skin that looked like the sun had burnt it on one too many occasions; it was the rich brown colour of young trees. His face was quite young, but old at the same time. He had deep lines on his face that did not leave when he relaxed. I certainly would not have called him handsome, but his eyes were striking. They were almost like mine, only his were coloured with jade green and warm pale browns.

As expected, my guards were barely polite and the greetings between the group in front of me and the guards at my back were barely civil. I took a moment and sent a thought to them all, and I asked them to do this for me. I softly added a "please," asking them this time and not telling them. I also directed my thoughts to Theo alone, pushing through his resistance. I knew that it made him slightly uncomfortable, but sometimes it was the only way I could communicate with him privately. I explained that we might be able to use this experience to learn different techniques. Theo had always been keen on the arts of defence, and this would provide a unique insight into the way that the Forest Dwellers protected themselves. I also told him that Alex and James would follow his lead and that I needed us all to learn because we might have to enter other forests in the near future, especially with the upcoming hunt for the other Element. I glanced backwards and saw him nod gently, and felt relieved as he stepped forward and smiled a new greeting at Thomas.

The visiting party stepped back and allowed us to leave the apartment. As I left I grabbed my jacket and walked ahead with Thomas. I asked him if Heather would be joining us later. I was surprised, even though I shouldn't have been, to learn that she had left to join Mia and Patrick. He informed me that Mia had called for her shortly after her arrival in the Irish Territories, and as the sister of the Life Partner to be, Heather had left straight away, excited at the prospect of helping with preparations that were in full swing for the upcoming Commitment Ceremony.

We walked out of the castle and took a castle vehicle to the forest situated to the south of the castle. Thankfully, after the recent cull there were very few photographers and media present, and those who were there were given very little time to ask any questions.

There was only one vehicle waiting for us, so we all had to share it. During the short journey to the forest, we all sat in complete silence. I tried to start up a conversation with Thomas, but he didn't reply; in fact, he looked every bit as uncomfortable as we all did.

I was relieved when we finally neared the outer limits of the southern forests; however, as I looked out of the window, I almost changed my mind. The ancient trees of the forest loomed neck-creakingly high above the car, blocking the brightness of the blue sky.

Once we arrived at the forest's outer limits, the driver parked the car and opened the door. We got out and a plan was made. Thomas seemed to take charge for a while and explained that apparently I was to walk with the Forest Dwellers through the forest and David, Theo, Alex, and James would try to attack me and take me from them. My bodyguards smiled, quietly confident. They seemed to think their task was going to be easy, and looking at Thomas's face I would have agreed with them, but it was Adair who held my attention. He wasn't smiling. His face looked deliberately devoid of emotion and disinterest, which made me feel a small shiver of fear make its way down my spine.

As Thomas explained what was going to happen, I realised that it was almost the same as the hunt I had seen a few years before, only I was the one being hunted. The thought made me feel slightly uncomfortable, but I tried not to dwell on that particular memory. We were going to be given a sixty-minute head start, so I kissed David and said good-bye as he went back to the vehicle to wait inside while I moved ahead with Thomas, Marta, and Adair.

Chapter 18

When they were completely gone from our sight, we walked a little farther into the forest until Adair indicated for us all to stop. He then pulled a large grey sack from the natural hollow of an old tree and started sorting through the bag. After a moment, even though I was already wearing suitably warm clothes, Adair came forward and handed me a dark green and brown cloak.

"You will need this if you are to be given any chance of survival in here. You are far too conspicuous as you are," he said, looking me up and down with barely disguised contempt.

The cloak looked heavier and dirtier than it actually was, and because of its appearance I was at first reluctant to put it on, but with one look at Adair's face I threw it around myself. I was pleasantly surprised. The colours of the cloak perfectly matched the lush, rich auburn colours of the surrounding forest.

The cloak shimmered and clung to me as I moved. Almost covering me from my chin down, it had a hood on the back and a soft belt at its waist. Begrudgingly, I realised that of course Adair was right; the cloak was definitely going to be my first defence. I realised, too, that whether I liked the Forest Dweller or not, my safety depended on him and his knowledge. Because of his general attitude towards me, I doubted myself for just a second, wondering if I had made the right decision, but then as I looked at the smiling encouragement on Thomas's face my doubt gave way again to curious excitement. As I wrapped the cloak closely around my shoulders, Adair continued to look at me, his face devoid of expression.

"Thomas and Marta have told me that you may be a being that has been anticipated for quite some time. Do you really believe that? Do you believe that you are something more than you appear to me to be? Perhaps you think yourself to be something special?" Adair spoke quietly, his voice out of the range of the others' hearing. I didn't even bother to answer him since his tone clearly reflected his disbelief and disapproval. "They also tell me that you have talent and that your senses go beyond what is normal for your kind. You may need to demonstrate those talents if you are going to survive today. You continue to remain human, and only that, even with the mark placed upon you by my ocean brothers."

I looked at Adair in response then because it sounded as if my trial would begin with him. I was going to respond, but I became aware of Thomas as he moved closer to me; even if he could not hear Adair's words, he must have felt that something wasn't quite right. The atmosphere had turned cold and the tension had become palpable.

"I am sorry, but I thought you were here to protect me. Why do I have the feeling that may not be the case?" I said, feeling more than a little nervous about the menacingly tall Forest Dweller.

"Adair! Be careful with what are you saying. She is protected by the emperor himself, and no harm will come to her while she is in our care," Thomas said sharply, stepping slightly in front of me to protect me.

"This behaviour is unforgivable and is not what we had discussed at the meeting with the Council of Dwellers. If my memory serves me right, and it does, it was decided to go ahead with this only if the princess was not to be placed in any immediate danger. You must know the consequences for us, and indeed all of our kind, if she comes to any harm. Are you willing to undo all of the recent progress made by the council?" Thomas's warning was clear.

"If she is who you think she is, then she won't be in any danger, no matter how she is tested," was Adair's defiant reply.

"But you said it yourself. She is still human," said Thomas, looking at me with an apology on his face, as if he did not mean to make my humanity sound as if it were a weakness. I smiled back at him with reassurance, not really understanding what was happening. More words followed and the conversation picked up speed, but I lost track of what they were saying; I understood that whatever they were saying didn't sound like anything good. The pair of them glared at each other for a while, and then Adair turned away and looked down on Marta, who had stepped forward to join Thomas.

"We will observe, but I command, as your elder, that neither of you are to use what you know to protect her. She is to prove her own worth to me on this day. Have I made myself understood?" Adair said with authority. I knew that he was giving them no choice and expected them to obey his request. When I saw Thomas back down and nod, and Marta follow suit, I felt the first real stirrings of fear trickle down my spine, but this was my own fault and I knew it; I was the clever one who had practically insisted on being put in this situation.

My heart sank a little lower in my chest as I thought that most of the lessons I had to learn had almost killed me until I was able to muster my senses and sense of self-preservation. My sense of foreboding did improve when I looked at Thomas. I could see that he was conflicted by what was happening; his gaze was both torn and apologetic, and I knew that he would have almost as much difficulty in the next few hours as David would have if he had heard the exchange with Adair. Thomas also knew that Mia would actually kill him if she knew what was about to happen.

It was Theo's reaction, though, that worried me more. I knew he would be seething if he found out, and I couldn't even begin to think about his reaction if anything did happen to me. The Forest Dwellers would be annihilated and David would withdraw any proposed freedoms he intended to extend to the Forest Dwellers. Theo would do his part by literally ripping the forest apart in his search for me. I turned to look at the Forest Dweller again.

"Is that it, is that your plan? You are just going to leave me here to fend for myself? For your own safety I suggest that you stop this now, because if they find me unprotected my guards will not be happy," I said with more authority than I felt, looking at Adair.

"It is not I who wants to test you, Princess, it is the forest. If you are who it is said you are, this particular forest has been waiting for you for a very, very long time," Adair said cryptically, his face giving nothing away to me.

As he spoke I felt a sharp pain in my neck, almost as if I had been bitten by an insect. My neck suddenly felt hot, a rushing sound grew in my ears, and I felt as if the ground beneath my feet was shifting. I felt dizzy as the forest seemed to swirl and change around me. The last thing I saw was the tall Forest Dweller taking a step towards me, and then there was nothing. Everything went greyish black.

Chapter 19

The next thing I remember when the grey mist finally started to clear from my mind is waking up in a sitting position with my back against a tree. As I looked around I could see only a very small sliver of daylight, and the sky appeared to have changed from pale to royal blue, marking the onset of late afternoon. I could hear very little noise; even with my improved senses the forest around me appeared unusually quiet, expectantly watching me.

I took a deep breath and gave myself a cursory health check. I didn't feel as if I was hurt or as if I had been sedated in any way; in fact, as I opened my eyes fully, my head felt strangely clear, alive, and aware. I sat there for a short while listening to and smelling the forest around me. After a few moments I sat forward and readjusted my position so I could get a better look at my surroundings. As soon as I moved, though, I felt chilled and pulled the cloak that Adair had given me around me, then I turned my body slowly and looked up at the tree that was supporting me. I could not see the top of it, but it appeared to be a large, very old oak tree. I didn't know how I knew what kind of tree it was—I just did.

The tree felt good and safe; not sensing any danger close to me, I stood up. Even though I knew I should have been afraid since I was on my own and unprotected in a place I did not know, I was keenly aware that the forest was neutral, waiting like everyone else. I stayed there for a few moments, contemplating my next move. I had already been warned in advance by Sarah;

she told me that this test was going to happen and I was going to discover something important.

I started to walk towards what I thought was a gap in the trees. I felt a little uncomfortable moving away from the tree without the solid support at my back. I made sure I stepped carefully so as not to disturb anything. Strangely, a sense of awe and reverence for this ancient forest began to flood my consciousness. I was beginning to feel happy and welcome, and amazed that I felt so free for some reason. The farther I walked, the more at home I felt, and then I knew that I had lived in a forest when I was a very small child. I still remembered some of the stories about the ancient forests that my mother had told me, and my mind began to wander through those memories as my feet stayed the course that I had chosen to follow. The carpet of moss and leaves on the floor was soft and spongy beneath my feet, and I could smell the heavy, slightly perfumed scent of the forest's plants and flowers and the musty but pleasant smell of old plants dying to let the new growth sprout from the decay.

I felt like I was walking in another time or that I was living in one of my dreams, like the one where my mother was still by my side and others walked in the forests with me. I recognised not only mother but also Lillie and Molly, whom I had known in my early childhood.

The path that I thought I needed to follow appeared to lead me forward towards a clearing, and I continued to walk happily forward in a straight line until I was almost at the edge of it. I stopped walking as I sensed something or someone behind me. I turned and caught a glimpse of the Forest Dweller Adair standing and staring straight at me. He was barely visible, with his own cloak camouflaging him against the dark of the vegetation.

There was no look of recognition on his face. His eyes looked cold and distant, and his forehead was creased in concentration. I could see his lips moving, but I couldn't hear the words he was saying; he looked like he was chanting or perhaps saying some type of prayer. I decided to ignore him and continue on my chosen path towards the clearing, but when I turned back around I could no longer see the open space; it was as if that part of the forest had moved. Instead there was now in front of me a darkened pathway, and at its end was a dense green wall. The scene was sinister, and the thick overgrown vines that hung from the branches of the trees above made it even more so. I felt the first inkling of panic since I knew where I had been before I had seen Adair and I knew that I hadn't moved off my chosen path. The clearing should have been there, but suddenly it wasn't; instead there appeared to be a wall of vines.

I didn't know how deep or impenetrable the vines were, so I reached out to touch one. To my surprise and horror the vine shrank away from me. Suddenly the forest was no longer what I had thought it to be. It was a living, breathing thing and I didn't know who or what it was. The illusion of safety and peace I had felt before faded and suddenly the forest didn't seem friendly anymore. It had become menacing, dark, and unwelcoming. Even the cloak I was wearing seemed to grow heavier. Not knowing what was happening, I closed my eyes and took some deep breaths to stop my panic from growing.

I tried to formulate a plausible explanation. I knew instinctively that the clearing was still there because logically it had to be, so ignoring my misgivings, I decided that I would stay on the path I had already chosen. I had a feeling, though, that whatever path I chose, there would be other obstacles, other tests, awaiting me.

I took a small step forward and then another. The vines appeared to move at my pace, keeping the same distance between themselves and me as I moved. I continued walking, acutely aware of my surroundings. Every little noise, even my own footfalls on the carpeted floor, had become louder. I sensed other movements behind me, yet each time I turned I failed to see anything.

It took a while for me to understand what was happening, but after a few minutes of concentrating and being careful, I saw out of the corner of my eye one of the vines that hung from the branch of a tree slowly unfurling itself, stretching forward and almost creeping up behind my back. The fact that there was no noise made it all the more ominous. I felt unsure, perhaps even vulnerable and humanlike again.

I felt I had no other option, so I stood still where I was and closed my eyes for a second and concentrated. I had never tried to sense anything other than the beings that surrounded me. It was difficult because I had no idea what I was sensing, but as I concentrated I got a faint connection with whatever was surrounding me. It appeared to be neither a bad thing nor a good thing; it was an ancient thing, and although its curiosity was almost childlike, it was a thing of great presence and strength. If I would give it a recognisable image in my mind, it would be of a white mist that touched everything and everyone that walked or lived within the boundaries of the forest, brushing passersby and gently sensing their intentions within the forest.

Because I felt no malice from it, I made the decision to remove the cloak from my shoulders. I knew I needed to get my fears under control, so I did the exact opposite of what any normal being would do: I laid the cloak out and sat down on the floor of the forest. I sat still and closed my eyes. I already knew that whatever it was that had me surrounded was not unfriendly; it was simply observing me.

It crossed my mind that Adair must have communicated with it, but not knowing how he had portrayed me worried me a little. My thoughts reached deep down inside of me, and my coiled dark inner strength became alert; I could sense it was ready. I knew without opening my eyes that I was strong enough to deal with whatever 'it' was.

When I was calm and fully in control, I opened my eyes and let them adjust to the dimness of the forest. It came as no surprise that the vine had seemingly slithered a little farther forward, with some of its tendrils within easy reaching distance.

With my eyes open I couldn't sense the vine properly and knew that I would have to touch one of its tendrils to understand what it was that threatened me. I chose one of the smaller, thinner ones and reached out, gripping it gently but firmly, not knowing what to expect. At first I felt coldness spread over my hand, and then my hand was burning. The burning was intense and spread a numbness that made me want to let go, to release it. Stubbornly I held on. I knew that the vine was merely protecting itself. When I looked down at it moving and pulsating in my hand, I could see that it was slimy and not dry as I had at first thought. I realised that it was covered in some type of sticky fluid, and from the sensation that was now travelling up my arm I suspected that it might be poisonous. I wanted to drop it but couldn't let go, and I knew then that it wouldn't let me—it was as if my hand had become stuck to it. When the heat reached my shoulder I felt like

I was going to be sick. I felt dizzy and hot, but was grateful that I was already sitting down. I couldn't even scream. I knew that if I did, David and the others would hear me and come looking for me. I didn't want to admit defeat just yet, so I bit my lip hard, hard enough to cause it to bleed a little. I was supposed to be part of the solution, and if I screamed I would have certainly caused a problem, but then it got to a point where I couldn't hold it any longer. I wanted to throw it away, and as the pain and my frustration grew, so did my anger and my strength.

As I battled to control the pain, I began to reach deeper into myself, peeling quickly away at my barriers. I could feel the darkness within me growing and feeding on my anger and fear, waiting for me to allow it to surface. I knew it had been growing restless and could feel its desperation to rise up and leave the restraints I had placed on it. I had grown up a lot since I had first discovered it and knew I should be able to control it. For the first time, in that forest, I felt that control rising with the darkness within and calming it. I felt elated at its release and the surge of power it gave me. When I felt it was almost ready to erupt from me, I turned my attention to the vine within my hand.

"Let go," I said as I leaked some of my own darkness into the vine, knowing somehow that my darkness would produce its own brand of poison if it needed to. The vine became still, and then without warning it started shuddering and wriggling frantically to get away, almost pulling me to my feet as it tried to retreat. It was my turn to grip the vine. I recognised that, at last, it seemed to fear me as a recognition of my inner strength passed through its limited intelligence.

The vine wasn't strong enough to get away from me, and I didn't want to release it, not because I wanted to be cruel but because I wanted it to know and accept me. This was important because I understood that Adair had expected me to fail. I did not want the vine to fear me; I did not want it to associate me with just fear. I understood that if the vine only associated me with fear, I would never be truly welcome in its forests.

I began to think about another challenge. I figured that I had probably been taken to a part of the forest that was unknown to all except the purest of the Forest Dwellers and that it would take even my worried, searching vampire bodyguards days to find me.

Because of my enforced connection with it, I realised that the vine in my hand was my protection within the forest and that what I was holding was as old as the earth that supported the trees that surrounded me. In my hand was the real power and magic of the forest. I knew that if I could form a relationship with it, nothing could harm me there. I loosened my grip but still did not let it go. Instead I tried to encourage it to recognise me as I had suddenly recognised it.

I remained seated on the soft, mossy floor of the forest, no longer feeling anxious and no longer in any hurry. The silence of the forest was comforting, almost as if the forest itself was holding its breath in anticipation of the exchange taking place between me and the vine. With my other hand I gently touched the vine again. It had stopped squirming and appeared to be still, seemingly concentrating on overpowering me, but as it increased its poison, I increased mine.

It finally became a simple primitive battle of wills. The vine was very much a living thing, and I knew it could feel and definitely did not like what I was putting it through. Eventually I began to feel it weaken, and as it did so I continued to lessen my own poison, mentally neutralising it into something that would soothe the vine and repair any damage and pain I might have caused it.

It was difficult at first to withdraw the power of the darkness, especially after I had acknowledged to myself how much I liked it, but I kept telling myself I was in charge and the darkness was a part of me that I had to learn to control. I had to control the surge of elation I felt at the vine's defeat, and I concentrated on reining in the darkness within. As I withdrew the darkness slowly, I felt the vine continue to relax, but I kept my guard up and continued to gently touch the vine with my other hand, maintaining a gentle contact until I felt no more poison seeping from it.

Finally it was my turn, so I took a deep breath and began to relax. I coaxed the last of the darkness within me back to its hiding place. The vine was quiet and placid in my hand now, and I reached out to it with my mind. I sensed that it was no longer angry and no longer saw me as a threat but as something superior. I couldn't exactly connect with it since it was too primitive to have any understandable thoughts, but it did have basic feelings and I could sense those. The pain in my hand caused by its poison was still excruciating, but I knew that it was more important for me to bond with the vine. I don't know how long I sat there gently stroking it, but I didn't move until I sensed it was time to attempt to communicate to it that I meant it no real harm. I also tried to give it a memory that if it ever tried to hurt me again, I would destroy it.

I waited until I was certain that the vine understood, and when it suddenly wrapped itself around me I was not afraid, even as it lifted me into the tree. I felt exhilarated when I realised that it wanted to play a little and couldn't help but laugh when it moved me gently through the forest. Even though I had never flown before, I imagined myself flying as it glided me gently through the top branches of the trees. The vine eventually placed me down in a little clearing next to a plant with large leaves, situated a few feet away from a small pond.

The leaves looked very familiar, but it took me a while to think where I had seen them before. A long-forgotten memory came flooding back. I realised that I had seen my mother with a plant like this once, at a time when one of the other settlers had been injured. My mother and Mother Lillie had covered the wounds with the leaves before bandaging them. I understood then that the vine was trying to heal me. In a show of faith, I walked forward, gently pulled a leaf off the stem, and wrapped it over the deep groove that the vine had made in my hand. I felt an instant relief from the burning pain that had radiated up and down my arm.

After the pain had subsided and without knowing why, just knowing that I should, I used my hands to trickle a handful of water over the plant. Then I took another leaf from the plant. I wrapped and secured the leaf around my hand and walked back to the waiting vine. I let it gently curl itself around my waist again and showed it my feelings of happiness as it lifted me into the air. We continued to enjoy ourselves as the vine showed me parts of the forest that probably had not be seen by human eyes in centuries. There were ponds and brightly coloured flowers; there were animals that I didn't know existed. Deer and their fawns, rabbits and their young, played happily deep within the forest, protected.

The vine's coils were warm and gentle as I gave it my trust. I caught a glimpse of a darkening sky and realised that it was time for me to return to David before he got worried. I placed my hand palm down on one of the thicker vines and sent it an image of where I thought David and the others had been left. It seemed to understand what I wanted because we moved away almost immediately.

Before a few minutes had passed, I was back where I had started and I could see them all gathered together, ready and waiting to start their pursuit. Even though my approach was silent, David turned in my direction just as I was placed in the branches of the tree nearest to him. I don't think he saw me because he turned his back as he watched the solemn approach of Adair, flanked by a visibly shaken Thomas and Marta.

"Where is she?" I could hear David shout. "She is supposed to be with you!" I could see Theo starting to move towards them. Before they could answer and before the situation escalated, I decided to intercede.

"Hi, David, I am here—up here!" I shouted. I couldn't read the expression on Adair's face, but I knew that he was surprised and perhaps even a little angry at my appearance. I gently stroked the vine and settled myself back within its coils, letting it know that I wanted to be placed nearer to my friends. It seemed a little reluctant at first, so I tried to communicate that it was safe with me. With a slight shudder it did what I asked it to do.

When my vine set me down, it didn't leave me; it stayed as if it was protecting me from the beings on the ground. I must have looked a little frightening surrounded by the vine because everyone, even David, looked worried. The only one who didn't was my very own protector, Theo.

I turned away from them and faced Adair. "Is this not what you expected?" I asked him, smiling sweetly and observing with pleasure his obvious discomfort. I then looked away from him briefly, both of us knowing that I was far from finished with him. And then I stepped into the cool arms of my beloved.

Chapter 20

D avid's response to my return was one of heartwarming relief. With his cool cheek resting on mine, I relaxed into his arms, glad that Adair was no longer within my sight. I knew I would have to deal with him shortly, but my feelings when I saw him were too raw and uncontrolled. Although I felt anger towards him, I did not want to confront him in front of the others; I knew deep down that, like so many others before him, he would claim to have tested me knowing that I was safe. I knew that if I were to have any real impact on him it would have to be through a private conversation.

I turned back to face him after a few moments and simply asked, "Well?"

"I concede that for a human you are much more resourceful than I expected. I had obviously heard rumours or stories about you, but I did not have any reason to believe them until now," he said with a slight smile and a bow of his head. The way he smirked at me irritated me even further; I knew he thought he had got away with the ordeal he had put me through. I was also aware that the vine, sensing my annoyance, slithered slightly closer, and the coils of the darkness inside me tightened as I tensed.

Adair was foolishly oblivious to all this happening, but after he had spoken he seemed to beckon the vine. When I saw his gesture, I began to stroke the vine and asked it gently to stay with me since I knew that it now liked and trusted me. I also saw that it felt fear in Adair's presence. I could only guess that he had at some point used superior force to make it comply with his wishes, whereas I had used kindness, which I believed was a rare experience for any natural thing on the planet. The vine stayed where it was, coiling itself protectively around me and David. I watched Adair struggle to understand what was happening, especially aware of his loss of control, which I seriously doubted was something he was used to.

I decided it was time to show him a little of my own strength, so I sent the thought to him that if he ever tried to harm me or any of the people I knew and cared about, then I would come back and have my revenge. The look on his face told me that he had received my warning loud and clear.

Without taking my eyes from his face, I addressed Thomas. "Thomas, do you know these vines?"

"Yes, Liberty, I do. I know them to be as ancient as the forest that surrounds you," he said softly, still sounding unsure of what was happening.

"I want these vines protected. I do not want them harmed or diminished in any way, and I want you to communicate their protection to all other Forest Dwellers. I now appoint you as their protector," I said, trying to sound as royal and commanding as I could, even though I wasn't sure that I could even do what I was saying.

"That is not your decision to make, Princess," Adair snapped at me.

"Why?" I asked as I faced him again.

"You have no domain over here. These forests belong to my people," he answered defiantly.

"These forests belong to the planet," I answered with a smile that I didn't allow to reach my eyes. "And that means they belong to my beloved." I turned to David. "May I could appoint Thomas protector of these vines—in fact, of all of the forest's plants?"

David, no doubt equally unsure of what was happening, had begun to smile as he watched the exchange between Adair and me. He understood enough to see that I was being challenged by Adair and that I was also challenging him in return.

"Of course, darling," he said indulgently.

"Thomas, will you do as I have asked and protect them for me?" I asked again.

"It will be as you wish, Liberty," Thomas replied. With those words, he walked forward and gently uncoiled the vine from around us. At first it seemed reluctant to leave me, but after some assurances from us it seemed content to leave and retreat into the forest. I noticed that it seemed reluctant to go anywhere near Adair, who stood still, seething with anger.

"You thought she was just a mere human, did you?" David said to Adair, still smiling.

Adair didn't answer; he just looked uncomfortable and unsure. After a moment of awkward and uncomfortable silence, he turned his back and moved away from us, muttering to himself.

Surprisingly, Marta stayed with us and watched his back as he stomped away into the forest. "He is a fool. It is not only those of your kind who need to learn lessons in humility," she said as she looked at David. She then turned to look at me and said simply, "Well done, Princess. It appears to me that as you learn, we will have to learn." With those words she stomped back into the forest, where she disappeared.

As I watched her leave I felt an overwhelming urge to run after her and hug her, but I didn't think she would understand. It made me happy, though, that the more we saw of each other, the deeper our bond seemed to become. When they all had finally left, I felt the energy leave me. I kissed David gently again on his smiling mouth and then threw myself into Theo's waiting arms. "It is good to be in safe hands again. I would have said the forest is no place for any being on their own," I said, and meant it.

I smiled to myself as the tension seemed to disappear from me, and then it returned as David saw the leaf on my hand. "What is that?" he asked.

"It is nothing. I just cut my hand slightly when I was in the forest with the vine," I assured him as I placed my injured hand in his and he began to remove the leaf bandages. I steeled myself for the reaction I knew David would have if he thought I had been hurt. I felt the other guards tense as well, but there was no need to worry; even I was surprised when I saw that there was barely a mark. The only thing that seemed to be left was a small silvery mark slicing diagonally through the centre of my palm.

David did not comment as he looked at my hand, and we soon made our way back to the vehicles since it was getting dark.

Since Theo was driving, he gently handed me over to David, who took me in his arms equally gently. He sat with me in the back of the car as we travelled back to the castle together. As we neared home, I quickly sent a short but happy message to Mia, and although I knew that Thomas would probably tell her of what he had seen in the forest, I chose not to.

It felt so very good to be in David's arms again, and even though I was exhausted I didn't stop him when he began to gently kiss my face; in fact, all that excitement must have awakened some of my other appetites. . . .

As soon as we arrived back at the castle, David and I retired to the bedroom, with David giving both Alex and James strict instructions that we were not to be disturbed under any circumstances.

David and I spent another blissful night together, both of us sharing time, both of us knowing that after the short separation to come, our time would not be as free.

Chapter 21

I woke up sometime in the early predawn hours of the next morning, fully rested after the excitement of the day and evening before. I was a little surprised to find myself alone in the bed. I could sense David was still close, so I knew that he hadn't left for his commitments yet. I opened my eyes fully and gave myself a moment to let the sleep-fog clear and looked around. I saw David sitting out on the bedroom balcony with his back to me, but I already knew that he was sitting with the shell. His head was tilted back slightly, and he held the gift from his people loosely in his hands.

I felt absolutely famished, so I got out of bed, wrapped the sheet around me, and grabbed some fresh fruit before I went to join him. He appeared not to hear my approach. His face was almost dreamlike as he concentrated on the beautifully polished surface of the shell that he was gently massaging in the smoothness of his hands. I hesitated for a while, content to watch him. He looked so beautiful and at peace. The early morning was warm and the sky still a rich, dark clear blue with a perfectly round moon and shiny stars.

He looked up as I stepped through the door and smiled. "I will be leaving later today," he said softly. I closed the door behind me and walked over to join him, still wrapped in the sheet from our bed. I placed my hand in his, my betrothal ring glowing warm at our contact.

"I know, I had a feeling that your leaving would be very soon," I said.

"It seems that the World Council has decided that the first of the meetings cannot be delayed further, and rightly my father has agreed with them. That means that the meeting will take place within the African Territories tomorrow. I therefore have a lot of preparations to make and must leave you soon," he said, a hint of sadness in his voice.

I pulled a chair close to him and sat with him for a little while, understanding his serious mood because sometimes our times apart were almost as painful for him as they were for me. I sat as close to him as possible and placed my hand over his hand, which still rested on the shell. As I did so, I heard a rush of water and realised that the sound was coming from the shell. Although I had not heard the noise before, I did not remove my hand. Through the sound I heard David instruct me softly to close my eyes. I did as he told me, and although the picture in my mind was unclear, I did envision blues and greens swirling within mists and faint but unclear images of sea creatures that appeared startled by my intrusion. The feeling of floating that I had experienced once before, when I was submerged, returned. I felt at peace, eternally grateful for the life and experiences I was privileged to have.

When the connection was broken and I opened my eyes, I simply smiled at David in understanding of what the shell meant to him. It appeared that the scar behind my ear had finally begun to open my senses and allow me some insight into the kingdom of the Ocean Dwellers.

"Although to me you are more precious than eternity itself, I have a need to protect you, to keep you away from situations of danger, and to try to curb your curiosity. You appear to have a strange ability to place yourself within danger's grasp, although I suspect that it is something you do intentionally. Something, a rumour that I have heard whispered through the walls of the castle, has been on my mind lately, a thought that perhaps you really will be the one who frees us. I am sure of it—not one door has closed on you yet," he said softly.

There was nothing to say, so I did not answer him. We stayed like that, each of us lost in our own thoughts until the spell was broken, when David finally placed the shell on a table in front of him, freeing his arms to embrace me.

"What will you do to occupy yourself in my absence? You know, obviously, that I would prefer it if you kept yourself away from beings and situations that would cause you any form of harm," he said softly into my hair as he pulled me tighter into his embrace.

I was a coward; I didn't say a word, not about Elathan or the fact that I would continue in my search for information. I couldn't. The time wasn't right and his meeting in the African Territories was too important for him to be distracted or delayed any more, especially by me. I convinced myself that I would know the right time to tell him of my bond with Elathan. I understood that I wasn't quite ready to give up that bond, and I knew that something between Elathan and me had not yet happened; I still felt as drawn to him as I had when I first arrived at the castle.

My mother told me once that it was wrong to fight destiny and that everything happened for a reason. She told me that at a time when everything I had ever known had been changed forever. I had held on to that memory and her belief, even though so much had happened to me in such a short time. For me this justified my link with Elathan. He was part of my destiny; it had to be because I wanted it to be.

He was the true owner of my home, and he had lived at least as long as Emperor Marcarius, if not longer, and after recent events and discoveries I knew, should he wish to help me, that he could answer many of the questions I now carried constantly in my head.

As I let those thoughts fade to the back of my mind, I pulled the sheet tighter around myself. It seemed as if it had become cooler outside. The last remaining darkness of the night began to lift, giving way to what looked like quite a stormy day. Suppressing a shiver, I walked back inside to get warm.

David followed me back into our apartment, and again we took comfort in each other's bodies, taking our own sensual time, our eyes tracing the fine details of each other's faces as if to memorise every single detail again.

When we were both satisfied, we got up and I helped David put some clothes in a bag. He tended to some last-minute arrangements as I sent a couple of trusted servants to gather gifts for the African king and his queen. I had chosen a delicate gold

121

vial with an ornate carving of a lion and his pride for the king, knowing that he had an eye for the unusual, and some specially created perfume made from rare spices for the queen, who I had heard was a real lady.

By the midmorning David had finished what he had to do, and eventually there were no more excuses left for him to delay any further. Just before he left, David threatened Alex and James with unspeakable tortures if I wasn't in perfect condition when he returned.

With a chaste kiss for the benefit of those assistants who were less than comfortable with our displays of affection, and a less than innocent smile for me exclusively, he walked towards the door. Cassius arrived and they left together. He was gone; the silence in the room was suddenly heavy and oppressing. I sat alone and waited for a while, not really knowing what I wanted to do; Mia was still away arranging her own Commitment Ceremony.

I had a shower and put on some casual clothes. I had decided to go and see Rachael at the library and find out if anything else had been discovered. I put on a warm jumper and left the apartment, followed by Alex and James until we reached the library.

Chapter 22

Alex and James stopped as I entered the library and stayed outside, guarding without intruding as they were supposed to. As I expected, Rachael was elbow deep in ancient books and scripts. I stood for a moment watching her. She still managed to look extremely beautiful and almost feline as she reclined among them, unaffected by the age-old dust, not a hair out of place.

I wasn't too surprised to find Theo with her, although the library was not a place in which he ordinarily would be at home. He appeared to be simply flicking through some geography books, not really concentrating on any one of them in particular. As soon as they heard me approach, they both looked up and smiled. Rachael gestured for me to join them, so I smiled back and made my way over to them.

When I reached them, Rachael, not saying a word, handed me a faded old photograph. As I took the photograph and looked at it, I knew that it was perhaps what we had been waiting for because I knew both the woman and child who were posing, smiling. Although many of my childhood memories had almost disappeared from my consciousness, the memory of who these people were and their importance hadn't.

I knew them from a lifetime ago. They both had white hair, and I knew that they had both shared my personal space with me during the time I was with both my parents. The woman and child were standing in front of a concrete archway which appeared to be the only remnant of a majestic building that had been overgrown and hidden deep within a forest. They were dressed in warm practical clothes that were camouflaged for travel within the forest areas. They had what appeared to be bags of supplies and looked as if they were about to go on a journey.

As I looked as the photograph, I felt a shiver race up and down my spine. My mind's eye flickered with flashbacks, and I knew with certainty where the photograph had been taken. I recognised that archway; it was the entrance to the settlement in which I had been born. All my senses appeared to come alive as I was momentarily transported back to the time of sweet-smelling long grasses that bent in the breeze. Everything was so vivid, real—and then, just as quickly, it was gone and I was snapped back into reality.

"Where did you get this?" I asked Rachael, suddenly very excited and very much awake.

"It fell out of one of the new books I had delivered from the Irish Territories. Heather has been kind enough to send me anything that she suspects is of historical relevance. I can see that it is important to you, and I would like it if you would explain why," she said as she watched my face closely.

"I don't know exactly, but I remember these two people clearly even though it was a very long time ago, before even the Enclosure. The old woman would visit my mother, and sometimes she would have that little girl with her," I explained. "I am sure she is or was a Forest Dweller, and the place where they are standing is the place where I was born, where I really came from."

"What you have said is certainly of interest. Do you mind if I make some enquiries? I will take a copy of the picture and send it straight back to Heather, and we shall see if she is aware of this old Forest Dweller," she told me, smiling. Rachael calmly laid the photograph against the dull grey of the table and scanned it with her mobile phone. She sent the photo to Heather and we waited.

To occupy myself while we were waiting, I wandered down the nearest aisle. I couldn't help but notice the book I had removed recently, even though I was sure that it wasn't in its original resting place. Seeing the book reminded me that I had wanted very much to see Elathan; I made up my mind that if he wasn't willing to see me, then I would force him to come to me. I would use one of his own gifts to call him to me. My mind was brought back to the present when the extremely loud answering bleep of Rachael's phone sounded in the silence of the library. Rachael gestured to me to remain silent as she got my attention. She then placed Heather on speaker phone so that all of us could hear. She connected her phone to one of the research computers so that we could all see Heather as well as hear her.

After greeting us, Heather became her usual calm, businesslike self. As she spoke to us she pointed to the photograph of the old woman just to confirm we were all talking about the same person. "This woman here is my mother. Her name is Anu, and she is also known to humans as Mother Earth," she said, looking as surprised at the photograph as we were. "May I ask where you found this?"

"It was inside the cover of one of the books that you sent to me," replied Rachael softly.

"How strange that I did not see it myself. I thought I had read through all the books before I sent them to you, even taking the time to earmark the pages and paragraphs that I thought would be of interest," Heather said, frowning slightly. "There are many stories about my mother—some are true, some are not. She has been given the title Mother of the Earth by many Forest Dwellers, and according to some of the more inventive stories, she was the younger sister of Mother Nature."

Heather didn't have too much to say about the small child who was also in the picture, but we all seemed to have the same sneaking suspicion that she may well have been a Sky Dweller, perhaps even the last Sky Dweller.

When Rachael pressed Heather for further information, she told us that her mother had often told them of a family that was in need of protection, and a short while before she had left them, she had told them that she was going to have to collect a very special little girl who would need to be kept safe because she would be needed in the future.

I thought I could hear the pain in Heather's voice as she spoke of her mother's decision. I asked Heather when she had seen her mother for the last time, and she replied that it was before Mia had been taken. I immediately felt for Heather. First her mother had disappeared and then her twin sister, Mia, had been taken and infused. I had a feeling that I had seen her mother more recently than any of them had.

When Heather had finished speaking, Rachael beckoned to me and sat me in front of the computer screen directly in front of Heather. "Tell her what you know, child. I think your words may ease her," Rachael said quietly.

"Heather, I know your mother, or at least I knew her. She used to visit my mother when I was very small. I believe she called herself Lillie. I don't really know why I say this, but it is what I remember. I also know she often brought this child with her, and I last saw her only twelve years ago. She was well and safe among us," I said, not really knowing what else to say.

"Thank you, you have said enough. At least we know now that she left us for a good reason," Heather said gently. "Again, Liberty, without knowing why, you have given me comfort," she added with a warm laugh. "Are we all agreed as to who we think that child is who needed her protection?"

"I believe she is our missing Element," said Rachael in a voice that left us all with little doubt.

"Do we know where this picture was taken?" Theo asked, quietly breaking the thoughtful spell that we all seemed to be under.

"I know," I said, again bringing everyone back into focus. "It is somewhere in the British Territories, and it is where I was first born."

"I do not know if she would have remained there. She probably moved around the other territories to protect the child. I will contact Thomas and have him make some inquiries. If anything comes to light, I will keep you all informed. And now I must say good-bye, as I believe I am being summoned by my sister," Heather said quickly.

"How are things going? Is everything going well?" I asked quickly before she could leave, missing them both immensely.

"They are developing," she said, not looking back at the screen, and then the meeting ended.

Once the screen was blank, Rachael gathered all of her researchers together and gave them a copy of the picture, instructing them to memorise it and concentrate on finding any information on the two beings in the photograph.

Everyone seemed to become busy then, so I left them. I felt hurt by Heather's sudden departure and decided to go to the Temple of

Thought with a copy of the photograph. I now knew that Mother Lillie was another ancient being who had a major part to play in the fate of the planet, and I wanted to share the knowledge with Sarah since she might know something of Mother Lillie. I also felt that Sarah should know what had happened recently. I informed Theo where I was going and left the research library quietly. Alex and James followed me as discreetly as always and positioned themselves outside the entrance to the temple.

When I entered the temple, I sat down and waited for Sarah, and as always I didn't have to wait long for her to appear. "I believe we have made progress," I said, showing her the photograph of the woman and child.

"What have you brought me?" she asked.

"It is called a photograph, Sarah. It is taken with a camera so that people can have a picture of their memories," I explained. "Do you know her?"

"Yes, I believe I have seen this woman in my dreams. Who is she?" she asked as she continued to handle and inspect the photograph.

"I only know her as Mother Lillie, but apparently her name is Anu. I am told that she is the queen of the Forest Dwellers, and she has also been known in the past as Mother Earth, the younger sister of Mother Nature," I said, trying to give Sarah as much information as I could think of.

"Ah yes, I have heard of such a being. And the Sky Dweller who is with her—where is she? Is this the Element you are seeking?" Sarah asked.

"We don't know yet, but we are going to have to look for her. This photograph was taken when I was very small, and it was at a place that is not far from here. It is the only clue we have," I explained patiently.

"You understand that we need to hurry. I sense that the time is coming when we will have to move together in order for good to be done," she said softly, knowing that I had heard her say similar things many times before.

"Yes, I understand, and now that we have this information, we can because we actually have a starting point," I told her quietly.

There was really nothing else for us to say, so I closed my eyes and let my mind wander back to the present as she faded. I felt tired. Sometimes my relationship with Sarah seemed to be as strong as ever, but with no new developments we had very little to say to each other, and sometimes the lack of progress made being with her a little strained.

After leaving the Temple of Thought, I went back to our empty apartment and had a small bite to eat. I changed into my sleeping clothes, knowing that I would not be leaving the apartment again, and watched my plasma device. While listening to the latest song from the Fairest Folk, which was my new favourite girl band, I must have fallen asleep.

While I slept, I dreamed. I dreamed of dark forests whose vines did not know me and hindered my way. I was trying to run to catch fleeting glimpses of Mother Earth, who seemed to appear just at the edge of my vision. I knew without seeing that in her arms she held a child and that the child was the future. I chased her because I felt a need to see that child, but as hard as I tried, it never happened. I woke feeling alone and frustrated.

It took me a little while to recognise the sound which had awakened me, and when my head cleared a little, I realised that the sound I was hearing was my phone. The call was from David, and for the next hour I chatted to him about all that had happened since he had left. It was a fantastic call, and afterwards I felt refreshed and alive. It was the way he always made me feel lately. I laughed when I told him about the dream I had been having, and he laughed with me. I told him a few times how much I loved him, and we blew kisses to each other before I hung up the phone. I also sent my regular message to Mia, telling her all was well and that David had arrived safe in the African Territories.

It was still dark outside, and I knew instinctively that it was nearing the right time for me to do what I knew I would do. Feeling a little guilty, I made a promise that I would speak to David as soon as he returned—there would be no more secrets between us. I decided to go and speak with Theo personally about having the alone time I needed.

As soon as I put my jacket on, Alex and James rose with me and, rather than just following me, walked beside me as I had asked. I liked the fact that they preferred to communicate without speaking; they were no longer so very serious and rigid around me.

Chapter 23

Alex and James were engaged in a casual and very funny stream of playful banter, which kept me quite amused until the time came and I had to interrupt their thoughts. I spoke out loud and told them that I still had some small errands to run and added, with a smile, that they didn't need to accompany me since I was staying within the royal wing. Predictably, they simply smiled back at me and ignored my suggestion.

It was a comfortable and very short walk to Theo's apartment, which was just down the corridor from ours, situated near the end of the heavily guarded corridor that separated the royal apartments from the rest of the castle. He had been upgraded to it when he had been appointed head of my security. His apartment was a large arrangement of rooms, most of which were secured. They also included rooms that were equipped with all the relevant computerised castle defences. There were more rooms, too, that could be reached via a hidden underground stairway; these rooms, which were off-limits to all but Theo and the emperor, were equipped with enough vials for all of the existing royal families to go into hibernation and re-emerge decades later if any conflict or natural disaster ever happened.

I sometimes felt a little intimidated and small when I approached the doors that led into the apartments that were linked to castle security. They were massive and painted a dull metallic grey; there were no visible external handles for opening, nor were there any bells or anything one could use to knock. There was, however, an intercom system where visitors pushed a button and announced who they were. A voice from within would then command them to stay where they were. Theo had told me once that within the thick doors lay a scanner as extra security. Usually visitors were expected to wait for however long the security guard on duty decided to keep them there; it was the first line of intimidation.

I never had to push that intercom button because Theo always seemed to know I was there. He had always had an extraordinary sense of me; even as a younger child, I always had a sneaking suspicion he was roughly tuned in to me and my whereabouts at all times. He did not like communicating with thoughts; he felt invaded whenever I tried.

I stood in front of his door and waited patiently. After a few moments I thought I could hear movement on the other side and took a few steps back, ready for him to open the door and appear. After just a few more seconds he opened it.

As he opened the door, I quickly took those few steps forward and launched myself at him, since he always caught me easily. I don't know why I still felt the need to jump at him—I was no longer a child—but it was just our thing to do it for fun. I loved the feeling of security that his huge arms gave me as they encircled me.

Sometimes Theo would laugh, equally happy to make that contact. His laugh was like a roll of thunder that started somewhere in his chest and radiated outwards to fill the corridors. It was natural and infectious. He cradled me gently against his massive chest, which was as hard as stone. I had a feeling that if I was destined to do great things for the planet in the future, then Theo was destined to be at my side to protect me.

When others were around he was always so serious and I was expected to behave in a certain way as the Everlasting Life Partner of the emperor's son, so we tended to keep our moments private, as I was certain there would be those both within and outside the castle who would have thought our behaviour inappropriate, perhaps even punishable. The difference between us was that it would be Theo who would have been punished and not the human princess, and I would have hated that. I kissed his cool, slightly rough cheek a number of times until he laughed again, the same joyful laugh that he always gave when my affection

130

took him by surprise. The bond between us was indescribable, and something very different from the love I felt for any other being, including David.

"What brings you here, Princess?" he asked, carrying me gently into his vast apartment. As he placed me on the floor, I noticed he was dressed in casual soft clothes as opposed to the black jeans and shirt that he almost always wore. I also noticed he had nothing on his huge feet; it was almost as if he had already decided to take this night off. This was the first time I had seen him dressed so casually, and it suited him. As always, the clothes did nothing to mask the muscles that rippled down the length of his arms and across his chest with every step that he took. Of course, I was also pleased that he appeared to be off-duty since that was exactly what I had been hoping for.

We entered the reception room to his apartment, and without even looking behind him and acknowledging Alex and James, Theo left his apartment door ajar and they followed us inside; the door closed of its own accord behind them. Once they were in the apartment, Theo did not invite either of them to be seated, so instead they stood at either side of the door like statues, seemingly unmoving, unhearing, and unseeing.

Farther inside the room I saw that Theo had other company. Rachael was sitting, curled up on one of his oversized chairs reading a book. No wonder Theo looked so relaxed; Rachael was good for him. She looked up and smiled when she saw me but didn't say anything. If she was surprised by my visit, then, as usual, she didn't show it. I wasn't surprised to see her because I knew they had been getting closer, but having Rachael there now made me feel a bit uncomfortable. I wasn't exactly going to lie to Theo, but I had no intention of telling him exactly what my plans were. Rachael had now become the person I would have to convince that my plans were innocent, and while I knew she trusted me, I was aware that she, more than anyone, could tell if I was lying.

Theo sat down with me still attached to him and just looked at me, not speaking, waiting for me to tell him the reason for my visit.

"I came here to tell you that I need some time alone this night," I said in a voice that I thought reflected sensible strength, yet perhaps a little bit of loneliness, as if I was missing David, which was true. I was very careful to ensure there was no weakness or anxiety in my voice.

Theo looked at me for a long time, as if he was trying to understand the meaning behind my request. I knew that he was not the most perceptive of beings, and I found it heartbreakingly easy to keep things from him. I managed to keep my face from betraying me as I looked back into his searching eyes, hopefully revealing nothing.

Guiltily, I knew that Theo would not deny me anything, and because he was in charge of protecting me, if he told the others to give me peace, then they would have no choice but to carry out his commands. I knew that of all the ones that I surrounded myself with, it would be Theo who would feel the most disappointment if he learned that I was withholding the full truth.

Before I could open my mouth to speak again, Rachael interrupted my thoughts and spoke. I was expecting it. I knew she was not as easily fooled and therefore not as easy to convince of my innocence as Theo was. "May we ask why, Liberty? Are you unhappy? You seem quite contented of late even though we as a group are incomplete," she said, still smiling.

I looked down as I replied, "You are right, of course. I am content and there is no other reason except that I just need my own space tonight. With everyone leaving anyway, I thought I could have a little alone time without upsetting too many beings. I need time to think and adjust."

Rachael, placing her book down as she turned her full attention to me, asked, "How much space is it you want?"

"I just want some time on my own, just for tonight. I want to be allowed to walk the corridors of the castle without being trailed by any of the guards, in the way I used to. I have read a lot lately in the history books in the library and I want to spend time finding the places of interest I have read about. Look at it as a practical history lesson. At least I might be occupied in a constructive way."

I could feel myself becoming a little worried and even irritated by her, knowing that I would be unable to keep a secret from her if she persisted in questioning me about specifics, but she continued to smile and I tried to calm myself.

"We have all had this discussion when David was here, and you all agreed to obey and respect my wishes on certain occasions. I am linked to you all, so I am perfectly protected from any other being or danger. It is not like I have requested to be allowed outside the castle walls . . ." This time my speech was delivered with the edge of my sudden stubbornness clearly sounding in my voice.

Her smile became even bigger at my little outburst, and I began to feel a little confused by her reaction. I wanted this freedom, and I was only asking for one night. I wanted those moments to do as I pleased without being watched and, more importantly, I really wanted to see Elathan. The need to see him was becoming almost overwhelming and very necessary to me, so I was not going to give an inch, even when gently provoked by a smiling Rachael.

"And what about yourself, child? Do you not think you need protecting from yourself?" she asked quietly.

I noticed with annoyance that she was beginning to place emphasis on the word 'child.' I found it even harder to maintain eye contact with her because under her gaze I felt like a child; it felt as if she knew something.

"I don't think so—do you?" I said, laughing as I rested my head against Theo's warm shoulder, choosing to look at his neck rather than at her.

I continued to feel uncomfortable as the seconds passed under Rachael's scrutiny. I was almost ready to give up, but as soon as those thoughts entered my head so did the image of Elathan, and with his image my determination came flooding back.

"Look, I am not sure if I need protection from myself, but I won't find out unless I am given the freedom to know. I am sorry, Rachael, but I feel that I should have the time to find out who I am. I want what you all want, I promise, but I don't really know if it is because I have been nominated and manipulated into doing it or if I truly am that person you think I am."

"I did not mean to question you, little one, and I believe I understand what you are saying, but I am also telling you to be careful. You certainly have changed from what you were, and you may think you are strong, but remember you remain far weaker physically than nearly all others within the castle," Rachael reminded me softly.

"I know, and of course I will be careful," I said, relaxing back against Theo again and smiling at her again until she smiled back. Eventually she laughed and shook her head slightly. She picked up her book again, indicating that her contribution to the conversation had been made, and now that she was satisfied it was over.

I finally breathed a sigh of relief, knowing that the hard part was over as I settled myself against Theo again, waiting for him to give me the breathing space I knew then that he would.

"For tonight you will be left alone. I give you my oath that there will be no eyes on you, but you must in turn promise me that you will only go to the places you know and where you have visited before. Remember, you are not safe while you are walking the corridors on the lower levels," he said solemnly.

That was such an easy thing for me to agree to that I answered him straight away; I didn't even have to lie to him. "Of course I will be careful," I said, and then I gave him a huge hug. "Can I leave the boys with you, then?" I asked, trying to be adorable.

"They will escort you back to the apartment, and then they will return to me for the rest of this night. They will resume their duties watching over you when they have finished resting," Theo said with a laugh as I kissed him gently on the cheek.

I stayed with them for a while, noticing that the mood became more relaxed as the minutes passed. I waited until I felt like it was okay for me to go and then, with one final hug for Theo and another solemn promise to Rachael that I would be careful, I left.

Alex and James did walk me back. I imagined that they were curious as to what I was going to do, but neither of them said a word. Instead of entering the apartment with me, they wished me a good night and then went away in the direction we had just come from.

I didn't do anything for quite a while. Once I entered the apartment I sat down on the large sofa and sat still, barely breathing in the absolute silence of the royal apartments. I knew I would have to be very careful and that there were cameras and spying eyes in every place within the castle which fed into a security system that was situated on one of the lower levels. I also knew that if Elathan sensed me, he could cloud those cameras and prevent others from seeing where I was.

I sat still for a little while and wrapped myself in the absolute silence around me. I closed my eyes and used all of my senses, but there was nothing to sense—I was actually alone. The only thing left to do was send my message to Mia. I knew that she would be curious as to why the message was early, so I told her that I was going to bed earlier than usual. She responded with a simple "Good night."

I let myself begin to feel the excitement that I had been suppressing and couldn't help laughing to myself as I ran a bath. I was going to do something that I wished to do, and suddenly I felt free. I tried not to rush because I knew I had the rest of the night and early dawn, but when I started getting ready, all night did not seem such a long time anymore. I enjoyed the heat of the warm scented water as I immersed myself and thought about my carefully chosen outfit: a black and crimson sleeveless bodice chosen for its front-fastening clasps.

I chose it because it looked good and I would need no help doing it up. It was one thing to ask for my space, but I think I would have had difficulty explaining the reason for my chosen outfit, especially as I had insisted that I only wanted to go exploring. I intended to wear it with equally figure-hugging black trousers and black thigh-high boots. I thought Elathan might approve.

I dried myself and got ready, taking care to look perfect for when I finally came face to face with him. I chose to wear my hair piled on the top of my head away from my neck so that nothing would distract the eye from the necklace I intended to wear. I knew that my neck and shoulders were two of my best features. And last but not least, I selected my makeup very carefully, choosing to use mainly pale colours on my skin for a minimalist effect. I was only satisfied when my skin looked flawless, and when I finished with black mascara and eyeliner to widen my eyes slightly, I used a little charcoal diamond dust on my eyelids to make them darker.

The last thing I did was to take the black box, which contained the necklace, from my secret drawer. As soon as I opened the box, I felt thrills of excitement that had been gently nestled in my stomach erupt into butterflies; it was the same way I always felt when I knew that I was going to see him. I didn't put the necklace around my neck straight away, just in case someone in the castle spotted me wearing it as I made my way towards the lowest of the corridors. I couldn't take the risk that one of the other beings might see it; some of those who roamed the levels where I was going were certainly old enough to recognise it.

Lastly, I felt fear. The thought crossed my mind that since the ceremony and his last gift, he may not want to protect me anymore—I knew that I had neglected him and had not acknowledged his shadows.

I left my apartment, covering my bare shoulders with a large crimson wrap, which I fastened with a black diamond broach at the neck, and slowly walked the length of the royal corridor, which led back into the main part of the castle. Even though I knew that they would all leave me alone, it was difficult not to look back over my shoulder, but I didn't; I tried to look straight ahead, doing my best to look both innocent and confident at the same time.

I did hold my breath as I walked past Theo's room and tried to look calm and purposeful as I passed the guards near the entrance of the royal corridor. They didn't even look at me as I passed them, but I didn't start to breathe properly until I had passed through the doors which led to the rest of the castle. I finally began to smile again as I realised that I was back in the well-used, more common corridors of the castle.

Though I knew that I wasn't being followed, I was still careful and tried to remain unobserved by anyone, staying in the shadows and using various routes to avoid the more populated areas as I followed the corridors that took me down into the lower basement levels of the castle.

The corridors became darker and more enclosed as I continued. When I was satisfied no being had followed me I stopped and hid myself within the shadows. I gently placed my hand inside the box and briefly touched the necklace, hoping that Elathan felt me and that he would be willing to protect me from those who lurked on his levels as he had done in the past.

After a few more twists and turns, at last I found myself at the top of a slanting corridor that I recognised and knew very well. I eventually took the necklace from its box and placed it around my neck, the ends clicking quickly together as if they were magnetic. I tucked the box back into the small secret pocket hidden within the folds of my wrap.

There was no sensation of weight from the necklace when it hung on my neck, but there seemed to be an intense coldness where it connected with the skin of my throat that caused goose pimples to rise on my arms. The moment the necklace touched my skin, I felt my commitment ring loosen slightly and grow cold on my finger, and even though its reaction startled me, it did nothing to rein in my determination because as soon as the necklace touched my skin, I felt his presence. In a way the ring's reaction was right—I knew that David and Elathan would never be able to share the same space with me.

Chapter 24

I stopped for a moment at the beginning of the corridor
leading down to the door that I knew for certain led to his
rooms; it was hard to control the growing excitement that
I already felt. My heart was pounding, and my breathing got
faster with every step I took and with every second that passed.
I moved slowly but confidently forward. As I approached I
finally began to sense him, and my sense now of him was much
stronger than it had been without the necklace; he was almost
with me. I felt as if he was standing waiting for me, or at least he
was there guiding and directing me. I also felt as if we were on
a collision course and sensed some reluctance or disapproval
from him. It was as if he did not like being manipulated in
the way I had chosen, which made me hesitate, but only for a
moment; I didn't take the necklace off or break the link. I had
come too far to turn away from him, even if it meant facing his
anger.

I stopped a little way from the door and waited as I always
used to. At the back of my mind I half expected (wanted) him to
appear in front of me in the usual manner, but he didn't. Instead,
for the first time since I had been going there to visit him, the
door in front of me opened slightly, showing me a dimly lit
corridor beyond. The door stayed open and unmoving, waiting,
silently inviting me to walk through. I nearly didn't walk through
because I chose at that point to question why I was there. I knew
he was challenging me, my commitment to him, and it was as if I
knew that by walking through that door, I would change things

between us because I was willingly entering his personal domain rather than being led there by him.

I realised that perhaps I really hadn't thought about what was about to happen, but I could not make myself turn around and leave. The urge to see him was as strong as ever. I felt as if my will were not my own and had a slight, needling suspicion that I was being manipulated. Before I really knew what I was doing, I started to move forward until I had placed my hand flat against the door.

I began to push it back slowly, opening it wide. I was only slightly surprised that there was no resistance or noise, even though the door appeared to be part of the original castle and therefore quite old. I could have opened it using just my fingertips. I had to smile. Again the symbolism of the door wasn't lost on me because it was such an easy step to take; it took me over the threshold into the exciting danger of his domain. I stopped pushing the door when I felt it rest against the wall and I could see as much as possible of what lay ahead for me.

I stepped cautiously forward and entered the corridor. It was poorly lit, with a dim strip of light that ran down the centre of the ceiling. I pushed myself onwards, hesitating only briefly when I noticed shadows beyond. It felt like the corridor was suddenly never-ending, almost as if it lengthened with each of my steps, with the door at the end never getting any closer. I didn't know how long I had been in that corridor, but it seemed to have been quite a long time. Eventually I decided I had had enough. Although I was no longer scared, I was becoming tired and could feel my earlier excitement slipping away. "Elathan," I called, "where are you? I want to see you." I stopped walking and stood still.

"I am not leaving, so you might as well show yourself. You must know that I wear the necklace and I have done my research, so I know you have to respond to its call!" I added, surprised at how soft my voice sounded in the long corridor, as if the walls were muting it. Although I remained still, the door at the end of the corridor appeared to be moving towards me. It was moving fast enough to force me to take a step back. When the door was just roughly an arm's length away from me, it stopped and opened, showing me another area of darkness that lay waiting beyond.

I am still not sure why, but I took the necklace off my neck then, knowing that I had arrived and that the necklace had served its purpose. I knew that I would be seeing him in a few minutes; I could also sense his amusement at my excitement. I paused for a few seconds and made sure that my hair was in place, and I smoothed down imaginary creases in my bodice. With my heart pounding loudly in my chest, I took the first step forward.

I stepped into a small, dark entranceway. Beyond it was an enormous, cavernous but surprisingly well-lit room. One of the first things I noticed was a huge fire burning in a hole in the wall at the far end of the room. I understood then something I had always suspected: that Elathan may not have been a vampire, that he may have been something else entirely because, without exception, all of the vampires I knew recoiled from and showed a real fear of fire. In fact, I believed they feared it more than silver.

As I stepped farther into the room, I saw that at its centre was a long, dark wooden table with chairs of dark, ornately designed metal positioned around it. The room itself was decorated in such a way that suited him; it was a room fit for the Celtic Lord of Darkness. At the centre of the table was a large black glass bowl with small cups hooked around its sides. I saw that the bowl was half filled with a dark liquid, and I shuddered at the thought of what it could be.

Along the walls were various pictures of Elathan. In some of them he appeared to be part of hunting parties within the grounds of the castle. He looked as he did now in the present day, although according to the history books, he had not been aboveground for around three thousand years.

I couldn't help but notice a series of gaps in the gallery, as if pictures had been removed and not replaced. There were several closed doors on either side of the room. I noticed some of them didn't have handles, and on closer inspection I found that some of them were surrounded by what I assumed were ancient runes.

"Elathan?" I called, suddenly unsure of what I should do now that I had arrived.

"Princess!" his voice sounded from somewhere close behind, yet I did not hear his approach. I heard a door shut behind me and turned to face him. As always, he took my breath away.

I had forgotten how beautiful he really was. He was wearing a crimson silk shirt which was unbuttoned at the neck, exposing the smoothness of his perfectly toned ebony chest. The shirt was tucked into a pair of tight black leather trousers under which he seemed to be wearing a pair of low boots. His white hair that hung down almost to his hips was tied back from his face and plaited neatly. I realised that I hadn't really seen him with my new, improved vision; all of our meetings since my return to the castle had been extremely brief.

Although his eyes were crimson, they still had softness about them, as if seeing me pleased him also. He bowed to me, smiling slightly. "Princess."

"Elathan," I answered breathlessly, so happy to see him again.

"May I ask what you are doing here? Why the sudden need to see me? Are you not happy with your life in the corridors above?" he asked, still smiling—although the smile faded slightly in his eyes.

"I am, really I am. What if I told you that this visit is because I missed you? Would that be enough of a reason for my visit?" I asked, my voice soft.

I could not hold his gaze for longer than a few moments. As I looked into his crimson eyes, I could see them becoming deep pools of darkening reds, the smile returning to them in an instant.

"It will do for now, Princess. Please come in and be welcome," he said formally, trying not to laugh. As he spoke he offered me his hand and I took it.

I had never been in physical contact with him before. All the times I had been in his presence, we had never touched. Unlike David's hands, which were always cool, Elathan's were very hot. I should have known. The heat from his hand tingled up my arm; it felt unusual but not uncomfortable, and I resisted the urge to pull away.

I let him lead me over to the large table, where we went to the farthest end nearest to the fire. "Where is the necklace?" he asked, still smiling.

I handed it to him immediately, and as he placed the necklace on the table, his smile faded and he frowned slightly. When I saw the look on his face, I said simply, "Sorry." Both of us seemed to know that I had crossed an invisible line when I had used the necklace to call to him.

"It was just that I wanted to see you—you have not been close to me since I became David's Everlasting Life Partner."

"Come sit with me. Unlike those above, I prefer the heat to the cold," he said as he pulled another chair closer to the fire and next to his. He finally let go of my hand as he sat in his chosen chair. I sat down and let the wrap fall from my shoulders; I had never thought of David as cold, but sitting there in front of a real fire I realised that the world I lived in, the world of my friends, was rarely warm or hot. I sat staring at the flames for quite a while, finally alone with Elathan and not knowing what to say.

When I looked at him, he was staring at me intently as if he was waiting for a further explanation, but as far as I was concerned there was none to give, so I simply turned and watched the fire.

"You have gone to a lot of trouble to come to me, yet you do not speak," he said softly. "Why after this length of time do you choose to come and see me?"

"I told you I missed you. I think of you often, and despite all that has happened recently, I still feel as if I am linked to you. There is a place for you in my destiny," was the only answer I had.

"I will ask you again, then—are you not happy and occupied with your chosen partner?" he continued, seemingly unaware of my growing uneasiness.

"I was . . . I mean, I am, really I am . . . I just think about you sometimes, although lately it seems a lot more often, but that was all. Up until recently I had the rose and obviously the necklace, and they were enough. I am not saying that I didn't miss you, but I managed without you—if you know what I mean." I knew that I was beginning to sound a little upset and childlike, but it was becoming harder to explain to him without sounding like a silly little girl.

"What changed?" he asked softly, as if finally understanding my discomfort.

"A book, it was a book that I found in the research library a few days ago. It changed me and reminded me of how much you mean to me," I said quickly, looking at the fire again.

"A book changed you?" he persisted.

I couldn't even look at him as I spoke again because I could feel my face becoming hot with my own awkwardness. "Yes, I was in the research library and I found a book. Well, it sort of found me. As soon as I saw it, I felt compelled to pick it up and read it, and even though I didn't really read it a lot, there were just some interesting things in it, things about you that I didn't know."

I knew I was speaking too fast, that the words were pouring from my mouth. I was becoming irritated with myself at how I was handling this meeting but continued, "It was a very old book. It is hard to explain because it didn't look like it belonged there. It was plain and old-looking among the newer books in its section. But it was about you and the castle. In it I read that this was your castle and your kingdom before some battle that you fought with Marcarius, which led eventually to Marcarius's victory and your loss.

"The book also told me something about the gifts you had given me and how they secretly bound us together. And after reading that I couldn't stop thinking about you and how much I missed you and wanted, or even needed, to see you again," I said finally, taking a deep breath but still unable to look at him.

"I see. Well, isn't that interesting. Do you still have the book with you, or at least do you know where the book is now?" he asked, suddenly sitting straighter in his chair. I could tell he was trying to look nonchalant, but it was clear he was very interested.

"I put it back where I first found it. It should still be there in the library. Elathan, did I do something wrong?" I asked, watching him as he leaned back and closed his eyes.

He didn't answer me; in fact, he didn't move for a few moments, and when he opened his eyes he smiled again. "No, Princess, not you."

I heard a door open and close somewhere behind us, and I heard someone approach. I resisted the urge to turn in my seat; instead I continued to study him. I waited until the footsteps sounded close. When I did turn I saw a girl who appeared younger than I was. She was smaller than I was with short, curly black hair and large, cute dimples on her face. Her build was slim and perfectly proportioned; her eyes were dark, almost black; and her skin was white and smooth like porcelain.

She was dressed from head to toe in black, and the all-in-one outfit she was wearing clung to her from the top of her neck to her fingertips and down her body to her ankles. I should have been able to say that she was beautiful or even cute, but there was something about her that stopped those thoughts; when she looked at me I saw that her eyes were merely black cavernous pools and that they lacked soul.

I couldn't for a moment think what was wrong with her, but then I remembered she reminded me of someone that I had seen when I had first arrived at the castle. I understood then that she was decaying and that there was something rotten within her, something that was slowly eating away at her inner life force. I knew then exactly who she was because I had read about her in the book. I found myself staring into the face of Lillith, the Princess of the World Beneath. I suppose she was my equal within that world.

"Lillith, how good of you to finally join us," Elathan said quietly, not looking at her, his voice dripping with undisguised sarcasm. I watched him as he spoke the words; his eyes were filled with venom and loathing.

"You summoned me. What is it you want? Bear in mind that I did not wish to be here, but now that I am, aren't you going to introduce me to your friend?" she said, smiling sweetly and ignoring his almost hostile tone.

"Lillith, this is Liberty. Liberty, I would like to introduce you to one of my—until recently—more favoured subjects, Lillith," Elathan said, not looking at either of us, instead staring into the flames of the fire.

"I believe the pleasure of this meeting is going to be all mine," I heard Lillith say as she removed one of her gloves and held out her hand. I suddenly felt an overwhelming urge to touch her, to place my hand in hers, but before I could Elathan stopped me, taking my hand and lowering it. At first I was surprised, but then I remembered having read that her touch was poisonous and felt ashamed that I had been so eager to shake her hand like a silly girl. The thing is, I had not been able to stop myself from offering her my hand, even with all my extra strengths.

"Spoilsport," I heard her mutter.

"Hello, Lillith," I said, politely keeping my hand in my lap.

"Nice to meet you at last, Princess. I have heard many things about you. You are not as big as I thought you might be," she said as she turned to face Elathan. "So I am out of favour, my lord. May I ask why?" she asked as she moved closer to him, seemingly unafraid and choosing to ignore the look of anger on his face.

Among them I suddenly felt very small. I could sense a growing power within the room, and even though I had felt the superior power of the vampires, it was nothing compared with what I sensed then.

"It appears that Liberty has been given a small nudge in my direction. She tells me that a book that should have been in my library has appeared in hers. Do you know how it could have gotten there?" Elathan asked, barely able to contain his anger.

"I am unsure, Master. I merely replaced one of the old history books that has always belonged in the research library. I placed it back within the restricted archives, and she should not have had access to such an area," she said, frowning as if still not understanding why there was a problem.

"Why did you choose to interfere? I gave you all specific instructions not to," Elathan questioned as he stood and faced her, this time towering over her. I couldn't work out if it was because she was shrinking back from him or if he had suddenly grown before my eyes. There was a coldness in his voice that made me feel almost sick.

"It belongs there, Master, and you are the rightful owner of this castle—you are its history—not those who dwell above." Lillith sounded slightly defiant as she spoke loudly, even though she looked at the floor as she spoke. "The time is coming when the true way needs to be known. I simply wanted to make certain other of your friends were aware when I moved it, but I would never have been so direct," she continued, looking at the floor.

Elathan seemed to forgive her a little because he sat back down. "Then who is responsible for placing it in her way? Find them and bring them to me. Now go and leave us," he said, dismissing her. Lillith bowed a small bow, and I heard her walk softly away.

"What did she mean by the true way?" I asked.

"Not now, Princess. You are my guest, and suddenly I feel as if I have not been a very good host." As he spoke he smiled his beautiful smile, and I felt as if the last few tense moments had almost never happened. We spent the rest of that night together, mainly with me telling him how I felt being a real princess. He laughed at some of the stories that I told him, especially some of the more endearing ones that pointed out my more accident-prone traits.

He appeared quite interested when I told him about my bodyguards; he seemed pleased that I was well protected. I avoided speaking too much about David. I found that while I was with him I didn't want to. When he noticed the slightly green mark on my hand, I explained to him what had happened, and it surprised me how delighted he seemed when I told him what had happened between the vines, Adair, and me.

I mentioned how hot it was within his apartment. He used a mobile phone in a similar way that I would have to order me some water. It was brought to me by what appeared to be a young boy, almost a twin of Lillith. Again I knew who he was before Elathan introduced him as Dominic.

Dominic did not say a word, but he did smile at me when I took the water. The smile made me want to get as far away from him as possible, yet as with his sister there was a hypnotic quality about him that seemed hard to resist. Elathan laughed when he saw my face and told me that Dominic was not to be feared—at least not as much as his sister. He dismissed the boy quickly and we continued to talk.

After that the night seemed to pass too quickly, and before long we could both see that the dawn was on its way. "I need to go back," I said, standing at the same time as he got up from his chair.

"I know," he said.

"Thank you for not sending me away earlier. It has been good to spend some time with you." As I was speaking, without even realising it, I had been taking small steps towards him until I stood within touching distance. I stopped speaking and held my breath as he reached out his hand and gently touched my face. "I would like to visit you again—if that is okay?" I said.

"Princess, you are welcome here, but there will be a price to pay for these visits," he said, smiling as he took a step towards me so that our bodies were almost touching.

"What is the price you had in mind?" I asked in a voice that was barely louder than a whisper, guessing already.

I didn't move—I couldn't have moved even if I wanted to. The beauty of him kept me mesmerised and rooted in place, though somewhere in my head there seemed to be someone or something screaming at me to just leave, to go and never return to him, ever.

Even then I knew that it was never going to happen, that I could not or would not deal with the thought of never seeing him again. When I didn't move I could feel the heat from him grow stronger as he leaned down and gently kissed me on the mouth. At his kiss my mind exploded with bright, wonderful fireworks. Whereas David's kisses had a cool, coppery sweetness, Elathan's tasted like hot, fiery copper. Both were similar in a way but, in another, vastly different. When his lips first made contact with mine, I placed my hands gently on his head and pulled us together until I could feel the level of urgency between us growing. As it started to build, he placed his arms around me, locking me in place until I simply couldn't breathe. Unlike the gentle bubble that David and I felt wrapped in, the passion I felt from Elathan was heated and dangerous, and I wanted more—or at least I recognised that the darkness within me wanted more. It was he who broke away from me, as if he understood that I was losing control, almost to the point of no return. As he held me at arm's length, he shook his head and started to laugh, softly shaking his head as if to clear his thoughts. "You will destroy us all, Princess."

I thought I knew what he meant, and I had to look at the floor to hide my embarrassment at my sudden lack of control. "I am sorry, I don't know what happened. You are just so . . . tempting," I said quietly as my breathing and heart rate slowed to a normal level.

"Elathan," I said softly, not looking at him, "I think we are going away soon because there is something that I have to look for and it is important. I am telling you this because it also said in the book that you are tied to the castle and your kingdom, and until you rule above again you are unable to venture beyond the lower levels."

"You certainly remember a lot from a book you just happened to glance through. You must have studied the history part a little

147

better than you first thought," he said, his smile beginning to fade from his face.

"It just means that it will be a while before I can see you again," I said quietly, finally looking up and into his eyes.

"Wait then, Princess, because I would like to give you something. It is something that will remind you of me. It is no more than a trinket, and just so you won't forget me during your time away, busy looking for that something important that the castle seems to be caught up with." As he was speaking he walked away and went to a little drawer that I hadn't noticed before situated in the underside of his large wooden table.

When he came back to me, he held in his hand a simple bracelet; it was more like a thin, soft mesh bangle. It appeared to be made of gold threads woven together and roughly shaped into a circle. At the centre of the gold lace was what looked like a tiny black teardrop made from some type of glass or crystal, the inside of which appeared to move and swirl when I looked at it closely. The crystal seemed to be full of a strange, compelling beauty that responded and moved with an inner and unexplainable life.

"Once this is on, I want it to stay on. I see that you carry with you the prince's ring and his family's crest around your neck and drawn into the skin on your shoulder, yet I know you have to hide away my gifts." He paused for a moment before he smiled and added, "Perhaps that is wise, as they are easily recognisable." He spoke to me while he fastened the bracelet around my wrist, on the same hand that carried David's commitment ring.

The bracelet, like all the other gifts that adorned my body, seemed to fit exceptionally well. It was soft and flexible, and when it was fastened it appeared to be where it belonged. It moulded itself to my wrist softly, almost disappearing against my skin. As Elathan stepped back from me, I reasoned that he knew what he was doing, since by placing it on my left wrist it would never come into contact with David's ring, which gave me comfort knowing that it would not be a problem for me to wear it.

It was beautiful. I wanted to stay longer and thank Elathan properly, but I knew I did not have long before the others would want to resume their duties. (Besides, I no longer trusted myself with him.) I went up on my toes and placed my hands on either side of his face before I kissed him again, but this time the kiss was briefer. I let go of him and turned away, moving forward down the corridor towards the door that would lead me back into the corridors of the castle.

When I reached the door, I couldn't help myself—I had to stop and look back. When I did, he was already gone and his door was closing softly.

Chapter 25

As I walked back to my room, I barely noticed where I was walking. I just pointed my feet in the direction I wanted them to take me and moved forward; it was as if my feet and my body had taken over and I trusted them to guide me to the safety of my apartment. I couldn't tell if the corridors were warm or cold, light or dark; they just were the way back to where I existed within my 'normal' life. The feeling of Elathan's heated lips still lingered on mine, but with each step the heat seemed to subside. I knew I was still smiling, although it was difficult to figure out why.

As I moved forward, a voice somewhere in the back of my head was growing louder. The farther I moved away from him, the higher the volume became until finally I could understand a little of what the voice was screaming at me. I had to stop for a moment because it was making me feel a little unsteady. I closed my eyes and sat down in the corridor.

As the voice became clearer I realised it was Sarah. She sounded hurt and upset. She was afraid because she could not find me; apparently the links with my friends were not the only things that were severed when I was with him.

It was both nice and frightening at the same time, knowing that with Elathan I could disappear from all those involved in my life in the upper levels, even from a sorceress like Sarah. But a little warning at the back of my mind tried to imprint through my thoughts that it was also dangerous to be cut off from those who had sworn to protect me. I knew Elathan, and I knew that for the moment I was as much an intrigue to him as he was to me. He had no intention of hurting me, but I did not know him well enough to guess what the future held.

Sarah was shouting because she had wanted one of our usual updates and had been unable to reach me. For a while I let her thoughts roam through my head while I tried to keep my thoughts focused only on the corridors of the castle, a technique I had been practising much more lately.

Although I believed she was a powerful sorceress, Sarah was also quite primitive in some of her abilities. I found it easy to block my thoughts from her, which was not the case with my friends who knew me better. It seemed that Sarah almost believed too much in her own powers and felt it unnecessary to probe too deeply into the thoughts of a human. I smiled to myself; the one weakness of all the beings that I was surrounded with was their arrogance and indulgent superiority over human beings.

When she could not find anything to explain my absence, I felt a familiar pressure but kept myself in the present, even though I knew that she wanted me to let go and visit her in her cave, where she was much stronger. I sent some calming thoughts and told her the same thing that I had told all of my beloved companions: that I wanted some time alone occasionally. I dared not even allow myself to think why I wanted the time, even though it was the perfect opportunity. I knew she would not understand in the same way, as I knew that none of the others would understand either.

It didn't feel bad to me when I was with Elathan; in fact, it seemed to me as I walked away from him that my own inner darkness was contented, more than it had been for more than a little while since its awakening in the forest. I knew he had to remain a secret, my secret.

I managed to calm Sarah by reassuring her that I did know that once I decided to be alone, I could shut myself off from her as well. I stayed where I was for a few minutes until all the anxiety I had felt from her subsided, and then I got to my feet and continued on my journey back to the royal apartments. As I continued back unaccompanied, I took more notice of my surroundings again as I spotted some barely noticeable shadows. I began to understand how Elathan could have survived within the castle. I had no doubt that Emperor Marcarius was aware of his existence, but I finally began to see how Elathan was able to roam on the upper levels if he wished to.

I barely noticed the two guards at the entrance to the royal corridor as they stood to attention and saluted me as I approached. Without a word to me, they opened the two large entrance doors before I had even reached them. I wanted to get back to my rooms before anyone saw me and had the chance to question my night or where I had been. As I entered my room I realised too late that although I still had the box, I had forgotten the necklace. I knew I didn't have time to go back and wondered whether he would ever return it to me. I knew deep down that after that night I would not need it again, but still I missed my gift.

As I thought of him I placed my hand over the bangle that he had secured on my wrist and imagined I could feel his heat from it. I put the box away in its usual hiding place, more out of habit than worry because it was now empty — it held nothing to hide.

I walked through my rooms to the bathroom, knowing that I would have to relax and try to remove the thoughts of Elathan from my mind, especially if I was going to get any rest before the day was to begin properly. I wasn't expecting any visitors but I knew it would look odd to those who knew me for me to stay in bed all day, so I planned on trying to get just enough rest to see me through the day. As I started to remove my clothing I noticed that my betrothal ring on my hand seemed to wake up to me again and started glowing slightly, as if it approved of my coming back here. When I looked at it more closely, I could see the crest, my family crest, glowing deep within the blackness of its onyx.

I wondered then if the bangle that Elathan had given me would glow warm or give some other indication if he was near or if I was near to his apartment. I loved the bangle but was unsure if it was wise of me to wear it, so I began to look at it more closely. I soon saw that there was no way to remove the bracelet. It was too small to go over my wrist, and there was no longer any evidence of a clasp even though I had seen Elathan fasten it in his apartment. There was nothing I could do about it, so my thoughts ran to how I would explain it. I needed a reasonable explanation as to why I was constantly wearing it, and I knew it would have to be a lie.

I made sure that the bath I ran was almost uncomfortably hot and stayed in there until I was tired and drained enough from its heat to sleep. I put on some comfortable nightclothes and prepared myself for a good sleep. When I got into my bed and closed my eyes, I dreamed of nothing and when I woke up I felt slightly revived.

Although I remembered everything from the night before, it didn't seem to have the same impact on me anymore, and though I knew we had shared a kiss, it didn't feel that important now. Instead I woke up feeling more excited that David was going to be home the following morning and then stayed in bed for a few moments, enjoying the warmth of the soft space.

Eventually I knew I had to do things, so I got up and quickly put on some casual clothes, knowing that I faced a busy time ahead. I needed to prepare for David's arrival. I chose a shirt with sleeves that fell down to my fingertips, covering my newly acquired piece of jewellery. I also chose to wear soft trousers rather than my normal jeans, knowing that the more comfortable I was, the less irritable I would be when I became tired later.

Now that something new and tangible had been discovered about the missing Element, I knew that there would be a purpose to our time left at the libraries; I now knew how to fill the time until David returned, especially since my longing to see Elathan seemed to be satisfied for the present time. I picked up my phone and called down to the kitchen for some food. I decided to have them cook me something hot for a change since I felt lightheaded and extremely hungry. Shortly after I put down the phone, I heard a knock at the door and, although it was quick, I still expected it be my breakfast or one of my usual guards. I opened the door without checking. I was surprised to see the boy Dominic standing in front of me holding the necklace in his gloved hand. I didn't want him to enter my apartment, so I didn't invite him in. He did not belong up here in my life on the upper levels.

"Dominic," I said quickly, glancing up and down the corridor, aware that it was almost evening and that my guards would be on their way shortly. "Why are you here?" I asked, trying to smile.

"I was sent here because you left this behind," he said as he held the necklace out to me. I noticed that he was dressed in clothes similar to the ones his sister Lillith wore.

153

"Thank you," I said as I reached out to take it. I took it without actually managing to touch his hands, even though they were covered. Now that I was back in my world above theirs, I actually felt repulsed at the thought of touching him.

"It is my pleasure to serve you, as always," he said, smiling as he bowed and backed away from me.

"Thank you, but you must not be seen here. I wish you no offence, but I want you gone," I said without taking my eyes off him. I then took a careful step backwards into the safety of my rooms and closed the door. I moved quickly to place the necklace back in its box without taking time to stop and admire it. I was relieved to have it back and even more relieved when I checked the corridor and saw no trace of Dominic. The next knock brought my breakfast of fried hen eggs on thick slices of toasted bread.

Alex and James arrived while I was eating, and with their arrival my world seemed to adjust and become normal again. Neither of them asked me any questions about what I had done, and they almost behaved as if they had been with me as usual the night before. As soon as I had eaten, I put on a jumper and went with them to the research library.

Rachael and Theo were already there, as was their own full complement of trusted researchers. Rachael was immersed in some books and was glancing at various maps that had been laid out flat on the tables surrounding her. Theo looked a little less enthusiastic about whatever she was doing, so I went to him first to say hello. He gently bent down and picked me up so that he could look into my face as he spoke to me. "Well, Princess, did you enjoy your night of solitude and freedom?" he asked, smiling at me.

"Yes, thank you, although I didn't really do much. I went for a walk and just visited some places in the castle that I hadn't visited before," I said, sighing as if I really hadn't done anything of interest. When Theo frowned at me, I realised that what I had just said was probably not the best thing to have said to him, so I quickly added, "It's okay, don't be worried—I didn't go anywhere I wasn't supposed to. Besides, you know me. I am not the most adventurous of beings. I have come to know my limitations, and I know better than any other person here not to visit any of the lower levels." I said the last part as if I was repeating a lesson that had been told to me on many occasions before. Although Theo looked a little dissatisfied at my explanation, he seemed to accept it and no more was said. I dared a quick look at Rachael as I went to take a seat, but she seemed intent on whatever she was studying in front of her. I spent the entire day with them, searching and reading anything the researchers could find on the presumed extinct Sky Dwellers.

There was a lot of discussion on how human beings had been responsible for the demise and near extinction of the Earth Carers and Dwellers, and how the invasion had taken place almost too late for the Sky Dwellers. When I tried to speak, I wanted to question their interpretation of history because my mother had always seemed to think that the invasion had not been as beneficial to the Dwellers as the vampires had, at first, promised. Even my own experiences with Thomas and the fact that David was working to change our laws showed that vampires were at fault as well. I knew that they heard me, but they ignored my questions. Rachael and Theo were less than enthusiastic about my views, and in time I seemed to become mildly irritating to them.

I found myself randomly checking on the bracelet that Elathan had given me because the more irritated I became with my companions, the more I wanted to feel it—to make contact with it. When Rachael asked me what was wrong with my arm, I defiantly lifted my arm to show her, but she didn't appear to notice anything. I quickly put my arm down, not sure why she did not seem to have seen the bracelet but relieved that I wouldn't have to explain where I had gotten it and why I couldn't seem to take it off.

Rachael then became distracted by a phone call from Heather. After the call ended she began to speak with her researchers, and from the instructions she gave I understood we would all be travelling to the Irish Territories as soon as David had returned. Still, I wasn't really included in any of the decisions that were being made, and just when I felt like wandering away, one of the researchers finally noticed me and seemed to feel some compassion. He found some history books for me that told of famous human beings who had shown strength and had appeared to care. Among the books that he handed to me was another book that looked as if it did not belong, but when I went to hand it back to the researcher, I saw him look at my wrist. I was intrigued; he must have noticed something, and he looked slightly afraid. He shook his head slightly, as if he did not know or understand fully what he was seeing, and he looked a bit fearful. When I tried to hand the book back again, he kept gesturing it away from him and, at the same time, kept nodding at it as if I should take it and read it.

It was a small handwritten book easily concealed under my clothing, so rather than risk discovery I told the researcher to calm down and I discreetly hid the book, intending to take it back to my room before I opened it and examined it further. I started to look at the rest of the books that he had given me, creating my own little research corner out of the way, and only stopped reading to eat when Rachael, who seemed to know instinctively when to feed me, brought me some food. When I had become too tired to stay there any longer, she told the researchers to help me pack the books away.

Theo seemed to react to a look from Rachael and offered to carry me back to my rooms. Even though I would have probably enjoyed the ride, I stubbornly decided to walk back. It felt good to be tired, knowing that when I woke David would be with me again. I was back in my real world, and all thoughts of Elathan's heat were already fading.

Once I was back in the apartment, I pulled the book out from underneath my jumper and looked closely at it. I wondered why the researcher had given it to me but was simply too tired by then to worry, so I placed it in my secret box and put it away. I discarded my clothes altogether and climbed into my bed, all thoughts of the previous night and of the book forgotten almost immediately as I drifted into a deep, dreamless sleep.

Chapter 26

Iopened my eyes when I sensed David sitting in a chair next to my bed. He was smiling and looking at me as if he was just as happy to see me as I suddenly was to see him. Before I could make a move to get up he was at my side, holding me and squeezing me gently, though hard enough to take my breath away, giving me goose pimples with his coolness against my skin.

"It is good to be home. I have missed you this time, my sweet beloved, perhaps even more than I thought I would," he murmured, nuzzling his soft lips into my hair. I shivered slightly as I could feel him breathing me in.

"And I have missed you," I said, pulling back so I could look at his intensely serious face. I had to laugh because it just felt so very good to see him again. Even the coolness from his touch felt right. He looked happy and rested, and as if he had achieved something during his time away.

"Did your visit go well?" I asked.

"It went better and quicker than I expected," he said, still holding me close. "Our hosts were more than hospitable, and they made us all very welcome. In truth, I was a little worried about how their culture might conflict with our version of the Universal Laws, but my worries were unfounded because they have adapted to them easily and well. They were extremely welcoming of the new Enclosure proposals."

"That's good. I am glad—I like King Bello and Queen Abiba. I am glad that they are both well. Did they like their gifts?" I asked, smiling.

"Yes, and they seem to like you very much, too, and have extended an invitation for you to join me the next time I pay them a visit, official or unofficial—it doesn't matter. They have both assured me that they will be able to find something for you to do. They really loved their gifts. In fact, Bello insisted on using his new vial throughout the council meeting, and I am afraid you may have started a tradition. My next visit should be with Eduardo and Margarita of the Spanish Territories. Actually, Eduardo had a quiet word with me at the banquet, asking if I would be bringing them gifts as well," he said, smiling and hugging me tightly again.

"But I have never really spoken to them. I don't know them—what shall I buy?" I said suddenly, feeling a little unsure of the new gift tradition I appeared to have started.

David laughed at my sudden insecurity. "Mia knows them well. You will have to ask her when we see her. I hear that you and the others have been busy finding clues in my absence, and we are all to be joining my sister in the very near future," he said, smiling and hugging me against him again.

"You know, if you let me go I can get out of bed and we can talk while I have something to eat," I said, pushing at him playfully. Of course, there was no point since it was like pushing at a wall. He held on to me for a few minutes longer before loosening his grip on me. "Actually, it would probably be better if you spoke to Rachael. She knows so much more than I do about what has been found and needs to be done, and she has everyone organised. She is also overseeing the travel arrangements for our group to attend Mia's ceremony."

"I know," he said. He kissed the top of my head before moving away to allow me to get up and take a shower before my breakfast arrived.

I tried to shower as quickly as I could, not wanting to leave David for any more time than necessary but still wanting to emerge from it looking and smelling ravishingly fresh to him.

While I was showering, my thoughts turned again to the gift that Elathan had given me. I thought it was odd that Rachael had not noticed it and neither had David. If Elathan had done something to obscure its presence from my friends, then I would do nothing to change that. I decided that if the gift was going to be permanently attached to me, then I would have to learn to ignore it and not draw any unwanted attention to it, although I didn't quite understand how a human researcher, the one who had handed me more books to pore over, had seen it but Rachael hadn't.

Once I was clean to my satisfaction, my skin tingling after the fierce spray, I dried myself and slipped into a pair of comfortable trousers and a soft jumper, and then I went outside. I had a feeling that David and I would not be straying too far from our rooms for most of that day.

When I reappeared refreshed and ready in our communal room, I heard David speaking to Rachael on his phone so I went and got myself some food from the breakfast tray that had arrived while I was showering. I sat down to eat while David made a few more phone calls. It took me a while to realise that Alex and James were not at their usual place on the sofa in front of my plasma device.

It felt odd for them not to be there, but I knew that they were absent for a reason—probably David's wishes. I ate my breakfast and waited patiently for David to finish speaking to the people he needed to. Eventually he came over to me and sat down. We spent the better part of our late morning together cuddled up on the sofa watching silly programmes on the plasma device. I didn't ask about my guards not being there or the lack of visitors; I was grateful for our time alone.

Shortly after lunchtime our peace was finally over and our travelling companions started to arrive. After the initial greetings we sat quietly while Rachael explained about the most recent findings and the plans she had put in place. I slipped away before she had finished because I already knew most of what she was telling us, and I wanted to start packing my personal bag.

I chose one of the bags that Mia had given to me when I was younger. I chose that particular one for its pockets within pockets and quickly took the book from its hiding place. At a quick glance the book appeared to be some sort of diary, and there were handwritten notes on every page. I felt myself wanting to sit and read it as soon as I touched it. Before I realised what I was doing, I sat down with the book, but a noise outside distracted me and my senses returned quickly. I shut the book and placed it at the bottom of the bag among other items, and placed the bag on my bed. I pulled up a larger bag and started to place some clothes in it, trying to make it look like I had actually accomplished more packing than I had.

I heard Rachael beginning to issue instructions to late arrivals, and when she was done speaking she joined me in the bedroom and began to help me pack the rest of my clothes. I felt a little awkward at first, as if I had grown apart from her. I knew that it was partly because we were both busy with other things and partly because I was growing up. I never really saw her socially anymore, and when she wasn't at the research library she was with Theo.

I missed her. If Mia was like my sister, then Rachael had been like a second mother to me. Rachael was the one who had nursed me back to health after I had been poisoned and had also played a big part in helping me to re-enter the castle and David's life. She, more than any other being, had saved me and helped me to prepare for the world I was now living in.

Rachael also made life for my mother as easy as possible, especially when I was taken from the Enclosure. She had stayed with my mother as my mother began to fade and the life slowly left her. Rachael also took me when I was back to the place where the Forest Dwellers of the area had created a mound as a tribute to my mother. I had a lot to be grateful to her for and loved her intensely. I didn't know what to say so I worked with her, listening to her instructions about the clothing I would need. When we were finished, she turned to leave and I reached for her hand. As I did, she surprised me by reaching for me.

"I have missed you too, child," she said. "But someone has to stay focussed around here, and you are both alarmingly distracting and endearing, especially around your guards. I believe what I have read is correct and that something important is about to happen. However, I do not believe that this planet will come to an end, as some of the articles I have read seem to indicate, but I have a sense of foreboding and it unsettles me. We all, it appears, have destinies of our own to follow."

I didn't know what to say — there was nothing really to say, so I just hugged her back, knowing she was right and I was probably being overly sensitive. After a few moments together she kissed the top of my head and pushed me gently away in her usual 'get back to what you were doing' way. As we left the bedroom with the bags, I had the bag with my personal belongings tucked safely and firmly under my arm. We placed the bags next to the others that had been placed by the door. The rest of the afternoon was spent finalising plans, and after a short while Rachael left us, saying that she needed to organise her research staff.

Theo stayed behind because he was our official head of security as well as my protector. He said he had things he wished to discuss with David, but his eyes never left Rachael as she left. I did what I could to contribute, but mostly I let my family do what they do best and arrange the finer details for the upcoming trip. Everything that could be arranged was done by late afternoon. David and I decided to pay his parents a quick visit, since it might be a while until we saw them again. After everything was done and everyone had left us, I changed into some more appropriate and less casual clothing.

Alex and James were standing outside of our door, where they had been for most of the day. When I asked David why they were not invited inside to listen to what Rachael said, he told me that they had been asked to stay outside as added protection. David nodded to them both as we passed, and they smiled a greeting in return. They were both at ease; seemingly no one had approached during our discussions. David and I stopped walking long enough to issue them both instructions. They were coming with us officially as my royal guard and were required to wear palace uniforms at the ceremony.

When they both looked a little alarmed, David turned his head and winked at me. I realised that at moments, when we were alone and being just us, not the prince and the princess, nor the vampire and human, that I was really very much in love with him. I held his hand, our palms pressed flat together and our fingers entwined tightly as we walked slowly together along the corridor until we came to the entranceway to the emperor's apartments.

Their guards were already expecting us, so we walked straight through to the emperor's royal suite of rooms. The Empress Constantina was already seated in her reception room, and she rose from her chair when she saw us. She still took my breath away. I felt insignificant when I was near her. She moved elegantly and was effortlessly graceful. She was stunningly beautiful in a darkly exotic way. On that visit it was one of the first times I had ever seen her dressed so casually. She wore long satin trousers and a wraparound top that emphasised her perfect shape. Her long blue-black hair was loose and flowed over her arms and shoulders; her makeup was dark and dramatic to make her eyes look less rounded and more feline.

She looked different in other ways. To me she looked more human than vampire. When she noticed me staring at her, she must have guessed what I was thinking and she smiled lovingly at me. "Finally, in a short time, Marcarius will be passing on his legacy to our son and his son's beloved partner. Therefore it is time for me to recognise and reconcile myself to the being I was before," she said softly.

"Who were you?" I asked, leaning forward and unable to stop the question from leaving my lips. I could feel David tense beside me as if he disapproved of the way the conversation was going.

As if she sensed the change in atmosphere, Constantina leaned forward, glanced at her son briefly, and said, "This can wait. Perhaps we will have this conversation another time."

I did not know how to respond. Instead I found myself going to her and hugging her gently because, although she was the Everlasting Life Partner of the ruler of our planet, she was always lovely to me and it just seemed to bring me closer to her now that I realised she had been human before she had been infused. I felt that something was changing between us; a bond that had nothing to do with her Life Partner or son was forming. "Actually, I think you have never looked so beautiful or human, and I think it is good to see you as you were," I said, sitting on a chair next to David.

"How is the emperor? Is he finding it as easy as you to find the person he was?" I asked, genuinely curious.

"No, Marcarius is as he has always been since I met him as a girl. He took me and showed me a world that I had only dreamed of," she said, smiling serenely as she looked at something somewhere above our heads, appearing to remember that first meeting.

I would have liked to know more, but before I could ask another question David again changed the subject and offered me something to drink. In doing this he seemed to break her spell and make me forget what I was thinking. When I turned my attention back to the empress, I had already forgot what I had intended to ask her. I did, however, notice a look that passed between David and his mother and was surprised to see her drop her gaze. After this, we spent a quietly respectful time with her speaking of our plans for our future, and we stayed to join her in some light refreshments.

Just before we were about to leave, the emperor made an appearance and, as he communicated directly with David, I suddenly felt almost unbearable pressure in my head. I had to hold on to David just to keep myself upright. I understood then how much David's power was growing because he could tolerate communicating with his father without any shielding from the empress. I had felt some of the emperor's power when I had first arrived at the castle, but it had been a mere fraction of what David could endure. After we had their blessing, we left them to go to the Temple of Thought.

This was the first time he had accompanied me to the temple. He had to wait for me outside because, surprisingly, he was forbidden entry; the Temple had never accepted him. I went in and had a brief but informative conversation with Sarah. I informed her of our plans and how we intended to pursue any clues about the scripts straight from the Irish Territories. Sarah appeared happy with the decisions we had made, and as I was about to leave she promised to come to me if I called. When I asked her how, she mentioned that there were many shrines to her within the Irish Territories and told me that she was known among the Irish as the Sorceress Sorica, which was another of her ancient names. She told me that she could connect with me in any one of her shrines. I went back outside to David, and we walked back to our apartment.

When we finally got back to our apartment, we made final checks with the rest of our group, and when David was satisfied with everything that had been put into place, we decided to have a few more precious moments together and went into our bedroom. Even though David was fully rested, he lay on the bed with me and covered me with our quilt. I fell asleep in his arms.

Chapter 27

We decided to begin our journey at the first light of dawn. David woke me gently from a deep, contented sleep. As I felt his lips brush my forehead, I opened my eyes and felt a thrill of excitement. The thought of seeing Mia again soon made me want to laugh out loud, even skip around the room. I dressed quickly in some warm clothes, grabbed my bag, and went to join the rest of our group, which had already begun to gather in the apartment.

The castle guards were already collecting our luggage, taking it from the pile in the centre of the room. I had kept my luggage to a minimum, as Rachael had suggested. When David had questioned the minimal amount, Rachael starting rolling her eyes and informed him of the many upcoming shopping opportunities I would have during my stay within the Irish Territories. We all laughed when she pointed out that it was Mia whom we were going to see.

The predawn morning was still dark when we left the castle. We used the castle jeeps to ferry our luggage and us to the waiting planes. Because of the hour we had chosen to travel, we saw very few beings of any kind on the first leg of our journey. This was mainly because predawn was usually the time when most vampires were going about their business while city humans and Dwellers were usually staying safe behind closed doors.

We had arranged for Lisa and Nick to travel ahead of us and to record our arrival in the Irish Territories. There were just a few photographers at the nearby airport, but Theo cleared a path for us and shielded David and me from them. Once inside the airport building, David and I were introduced to the pilot and his Adwar crew, who had been especially lined up to greet us. Afterwards we were guided onto the castle's private plane. On the plane I slept again, wrapped in a blanket in David's arms, and the journey was peaceful and uneventful. Rachael woke me before we were due to arrive so that I could freshen my appearance and apply some makeup. We knew that word would have spread that we were travelling, so we expected the media within the Irish Territories to be on high alert and out in force to get the photograph of any visiting royal family members. Queen Sinead also loved and encouraged any form of publicity. She held the title of the most photographed royal on the planet. Mia and Patrick's Commitment Ceremony was the biggest vampire event to happen in the Irish Territories in many centuries, and already there had been almost daily reports on developments as they happened.

Once I was presentable and groomed to Rachael's approval, I sat back down next to David and placed my hand in his. In my other hand I clutched my bag, and even though David looked at me a little strangely he did not say anything. I could see the lights of the airport in the distance, but I asked David if we could travel a little more before we landed. I explained to him that I had heard a lot about the Land of the Green and would like to see if it lived up to its name. David sent a message to the pilot and we ended up flying lower over the land a couple of more times as the sun was beginning to rise over the horizon.

Because the sun was bright, the shades within the plane automatically lowered, but I could see everything clearly and it was beautiful. The land did live up to its name. It was very green, but it wasn't just one shade of green; it was many shades. There were vast areas of forest, rolling hills, and what looked like meadows that contained large mounds. The meadows were what caught my eye and held my interest. I couldn't recall ever setting foot in the Irish Territories, but when I saw the mounds I got a vague sense of déjà vu. I knew then without any doubts that I had visited places like this with my mother in another time. I knew that the mounds were created as tributes to the forests and to the ancestors who had cared for the land.

Once I felt I had seen enough, David instructed the pilot to land the plane. When I looked out of the window at the airport below, I realised that it was gently raining. We landed without incident, and as the plane gently rolled to a standstill, we prepared to meet the crowd of photographers and others who were waiting for our arrival.

I could hear the sound of music as the steps were lowered. It sounded like a traditional Celtic melody played by a group of Forest Dwellers. There were also groups of young human children dressed in brightly coloured robes, with bunches of handpicked flowers scattered around them at the base of the steps. I had to smile when I saw them; even though their Adwar vampire supervised them, they appeared to be very happy and free; none of them appeared afraid as they moved among the crowds of vampires and Dwellers. At the bottom of the steps I was handed some flowers, which were taken by Rachael. I did try to thank the child, but the noise from the crowd was almost deafening. I followed David closely, and I felt Alex and James move closer to my sides.

We walked in a tight-knit group, only pausing when David stopped for a smile and a wave. He pulled me forward when he was asked about me, and even though I couldn't make out whom I was waving at, I followed David's lead, smiling and waving as we made our way quickly towards the airport building. Although it was raining, there was still a hint of sun preparing to rise on the horizon. After a short period of time, a group of guards came forward to escort us across the tarmac towards the airport building. They greeted us briefly and ushered us efficiently forward, only pausing occasionally for a strategic photograph call. I felt Theo move up so that he was close behind me, and Alex and James resumed their position close by my sides. Cassius moved up ahead of me to walk with David.

With the guards' appearance our arrival had become a more serious and formal occasion. A wall of vampires intent on protecting me suddenly surrounded me. I had not travelled much outside of my territory, and this really was our first official visit together to another territory. We moved forward steadily until we entered the building.

Once we were inside, the noise stopped and I could hear the guard in front explaining to David that they had been sent by the queen to escort us safely to the place we would be staying. We walked straight through the building and out the other side. The rain was light and warm, and it felt refreshing to all of us. We started to relax under the huge black canopy the queen had erected to shield us from the weather. Soon, though, we were ready to go forward. As we started walking I could see lights ahead and could just about make out another open-fronted building. I heard animal noises, and when I looked at David he smiled and winked. As we neared the building, a Forest Dweller approached us slowly and we stopped walking.

He bowed low to us but spoke to me directly, saying, "I understand that it is your wish to see a horse before its senses are protected." His voice was tinged with the soft, lilting accent that I had heard before when Patrick spoke, and it reminded me again of where we were and what we were about to do. I instantly felt comfortable with the Forest Dweller in front of us.

"If that is possible, it is very much what I would like. David, may I? Where do we go?" I asked him, trying to see what was beyond him.

"I am sorry, young mistress, but the prince cannot accompany you, nor can any of your vampire companions. I mean no disrespect to any of you, but our horses do not cope well with those who might drain them," the Forest Dweller explained sincerely, looking apologetically at David.

"No, that will not happen," David said, equally pleasant and still holding my hand tightly.

"It's okay, David. I will be safe, and all of you can see me. I won't be that far away," I said to reassure him, wanting desperately to see the horses and automatically trusting the Forest Dweller.

"No, you will not go unattended," he said stubbornly, not even looking at me, his voice inviting no argument, his eyes never leaving the face of the Forest Dweller in front of us. For my part I simply looked at the Forest Dweller, willing him to find a solution to the problem. He seemed unsurprised at David's reaction; it was as if he expected it.

I knew that I could not go against David's wishes. What we did in private was no one's business, but here we were in front of his subjects, and even though I was his Everlasting Life Partner, I was also his human—and his inferior.

The silence seemed to stretch on forever, until the Forest Dweller finally spoke, searching for a solution. "If I left my mate in your care, would you trust me with yours?" he said, looking straight at David and smiling with confidence. It was as if what he asked was a perfectly reasonable request, one that would solve everyone's problems. I waited and watched and felt David relax a little. I realised that he seemed to also like the man in front of us, and it looked as if he were actually considering the Forest Dweller's proposal; this was confirmed when he smiled and nodded.

"Bryna, come to me, my love," the Forest Dweller called tenderly. After a few moments a heavily pregnant human girl appeared and walked slowly towards him, her eyes never leaving his. When she was at his side, he placed his arms protectively around her shoulders, and the look they shared was full of love and tenderness. When the Forest Dweller saw me looking at her, he explained, "She was a gift from our queen, given for a good deed, and although she was a gift she is my most precious one—one that I would see no harm come to. She is carrying my firstborn, and I am entrusting them both to you. I must point out that she is every bit as precious to me as the princess is to you," he said, looking directly in David's eyes.

"It is agreed. I will care for your mate as you will mine," David said as he let go of my hand. I took a step forward as the girl Bryna moved away from the Forest Dweller and mirrored my move.

"What is your name?" David asked the Forest Dweller.

"It is Malachi, my lord," he answered.

I walked and stood with him as Malachi's mate joined the members of our party. We stood still for a few moments while he seemed to reassure himself that Bryna was in safe hands. As I walked away with him, I could hear Rachael calling for a chair. I smiled, knowing that she would do everything in her power to lessen the fear that the human woman must be feeling. I knew that to a vampire any child is precious, and therefore they would protect Bryna with as much energy as they protected me.

Malachi looked at me for a moment and said, "She will be all right. She has had many experiences with vampires. She belonged to one before she was mine, and I would not have left her if I did not trust your master."

He said nothing more as we walked into the shed; it took me a little while for my eyes to adjust to the light. When I looked at Malachi he pointed to the far corner, where a human was attending to a large brown horse. The horse was much bigger than I had ever imagined; I could barely see the top of its back. I walked slowly towards it, and the horse made small whimpering noises, taking small steps backwards. When I looked slightly worried, Malachi explained that the horse could smell the vampire scent on me, and it also sensed my fear.

I knew I could do nothing about how I smelled, but I could relax and push my fear to the back of my mind, so I took a deep breath, calmed myself, and put my hand out, palm flat, in a gesture of peace. The horse stopped fidgeting, and when I reached for it, the horse lowered its head and nudged me slightly, making me take a few steps back. I heard Malachi laugh beside me. He put out his hand and the horse immediately nudged his hand, obviously looking for something to eat.

"He won't hurt you, will you, boy?" he said, gently rubbing the length of the horse's head. He pulled some leaves out of his pocket and placed them in my hand. He held my arm as I held out the leaves for the horse, which took them carefully, eyeing me warily, not sure if I was a friend or enemy. I found myself looking directly into the horse's rich brown eyes. There was a wisdom there that I hadn't expected. There was no fear then, just a look of curiosity.

We continued to stare at each other, comfortable in each other's presence, until the horse had taken the last leaves from me. When the leaves were gone, Malachi gently led me away, but it was hard for me to leave. I wanted to spend more time with the magnificent animal.

"I am sorry, but I do not like being away from Bryna for any length of time, and I am sure that your master feels the same way about you," he said.

"I understand, thank you, but David is not my master. He is my Everlasting Life Partner," I said, smiling up at him.

Malachi laughed slightly as he said, "You are a human and he is a vampire. I know that he has taken you as his mate, but on this planet among its beings he is and always will be considered your master," he said.

"As it is with your 'gift,' are you Bryna's master, then?" I asked him in return.

"Touché, Princess," he said, laughing.

We continued silently and quickly back to where the others were. I was amused to see that Rachael had taken over the full care of Bryna, sitting with her and speaking softly as she gently kept her hand on the pregnant girl's stomach. I wasn't too surprised to see Theo, with a face like thunder, standing off to one side with an equally unimpressed-looking Alex and James.

"It appears that not all of your party is happy with your being placed totally in my care," Malachi muttered as we approached them.

"They are my bodyguards, and they are always like that," I said, laughing suddenly, the mood between us lifting with the sound.

When I approached the group, Rachael helped the young woman to her feet and we both walked forward to stand beside our partners. As we passed, we smiled at each other.

"Thank you," I said again as they turned to leave.

"It was no trouble. If you wait here, your carriage will arrive shortly," Malachi said.

"Did you get to do what you wanted?" David asked as he hugged me close.

"Oh David, you should have seen it. The horse was huge but very gentle. Malachi gave me some leaves and it ate them from my hand. Was Theo really annoyed with you?"

"It is nothing he won't recover from in a second," David said, laughing. "He appears to value you as much as I do."

A few moments later a large carriage arrived, pulled by the horse I had fed earlier. This time, however, the horse had a hood over its face. The only parts of the horse's head that were left uncovered were its ears. The carriage was open, but it had a hood pulled up over most of it to protect us from the soft rain. We climbed into the carriage together, with Cassius climbing in first, then David. I ended up sitting between David and a still aggravated Theo, with Alex, James, and Rachael sitting opposite us.

The journey we had was magical. It seemed that Queen Sinead liked her lands to be left mainly as nature intended. The horse trotted at a leisurely pace down small winding roads. When I asked David why I hadn't seen any Inner Districts, he told me that he had arranged for us to travel the scenic route.

He explained that the Irish Territories were no different from the other territories with their own cities, districts, and Enclosures. I stopped talking for the rest of the journey. I spent the rest of the journey simply enjoying the views and getting a feel for the territories where my mother's family had come from. Eventually we turned off the road we were on and started up a small winding lane that was lined with luscious green trees. The farther down the lane we travelled, the less dense the trees seemed to become until eventually we were in a clearing. At the centre of the clearing there was a large lake, and beyond the lake there seemed to be a collection of picture-perfect cottages. I sat up as we neared because I could see people standing in front of them waiting for our arrival.

Chapter 28

As we got nearer to the cottages, there were many more breaks in the trees and I could finally see what lay ahead of us more clearly; as we continued slowly forward, I shouted for the unseen person driving the horse to stop the carriage.

I couldn't help myself; all tiredness suddenly left me and I called out loudly because I could finally see her. Mia was standing in front of the gathered welcoming group, she obviously wanting to be the first to greet us. Even though she had always been a small being, she still looked formidable; she had a magical presence about her that had never appeared more obvious than it did in the centre of the clearing as she stood watching the approach of the carriage.

Unusually, she had let her hair down and with the breeze, which seemed to add a frame of wild orange fire to her background. She was wearing a large dark green cloak that was fastened at the neck and hung to her ankles, a little different from my normal trench coat. Seeing her there dressed like that gave me goose pimples, and I realised that for the first time since I had known her, she looked the part of a pure vampire.

As soon as the carriage slowed sufficiently, with a little help from David, I was out and running towards her.

Before I could get too far, I felt Theo; at first he was simply running to keep up with my pace, but then he reached forward to sweep me off my feet into his huge arms. This time I didn't mind because I knew that I would get there faster with him running. I could hear David laughing and calling out behind me that Theo would not let me get away from him for a second time that day. Theo took no notice of him and ran effortlessly with me in his arms to my intended destination. When we were a few feet away, he gently placed me back on my feet. I took a few moments to steady myself and then I turned towards her. As soon as that happened Mia was with me, holding me against her with both of us almost crying with relief. After a few private moments, I felt the huge arms of Theo encircle us both. I knew that he considered her to be a sister, and even though he was a vampire, he was probably just as pleased to see her as I was. Although she held on to me, I felt her stiffen slightly at Theo's embrace, as if it was something that she didn't expect or want, but the embrace was over in a seconds, before I could issue her an enquiring look.

It was good to see her again. She looked wonderful, and it was obvious that staying with Patrick in the Irish Territories had agreed with her; she looked almost healthier—her features appeared more vibrant and more beautiful.

"I have missed you," I said as I hugged her tightly again.

"And I have missed you," she responded. "And you, Mountain Dweller Theo." As she spoke to him she pulled away from the both of us and bowed to him formally from the neck.

"That's a little formal, isn't it?" I said, laughing nervously.

"Yes, it is. I am sorry, but I have been away from you all and your customary embraces and loving demonstrations of affection for a quite a while, and I feel a little different—please forgive me, Theo," she said as she lowered her guard and hugged him again, this time without restraint. The embrace was heartfelt but brief, and Mia seemed to be on her guard again.

Glad that the moment had passed, I continued to speak. "How is everything? Is it all arranged? I am so excited to be here, to see you again." I could not help but hug her again. I knew I was babbling, but I couldn't help it.

We finally pulled apart as the carriage pulled up behind us. Everything became a little chaotic: Janet, her sister Georgina, and Heather all came out of one of the cottages to greet us. Patrick was there as well, and for a while the men shook hands and the women gave each other hugs and kisses.

There were other vampires, both male and female, all of them ranked Hiltian and above, who seemed to want to greet me. I didn't know them, so I retreated closer to my friends and protectors.

While the greetings took place our luggage was unloaded and Mia broke away to organise their distribution to the various cottages. As I watched her I realised that she had changed quite a bit; she seemed so much more mature, laughing and joking with the strangers who had come to greet us. After a long conversation with Rachael, which appeared to involve something about me (I caught them both looking in my direction more than once), Mia eventually came back over and took me by the hand. She led me away from the beings that continued to mill around me, towards one of the central cottages, and pulled me inside.

"I have chosen the cottage that I thought you would like the most, and I have added some things that I thought might appeal to you," she said, smiling as she opened the door.

The cottage was beautiful and full of soft, warm colours and furnishings; there was an illusion of a warm welcoming fire at the end of the main communal room. I had to smile, as it reminded me of the cabin in the mountains where David and I had spent time on our first date. There were the obvious creature comforts like a music centre and a large plasma device, in front of which was my customary oversized chair. The room also had a glass-fronted chilled cabinet which seemed well stocked with various bottles and a variety of snacks. There were two doors to the left of us as we entered — the first had stairs leading up, and after a quick look round the communal room, Mia took me to the upper level.

On the upper level there was a luxurious-looking master bedroom which had a large walk-in wardrobe. There appeared to be a selection of clothes already hanging in clear plastic covers, and when Mia saw me looking at them, she innocently explained that she had gathered a few things she thought I might like. There was also a huge four-poster bed in the centre of the room, and when I looked at Mia again, she shrugged and smiled, her eyes sparkling, as if it was perfectly normal to have such a huge bed for one person with the occasional resting partner.

Covering the bed were various large cushions and fur blankets, and between the posts were thin sheets of netting which appeared to have threads of reds and golds entwined through it. I had to laugh because it appeared that Patrick had been influencing her. Since they had been planning their commitment ceremony, she had been afflicted with a few new romantic tendencies.

The view from the large curved window at the far end of the room was beautiful; it overlooked the lake and the green fields beyond. Next to the window was a small table with a large bowl-like vase that was filled to capacity with fresh wildflowers.

There was a fully equipped bathroom next to it that seemed to be already well stocked with my favourite bath oils and scents.

When we had finished looking upstairs, she led me back into the communal room, and as we entered Alex and James came through the door beside us. When I looked enquiringly at Mia, she told me that there was accommodation in the lower level for my two royal bodyguards. She explained that Theo and Rachael would be sharing accommodation with Cassius next door on one side, and Janet, Sebastian, Georgina, and Heather would be on the other. She added that she and Patrick were staying up at the palace per the queen's wishes.

The first few hours following our arrival were a blur of greetings and excited welcoming conversations as we all crowded into one of the cottages and swapped stories.

Patrick was his usual charming, handsome self, and he seemed genuinely happy to see us all together again. Mia took up her customary place at my side, though when Patrick addressed her she let go of my hand. Apart from that, it was a good, happy start to our visit. As the afternoon wore on, I began to get hungry and asked Mia for some food to be brought to me.

When it arrived I ate a variety of meats and fresh vegetables, but when I offered Mia some to nibble she refused, telling me that she had not eaten food since she had left the castle and that she preferred to stay with the true vampire diet. She explained that none of Patrick's family bothered with human food anymore. I noticed she looked less Forest Dweller and more vampire than she used to, and when I looked at her face closely, I imagined I could see a widening of the black ring surrounding the iris of her eyes. I returned her smile when she saw me looking at her, but I could not help but notice the look that her sister gave her back; it was one of loss and possibly regret, as if Heather also knew that Mia was finally succumbing to the vampire essence and her Forest Dweller heritage was finally diminishing.

Once I had come to that conclusion, I began to notice other subtle differences. Although she and Patrick shared an obvious closeness, there no longer seemed to be any physical contact like hand-holding. Before they had left, they had held hands as much as David and I did.

When Mia felt the eyes of her sister on her she turned towards her, but there was no warmth—just determination in the look she returned. It unnerved me; I knew then that something had happened between them. I found myself moving closer to David, away from Mia. I reached towards him, gently touching his hand, and comfortingly he responded by picking my hand up and enclosing it in his. He did this even though his attention was directed away from me; his was a subconscious and natural gesture between us.

There was no doubt in my mind that Mia still loved me—I could see it in the way she smiled and looked at me—but I didn't know enough about a developing vampire to be sure that I was entirely safe. I had only recently, during one of my free afternoons, read about this different type of vampire. I knew that developing vampires were ones that had been something other than merely human before they had been infused. For a while, sometimes forever, they retained both elements of who they were previously, and some never did lose that original element. I had always been conscious of the Forest Dweller that remained at the heart of Mia.

However, I had read that some of them let go of their pasts and succumbed to the essence, and in doing this some of them become pure vampire and quickly developed a craving for human blood. I was certain that Mia was developing, but I didn't know how much control Mia had or whether I should be wary of her like I would have been with a newly infused vampire. They were also known to be stronger and sometimes faster—more vicious that 'human' vampires. I felt a little sad, as Mia had been my playmate, big sister, and best friend since I had arrived at the castle.

She explained that a banquet was to be held in our honour by Queen Sinead. When we had been together at the castle, she would have been jumping with excitement, but now, with a quick glance at Patrick, she made the announcement in a more formal manner.

As we got up to leave and rest before the formal banquet, Mia came over to me again and hugged me to her, promising that she would be there to help me choose my costume for the banquet the following evening. She also promised that she had a surprise for me.

Then she was gone. She went to Patrick's side, and they got into a waiting car and sped off down the little road.

David, Alex, James, and I went back to our cottage. Alex and James sat down and started looking through the channels on the plasma device, stopping and studying with interest any of the news reports that mentioned our departure or arrival. They studied faces in the crowds, looking for potential threats.

David and I went upstairs. It was almost night but we were both in need of rest, so instead of enjoying the view we closed the blinds and lay down together on the bed. I lay in his arms as he rested, and I watched him as he closed his eyes and became still, his features relaxing. I got off the bed to remove my clothes, and when I lay down next to him I covered myself with the fur blanket provided.

It wasn't long before I fell asleep.

Chapter 29

I wasn't sure exactly how long I had slept, but I was awakened suddenly by the sound of quietly controlled arguing. It took me a few moments of intense listening before I realised that Alex had just prevented Mia from climbing the stairs that led to our bedroom. When James eventually joined Alex, I heard her voice fade. They really didn't view her with any kind of subservience, and I knew that she would not be happy at being turned away, but I didn't want to distance her any more than necessary. I already had a feeling that I may have lost a part of her already without adding her exclusion from my private quarters as well.

I phoned Alex and told him gently that I wanted her to come up, and that while we were within the Irish Territories she was to be allowed unrestricted access. I made the excuse that she might want to discuss urgent matters concerning her upcoming ceremony. I heard him sigh, and he seemed distant. I closed my eyes and took a deep breath, and then thanked him for doing his job so well and apologised for changing my own rules, but it was important.

Knowing that Alex was irritated made me suddenly tired. It seemed as if I was going to have a hard job this time pleasing all the vampires at once. I reasoned that for beings that had been on the planet for centuries, they were a little childlike in their behaviour sometimes. This was not quite what I had been expecting or looking forward to.

I got off the bed, still wrapped in the fur blanket, and opened the blinds that shielded us from the view of the lake. Another day had almost gone, and the sun was gently turning orange in the darkening sky. The lake was still and dark in the distance, but I could see lights, some moving and some still, but all intriguing. I wasn't aware that David was awake until I felt him behind me; I shivered slightly as I felt his cool arms wrap themselves around my bare shoulders.

"Come and lie with me again," he whispered in my ear, his cold nose gently tracing the artery in my neck.

"Mia is on her way," I said as I gently laid my head back against his shoulder, resting my face against his.

"Mia is here. Hello, Sister," he said as he kissed my neck softly, breathing me in one final time before he removed his arms and moved away. As he moved to greet her, I took the opportunity to slip into the bathroom and run myself a bath. I gathered from the sudden coolness of his greeting that they both had some things to say to each other and didn't think that my presence would be helpful in any way. I sank into the water and relaxed, but the door was open so I concentrated on what I could hear in the next room. I felt the need to hear their conversation; it was becoming increasingly irritating to be left in the dark about what had happened or was happening over there.

"David," I heard her say, "am I still to be expected to ask your bodyguards for an appointment here as well?"

"You will do whatever is necessary to protect my chosen partner and your best friend, Sister. You know that. We all know that," he retorted.

"Of course I will. I am as duty bound as you, as we all are, to protect her," she answered.

"Is that what she is now—a duty to you?" David said curtly. I heard his voice lower as he spoke.

After a few seconds of silence, Mia spoke again. "How dare you suggest that? She is the one being that has taught me to feel. She has taught us both to feel again," I heard her hiss at him.

I dared not move, but the hairs stood up on the back of my neck. I sensed that the atmosphere within the room where they were speaking had perceptibly chilled.

"Step away from me, Sister, or I will be forced to reprimand you." David's voice was barely a whisper, and I strained hard to catch his words. Both of their voices were filled with cold threats.

I held my breath, wanting to get up out of the bath to stand between them, or at least try to make things right again, but I felt afraid to move—afraid at what I might be witness to.

An image of Elathan flashed through my mind, and suddenly I wanted to be back at the castle again. As fast as the image left my mind, the tension in the next room seemed to fade just as quickly, and I imagined both of them were softening.

"I am sorry, I forget myself sometimes, David. It is different here. I have felt different here," I heard Mia saying finally.

"I can see the change in you and so can Liberty," I heard David respond, equally quiet.

"I know. I will speak with her later, but I believe she is probably the one who will understand the most," Mia said.

"What makes you believe that?" David asked.

"I know she has felt as I do," was Mia's response.

"Is it still difficult with Heather?" was David's next question.

"Not as bad as it has been. I believe we are improving." I heard her sigh.

I ducked my head under the water to stop myself from listening any further, and when I lifted it again they had obviously changed the subject.

"Liberty is beautiful, as she always is, and she has remained a full-time occupation, especially since you left her to her own devices. As far as I am aware, she has only requested one evening to herself, and though it is not completely understood what she did or where she went, she returned safely," David said.

I could hear the smile in his voice and I heard her laugh; I was sure that she understood perfectly what he was talking about.

"I can hear you," I called from the bathroom.

"We know," they both answered in perfect unison.

Mia walked into the bathroom with a large towel, which she held up as an invitation to me to get out of the bath. "It is time for you to get ready. I have chosen a selection of Janet's latest designs for you to have a look at," she said as I stepped out of the bath and into the towel.

"I see you have visited the forests while I have not been with you," Mia said, taking my hand and looking at the small silver scar on my palm.

"Yes, I thought it would be a good idea if I proved to David and the others that I would be safe and protected by the Forest Dwellers. It didn't quite work out the way I planned it, but I think I may have made a new friend for life," I said, smiling at her, not wanting her to be upset with me.

After a moment's hesitation she smiled and said, "So I see. Now, let us see what Janet has prepared, shall we?" she said, effectively finishing the conversation.

"I have missed her too," I said as I shivered slightly in the cool afternoon air.

For the next few hours we banished David from the bedroom, and it was like we had never been away from each other. I tried not to notice the little changes in her, and she tried to relax and enjoy herself and be the being she usually was with me. We tried on and disagreed on more than a few outfits. The one that we finally agreed on was a long, flowing dress that was crimson in colour. It consisted of a tight bodice beaded with black diamonds that made it almost impossible for me to breathe. It had a skirt with many layers of sheer material that flowed behind me like a trail of crimson mist. Mia wore a similar dress in dark green. I then chose to wear black and gold soft flat shoes on my feet because Mia had told me that it was going to be a long night.

My makeup was strikingly dark, and Mia used crimson to accentuate the dual colour of my eyes. I added no more jewellery to my existing jewellery, and Mia startled me a little when she referred to the bracelet I was wearing. I thought that Elathan had somehow made it invisible, but clearly not to all beings. I told her that it was just something that I had picked up. I didn't look at her, and I pretended to have found something of interest in the bodice.

She went to take a closer look, and she frowned and mumbled something about it being too old. I just placed my arm behind my back, out of sight, trying not to give away the fact that I was lying. To my relief, even though she continued to frown slightly and appeared to want to say something more about it, she changed her mind. When we were dressed to her satisfaction we walked down the stairs to join the others.

As we got closer to our destination, Mia quickly explained that although Queen Sinead was a liberal and tolerant ruler, vampires were expected to be vampires, and even though I was a human, for this occasion I was the Life Partner of the next in line to the vampire empire.

They were all there as I expected, chatting in small groups. I saw that Cassius was having an intense conversation with Heather and Georgina. Georgina had her arm around Heather, protectively, as if Heather needed comforting. At the back of our group standing alone were Nick and Lisa, who were the only other humans present. Mia knew who they were, so she had allowed them certain photograph opportunities. I found David near the front of the room having a conversation with Sebastian and Janet.

Everyone looked really wonderful—the bodyguards looking stylish and menacingly handsome, and all the females in flowing gowns in a variety of colours, but all of them looking very much like traditional vampires.

David looked breathtaking, as he always did to me. He was wearing his traditional black suit with a crimson waistcoat and thin gold tie. Over his arm he carried a ground-sweeping cashmere trench coat. He must have sensed me admiring him because after a few seconds he turned and looked at me. I made my way down the stairs towards his smiling face, and when I reached him I kissed his cheek.

Mia said a brief good-bye, kissing me gently on the cheek and telling me that she would see us all at the banquet, and went to join Patrick. As she passed Heather I saw her look at her sister as if she wanted to say something; her eyes showed sadness, but Heather turned her face away and Mia left.

When she had gone, David assigned a vampire to protect the humans in our group. Cassius was the obvious choice to protect Heather, while Janet and Sebastian would protect Georgina, and Alex and James would protect Lisa and Nick. Although they were among our party and should have been protected automatically, we were still a little unsure of the reception they would get. I am sure David truly believed it was better to be safe than sorry.

It was also decided that Theo and Rachael would remain with David and me throughout the night as our joint bodyguards. We sat quietly, most of us so very happy to be together as a group again.

We didn't have long to wait before our carriages arrived. We were transported to the meadow where the banquet was being held in the open carriages at an unhurried, leisurely pace. The night was warm, with the slightest of breezes blowing; it was perfect and added to the growing excitement. On arrival at the event, we were ushered to the front of a line that had already started to form on the path leading to the arched floral entrance of a large marquee.

As I stood waiting with my friends, I realised how much I was really looking forward to the upcoming event. The welcoming atmosphere was filled with happiness that was infectious. Soon even Heather was smiling as Cassius stayed protectively close to her.

The pathway was lit with small, shiny orbs of crystal that were scattered along its edge. As we moved up, ready to be announced, we arranged ourselves into our pairs and adopted a more formal manner. It was becoming second nature among us, and just before we reached the front, all smiles left our faces and we became the party of the future ruler.

When David and I stepped through the entrance, I felt like a child who had suddenly entered a fairy-tale land. I felt as if I had been transported to somewhere magical, somewhere enchanted. We were standing at the entrance of a picturesque meadow. Throughout the meadow I could definitely detect the playful influence of the queen.

There were small lights strewn throughout the protective canopy of trees surrounding us and protecting the guests from prying eyes, and among the long grasses there were more glowing crystals that reflected the lights and stars above, making the grass appear alive as the crystals moved within. The meadow was large enough that it had a number of groups of musical Forest Dwellers playing at either end in huge black and green marquees to a variety of beings. There were various magicians, contortionists, and entertainers walking and performing among the guests. There were human children running around in little fairy costumes, carrying trays of vials and human foods.

Later I discovered that not all of the children were human because some of them had been infused. David explained that it was the vampire children who watched and protected the human kind. I knew then that these vampire children were the possessions of the vampires in attendance, and I should have been horrified, but they looked different from the children that I had seen with Mistress Vivien; these were running around the way children should. The human children who played happily among them were also different compared to how I had remembered myself; they looked well fed and well cared for. When Rachael saw me watching them, she told me that Queen Sinead thought that children, even her vampire children, should be given the opportunity to play and they all should be happy while they were still young. She believed it made them much better adult servants.

Then David and I were called forward to be announced. David took my hand and we stepped into the meadow. We began to circulate, stopping occasionally to speak when we were spoken to, not really knowing anyone outside our group. Our bodyguards did their duty well that evening. They became expert at guiding those who were unfamiliar in other directions. There appeared to be a lot of beings there that thought I was invisible, choosing only to address David.

It was both boring and annoying, but there was nothing either of us could do; we had to just smile and put up with it. At least David refused to let go of my hand, a gesture that didn't go unnoticed by some of those who surrounded us. Eventually, after it appeared that we had greeted or had been greeted by almost everyone in attendance, I spotted two familiar figures standing with a group of Forest Dwellers. When I pointed out the group to David, he nodded and we made our way towards them. I saw Heather move ahead and realised Thomas was standing among the Forest Dwellers. He greeted his cousin with a hug and spoke to her quietly before greeting Cassius with a handshake.

Malachi spotted our approach and stepped forward to greet us with his mate, Bryna. She looked beautiful and radiantly pregnant, and as soon as she saw Rachael she smiled genuinely. It seemed that they had bonded deeply when they had last met. I went with Rachael to greet her, and although she was a little hesitant at first, she began to relax with me almost immediately, especially when Rachael assured her that even though I looked a little different, I was definitely human. Bryna even managed to laugh a little when Rachael started to tell her of how hard it was to keep me from getting into trouble.

Eventually I wandered away from them as they discussed Bryna's unborn child, and I saw David speaking quietly with Malachi. Although I had only really had one conversation with him, it was enough for me to decide that I also liked Malachi. We smiled and greeted each other warmly. I waited until Thomas had finished speaking with Heather before I moved to greet him with an embrace of my own. He must have known that I had some questions for him, but he told me softly that the conversation I wanted to have with him would have to wait for a better time and a better place. I trusted him and knew that he would eventually answer them all, so I didn't ask.

When all the various and expected greetings had been dealt with, we all drifted towards each other once again and regrouped. We found a place at the far end of the meadow, near to one of the groups of Forest Dwellers playing some interestingly modern versions of traditional Celtic music. The closer we got to them, the more I wanted to move with their music. It was as enchanting to me as everything else was. Everyone was relaxed and laughing with each other; even Heather, who still had not spoken with me, seemed to begin to enjoy herself a little.

"What is it about this place? Is it really magical?" I asked David as we found each other again and embraced.

"I wondered if you would notice eventually," he said, smiling. "The meadow has been strongly glamoured, though it is done to protect the children and not to deceive the adults," he added as I pulled away from him slightly. I couldn't ask him anything else since a loud bell was sounded and the meadow suddenly became silent. The bell signified the arrival of Queen Sinead and her party, which included Mia and Patrick.

Queen Sinead welcomed all who were in attendance before sitting on the central throne on the newly erected podium in the centre of the meadow. I tried to look beyond the magic of the meadow just to see it as it really was, but I couldn't. I didn't have time to really concentrate because it wasn't long before David and our party were told that the queen had requested our company. As always she seemed delighted to see us all, especially when I ran up the steps to greet her, hugging her in our customary way. I had decided to embrace the glamour because I knew I was safe and decided to enjoy myself among the revellers and appreciate the efforts that the queen had made to make all her 'humans' happy. When I had ascended the podium, she had laughed without humour when a young vampire sitting at her side moved forward to shield her from me and held me tightly when I reached her.

"Lorchen, I am sure that I am perfectly safe being hugged by one of my newest friends. After all, she may be in line to be our empress, but she is still only a human." The little queen laughed lightly as she said the last part. As she held me close she whispered, "It appears you have been busy, both on the land and off. You must tell me of your newest adventures when we have the opportunity. You are fast becoming a friend of the Earths Carers, almost as if the planet itself is accepting your friendship."

Loud enough for Lorchen to hear, she said, "Forgive him, little one, as I will because he is young and impulsive, but too entertaining to be sent away just yet." She laughed and hugged me again, nuzzling her cold face in my neck, tracing the veins and breathing in my scent.

"It is a good thing that I have been well fed and catered to this evening." She laughed again as she held me at arm's length to look at me, her eyes shiny and happy but completely black, as if my smell was difficult for her to resist.

I had to laugh with her then. I couldn't help myself because, for a vampire, she was just so wickedly mischievous and, in a strange way, emotional. Because I had discovered that the meadow was overshadowed with glamour, I could concentrate on the reality. The lines of the fairy-tale setting blurred on occasion and the meadow seemed to darken and lose some of its vibrant colours. I was also becoming more aware that not all those who were surrounding us approved of our closeness. And although I saw a smile appear on Lorchen's face as he laughed a little with the queen, pretending he understood some intended joke, I knew without a doubt that he did not like me.

As Alex and James approached I silently let them know that Lorchen was obviously not a fan of mine and told them to keep him at a distance. I had already had my fill of ignorance during the entire greeting session earlier. We spent the rest of the evening on the podium with the queen and her intimate group of friends. There were times when I felt Lorchen would have liked at least to get a little closer to me, but every time he took a step in my direction, Alex and James would head him off with a little prompting from me.

I also noticed that Heather and Mia continued to keep their distance from each other. I couldn't stand to see them so unhappy, so I decided to do something about it; Heather was as much as a sister to me as Mia was. I could see that Patrick and the queen kept a close eye on Mia when she was with us, so I quietly asked David and Cassius to speak to them, to distract them so that I could try to speak with the sisters together for a moment.

I then asked a reluctant Thomas to help me separate the sisters from the groups where they were conversing. Eventually I managed to find a spot to meet with them, away from the main body of our group but still near enough to it to satisfy Theo.

Heather came to me first. She looked tired, as if she had not been resting too well. When she approached she didn't speak; she just looked at me and waited. I didn't know what to say to her, but I knew from her face that she had probably heard every possible explanation of what was happening to her beloved sister. I got the impression that she had expected something different from me.

Before long, the decision to speak was forgotten as Thomas approached with his very unhappy cousin Mia. We stood there awkwardly for a few moments before Thomas spoke softly, addressing them both: "You are sisters, you will always be sisters. Just because you are changing and growing now in different ways, it should not change the love you both have for each other."

"He is right. Don't you think it is about time you both talked? I have only been with you both for a short time, but the space and sadness between you is almost unbearable," I said, coming to stand beside him. "Please," I continued, "I love you both, but my love is nothing compared to the love and loyalty I know you both feel for each other."

"I simply feel as if the sister I once knew is lost to me. The heritage we shared and have worked to sustain has finally been lost to her, and it is that which makes me grieve," Heather said sadly, facing Mia. Tears began to trickle silently down her cheeks. "I do not know if the being she is finally becoming is . . . is . . . is

187

a sister that I really want or one that I can truly love," she said, faltering.

"Of course I remain your sister—it is you who wishes to avoid me," Mia said, with no hint of the sadness that Heather seemed to feel, although anyone who knew her well would have been able to see how hurt she was; she seemed determined to keep that pain contained. "I feel nothing but love for you. You must know that, but my love for Patrick and my wish to be a worthy Everlasting Life Partner is greater."

"It doesn't have to be, Mia," said a gentle voice from behind us. It was Patrick, who had obviously missed Mia and come to find her.

Mia turned to him. "I feel as if I am a newborn again. I have spent my time over here embracing the essence that flows through my veins as you and the queen have wished me to. I do not know anymore how to please you all," she said, walking away from us all.

That was it for me. I ran up to her and threw my arms around her. She didn't shrug me off, but she didn't turn around to face me either. The only thing I could do was hug her from behind. Not really thinking, I started to speak. "Mia, you are who you are. You were once a Forest Dweller, and from that time you have a sister. Now you are a vampire and you have Patrick. Why can't you be both things to them? After all, I don't really mind what you think you are, but you will always just be Mia to me, so can we stop all this, at least while I am here? I am getting tired, and this isn't exactly what I expected when I left the castle." My words were almost running into each other; I wanted so much for her to understand what I was saying. By the time I had finished, everyone was simply standing and staring at me. I didn't realise myself how agitated I was becoming until the words spilled out of my mouth, reflecting all the impatience that I obviously felt.

It was Patrick who finally spoke. "She is right. Of course, you can be whoever you want to be, but it will take some time, my beloved, that's all." Patrick ventured a small laugh to try and change the heavy atmosphere that surrounded us. I noticed, too, that the meadow was darkening again. In a second, though, Theo distracted me as he approached, seemingly oblivious to the intense conversation that was taking place among us all.

He stood in front of me and winked as if he knew that now was a good time for me to leave them. He put out his arm and I took it as we walked past my friends and back to David, who was still chatting (and perhaps flirting) with the little Irish queen, much to the obvious annoyance of Lorchen, who constantly seemed to be hovering on the outer edges of our circle.

When I joined David he reached for my hand, giving me a tender but not overly concerned look, as if he was trying to tell me not to worry and that things would work out eventually. We stayed with the queen, enjoying her company and her hospitality, until the first signs of dawn started appearing in the night sky. She even insisted that I squeeze myself onto her throne with her, much to the amazement of those who surrounded her. She really seemed to like upsetting her 'yes' people. Bryna left with Malachi just as the sky was lightening, and her going made me realise just how tired I was feeling. Just before the first rays of sun appeared over the horizon, our darkened carriages arrived and took us back to our cottages. We said our quick good-byes and went our separate ways. David carried me up the stairs and placed me on our bed, and that is all I remember of that sad but magical night.

Chapter 30

L ater that morning we rose to find our rooms filled with fresh, beautiful flowers of all colours and sizes. I concentrated hard, trying to sense if there was anything amiss with them, as the feeling of euphoria was a little unexpected, but I could not detect any glamour on them. They were real and quite beautiful. My mood dropped a little as I remembered what had happened between Heather and Mia the previous night. I had to believe, though, that their sudden differences would eventually resolve themselves.

David was deep at rest, so I got up from the bed and quietly retrieved the notebook from my bag. I leaned over and checked that David was still deeply asleep before I dared to open it. I turned it over in my hands and studied it. Although the book was very old, the written extracts inside were clear and concise.

I understood very little of the ancient language, but I knew enough of the vampire language to know that what I was seeing was something different, something that was not meant to be on display in the library. I tried to decipher the words but could not. I knew I would have to find someone from the library to help me. I thought that perhaps when I returned I would seek out the researcher who had given me the book and ask for his aid.

I now had a reasonably interesting new subject to study: the ancient vampire language. I wanted to be able to understand it because, although we all spoke the universal language, those on the outer edges of our group were not averse to conversing quietly in the ancient language when they thought I was within earshot of them.

As David began to move slightly, I hurriedly placed the book back under the belongings in my bag, hiding it again thoroughly. As I sat watching David settle himself again, I breathed deeply. I closed my eyes and allowed myself to absorb the perfume of the flowers. I stretched among the fur blankets that covered me, too awake to rest any more. I decided to go and look for my friends. As I rose from the bed, I took the fur blanket with me, uncovering David in the process.

I had to smile at his perfection and found him wildly distracting; I almost changed my mind so I could lie back down next to him and perhaps take advantage of him. While I stood watching him, I realised that David had rested twice since we had arrived; it was as if he had found a type of vampire peace, or perhaps he knew that I was somehow safe there.

Even though I could see the sun shining beyond the blinds, I didn't draw them back. Instead I went quietly to my wardrobe and gathered up some clothes, which had been unpacked and arranged while I had been out. I chose a pair of my favourite, and oldest, blue jeans and a well-worn cotton shirt and underwear before heading in the bathroom to take a shower. I showered quickly and managed to slip quietly out of the room without disturbing David.

I made my way quietly down the stairs and entered the communal room. I was surprised to see that it was still empty and quietly peaceful, and that it had also been filled with freshly picked flowers. I spotted some food on the table, and there was a glowing heat coming from the fire illusion at the end of the room. I grabbed some food, flicked on the plasma device, and sat by the warmth of the 'fire' for a while.

As predicted, most of the major news channels were featuring our arrival. Most of them discussed the way we were dressed and how we looked, but some went into detail about why the future ruler and his human Life Partner had arrived early, days ahead of the ceremony. Again the focus switched to my long friendship with Mia.

Although I had never said anything to anyone, I found it irritating that I was never described as just David's Life Partner;

the word "human" seemed like a necessary qualifier, and one that denoted inferiority. Every time I heard the phrase, a little voice inside me told me that I was so much more than merely a human on this planet. Someone had even managed to find some pictures of me as a child, which was surprising since I had not been aware any had been taken. One photograph was of a child (me) on what looked like a holiday. For a moment I thought of my friend Daniel, promising myself that I would write him a letter when I returned to the castle. There was nothing else of interest really said, so I very quickly became bored with listening to the reports.

At first I wandered aimlessly around the room, smelling the flowers and picking up various magazines and newspapers. I took my time nibbling at the food, and after I had finished eating I decided, with no one around to argue with me, to go for a short walk, just to the lake. It had looked too pretty to ignore the previous day, and in truth I didn't like sitting there on my own; the room was too quiet. The lake remained in full view of all the cottages, so I knew that I would not get lost and would be easy to locate if any of the others woke up suddenly and sensed that I had gone.

As these thoughts ran through my head, I suddenly felt brave, impulsive. I felt my first thrill of freedom since I had landed here and, at the same time, definitely in need of some fresh air. I grabbed one of the winter jackets that was hung by the side of the door and put on my boots. I left the cottage, quietly shutting the door behind me.

The early afternoon was warm, but it was drizzling just as it had the day before. As I pulled the jacket around me and started to walk, I wondered if the constant drizzle was the reason the Territories were so green, and if it was why so many of the vampires that I knew enjoyed taking short breaks there. Of course, it simply could have been because the queen was renowned for being a spectacular host; even among vampires her parties and celebrations were legendary.

I started walking towards the lake. It was peaceful outside, and I felt completely free and unthreatened by any of my surroundings. I tried to keep my mind focussed and to be aware of everything around me. It was good to have one of those rare moments to myself. My thoughts soon turned to Elathan, knowing that he was the usual reason for my solitude, and wondered if he missed me—but I doubted it.

I shrugged off those thoughts and continued to enjoy the freedom of being outside by myself. When I got near to the lake I heard a noise. I took a step forward and parted some tall grasses only to be delighted by the sight of birds on the lake. The lake was grey green in colour, large in size, and circular, looking almost as if it had been made as a centrepiece for the grounds. Surrounding it were many plants of all sizes and types, displaying a huge myriad of different colours, their vegetation thick and vibrant; many of the plants had their roots below the surface of the water.

The birds in front of me appeared to see me as soon as I saw them, although they appeared to be calmer and less delighted than I was. I presumed that the birds were ducks because I had never actually seen any waterbirds before. They looked like ducks; they were small and brown with colourful feathers just beginning to show beneath the brown ones. Once they saw me they turned and looked straight at me. When two larger, more colourful ducks appeared I realised that the birds I had initially seen were probably young birds; the older birds were much more colourful, with vibrant bright red and blue feathers fanning out from their tails. I found myself fascinated by them and wanted to see more, so I walked slowly forward as quietly as I could, trying not to startle the smaller birds, which were closer to me. However, they did not seem to be at all startled or afraid of my approach; in fact, they seemed to be moving forward just as slowly as I was. I eventually stopped because the closer I got to them, the more I realised that there was something about them that made me feel uneasy and want to back away. Their eyes, which I finally noticed were totally black and devoid of any colour, never left me as they moved forward. I suddenly felt threatened, like prey.

Without taking my eyes off them, I took a small, slow step back. As I did I felt someone close behind me and froze, my heart suddenly rising in my chest, blocking the wind from my throat so that I couldn't even scream. I tried to gather my thoughts, wanting to send them out hoping that someone would reach me before the ducks did. "Pretty little things, aren't they?" I heard Rachael say softly behind me. "Please continue to take those intended steps back."

I nearly collapsed with relief at the sound of her voice. "What are they?" I asked in a voice that sounded unsteady, mixed with fear and relief, as I did as she said.

"They are ducks, of course," she said, seemingly amused at my question.

"What is wrong with them? Why do I fear them if they are just ducks?" I asked in a quivering voice.

"Did you not wonder why there were no other visible securities here or why we felt we could finally rest around you?" she said, her voice close to my ear.

"I did wonder why I was left to my own devices this morning," I answered her, beginning to understand why I had felt fear when I looked at the birds.

"Queen Sinead really does love all of nature, but she has seemingly created her own species of hybrids. After the caretakers and familiars attached to her lands hand-raise the animals from infancy, inducing intense loyalties, she infuses certain creatures and allows them to roam free. They are no danger to those whom they are familiar with, but you are strange to them, and by wandering around you have placed yourself in danger. Thank you for also making my morning much more exciting, especially as they, like their vampire counterparts, have a thirst for human blood. Do you not think this is a perfect solution? They are part of the natural habitat and the landscape is not ruined by the presence of guards. Ingenious, wouldn't you say?" Rachael concluded.

All I could muster was to ask what we should do; I tried to relax as the ducks continued to move slowly towards us. "I will have to pick you up. I believe I can move faster carrying you rather than dragging you with me. While I do not believe they would attack me as such, I am unsure what they would do in order to reach you," she said.

"Okay," I said quietly, still unable to take my eyes off the birds that were now at the edge of the water. I continued to take those small steps and only stopped walking when I felt Rachael move closer behind me. Without her saying another word, I felt her strong arms encircle my waist and lift me off the ground as the ducks rose up out of the lake. The last thing I heard was a malevolent hiss before Rachael moved in and then everything became a cool blur.

When my eyes finally managed to focus, all I saw was the cottage in front of me coming at me very fast, so I simply shut my eyes and hoped for a safe delivery.

It took me a moment to realise that Rachael had stopped moving before I opened my eyes again. She had placed me gently down in front of the door to my cottage, and once I felt steady on my feet again, we both entered. The communal room was still empty, so while I took off my jacket and sat down Rachael fixed me a drink of hot sweet tea and picked up a small vial of blood, which she poured into a china cup for herself.

As she handed me the tea, she simply said, "Drink it."

I did as she said and began to feel a little better almost immediately. I hadn't realised that I was shaking until I took the cup from her hands.

"Whatever made you think that you will ever be safe on your own, child?" she said, looking at me with no smile on her face.

"Well, I just thought with all of you at rest the grounds must be safe. That's why I felt it was okay for me to leave the cottage. I never once disappeared from sight, so I knew I would be easy for any of you to spot once you had awakened from your rest. How does anyone control those ducks? Aren't they wild?" I asked, sipping the hot, sweet liquid.

"It is true that they are born wild, as they should be, but it seems that once they are infused they become more intelligent, and therefore easier to manipulate and control by those who have hand-raised them," she started to explain.

"If we are guests and they are intelligent, then why was I in danger? Surely I should have been warned. If it hadn't been for you I might have been hurt or even killed," I said, my voice becoming a little louder as I began to feel irritated by what had happened.

"And how do the Forest Dwellers manage with them? I noticed that the land and the surrounding trees were neat and well looked after. Surely that is more than a one-being job," I added, a little quieter as she raised her eyebrows and gave me one of her 'what makes you say that' looks.

"One question at a time," she said, smiling at me the way I remembered from what seemed a really long time ago. "You already know that, once infused, it is impossible for us to produce young. Well, that works, it appears, the same for any living thing. The animals that you saw on the lake are probably centuries old and have been tended to and nurtured by the same family of Forest Dwellers throughout their existence. Therefore, only one family of Forest Dwellers resides on each of the queen's residences. You have already met the keepers of this residence."

"Malachi," I said.

"Yes, Malachi. He is a much favoured member of the queen's extended family," she agreed, smiling. I knew she liked him; I could sense it, but I knew better than to ask why.

"But isn't that dangerous for humans like me who are invited to this place? They do not know me—the animals, I mean. I am not a human who nurtured them, and Malachi would have known this," I said, a bit confused.

"Yes, and it is not usual for any of the animals to be roaming during the daylight hours, when humans are usually awake. I believe that we should report this to Mia and Patrick as soon as they appear. In the meantime I will wake Theo and your guards, although I have some serious doubts as to whether Malachi or his mate had anything to do with placing you in danger," Rachael said.

I didn't answer as she moved towards the door. I planned to go and wake Theo, and they were back within moments. Theo wasted no time in going downstairs to wake Alex and James. After they had satisfied their needs with the variety of vials provided them, they made themselves comfortable and waited.

Before we could start discussing anything, a rather irritated-looking David came to join me in front of the fire illusion. He didn't speak—he didn't have to. All of us knew he wasn't happy by the look on his face. As soon as Rachael tried to speak he interrupted her, saying that he wished to wait for the arrival of his sister and the Forest Dweller Malachi.

As we waited, the silence in the room grew uncomfortable. All of the vampires seemed to adopt their statuesque stances as they settled in to wait. They seemed a little tense, but nothing compared to the way I had suddenly begun to feel.

After a few moments Mia, Patrick, and Malachi arrived. Without any greetings Rachael explained to everyone what had happened to me when I had decided to go for a walk unaccompanied and unprotected. Of course, that earned me the expected disappointed looks from my friends and protectors. Before she had finished, David left my side and stood dangerously close to Malachi. I called to him at the same time Rachael and Mia reached his side.

Although Malachi stood his ground, I could see his shock at what Rachael had just said and I knew she was right: he had known nothing about the animals being freed on the land. He looked at David and calmly explained that all the animals under his care, those infused, had definitely been enclosed before he had left for the welcoming celebrations. When David challenged him he continued to stand his ground, and as I watched I realised that David still liked him and wanted to trust his word.

What followed was yet another conversation about who would want to harm me, until Alex spoke. I could have kissed him when he questioned whether the ducks actually wanted to harm me; perhaps they had another being in mind.

A discussion then followed as to who might want to endanger Malachi and his mate, Bryna. After all, he was a much favoured subject of the queen and his mate was carrying the first half-human, half–Forest Dweller child. The child also was a being who induced a lot of curiosity and condemnation among those who considered themselves purists.

Although Malachi thanked Rachael graciously, he refused her offer to move Bryna into the cottages with us, explaining that although she was comfortable around vampires, she was nearing the end of her pregnancy term and she appeared to want to stay near her own home. I didn't doubt his words, but neither did I miss the look that passed between him and Mia. I didn't say anything but simply thought I would ask Mia later when things settled back down again.

As they continued to discuss the petty jealousies of the queen's court, I sat back and closed my eyes. My first day was already coming to an end and I had not achieved anything other than to create another tense situation among my friends. Mia must have seen the look on my face because she interrupted the conversation to tell me to put on some warm, respectable clothes because she and Rachael were taking me shopping. Rachael didn't react; Mia's statement was probably as much of a surprise to her as it was to me. When David started to say something, both his sister and his friend warned him to stay quiet and told him that I would be perfectly safe with them.

Mia also looked intently at Malachi, as if she was asking an unspoken question for him only, and if I hadn't been watching him intently, I probably would have missed the nod he gave her. Things were definitely becoming more intriguing; I had a feeling that Mia had arranged for me to have another surprise.

Mia explained to David that before she returned me to him, we would all be paying a visit to Malachi's dwelling, as Bryna was almost ready to give birth and would probably be thankful of some female company. While we were out we would be getting some things that she would certainly need. I saw the look that passed between them. I knew that they both knew something that I didn't. The nod of agreement that David gave her was almost imperceptible; a few years ago I would not have noticed it, but I knew that he was allowing something, something that involved me.

I listened carefully as I went quickly upstairs but was disappointed when I heard their conversation revert to what had taken place earlier and who might have deliberately placed me in danger. As always when something unusual happened, I had been put in a precarious position and had been left unattended.

Chapter 31

I dressed quickly and surprisingly efficiently for me. Usually it took me a while to choose what to wear because Janet, Mia, Rachael, or any other vampire I knew were always getting things they thought would suit me, and many times new clothes appeared in my wardrobe that I had never seen before.

I was in a hurry to rejoin my friends, only because I thought I might miss something and I wanted to hear and perhaps have a say in the decisions I knew they would be making about my safety. More than anything I wanted my day with Mia; it felt as if it had been too long. I chose the silver-streaked top and matching boots that I knew went well with my old-looking jeans. The jumper was both warm and loose, and the boots were low-heeled and comfortable. I put my hair up into a high ponytail and applied a small but effective amount of makeup. I also took with me a large black and silver woollen wraparound scarf instead of a coat, choosing to travel light but with enough glamour to satisfy any royal princess watcher. Once I was satisfied with the reflection in the full-length mirror, I hurried back down the stairs.

I was more than a little disappointed when I finally re-entered the communal room to see that most of the group had already left and only Rachael, Mia, David, and Theo were sitting around the fire illusion speaking quietly. Although my hearing was good, I could not make out what they were speaking about, and the conversation seemed to falter, perhaps even change direction, as I walked towards them.

I felt a little better when I saw that Rachael had also changed from the casual outfit she had been wearing earlier. She was now dressed in a black trouser suit that was more suited for her role for the day. The suit was tight-fitting and complemented her perfect figure. The trousers were tucked into shiny black high-heeled boots, and she had accessorised the suit with an eye patch studded with black diamonds; her other eye twinkled wickedly when she saw me smiling at her. Her hair was also placed in a ponytail, but hers looked much slicker and more severe. She was wearing her customary deep crimson lipstick.

Mia was on the phone when I entered the room. I heard her arranging our transport for the evening and got the impression that even if I asked I would not be told about what had been discussed previously. I sat on the chair next to David and without even thinking placed my hand in his. As always his coolness made me shiver slightly, and then he folded his fingers over mine and gently pulled me over to him. I rested against his coolness, almost regretting having to leave him soon. We sat like that in a comfortable silence and the time seemed to slow right down; I could feel each individual second pass. After a short while a message on Mia's phone told her that our transport had arrived and was waiting for us outside.

I kissed David, suddenly loving him intensely again for protecting me, and gave him a passionate hug good-bye. Although he looked a little surprised, he hugged me back and laughed. I turned to Theo and he picked me up so I could lay my head on his shoulder. I knew that for all of those who protected me, it was harder for David and Theo to let me leave; they both thought of me as someone precious, a being whom they both cherished and loved, though each in a different way.

After a few seconds, Theo placed me back on the floor and I went to the door and followed Mia and Rachael outside to the waiting car. The car that had arrived to collect us was similar in look to the castle cars; the only differences were that it was dark green instead of black and there were no royal crests on its doors. The afternoon had remained reasonably warm, but looking out the car windows at the lake, I noticed that in the afternoon shadows looked a lot less picturesque. I scanned the trees that were nearby and the surface of the water for any signs of animal life as a cool, feather-light touch of fear traced its way down my spine. When I felt the curious gaze of the other two watching me, I quickly got into the backseat of the vehicle with Mia while Rachael decided to sit in the front next to the driver. The car moved slowly at first, but it soon made its way out of the private road and onto one of the much wider, more public roads. No one spoke at first, but once the cottages were out of sight, Mia started to relax a little and she reached for me.

"Liberty," she said as she hugged me the way she used to, "it is so good to see you away from the others. You seem to have gathered quite an entourage. You have no real idea how much I have missed you," she added softly, her whole face suddenly filled with warmth.

"It is good to see you too, Mia, and I have missed you very much too. But forgive me for not appearing quite as at peace as you. I don't understand what is happening here, why so much has changed between people I thought I knew in such a short time," I answered her quietly.

"Actually, I think you will probably understand better than most what is happening and what has happened to us all recently," she returned gently. "Please say that you understand."

As she spoke I realised that with the softening of her face she looked more like the Mia whom I had known back at the castle. "I will try—I promise—though I still have no idea what you are talking about, what has happened," I said honestly.

"I have feelings for Patrick that I had not known I was capable of. When he is near me I believe I still am capable of having a beating heart. I know that you have a place there, but it is just a shadow of the feelings that I have been experiencing for him."

"Was it Patrick who asked you to let go of the person you were then? Because you definitely look more like a vampire than I remember," I said, gently pulling away from her so that she could see eyes that would tell her that I still loved her as much as I always had.

"No, it was actually the queen. Although she loves all things natural, she prefers things to be the way they should be. Therefore, to her I should behave like a vampire simply because I am one, and the essence is, as always in all things, dominant," she said, smiling wryly as she heard her own words.

201

"Is that why Heather is so upset with you now?" I asked her, quietly looking out of the car window for a second, trying to hide the fact that I had already begun to guess what she was going to say.

"Yes, she quite rightly thinks that I am giving up my heritage, and she worries that she will have no one left of her family. She now recognises that she is the last of my mother's pure bloodline, and unless she finds a mate among the Forest Dwellers of these territories, she will stay the last. Poor Heather—my sister has suffered more losses than most since our mother disappeared, seemingly to save another child, and now she feels I am abandoning her for Patrick."

"Oh, Mia, of course I understand what you are saying, but don't you have feelings for your sister as well? Can't you also be the sister she wants when we all return to the castle? It will be better, won't it?" I said, feeling desperately sad for Heather and knowing too that David and I also expected a lot from her.

"Of course I have feelings for her, but they do not have the same strength as the feelings I have for Patrick. I just wanted you to know that I am still Mia and I will always love you, but I am Patrick's intended Life Partner now and he is the most important being in existence to me. That is why I am asking you to understand me now when I tell you that it is not I who is destined to follow you further on your journey to gather the Elements and change the future. I believe now, in my newly awakened heart, that it is Heather's place to go with you. I will not leave these territories—I will not leave Patrick."

"Mia, what are you saying? She is not the only one who needs you. I need you," I said, hearing the desperation and panic in my voice. This trip was not going to plan at all.

"David told me that I should wait until after the ceremony, but I told him that you would understand. Please tell me you understand—I need you to. I will always be here if you need me, and all of you are welcome. You will always remain my family," Mia said.

As I looked at her I knew that all decisions had already been discussed and made. I knew Mia well enough to know that she was in as much pain as I was beginning to feel, but I also knew that there was nothing else I could possibly say or do to change what was happening.

"Does Heather know how you feel about what is said in the scripts? Do you think she will be willing to join us?" I said quietly, trying to understand what Mia had just finished explaining to me.

"Heather knows everything. I have made her aware of every change from the very beginning." She looked out the window and then said, "I believe that we have reached our destination."

With that, the conversation appeared to be over; as soon as she said the word "destination" the car seemed to stop. When we had all emerged Mia held out her arm, but for a second I hesitated, until Rachael came to me and placed my hand in Mia's. The connection between us was still there; I felt it. I knew then that this might be the only opportunity for us to spend some time together, before the ceremony—and before everything changed.

We spent the next few hours shopping for all those imaginary things that girls think they need. The tension that had been there throughout the journey disappeared, and before long we were chatting and laughing as we all used to. As afternoon gave way to evening, we spent our time meandering in and out of shops that had been cleared of nonessential beings for our visit. In every shop that Mia entered there seemed to be numerous staff members, both human and nonhuman, waiting to obey her every instruction. Mia eventually explained in a sheepish voice that Queen Sinead had announced that nothing was to be refused to the betrothed of her favourite nephew.

It was an unusual experience for me. Although the shop members knew who I was, some of them appeared to disregard me because the fact that I was human was just too much for them to tolerate. But it was okay; I welcomed the extra bit of space. Mia laughed a lot at the more obvious ones, who were barely able to disguise their disgust and disrespect towards me.

I found the accent of the Irish Territories both fascinating and difficult to understand at times, but Mia seemed to be able to follow every word that was spoken and thus prevented me from making more than a few silly mistakes and errors of judgment. We went to one shop where Mia had said she had found her very own 'Janet.' The shop was small and the girl who owned it was human. Mia told me that, like Janet, the girl, whose name was Geraldine, had captured the eye of the Nedas of the area, a vampire called Max. Mia also informed me that it was Queen

Sinead's final decision as to whether Geraldine could be infused. Sadly, Max had fallen out of favour with the queen, and so far she had refused their request to become a pair.

Geraldine was tall, with curly shoulder-length auburn hair and piercing green eyes. She was shy and nervous with us at first, but when we started to discuss her latest design she came alive. Her clothes were fairly demure for the usual tastes of vampire women, but her colours were vibrant and exciting. She spoke so fast that I had to ask Mia on several occasions what she was saying. After Mia had shown me some more of her favourite clothes and jewellery items, we got down to the serious task of choosing my outfit for the Commitment Ceremony.

After quite a bit of disagreement (where Rachael had to intervene), we decided to dress me in a loose-fitting gown made from sheer silver and white material. It was a simple but beautiful design that was not one of Janet's; in fact, it was one of Geraldine's. Mia told me that Geraldine was developing a new line of clothes for some of the more favoured humans who were emerging on the planet.

She had previously been responsible for dressing the queen's 'children,' who had been at the airport and at the welcoming gathering. When I asked Mia about her choice of colour and design, she said with a small apologetic smile that I could not wear crimson or any other bold colour because I was a human.

We chose some simple hand and ankle jewellery, which was really slave jewellery with the chains removed. Again Mia felt the need to apologise for the choices she was making, but it was all right. I had heard enough to realise that she had no choice in the matter either.

Once we were all satisfied that we had done and seen enough, Mia called for our car. When it arrived we sat in the same places we had on the ride there: Mia sat with me in the back while Rachael sat in the front.

Chapter 32

Again we were alone and comfortable in the car. The shopping trip had been fun, and although I was beginning to feel tired, it was just what I had needed after the incident with the ducks. I had come to terms with the conversation that Mia and I had earlier and felt at peace with Mia's decision. After a few moments of contented silence, it was Mia who spoke first.

"Liberty, thank you. I had forgotten how good it was to shop with you, and of course you, Rachael. I am sure you must be at least a bit tired from all the excitement, but before we go back to David I am going to have the driver take us to the Forest Dweller Malachi's cottage. I hope that is all right because I have obviously heard what happened to you earlier today, and while it is true that Malachi is responsible for the estate on which you stay, I truly do not believe he is responsible in any way for what happened with the ducks out by the lake this morning. Do you agree?"

"Um . . . yes, of course. I don't really know him that well, but he seemed nice to me," I said, suddenly feeling much more awake and not nearly as contented.

"Good, because our visit there is important, and I know there is something there that you need to see," Mia said quietly.

I knew that look on her face and sat there in silence, waiting, wondering if Mia was already planning another big surprise.

"It is okay. It's nothing you need to worry about," she said, smiling and reaching for my hand.

"What is it, Mia? I don't understand. If truth be known, I am hungry and tired and feel like I have had enough surprises to last me this entire trip, let alone today. No more mystery, please. Just tell me what is going on. Don't be complicated. I can take in more because I know that none of what has happened could have been predicted. Let's face it, when I was little and you helped me with David, you would have laughed at me if I told you then you would leave me and give up what we thought was your role in the quest for a boy." My voice was beginning to tremble as I spoke, trying to smile away the emotions that were dangerously ready to erupt. I turned away from her to try to stop the hurt I was suddenly feeling but was unable to contain it anymore. Helpless to stop them, tears spilled from my eyes.

It was true. When I was younger Mia had promised that we would always be together, and now that felt like a lie. Again, everything seemed unsettled. A part of me that appeared determined to make me grow up seemed to be embroiled in a battle with the child that still dwelled within. My heart was hurting because my perfect little world was changing again, just when I felt that I belonged where I was and that everything was just as it should be.

I knew I needed to cry. I always felt better when I cried. Besides, I was sick of holding my emotions in check. I pulled away from Mia and sat as close to the window as I could. I let the tears run down my face, only stopping when I saw Rachael silently lean over with a tissue in her hand. I didn't even bother to look at her as I took it. I knew now why she had chosen the front seat of the car; she knew what Mia had intended to say to me. My tears stopped eventually and I did feel a little better.

When I sat back against the car seat, I saw that Mia had a takeout bag of food in her hand. I didn't know where it had come from, but something inside it smelled really nice and my stomach was growling with hunger. I knew she was waiting for me to make the first move. She had always tried to allow me time for my more human habits—her words not mine. As I reached for the bag I tried not to, but I touched her hand.

"What is at Malachi's?" I asked as I took the sandwich out of the bag and started to nibble at it.

"You will see," she said, smiling at me, no doubt glad that I had gotten control of myself. I noticed that for the first time since I had arrived in the Irish Territories, the smile had finally reached her eyes, as if we all knew that all I needed was a good cry. She had known deep down that I would eventually understand.

After I had eaten almost half the sandwich, I wasn't really as hungry as I had first thought. I put the rest of it back in the bag and moved myself closer to Mia. I placed my head on her shoulder and she squeezed me closer to her.

"Feel better?" she asked.

"Much," I said.

We didn't speak again until the car turned off the main road and down a small tree-lined lane, not too different from the lane that led to the cottages by the lake. There were no artificial lights, so the lane was beginning to darken as we drove down it. After a few moments of near darkness, I noticed a collection of lights and what looked like a cottage at the end of the lane.

The car stopped outside the cottage, but instead of all of us getting out, Mia and Rachael appeared to sit back as if they were waiting for me.

It was Bryna who came to the car. She opened the door nearest to where I was sitting and got in. "Hello, Liberty. Mia, have you told her why she has been brought here?" she asked, looking past me at Mia.

"No, we had other things to discuss," I heard Mia explain.

"Tell me what?" I asked.

"Liberty," Bryna said softly, "do you know the name Eileen Kavanagh?"

At first I did not know what to say. Of course I knew the name, but it was from a place in time that was a very long time ago, a time that I had almost forgotten. "That is the name of my mother's mother, or so I have been told in the past," I answered softly, barely taking a breath, my heart beginning to flutter at the sound of her name.

"There is a woman in my cottage who tells me that is her name. She is very old and very frail. I have known her all my life—she has always been part of our forest ever since I have known it," explained Bryna in her gentle voice.

I studied Bryna for a while. She was human and looked no older than I was, but she behaved older, calmer, and she was with child. I wondered if her time with the Forest Dwellers had helped to slow the normal human rate of aging. After a long period of silence I became aware that they all were looking at me.

"Do you think she may be my grandmother?" I asked, desperately wanting to believe that she was. My heart was thumping; I was about to meet someone who shared the same blood as me. This was my real bloodline.

I had been around vampires all my life, and I knew that no matter what your bloodline is, the beings who gave you life are the most important thing in your heritage. It is your bloodline that truly defines who you are.

"Honestly, I cannot answer that—it is not my place to say— but I think, looking at you, she nor you will not be disappointed," Bryna said, smiling. "Unfortunately, she does not appear to appreciate those who are other than human, so I will ask that you enter my house without your companions."

When I turned to look at Mia for confirmation, she added quietly that I would be perfectly safe, that I was in the company of other humans only, and she added with a look at Bryna that among humans I was perfectly capable of protecting myself. When she had finished speaking, she eased herself out of the car and held the door for me. I got out, shut the car door, and linked my arm with Bryna's. We went into the cottage together.

The cottage was beautiful and natural, full of handcrafted wooden furniture and brightly coloured floral cushions. Their communal room had a real fire at the end of it, which made the room warm and welcoming. Even though the room was filled with the fragrances of the fresh wildflowers that were arranged on almost every surface, I could also smell the powerfully beautiful fragrance of fresh baking. The whole mood and look of the cottage had a fairy-tale quality that made me feel very young and safe. I had read about cottages like the one I was standing in; before then they had only existed in books and dreams.

"Please sit and be welcome in our home," said Bryna as she took the wrap from my shoulders. "I will see if Eileen is awake and ready to see you."

"Thank you," I said, taking a seat near to the fire. I sat waiting, not knowing what to think, my mouth drying with nervousness, my heart beating a little harder every time I heard a voice murmur. I tried not to get my hopes up. I tried to talk some sense into myself, but as I sat there it didn't work. I wanted the woman who was calling herself Eileen Kavanagh to be the real one, the one who gave life to my mother. I was staring into space, lost in those thoughts, when Bryna gently placed a hand on my shoulder.

"She is awake and wants to see her visitor," she said, taking my hand to lead me to the room with the open door.

Chapter 33

I got up and walked slowly towards the door, my hand gripping Bryna's. Just outside the door, Bryna let go of me and nodded to me encouragingly. I had learned not to look back, so I didn't. I put my hand on the door, pushed it gently, and took a step forward into the room.

The room appeared to be just as warm and welcomingly peaceful as the rest of the cottage. I took a deep breath and stood still, waiting.

"Close the door, child. I get cold too easily these days," said a quiet voice that still had strength in its soft Irish accent. The voice was soft and welcoming. I did exactly as I was told and took another step into the room, shutting the door quietly behind me.

The room was painted in a plain pastel rose colour, which gave the illusion of both space and warmth, and was lit only by a large window on the far wall. There was an empty, freshly made bed at its centre. In front of the window was a large, comfortable chair that had its back facing me. The voice had come from the direction of the chair, so I continued to take small, quiet steps until I was at its side. I felt so young and small knowing that the person in the chair was probably the most important person I was ever going to meet. When I looked down I saw a small old lady sitting wrapped up in soft, warm blankets.

I walked around the chair slowly until I was standing directly in front of her. Although her eyes were shut, I knew that she was awake because she had already spoken to me. I stood gazing down at her and already felt an almost overwhelming love for her because she was exactly what I had imagined her to be. I could feel myself becoming emotional because I knew deep down with a certainty that she was my grandmother. I had seen my own mother age before her time, and the woman who sat in the chair in front of me looked just a little bit older than my mother, but so much like her, the way she had been when I had last seen her.

She had the same eyes as my mother and I had, and even though her hair was almost pure white, there was still evidence of the golden colour it had once been. I tried to probe her mind a little, but I couldn't yet. I could sense no danger from her, so I stayed where I was and waited for her to speak to me again. She appeared small in the oversized cushions of the chair, and although her face was a myriad of fine wrinkles, her face was strong and mischievous. There was a fire in her eyes that was recognisable in my own and I was sure had been in my mother's eyes as well.

"Come, sit down by me. It is easier for me to see you if I do not have to look up," the old woman said, indicating the floor with her thin, frail hand.

I did as she said, immediately captivated by this lady who held the key to my existence. Neither of us said a word as I seated myself in front of her, but we both looked intently at each other.

"What is your name, child?" she asked, smiling and making the room appear brighter.

"It is Liberty," I answered.

Smiling softly as if she could read my thoughts, she said, "Of course it is—it was always going to be that. You may call me Grandmother, for you are definitely from my blood, although you smell of them." I smiled as I noticed her nose wrinkle when she said the word "them."

"Please tell me, child. I would like to hear your story. I have long dreamed of this moment. I would like to know more of you and of what happened to my precious daughter. It is a long time since I have allowed myself to even think of her." When she spoke her eyes glistened as she stared off into the distance. There was a sadness about her that we seemed to share, a sadness caused by our common loss. My heart sank and I felt a lump in my throat.

I began. I spoke of everything that I could remember, even the parts that made us both cry. At some point during my story, she reached over and took my hands in hers. Her hands were soft and warm. There was no fire in them, nor coolness. They were just hands, like mine. The hardest part was telling her that my mother had been on her own with no one to comfort her when she had passed away. I did speak of Rachael and her kindness, but Grandmother did not seem interested. Despite the sadness she felt at the lonely loss of her daughter, she seemed to smile again when I spoke of the tribute that the Forest Dwellers near the Enclosure had created in her daughter's honour. I told her of all the things I had learned from the Forest Dwellers, but she did not want to hear much of the life that I had now. Although there was a hint of bitterness to her voice when she enquired of the life I led within the castle, she also acknowledged that the child of her bloodline was a princess among vampires.

I spoke for quite a while, trying to remember every little detail, but felt sadness that I could not tell her more of her daughter. After a moment's silence had passed between us, she gently reached down and patted my cheek.

"You remind me of her in a small way. You are not as natural as she was, but you have had other influences since you were very young," she said, deep in thought.

"Will you tell me of my mother, I asked. "What was she like as a little girl?"

She smiled warmly as she looked down at me, and I moved as close to her as possible, gently leaning myself against her frail legs. The closeness felt good; we both knew that we were connected by blood.

The night was beginning to darken as my grandmother started to talk in her soft, lilting voice, making my eyes close. At some point I must have fallen asleep because suddenly I was no longer in the cottage. I was transported into a world that was filled with long, soft grasses and trees and flowers, but it wasn't the grasses I had known; it was somewhere different. At first I thought I was standing in the forests that surrounded the castle. The forest was dark and full of vines. Surrounding the cottages and protected within those trees, a group of young children was playing outside, chasing and catching each other, their laughter piercing the silence of the forest and bringing with their joy their own sunshine. I stood still as I heard the name 'Elizabeth' being called. I knew that

212

it was my mother. A child who had been running no more than a few feet away from me stopped and turned in the direction of the nearest cottage. In the doorway stood my grandmother, her hands on the shoulders of a small, intensely serious-looking boy with rich auburn hair and chocolate brown eyes. I watched as my mother walked slowly forward, shyly inclining her head as she approached her mother and the boy. I overheard my grandmother introducing the boy as Nicholas, and I realised happily that my mother and father had met when they were children and that they had probably grown up together.

Then the seams of my dream appeared to blur and I found myself standing in a clearing surrounded by trees and lush vegetation, large patches of small flowers, lilacs and blues, vivid yellows scattered throughout the surrounding areas, insects humming and buzzing and dancing throughout the patches. I became distracted as I watched a young girl whom I recognised as my mother, walk into the forest with my grandmother. Both of them had long, flowing golden hair that shimmered in the sunlight. My grandmother's hair was tied back at the nape of her neck, while my mother had hers loose, with it gently caressing her shoulders.

My mother was wearing a simple flowing white dress, and my grandmother was wearing trousers and a tunic top that I had seen many of the Forest Dwellers wearing. My mother seemed to be a little upset, and as my grandmother spoke softly to her, she placed her hand protectively over her stomach. I tried to hear what they were saying, but the conversation stopped as the Forest Dweller Ana walked into the clearing with a handsome young man. The young man, whose eyes were a warm chocolate brown, looked to be engaged in an equally serious conversation with her.

I knew instantly that he was my father; the four of them seemed to be on a collision course. When they came together he hugged my mother gently, his hand covering the protective hand my mother had already gently placed on her stomach. The last thing I saw before my dream faded was my mother and father saying good-bye and being gently led away from the cottages by Ana and my grandmother in the quiet of the night.

I don't really know how long we stayed together, but Bryna eventually came in to say that it was time for my grandmother to get some rest. She added that Mia was becoming restless and needed to return me to her brother. Although both my grandmother and I protested a little, I knew that Bryna was right and I helped persuade my grandmother that we were both tired and needed to get some rest.

Once my grandmother allowed us to place her under the warm, soft covers of her bed, I gently kissed her good-bye and promised to come back and visit her as soon as it was possible. As I left her side and left the room, I felt as if I was floating. Everything seemed different because I felt different. I felt more grounded, as if suddenly I had roots again. As Bryna closed the door of her room behind me, I turned and hugged her gently, taking extra care to avoid pressing against her swollen stomach. As I did I felt something push back at me, and I stepped back in surprise.

"He is active tonight. Perhaps he is greeting you, Princess. You know that I know a little of where you have come from, and that out of the sadness and sacrifice of your mother and her mother before her has come a child who has long been awaited. I know that I have been waiting a very long time for this child of mine," said Bryna, rubbing her stomach and looking at me intently.

"Thank you," I said, not knowing exactly what she meant but giving her another hug. There was no need for us to say anything else, so we simply just smiled and nodded shyly. I let go of her and we walked together to the waiting car.

Malachi approached with some freshly killed birds and rabbits. He had a large wooden hunting bow slung over his shoulder. I wondered if his weapon was the queen's choice, but he certainly looked the part of a forest hunter.

It was almost unnerving, though not sinister, to see what the queen was creating. I felt as if I was on the outskirts of a real-life fairy tale. As he placed his arms tenderly around Bryna, Malachi apologised for not having been at home during my visit and asked if I would visit again. I assured him I would. I got into the car and we drove off.

None of us spoke on the journey back to the others. I was exhausted from such an emotional day and needed quiet time to try to process all that had happened.

Chapter 34

When I returned to David later in what was already becoming the early hours of the next morning, I was exhausted but unbelievably happy. I couldn't stop the tears as I tried to tell David all that had happened. I started with the fact that Mia was not coming back to the castle. I was curious as to whether he knew why Mia had insisted that I come shopping with her without him. Had he known of her intentions? He didn't answer, so I carried on speaking.

I knew even as I heard the words tumble from my mouth that most of what I was saying didn't sound like it made any sense. I was babbling, each sentence reflecting the muddled-up thoughts and emotions I felt.

But David didn't seem to mind. He was gentle and tried hard to follow my words and understand what I was feeling. He held me close, and at some point he even got up to find me something to wipe the tears from my face. As I began to tell him of my meeting with my grandmother, he held me tight and seemed to share my happiness.

As I spoke about my grandmother, I felt as if I had found a part of me that I wasn't aware had been missing. I had found someone who was mine; my mother and I came from her bloodline, and she had remained human just like me and my mother. It was incredible. I felt a natural inner power as I understood the significance of my own bloodline, the thoughts of which ran through my head like the blood through my veins. I realised that my own bloodline had created me and given me my core strength (not the beings who moulded me), and now I was possibly destined to be the only human ever to sit on a throne beside the ruling emperor.

I stopped speaking for a moment when I realised that during my first visit with my grandmother she had told me much, but I still knew nothing about her—where she had been since my mother had left her and how she had survived. I knew, though, that the information would come and that Grandmother Eileen would become an important part of my life.

While I had been babbling, I got the impression that David already knew in advance about some of things I was going to tell him, but at that moment I did not care. I needed to tell someone I loved and who loved me, and who cared how I felt.

After I had told him about my grandmother, David held me gently and promised solemnly that after the Commitment Ceremony and before we left the Irish Territories, he would speak with Malachi and Bryna and make sure that my grandmother would be well taken care of for the rest of her life. He would provide whatever they needed for her care. I asked him if we could take her back with us, and after a moment of thought he agreed, as long as it was what she wanted and providing Queen Sinead allowed her to be removed from the territories.

I watched him as he spoke, and he looked as if he were almost in pain, as if he knew what the answer would be before he asked it. He knew that coming to the Irish Territories was becoming an eye-opener for me, that the little bubble of life that he and my friends had created within the castle did not exist in the world beyond. What actually existed in this world beyond was a vampire world where the only thing that protected me was David's attachment. It seemed clear that I was David's biggest weakness and an easy way to manipulate him. Exhausted from my day, I fell asleep in his arms.

That night David did not place me on the bed. He only moved to get a fur blanket to wrap around the pair of us. When I woke up I seemed to be still in the same position, although I was a lot hotter and stickier, still dressed in my clothes from the night before. David and I stayed there together, waiting until the sun's heat had passed its peak. I knew that David had not rested—he did not need to—but he remained very still with his eyes concentrating on something far away in the distance. When his attention finally focussed on me, he smiled, and for the first time in a few days, we didn't hurry as we created our own world of passionate intimacy. After we had been sated, he rose and carried me to our bed, where we spent most of the afternoon lying together to enjoy our own gentle privacy.

For the next few days my life seemed almost normal, almost the same as if it all had been happening back at the castle. I was kept very busy shopping and visiting various places, my photo taken everywhere I went. Sometimes we posed and sometimes we were escorted quickly into buildings by the queen's guards before any photographs could be taken.

The time I spent with David alone was romantic, calm, and at times a lot of fun, although our time together seemed to pass quickly. On our days when nothing had been planned, we were content to watch the plasma device together and follow the progress of the preparations. I admit that there were times when I missed the royal apartments and the castle keepers like Sally and Miss Davina, who I knew would also be missing us. Since her daughter, Alyssa, had been killed, Miss Davina had practically adopted me and treated me as her own family.

I tried not to think of the castle very often for another reason. The more I was away, the more I missed Elathan. I knew that I shouldn't, but there were times when his gift to me tingled like a little alarm and I felt as if he wasn't prepared to let me forget him.

Even though Malachi had enlisted more trusted Forest Dwellers to patrol the surrounding land, I still could not venture outside the door of our cottage without another being accompanying me. Alex and James had been instructed to stay close to my side, I was told, for my own protection.

I spoke to Bryna on my mobile phone about my grandmother almost every evening, and all continued to be well with her. There were times when I asked if I could see her again. There were so many questions forming and building in my mind that sometimes I felt as if my head would burst with them. I understood that she was old and that she needed her rest, but I could not hide my disappointment every time Bryna gently told me I needed to have more patience.

217

As soon as the final preparations for the Commitment Ceremony started, Rachael became the one in charge of the arrangements. She said that it would be wrong for Mia to oversee the arrangements for her own ceremony, and although I was willing to help as much as possible, the preparations had escalated to a scale that I knew I would not be able to deal with. One of the first things she did was to move Theo and Cassius out of their cottage; although they did try to protest, we all knew that she would get her way. She moved them into the communal room in our cottage. I didn't mind, really. I had missed having Theo and Cassius around. I loved them both, and it was nice for David to share time with Cassius, even if most of their time was spent huddled in various corners discussing castle business.

Rachael's cottage had now become a dressing room, and we had all of our outfits hung in various rooms. The gowns were all beautiful, although there was a definite contrast in gowns: Mia's, Rachael's, and Janet's were all deep red with crimson undertones, and Heather's, Georgina's, and mine were all white with silver trim.

Heather seemed to be at home out in the forest with Malachi, although Cassius did sometimes venture out with her. She gathered beautiful ferns and flowers and wove them through our jewellery. Rachael, Janet, and Mia spent one of the days with their hair wrapped in towels infused with natural henna dyes to enhance their natural hair colours.

After a lot of effort, Mia managed to persuade the queen's assistant that it was an old but necessary tradition that the being about to commit should be allowed to stay with her friends for the last two nights before the ceremony. Our evenings were spent together as group, including Patrick when his cousin would allow it. We usually gathered in one of the little cottages sharing meals—Heather's, Georgina's, and mine were obviously a little more solid than theirs—and watching the buildup to the ceremony.

Every day new dignitaries and representatives from the other royal vampire families arrived. Queen Sinead was the perfect hostess, greeting each of her guests personally as they arrived. It appeared that she did not need the company of Mia and Patrick either; she looked as if she was enjoying every single moment of it.

As time went on, I realised that although I still liked the little queen very much, I found her ideas to be a little sinister at times. She seemed to want to control and manipulate all aspects of her territories and subjects, including nature. She was creating something that was not quite real; although I had not travelled much within the Irish Territories, I had not seen any evidence of her Enclosures. I knew that they must exist because in our world every territory had them.

During the day before the ceremony, I spent a lot of time with just Mia and Heather. Everything would change with the ceremony, I knew, and therefore I tried to bond with Heather and separate myself a little from Mia. The sisters themselves seemed to have reached some type of understanding between them, although Heather still reflected a lot of pain in her eyes when she looked at her sister. As a distraction Mia would often guide the conversation between the three of us towards the search for the missing Element and the scripts.

On one occasion, as we were speaking I realised that I had not been in contact with Sarah since I had left the castle, but for some reason when I thought of her and was about to ask Mia about any sacred place in the area, my bangle tingled and distracted me, making me forget to ask the question When I hesitated, Mia simply gave me a curious look.

During the evening before the ceremony, Malachi turned up at our cottage and asked if I would like to join him and Bryna for an evening meal. He explained that my grandmother had not stopped speaking about me when she was awake and had expressed a wish to see me again. Although I was advised against going, David knew that nothing short of restraining me would prevent me from going with him to visit her, so when Theo started to protest, David interceded on my behalf.

Theo settled on threatening Malachi with unspeakable pain if he did not return me in the condition he had found me. When we got outside the door, I was expecting to see a car but there wasn't any. Instead Malachi gently took my arm and indicated that I should follow him.

We walked together to the end of the cottages. Once we were clear of them, I saw the method of travel we were going to use: the big brown horse that had brought us to the cottages.

I was sure of it, although this time there was no carriage, just a large saddle on top of his huge, broad back. Malachi took off his cape and wrapped it around me, explaining that there was a strong aroma of vampire on me and he did not want to have to cover the horse's senses. He wanted me to experience what it was like to ride this beautiful creature since it was supposed to be ridden.

Once the cape was fastened, without another word Malachi lifted me onto the saddle, all the while speaking softly to the big horse under me. The horse seemed a little restless when he felt me, and Malachi had to speak to him quietly to calm him. As soon as the horse became still, without any further effort he pulled himself up and sat behind me. With a little encouragement the horse moved gently forward. When we were clear of the lake, the horse began to move a little faster, trotting down the narrow road.

Once we were clear of the estate, Malachi leaned forward and asked, "Do you mind if we give him a little run?" Not really sure what he meant but already enjoying the feeling of freedom, I turned my head slightly and smiled, indicating that I was enjoying the ride.

"Hold tight," he shouted as the horse suddenly leaped forward and began galloping. I had never been on a horse's back before, but I managed to find that my rhythm and movements echoed the movement of the horse. My smile widened and I couldn't help but laugh loudly.

"I suppose we will be taking the long way home, then," I heard Malachi shout as he started to laugh with me. "This is who you are. I have seen the marks you bear on your hand, and the silver streak you have behind your ear. I have heard of your heritage—I sense it in you. You were born to be free."

I didn't know what to say. His words, although they were probably right, meant nothing to me. I was not an enemy of the forest, but I did not consider myself a true friend. I knew it was partly because of the territory that the queen had created, and she had probably spoken of the child mentioned in the prophesy many times, but it was just another fairy tale to me. Just a few moments later we arrived at the cottage and Malachi helped me to dismount.

Bryna was there to greet me with a hot drink and some toast and jam. I was about to ask her why when she told me Mia had rung to tell her I was on my way. The food was laid out on a tray, which she carried into my grandmother's room and as we entered the old woman was already propped up in bed. My grandmother and I sat together eating toast with butter and jam, a meal that she told me was also her favourite.

I felt so settled with her. She seemed to know that there were things on my mind, but when I started to explain how I felt, she stopped me and told me to remember who I was inside—just Liberty.

When I asked her to tell me something of her life and of her parents, she promised she would, but I was a little disappointed when she told me it would have to wait until another time. She was tired that night. She told me that she had been waiting for me for a long time, and if the stories she had heard were true, then I was going to have a busy life. She also told me that she believed I was on the right path and that she was very proud of me.

All the questions that had been forming in my head to ask her suddenly did not seem that important anymore, and as she spoke I seemed to forget most of them. I felt so happy with her words that I found it hard to speak. What she said made me feel strong and proud, and I knew then that I would do absolutely anything for her to stay proud of me. I stayed with her until she seemed to finally drift off to sleep.

Malachi took me home again on the horse. This time he did not need to ask me; I couldn't wait to get on. I held on to the horse's mane and we flew across the countryside. Theo was at the door to collect me—and obviously to make sure I had been returned in exactly the same condition I had left in. I had to laugh at the seriousness that showed in his face as I walked in the communal room and turned and jumped. He caught me and I planted a big kiss on his cheek. My protector.

Chapter 35

None of us had any time to ourselves the next day because it was finally the day of the long awaited ceremony. As always, it seemed that as soon as she sensed that I was awake, Mia came and got me. I barely had a chance to say good morning to David, who had suddenly decided to become a little irritated with my lack of time with him, but after a few stern words from his sister, he surrendered me into her care.

Just before I left, I hugged him and whispered quickly that I would be with him later, and then Mia and I left the chalet, leaving all of the males to their own devices, and we joined the other females in Rachael's cottage.

It appeared that Mia and Rachael had been a little busier than I thought. The upstairs room had now become a room of mirrors—every wall had been lined with them and the bathroom had become like a mini salon, providing various hairstyles and different makeup needs.

Although the cottage already seemed smaller, when the females attending the ceremony had arrived and were all vying for space, the atmosphere became almost claustrophobic for most of the morning and early afternoon.

Among us there was also an army of human women from the nearest Enclosure, who were under the constant supervision of the local Ophir and Adwar. They patiently catered to all our needs and did our hair and makeup until, I thought, we all looked stunning.

Sometimes it was difficult to be attended to by human beings. I was not used to being cared for by my own kind, and although they showed nothing in their eyes except kindness, I didn't feel very kind; I knew what their existence was like. I wondered, at times during that morning, how I made them feel and whether it was pride or jealousy in their minds and hearts. Throughout the day they brought food and vial, but only small amounts because Mia told us we should remain hungry for the feast, which would be happening almost immediately after the ceremony.

I remained slightly jealous of the way that vampires dressed. Janet and Rachael were both dressed in black figure-hugging floor length-gowns that covered them well but really left nothing to the imagination. Mia, on the other hand, was dressed in head-to-toe crimson.

Her design was looser, almost the same design as my dress. Once I was standing with Heather and Georgina and we were all dressed in our plain, flowing white gowns, I thought we looked beautiful, but more demur and definitely inferior. I didn't say anything or complain because this was Mia's day—she was the princess.

All of us wore jewellery. Janet, Rachael, and Mia chose to wear traditional and dramatic jewellery made from chains of small black diamonds draped around their necks and waists with earrings to match. I was constantly worried that one of them would notice the mesh bracelet that Elathan had given me, especially when one of the female human helpers put on my hand jewellery. But even I was surprised when the jewellery appeared to link itself to the bracelet, and as I watched I thought I saw the two pieces blend. They blended so well that it appeared as if they were one piece, and the thought did cross my mind that it was strange (but believable) that something that was inspired by slavery should recognise something that had originally belonged to Elathan. Deep down I knew that he must have, at times, had to live up to his dark name.

I missed him but knew I shouldn't see him again, not after the last time. I thought that it had been enough but knew deep down that I would see him again as soon as I could slip away after I had returned to the castle. I couldn't deny that there was a growing part of me that needed to see him again, even for a short time.

My feelings for him when they broke free from restraint were too strong to ignore.

I managed to stop myself from thinking of him any further and re-immersed myself in the growing excitement in the cottage. Something got my attention straight away: I realised that Mia's voice sounded angry. When I looked up I saw that apparently the human who was trying to do her hair was not listening. I recognised the danger because I had heard similar tones from her before. Even Heather was trying to placate her but was having little effect. It seemed that the more the poor human woman tried to do as Mia demanded, the angrier Mia became with her.

Mia, calm yourself. Sarah is with us. Can't you feel her? I sent the thought to her gently, knowing that if I tried to go over where they were it would add to the confusion. Although it was a gentle thought, it seemed to take Mia by surprise. She looked up and saw my reflection in the mirror in front of her. The thought seemed to have worked, and she took a few deep breaths and apologised to the poor girl who was attending to her.

She has come even though I will not be going with you and will no longer be part of her prophesy, she said, her thoughts mirroring the softness of mine.

She has come to give you her blessing. You will always be part of us, I thought smiling.

I had not communicated with Sarah for what appeared to be a long time, but as I grew I realised that if I needed her she was there and continued to stay with me in my heart and mind to guide me in her own gentle way, whether I wanted her to or not. I found the thoughts of her comforting.

She had also grown in her understanding of me and had learned that there were times when I needed to be free of her. She could not seem to reach me or guide me with any strength, especially when I was anywhere near to Elathan, but she had stopped questioning me about my 'disappearances.' Perhaps she also realised that I had my own strength within me.

I walked over to Mia and gently took the brush from the woman who was attending to her. I smiled and directed her out of harm's way, and then started to brush Mia's hair. It was as thickly beautiful as I remembered it. As I brushed it, Mia closed her eyes and I knew that Sarah was reaching out to her. She looked more at peace than she had for a while—at least since I had arrived at the Irish Territories.

It only took a few moments for Mia to return to what she had been concentrating on, and suddenly I was the one feeling under pressure as I tried to give her the hairstyle that she wanted. I wasn't too good at making it look elegant as I piled it on top of her head, but with Rachael's and Heather's help, we managed to make sure her hair look quite respectable; at least Mia seemed satisfied.

Just before the onset of evening a large royal car pulled up outside the cottage, and with a lot of manoeuvring we all eventually managed to arrange ourselves comfortably. There were more vehicles for the males of our group, which followed directly behind our car. Our procession was joined by various Forest Dwellers, some of them travelling in cars but many others travelling in horse-drawn carriages. All were dressed traditionally—I did not see a suit among them.

We were driven slowly towards the border of the nearest Inner District, and as we reached the outskirts, an escort of vampire guards joined us and surrounded us in a secure cocoon. Even though I was excited, the escort who greeted us was so solemn that I suppressed any urge to smile. The guards were all dressed in black but had emerald green and crimson sashes over their left shoulders.

At first they ran alongside our cars, but eventually they slowed down, as did our cars and carriages, as we all began to join the procession. The roof of our car slid backwards and disappeared into a compartment that was behind us. It was a warm, dry night and the cool air added to our excitement. The stars were bright and beautiful, and the sky was free of clouds.

Mia suddenly gripped my hand hard enough to stop me from daydreaming. When I looked at her face I had to giggle; it was the first time I had seen her look so frightened. I leaned over and gently kissed her on her cheek. "You will be fine. Patrick holds your heart. Remember, you are binding yourself to the one person you love above all others," I whispered softly in her ear.

From behind us Heather leaned forward and placed her hand on her sister's shoulder, giving it an affectionate squeeze, and I sat back to give them a moment while I still held Mia's hand.

Mia rested her head against her sister's hand and we stayed like that, knowing that no matter what happened, the bond we had always shared would forever remain intact; it was just that Mia had rearranged her priorities, and the love she held for Patrick was so obvious that we, even Heather, understood now why she was doing what she was about to do.

The roads we were driven down were lined with humans, both young and old. They all seemed very excited to be there. Scattered among them were vampires. I knew that some of the vampires I saw were there to watch over the humans, and some of them seemed to be there to see and support us. All of them were smiling and caught up in the celebrations. There were lots of pictures of Mia and Patrick hung up on huge banners strung between various buildings.

Among them I saw some pictures of me, some with David, but quite a few were of me on my own. It was good to think that by placing my banner among the others, Queen Sinead was, in her own way, paying me tribute as a member of royalty.

Eventually the procession stopped and the car door was opened. David came to my side and immediately offered me his arm. We stood at the bottom of some large, sweeping stone steps in front of the largest cathedral-type building I had ever seen. At each of its four corners were flags and banners representing all of the twelve royal families. The building had a huge but elegant dark stone archway for an entrance, and down the centre of it was a wide path of thick green velvet strewn with leaves, which were all representative of the colours of the forest in autumn.

David placed his hand gently over mine and we began to walk slowly forward, smiling and waving as we were expected to do at the silent crowds of vampires who stood watching our arrival. As we walked up the steps I spotted Nick and Lisa at the top. They had been placed discreetly at the side of the large central arch, but they had a clear view of the arrivals. Nick was clicking away with his camera, apparently unrestricted, and Lisa was speaking continuously into a little tape recorder. I was aware that this must be another 'gift' from Queen Sinead. I knew how very private some of the other royal families were and that they would not usually allow their photographs to be taken, but I also knew how persuasive the little queen could be.

At the enormous, ornately carved wooden doors that were already propped wide open, we were greeted by a fanfare of trumpets and I nearly lost my composure, almost laughing out loud at the sight of them and the brightly dressed beings that were blowing them. Queen Sinead had obviously done some research and had designed the whole scene, which I knew was not something that Mia would have particularly chosen; it was just a little too obvious.

As we walked forward to take our places at the front of the cathedral, small groups of children danced among us in fairy costumes, scattering tiny gold and silver petals. Even though they looked simply adorable, I barely managed to suppress a shudder. They appeared to me now as something very wrong, unnatural, and unreal. One of them, a little boy, had obviously just fed; he had a small bloodstain on his tunic.

As we continued forward I began to look around at the interior of the cathedral. Since my discovery that the castle was older than three thousand years, I had become fascinated with old buildings. I knew as I looked around that this cathedral was old, perhaps not as old as the castle but clearly a building of history, another building with a story to tell. Again I could feel myself maturing, growing, and becoming stronger as I walked up the aisle on David's arm. I felt as if I was drawing strength from the surroundings, as if the planet was nurturing me itself.

Inside the vast cathedral there were long pillars that reached from the floor to the ceiling far above us. Each of the pillars was made of polished stone and had the faces of formidable-looking vampires and other beings carved into them. The attention to detail was breathtaking.

Even from a distance I could tell that not all of the faces that were carved into the pillars belonged to vampires. There were many faces as well of Forest Dwellers, and as I studied the carvings I realised I was watching the development of a species. In the darker recesses farther back, the carvings were almost gargoyle like; it could have been because the craftsmen were not as skilled as those who did the later faces, but I didn't believe that then and I still don't. I recognised one face as that of Marcarius. His was the face nearest to the sacred altar, as if he had been added when he became ruler. I also saw the likeness of Elathan, or a being that looked strikingly similar to him, which didn't surprise me since I knew that there were areas within the Irish Territories which still accepted some of the teachings of the ancient Celtic races.

The cathedral was softly lit with hanging baskets, which were hung from the ceiling at regular intervals and filled with glowing orbs. The baskets swung gently in the night's breeze, casting long shadows throughout the interior.

As we walked at a slow, measured pace up the centre aisle, I felt a peace and knew it would be a place of strength for me should I ever need it within the Irish Territories. The pull of the cathedral was strong, and I had to resist the urge to leave David's side and touch the walls.

Directly in front of us was a selection of various-sized thrones, some of which were very ornate and decorated with gold leaf and large jewels, others smaller and simpler. The thrones were set on a podium behind the vampire minister who was going to perform the ceremony. The thrones reserved for David and me were placed at the centre of the podium and were some of the more ornate ones. I couldn't help but notice that my throne was set a little way behind David's and not beside his throne as I would have wished. Not all of our other friends were royalty, although at Mia and Patrick's request they were to be treated as VIBs (very important beings), and they were seated in front of us facing us farther back.

Mia's ceremony was totally different from mine. She entered the church in silence with Patrick escorting his chosen mate to the altar to receive the minister's blessing and his approval of her commitment. I admit that I did not understand many of the words that were spoken during certain points of the ceremony, even though the words brought smiles to the faces of the vampires who surrounded me and a tender glance from David.

The ceremony took a little over two hours and then another fanfare sounded. Before we left, Mia and Patrick both removed their fang caps and shared the blood of a willing donor human. There were those among the ancient royal dignitaries who surrounded me that seemed to come awake at the appearance of the human donor, so David quickly but discreetly reached for my hand—whether to protect me or comfort me, I didn't really know.

Although it was something that should have made me turn away, it didn't appear to bother the human. The donor, a woman, looked beautiful and at peace; she extended her arms willingly. She continued to smile throughout the blood donation and appeared honoured to have been chosen. The ceremony, in its own ancient way, was tender and beautiful, and it was not difficult to understand that the ceremony had been about love.

Mia and Patrick looked so perfect together, and true to myself, I felt the rise of my own love, tears, and emotions as I watched them walk hand in hand out of the cathedral. Once they had left the cathedral, those beings that were seated on the podium were allowed to leave first. By the time the ceremony was over, it was already at its darkest outside, nearing the midnight hour.

David and I were directed to one of the royal vehicles, which, as expected, was big and comfortable, and were driven slowly in a procession that followed the horse-drawn carriage that contained Mia and Patrick.

The commitment celebrations were held at the queen's castle, which was situated nearby. The castle was as big and as foreboding as the cathedral, though it did not hold the same power within as did my castle or the cathedral. I didn't find it as entrancing as either of them.

We were led to our places in a large ancient banqueting hall decorated in the same style as the cathedral. We all took our places and waited quietly for the newly committed couple to make an entrance. When Patrick and Mia entered, we all rose to our feet and bowed silently to them from the waist as a mark of our love and respect. They both looked stunning, their faces flushed from their recent feed. I understood that the pull of his love was far stronger now than the pull of the love she had for me, or for anyone.

Once we were all seated, the giving of gifts began. Patrick and Mia were sent gifts from all of the royal vampire families as well as personal gifts from all of us. David and I gave them matching pendants encrusted with black diamonds—each had a picture of the four of us within their tiny compartments.

We had a formal banquet with various foods and vials. David and I were seated at the queen's table, and I was both relieved and happy to see Malachi and Bryna were also seated at the same table. Lorchen was also there, but he seemed to be concentrating on the queen's every word, far too hard to notice me; in fact, I would have said that he was trying very hard not to see me. I knew he didn't like me and that he felt threatened by me because I was a human whom he could not control. He was probably used to controlling others, though; he would not have progressed in the queen's court if he was not powerful.

But thankfully the barriers that I had put in place to protect my mind from any invasion from a vampire or any other being were so strong that I no longer even registered any of the attempts that were still being made by some of the more curious vampires who wished to manipulate me. It also worked in my favour that Lorchen was definitely conceited and a lot weaker than he gave himself credit for.

The night was magical and Mia was beautiful. I had a wonderful time surrounded by all that I loved and sumptuous food. I even laughed at some of the more overtly obvious passes made at David by some of the more liberated vampire females in attendance, marvelling at their blatant sensuous natures. I ate a little bit but drank a lot of a wonderful fruit juice that David told me had been especially made by the local Forest Dwellers. He explained that at the end of summer it was a tradition among the Forest Dwellers to collect any of the berries that were left on the bushes within the forest. The berries were then pressed and sieved, and the juices were blended. I didn't understand why he was smiling when he told me, but it didn't matter because I liked it so much that whenever my glass became empty, it was refilled almost instantly.

The celebrations were wonderful. Everything seemed bright, and every being there seemed to enjoy all that the evening had to offer. I even managed to speak to some of the more miserable-looking royals, although I can't recall their appearing too happy to see me.

Chapter 36

I woke up alone in my bed late the next afternoon. I could not remember arriving back at the cottage, and although I knew I had slept, I still felt a little tired with a strangely heavy head.

I could hear voices speaking softly somewhere downstairs, so I got out of bed slowly, taking the time to steady myself before I could stand up. I put on some casual clothes that had been left conveniently near and made my way carefully downstairs to join whoever was down there. Most of the others were there, and all of them smiled when they saw me. David was at my side in a second, placing his arm around me and leading me towards the seat he had been sitting on.

"How are you feeling?" he asked quietly, gently.

"Okay, a little tired and very thirsty," I said as I put my arm round him. We then walked over to his place in front of the fire illusion and sat down together.

"What happened last night? Did I fall asleep or something, and how did we get back here? It is strange, but I can't seem to remember anything much after we arrived at the celebrations," I said, cuddling up to David.

"You don't remember?" Rachael asked, with one of her perfectly shaped eyebrows arched in apparent amusement.

"No, I remember having something to eat and I was drinking that juice made by the Forest Dwellers, and that really pretty vampire saying hello to David. She was so funny and you just ignored her, David. Other than that, I can't seem to remember anything else. I must have fallen asleep. Is that what happened?"

231

I asked, looking at David for reassurance, suddenly feeling a little unsure of myself as if something else, possibly something very bad, had happened.

"Yes, it is, Liberty. We forgot that the Forest Dwellers' juice can be a little intoxicating to those who have not had it before, and we didn't realise how much you had been sipping until you started to giggle and laugh—a lot," said Rachael, smiling even wider.

"It appears you were very taken with some of the more ancient vampires who seemed determined not to smile, and inevitably it appears that some of them became quite taken with you," laughed Cassius.

"Oh no, really? Please don't tell me any more," I said as I buried my face in David's cool shoulder.

"Don't worry. As soon as David recognised the signs, he picked you up and made the excuse that you were tired and brought you back here," said Alex, who was also laughing from across the room.

"David, I am so sorry. Thank you for rescuing me before I did something silly. I can't believe I did that. I could have made fools of us all. I am so embarrassed!" I said as I buried my head farther into his shoulder.

"Don't be," David said, softly nuzzling my hair. "It gave me an excuse for getting away from the queen's cousin Helena, who was becoming quite persistent with her advances.

"Is she a real cousin like Patrick?" I asked, remembering the beautiful vampire trying very hard to get David's attention.

"No, she is more like Vivien is a 'cousin' to me," he said, laughing.

"Honestly, Liberty, it was David who needed help. You really did rescue him," Theo said, laughing. "I haven't seen him look so uncomfortable for a long, long time, actually since he first arrived at your rooms for that first disastrous date with you the day after your sixteenth birthday." With Theo's comment everyone laughed. I looked at David, finding the fact that he had been as embarrassed as I was very endearing.

"Did Mia say anything? Was she angry with me for having to leave early? She seemed to be really enjoying herself, from what I can remember anyway."

"Actually, Mia did not have the luxury of spending time socialising among us. Queen Sinead seemed determined to keep her busy, introducing her to some of her newly acquired friends," said Rachael. I didn't miss the looks that passed between my friends, and I knew that all of us were going to miss her when we left in the next few days.

If it weren't for that serious moment, we might have missed Heather's knock. Alex and James were by the door before the handle had turned fully. "May I come in? I am not interrupting, am I?" she said, stepping through the door and removing her wet cloak.

"No, we were just informing Liberty why David had to bring her back here early," said Rachael, still smiling.

"Oh, our juice can be a little strong sometimes. Don't worry, Liberty, there was nothing else to remember. I myself left shortly after you," Heather she said, blushing slightly as she exchanged a private look with Cassius.

"But that is not what I came here to tell you. There are some very special Forest Dwellers who are being allowed to pay us a visit. They asked if they could meet Liberty in person. I am aware she will need protecting," she added, raising her hands to placate the others before anything could be said.

"Okay, who are they?" I said, getting up from the chair straight away. I was becoming used to and beginning to enjoy meeting others outside of my protective circle of vampires.

"It is the headman, Riley, and his mate, Brigid. They are bringing their son, Prince Fletcher, with them. It is Prince Fletcher who really wants to meet you—in fact, he has become quite difficult over the matter," she said, smiling, her face infused with an odd expression of indulgence.

"Of course I would love to meet him," I said, curious at her obvious adoration.

"I think that I have overheard you and Mia speak about him before. Can I just get changed into something a little less casual? After all, he is a kind of prince, and Queen Sinead would never forgive me if I greeted him dressed as I am," I said as I moved towards the stairs again. I felt a little unsteady still but better than I had earlier.

I managed to make myself look respectable, taking the minimum amount of time possible, choosing to wear black jeans, knee-high boots, and a black high-necked jumper, plain but effective.

As I came down the stairs, I heard David telling the others that they could have the day off and that we would be going with Heather by ourselves. The only one who disagreed with him was Cassius, who insisted on accompanying us. After a moment's silence David agreed that he could come. I smiled; it was good to hear him say that. As soon as I joined them we put on our coats and left. The day outside was warm, yet a fine misty ran continued to wet us through.

There was no transport. Heather explained that the Forest Dwellers would meet us in a secret location within the forest. She said that young Prince Fletcher did not behave very well outside of the forest environment. I could not help glance at the lake as we walked. David saw me looking and put his arm protectively around me.

When we got to the trees, Heather spoke softly in a language I did not understand. David looked startled by the sound of the leaves moving as the vines of the forest crept towards us.

"Liberty, it is up to you how you travel. David and Cassius will remain on the ground on foot, but I know that you carry the mark of the forest and that you are capable and will be welcomed by the vines here," Heather said as she reached out her hand and a tentative vine crept forward to greet her. I sensed its suspicion when it registered the others with her, and I knew it did not know me. I had to be careful, but I also knew that it would recognise the mark.

"David, would you mind if I travelled with Heather using the vines? I want them to know me," I said as I let go of him and took a step towards Heather.

"As you wish, but promise me you will be careful," he said as he prepared to run alongside Cassius below us.

I stepped up to Heather's side and put my outstretched arm, palm upwards, towards the vine. It seemed to take forever for the vine to come close enough for me to touch it, but eventually it did. As I gently ran my hand over it, I had to smile. I remembered that its mentality was very simple and almost childlike, and continued to stroke it gently, almost tickling it, until I felt it shudder with pleasure.

As I was getting to know the vine, Heather interrupted my thoughts by nudging me and explaining quietly with a wry smile that David and Cassius would be there to greet them before we would. As we laughed together, I allowed the vine to curl itself around me and lift me high into the treetops.

The journey went incredibly fast, and we overtook David and Cassius easily. I thought David was unhappy with my choice, but as we passed him in short order Heather and I were laughing, and I also saw the huge smile on his face. I had a feeling that he and Cassius were enjoying their run and the freedom of it as much as Heather and I were enjoying the gentle journey being cradled by the vines. A few moments later we were placed gently down at the edge of the clearing, and I could hear the sound of a small child laughing.

Heather and I straightened our hair and clothes and waited for David and Cassius to join us once again. After they had caught up with us and David had removed the few stray leaves that I still had stuck in my hair, we moved forward together, happy; there was something about the child's laughter which made us all smile. It simply had that effect.

In front of us was a young couple, both of them easily recognisable as Forest Dwellers, each with deeply warm red chestnut-coloured hair and strikingly pale jade green eyes.

When we were close to them, I noticed a small child hidden behind the legs of his father. It had been at least four of my years since I had met Heather; I remembered the first time very clearly. She had come to the castle to inform Mia of the birth. The child was still very small, but I also knew from the books in the research library that the Dwellers aged at a much slower rate than we humans did. They valued the development of their infant years above all others, and the infant years to the Forest Dwellers, and indeed all of the Earth Carers, were considered the purest.

As we all exchanged greetings, I saw a flash of the brightest, reddest hair I had ever seen. It shone like fire, even within the darkened forest, its bright shine could not be dulled. I lost all thoughts of the adults in front of me, their conversation and greetings growing quiet and fading. For some reason I felt drawn to the small child, who apparently wanted to play hide-and-seek with me behind his father's legs. Without thinking I dropped to my knees. The little prince seemed to grip his father's legs a little tighter and his father immediately took a small step back, keeping his son out of my reach.

"He can be a little shy," I heard Brigid, his mother, say softly. "Although he seems to like you, usually he is up in his father's arms when he meets someone he does not know. We like to think it is because he has understood your coming."

"I am sorry. I didn't mean to startle him. He is beautiful," I said. Even though I had not seen his face fully, I knew he would be beautiful but was surprised that I already thought of him that way.

"He takes after his father, then," said Riley in a heavy Irish accent that I could barely understand. I didn't respond, as I was again distracted by the little boy, who appeared to be getting ready to have another peek at me from behind his father's legs. I could barely breathe as the conversation carried on above my head. I sat and watched the child in front of me take a few tentative steps around his father's legs so that we could get a better look at each other. I fell in love instantly, and strangely I thought the feeling was mutual because the child no longer gripped his father's legs; he simply left his hand there, maintaining a safe connection.

In front of me stood a child who had a halo of burnished sun-filled fire for hair and the most beautiful dark emerald huge orbs for eyes that appeared to sparkle with life and all that was good. I smiled, thoroughly besotted with him, and waited patiently while he studied me. It was worth it because when the little one eventually smiled, he had deep-set dimples in either side of his face. His smile made my heart skip a beat. I couldn't move; I was totally enthralled with him. All I could do was stay kneeling, with the damp of the forest floor beginning to seep through my jeans.

I held out my hands to him, both of them extended with my palms up, and continued to smile. I was tempted to reach out and sense what was in his head, but I did not want to startle him or frighten him in any way. I wasn't expecting him to take my hand, and I don't think any of the others were either, but he did. The little prince took a small step away from his father and gently laid his hand in mine. I didn't feel anything except love. It was as if the child was still untainted by the world—a clean slate that was as beautiful as it was pure.

I wasn't the only one who seemed to be holding my breath anymore. At the moment he placed his hand in mine, I became aware that all conversation had suddenly stopped. I didn't move a single muscle as the child in front of me left the safety of his father's legs and took a wobbly step forward and sat down, making himself comfortable on my legs.

When I looked into his beautiful eyes, I saw nothing but an ancient love reserved just for me in that moment of time. I felt as if I had finally found a kindred spirit. My mind questioned whether I had been that pure when I was born. I wondered what he sensed from me, especially after all that had happened to me. Whatever it was, he seemed to still like me, to feel safe with me. Just looking at him made me happy; I would have done anything for that child sitting on my legs and smiling up at me with his curly hair and bright eyes.

I didn't know what to do other than place my arms around him gently and cradle him against me as I got up off the damp forest floor. Once upright, the little prince seemed content to be held by me, laughing at his smiling and obviously very proud parents. He gently tugged at a piece of my hair and played with the golden strand as I held him close.

We stayed together for a while, and in those moments when I held him, it was difficult for me to even think about giving him back to his mother, although I knew that I would have to. Thankfully, his parents seemed to completely understand my reluctance.

He examined and kissed the small silver mark on my hand and pointed, laughing, at the vines that seemed to be moving slowly closer to us. I walked over to a large collection of restless vines and watched as the prince patted and played with them. I sensed only love and adoration for him within the vines. It seemed that the forest was equally proud and as totally in love with him as everyone else was. It made perfect sense because he was perfect.

We stayed among the vines, with them ever circling us until there was a point where we were hidden from view from his parents. That was okay, though, because the little prince did not panic, and after a little encouragement I lay back on a cushion of vines with him cradled against my chest.

The vines began cradling us gently, swinging backward and forward as we relaxed against them, watching small shafts of light glisten on their sap. We stayed like that for a little while until the vines were parted by adult hands and our peaceful solitude was over. Eventually I had to pass him back to his parents. I felt a little lost without him at first, as if I had given away the sunshine.

As I was leaving, Riley told me he would be seeing me later at the 'meeting.' I wasn't really sure what he was talking about, and when we had left the clearing behind I asked Heather. She told me that she would tell me when we were all together.

Chapter 37

We didn't speak at all on the way back. We all travelled the way we had earlier, with David running effortlessly beneath me. I admit that I loved it, although I wasn't too sure if it was the temporary feeling of total freedom or whether it was because I was still so happy after meeting the gorgeous, precious child and had fallen totally under his spell. I felt free of worry, and for the first time in probably forever I felt as if everything that had happened and was going to happen was meant to happen, that in the end (whenever that was going to be) everything would be fine and I would be fine.

When we arrived back at the cottages, I saw two horses tethered to the trees beyond Rachael's cottage. My smile suddenly got bigger. This day was going from strength to strength. Even though the horses were hooded and were quite a distance away, they appeared to be a little restless at our approach.

"David, I think they can still sense you, so we need to go inside. Malachi is here and seems to have brought someone else with him," I said as I reached his side and gently released my vine, tickling it gently as a thank you. After we had all stopped, Heather moved away and made her apologies known, saying she had other business to attend to. As I watched her leave, I felt a little sad for her. I knew that the time was drawing nearer when she would have to say good-bye to her sister.

We could see the light from the fire illusion in our cottage glowing brightly, and for the first time that day I realised that the weather had definitely turned cooler, even though the sky was still cloud-free and bright. When we went inside the cottage, I saw Thomas sitting quietly and unsmiling with Malachi. As soon as he saw us, he was on his feet and came and stood in front of me, putting his arms out to hug me. The two of us stood silently, giving each other comfort, and it was Thomas who pulled gently away first.

"You seem to have become a little bigger, Thomas, since I last saw you. There seems to be even more of you," I said. It was true; he had grown in some way, even though I knew that he had been mature when I met him.

"I think it is just the padding of responsibility and a few good meals," he said, laughing and patting his stomach. I smiled with him, looking at him intently, perhaps waiting for him to share a little of the secret that seemed to have made his eyes brighter than I had last remembered them.

"It is really good to see you, and also you, Malachi," I said, smiling over Thomas's shoulder at Malachi, who looked a little tense and uncomfortable and could only nod back at me with a half smile. It was then that I had noticed how quiet the room had become.

"Oh, by all those who are holy and are looking down over us, what has happened now?" I asked, already irritated by the atmosphere, my glorious mood quickly fading.

"Nothing has happened, Princess," said Alex as he moved from the chair in front of the fire illusion. With his words I sensed that he was hiding something from me.

"Nothing? Then why do you call me Princess? Surely it's not something to do with me since, as far as I am aware, I have done nothing wrong recently," I said, facing him.

"The Forest Dwellers came with a request regarding you, and it was refused on the grounds of security," said James, who now stood beside Alex in a show of unity.

"What . . . what did they ask?" I responded, sighing, well aware that I was going to have to listen to their tired, lengthy explanations for preventing me from doing something that I would probably have enjoyed doing. I turned away from them without waiting for their answer, and instead I faced Thomas again.

"Why don't you ask me now that I am here and I will answer for myself? I will say this again, slowly for all of you to understand. I used to be a possession of David's, but now I am his Everlasting Life Partner. Have all of you forgotten that means, at the very least, that I can make some decisions for myself, doesn't it?" I tried to sound confident, keeping my voice low and steady. I always allowed myself to be guided, and the decisions were usually made for me, but since arriving in the Irish Territories I had begun to understand that I needed to start trying to make myself heard. I felt David move to stand behind me, knowing that he knew he needed to support me as his partner.

"As you wish, Princess," James and Alex said in unison as they seemed to move back into their earlier, more discreet positions. I had to suppress a shudder when they did their 'together as one thing' move.

"Thank you," I said, hoping my voice sounded as sincere and gentle as I meant it to. It must have, because I felt a sense of relief as Alex smiled and nodded. I hesitated for just a moment, trying to get the same reaction from James, who I knew was a little more stubborn about such things.

"Thomas, what have you come to ask?" I asked, turning my full attention to him again.

"As you know, I have been travelling throughout this planet trying to teach and inform others of my kind of the changes that will be brought about when David sits on the emperor's throne. And one of the changes that has been agreed upon is the formation of a Dweller Council within each of the territories. At present, I have only spoken to my fellow Forest Dwellers. It is the wish of the newly formed council within this territory that Liberty become an honorary member. She is bound to us here by her heritage and, although she is a new friend, she already bears the mark of acceptance by the ancient ones of our forest."

As Thomas spoke, the room became completely silent and my heart started pounding in my chest. I felt so proud and suddenly wanted very much to be part of the council because Thomas was right—it would be a permanent link to my past and my heritage.

"Thomas, that is wonderful," I said, hugging him again. "Of course I would love to become a member of your council. This place is where my family is from, and I have been reunited with one who still lives. But why do I sense tension? I know that nothing is simple among you, so I ask you again: Why do I sense tension among you?"

"We are not invited," said Theo, standing up and staring intently.

"Oh," I said, understanding the situation. "Although I am greatly moved and honoured, this is getting to be tiresome. What is the reason for this? This time you know that my bodyguards are trustworthy and that they only stand with me to protect me."

"It is not meant as an insult to you or your guards, Princess, but it is the wishes of the members of the newly formed council that there be no vampire present, wherever or whenever we meet. They are worried that any new decisions and plans made by the council will be leaked inappropriately to your community, perhaps before David has the opportunity to reject or endorse them," said Malachi, coming to stand next to Thomas.

I stood there for a moment looking at them all, and in truth all I saw was my protector with a diminished look in his eyes. I knew he had taken an oath to protect me at the cost of all others, including himself, but during the trip all I had done was leave him behind.

I walked away from David and stood in front of Theo, looking into his face as I spoke. "I am sorry, but I will not go without Theo. Thomas, you know that he has been a friend to your sisters and to you, and I feel it is right that if you want me to attend, then I must come with Theo." As I spoke, Theo placed his huge hands gently on my shoulders. I knew that my words meant a lot to him. The room remained silent, and it was a while before anyone spoke.

"I will make a phone call and relay your decision," said Malachi, looking apologetic as he left the cottage. None of us spoke, and even though I did have enhanced hearing, I could not hear the conversation that was taking place outside.

When he entered the cottage again, Malachi again looked apologetic "It will be as you wish, Liberty. However, he will only be allowed to stay on the outer circle, whereas you will be within the inner. He will be able to see you at all times." I felt Theo tense slightly, his muscles rippling against my back as he pulled himself up to his full height. So I quickly bowed to Malachi and agreed.

Thomas and Malachi agreed to travel with us in one of the larger castle cars. The queen apparently had thought of Theo's

242

possible resistance when she had given us the use of a huge jeep. We left almost immediately after I had said good-bye to David. I sat next to Theo while Malachi and Thomas sat behind us; the journey was thankfully a very short one. When we arrived at the clearing, I recognised it as the same clearing where the welcoming celebrations had been held on the first night. Theo was asked to stay at the entrance and was shown the boundaries of the inner circle by the Forest Dwellers that were also going to be standing guard. I could see Theo beginning to relax slightly, sensing no animosity from the other guards. There were tendrils of forest vines slithering backwards and forwards along the perimeter of the forest, but Theo did not appear to be either surprised or threatened by them. I suspected that he merely viewed and accepted them as a thing of nature. Once everyone seemed happy with the arrangement, I was gently led into the clearing. There were rows of chairs set in front of a podium.

There were many others there, and all of them appeared to be Forest Dwellers. I felt a little nervous as I realised that I didn't recognise many of them but was intrigued to see that there were Forest Dwellers of all ages, some appearing short and wizened with age, some who had covered themselves, including most of their faces, with hooded cloaks.

The cloaks seemed to hold an identity for each wearer. The cloak that I had worn when I had been tested by Adair was the cloak generally worn by most of the younger Forest Dwellers. However, I also saw cloaks of shimmering black and others in rune-covered grey. It was difficult to tell whether this was a mark of wisdom or age. The ones who were covered completely in black were given an extra wide berth by all of the others.

I felt honoured to be among them, realising that this was a privilege that few others ever experienced. For a reason that could only be known to themselves, most the population of the planet who encountered them only ever saw the younger Forest Dwellers. It was as though they wanted to protect and hide both their strengths and weaknesses. My own strength, my darkness within, stirred a few times when those in grey or black walked close by, as if it recognised one of its own.

I continued to wander, and as I walked among them I finally saw a few Dwellers whom I had seen during the celebrations.

Finally, I felt as if I had a group I could attach myself to, and I would have gone over to them until I recognised that one of these was Lorchen, the queen's latest favourite escort and probably my biggest threat among them. His apparent jealousy made him, it seemed to me, extremely dangerous.

As soon as he felt my eyes on him, he looked directly at me. The look he and his companions gave me was, unsurprisingly, not very pleasant and it made feel a little unsettled, but it was not enough for me to not want to be there. I stood close to Thomas, who seemed to understand my insecurity and held out his hand. I gripped it tightly.

"I took a little advice from my sisters," he whispered.

Thomas appeared to know and be greeted by almost everyone in the meadow. There were plenty of nods and smiles for me, and for the most part I felt welcome and sensed nothing but friendly curiosity from most of the Forest Dwellers in attendance. I was beginning to feel a little bit out of my depth when I saw Heather by the side of the podium, speaking to some other females. I nudged Thomas and gestured in Heather's direction, and we started to walk towards her. She greeted me warmly with a brief embrace and guided me to a chair situated to the right of hers. She kindly introduced me to some of the females, all of whom seemed really nice and were excited and upbeat, caught up in the anticipation of what was about to happen.

I noticed that in general the female Forest Dwellers did not wear cloaks. I later learned that many females never ventured outside of the forests, never feeling the need to experience the world outside their home. Thomas wandered off finally, given the freedom to socialise and discuss the upcoming meeting without having me hanging onto him. It wasn't long before the others started to take their seats and began chatting excitedly with their neighbour. Not really knowing what else to do, I just continued to look around until Thomas came and sat on my other side with Malachi. As they sat down, they both gave me reassuring smiles and Thomas patted my knee reassuringly.

Left to my own thoughts, I began to feel a little nervous again, but it wasn't long before we were on our feet again. We all rose as one as we heard the first notes of a traditional folk song. The Forest Dwellers sang the words to their song and the atmosphere in the meadow became almost electrified with pride. Even I had to smile when Heather whispered to me that Thomas had questioned all the Forest Dweller groups of the planet and they had unanimously decided to make this song their anthem. She went on to explain to me that it had been one of their ancient battle songs, although now it was called their Song of Unity.

The band led a group of headmen onto the podium, and at their centre was Brigid, holding Prince Fletcher gently in her arms. Again, as soon as I saw him my spirits lifted and I smiled and relaxed. I was certain that he saw me also and smiled his beautiful smile just for me.

Once they were all seated on the podium and a silence had descended, the various discussions and speeches began. I tried hard to pay attention and look interested in the various speakers, but it was difficult sometimes to concentrate when all I wanted to do was laugh at Prince Fletcher, who was oblivious to the seriousness of the speeches. He was in favour of jumping up and down on his father's legs while using his father's ears for support.

I became alert, though, as Heather and Thomas stood and Thomas reached for my hand, pulled me to my feet, and moved me forward. They stood with me in front of the podium and spoke for me, asking the headmen to allow me to join with them as a member of their group. The chief headman, whom I did not recognise at all, extended a hand and pulled me up to the podium. He introduced himself as Quinn and then asked the crowd behind me if they had any objection to my joining them. It came as no surprise that Lorchen and some of his associates stood and began to announce their objections. The biggest issue was my humanity, and they used the history of abuse that was well documented, quoting whole historical passages about how my race had impinged on their beloved forests and planet.

Thomas and Heather both argued back that it was the forest itself that had accepted me. Thomas even held up my hand for the headmen to see, showing them the small mark given to me by the vines. I felt myself becoming increasingly uncomfortable as a debate erupted about whether I deserved to be a member of the council. I felt myself wanting to draw away from the heated discussion, but thankfully it wasn't long before the little prince, who had wriggled down from his father's lap and had made his way over to where I was standing, distracted me.

Without thinking I leaned down, picked the gorgeous child up, and hugged him to me. He started to laugh since my hair tickled his face. Wrapped up in the happiness that was Fletcher, I didn't notice at first but then realized I was standing in absolute silence; the debate seemed to have simply fizzled out and a decision was made. It seemed that even Lorchen and his friends could not argue with Prince Fletcher's reaction to me and the obvious mutual adoration that was flowing between us. I remained totally distracted and could only manage a polite "Thank you" since I was constantly being kissed and nuzzled by the child in my arms.

Eventually the little prince found a comfortable place to put his head on my shoulder and started to breathe slowly. I didn't really know what to do and was quite relieved when Brigid pushed Riley aside and gestured for me to sit beside her. She made no move to remove her son from me but simply gave me a smile that was warm and welcoming.

The rest of the meeting went well, and just before dark it appeared to finish. However, instead of joining Thomas, who had rejoined Heather, I stayed cradling the sleeping prince. Eventually we had to move and I stepped carefully off the podium. I walked with the headmen and again we followed the band, playing their Song of Unity to the edge of the meadow.

It was there that I handed back the sleeping prince, who had barely moved. I said good-bye to all those that I thought I knew and stood waiting for Thomas and Heather. I still had a lingering sense of some hostility when I turned to see Lorchen approaching. Before he was close enough to speak to me, thankfully, I also felt Theo approach.

Theo stood with me, placing his hand gently and protectively around my shoulder as Lorchen walked slowly by. I smiled sweetly at him, which seemed to make the dislike in his eyes shine even brighter. I suddenly felt tired as we left, knowing that for each friend I made, I also appeared to have made an enemy.

Chapter 38

After the council meeting we stayed within the Irish Territories for just under another week, and although I had been occupied with visits from various curious guests and visits with my grandmother whenever I had the chance, after a few days I sensed a growing restlessness among the others; even I had begun to feel the same way. Realising that there really was nothing else for us to do, everyone, myself included, felt as if all that was supposed to happen had happened.

We all came together one evening and decided that it was time for some of us to leave; it was the right time to move on with the search for Molly and the Ancient named Ana. For the sake of simplicity, we had all decided to call them by the names I had given them when I had identified them in the pictures, although Heather simply called them the mother and child. The day after we made the decision to leave, we all travelled into the Inner District and visited the extensive library and research facility that had been recommended to us by Queen Sinead herself. Rachael immediately set about gathering any information that she thought could be relevant. She became a blur of activity, choosing her helpers carefully and dismissing any staff member who appeared interested in us as a group. Rachael left it to us to sort out what we thought was relevant and those snippets of information that were more relevant and up-to-date.

I was delighted when Mia and Patrick arrived shortly after us. They looked happy and were glowing with inner contentment. It was so good to see her as she went from one being to another, hugging each of us. She laughed when Theo told her about what had happened to me at the celebrations after her Commitment Ceremony, hugging me even tighter when I tried to apologise. That entire day was pleasant and filled with peace, love, and laughter. It finally felt like everyone had accepted that things between us had changed.

As a new, stronger group we read through the scrolls that Rachael continued to set aside for us. Thomas joined us later in the evening and told us he believed that a woman and child fitting the description of Molly and the Ancient Ana had been spotted living and travelling with a family of Mountain Dwellers in the snow-covered mountains of the South American Territories. After a lengthy discussion a unanimous decision was made that we should begin the next part of our journey as soon as possible.

The place, The Resort, held so many good and bad memories, and I couldn't help laughing with Mia when Theo started to moan and mutter quietly to himself, remembering that he had found it difficult to stop me from accidentally hurting myself as I hurtled uncontrollably down various mountains on skis. I had only been back for one day since then, so I knew that my skiing would need a little practice again, but that did not put me off the idea at all.

Although I knew that there were vast areas of snow-covered mountains within the South American Territories, I also knew that the resort was reasonably central to the area in which they had been seen. I knew we would be welcomed and could stay for an indefinite period of time if we needed to; therefore, with David's approval, I rang Daniel. Daniel was both surprised and happy to hear from me, and he appeared to be at least as excited as I was. After I had explained the reason for the phone call, we made definite plans for our entire group to be there within the next couple of days.

I couldn't help smiling to myself as I remembered that I had been there on my first ever 'date' with Daniel. He had been my first crush. In any event, I stopped smiling when I saw David looking at me with a slightly quizzical look on his face. Although he had never really spoken about it, I believe that deep down he regretted his behaviour towards me on that holiday.

Once the travelling plans and accommodations had been sorted, we stayed in the research facility, where we continued to read and share time together until it was dark. After a lot of pleading, Mia and Patrick returned to the cottages with us and stayed until after I had fallen asleep. My sleep was contented; I felt well and at peace, satisfied with all that had happened and all that I had learned there.

The following day, which was the day before we were due to leave, I went out without any male guards for the last time. At my departure they all seemed to have finally accepted the decisions made by Mia and Rachael. We visited all of the shops which I had become familiar with and left a few requests with Geraldine, promising to revisit personally to collect the ordered items. Then we continued shopping. I bought a few bits and pieces for the others and for myself.

I bought an ancient crystal charm bracelet with Celtic designs on it for the queen, knowing instinctively that she would like it. I stocked up on some extra warm clothes for David, Alex, and James, although I knew that they could cope with the coldness very well, much better than I could—but I liked looking after them.

As a way of conceding to my logic, Rachael obviously did the same for Theo, though we had a lot more difficulty shopping for him because he was huge. Following our time out shopping, Mia took me to see Grandmother Eileen at Bryna's cottage one last time. I had also bought them all gifts. For Bryna I asked Geraldine to design an exclusive range of clothes for both her and her forthcoming child.

For Malachi I did the same. Geraldine had been thinking of expanding the male design side of her business. I had to laugh out loud at his reaction when she volunteered Max to be her experimental mannequin. She had been spending some time with Janet swapping ideas and designs; Janet was extremely protective of her and often advised Max on her well-being. Knowing that Max absolutely adored his human partner, Mia had promised to have another word with the queen to see whether she could forgive Max for whatever he had done and allow him to infuse her, knowing that it was what they both longed for.

Janet had slowly, since being infused, become the stronger of the two in her relationship, but Sebastian was totally in love with his fiery partner and accepted whatever she did, and most of what she asked him to do. I knew that they had spent a lot of time with Queen Sinead when they had started out as designers, but they ended up being close friends. Now, with the queen's encouragement, they were both looking at taking a young child from an Enclosure to complete their family. I knew deep down that it was wrong, but I also knew that they were both very capable of loving a child.

For my beautiful grandmother, who was suddenly one of the most important beings on the planet to me, I brought the softest blankets and downy pillows. I also employed a full-time nurse to provide for all her needs. I knew that Bryna would take very good care of her, but I also knew that she would have another full-time job when her baby was born and did not want her to be put upon in any way. In fact, I had left it up to Bryna and Malachi to choose my grandmother's nurse, trusting them to select the best person for the job. They had eventually chosen a local girl; Bryna told me that Malachi had visited their local Enclosure himself and had, with the queen's blessing, selected the girl and had infused her with the queen's own essence.

I was glad to hear that the infusion had gone well, and Bryna was expecting a visit from her very soon. When I asked her name, Bryna explained that they would allow my grandmother to give her a new name. I left my grandmother as she drifted off to sleep, but before I left I whispered to her, telling her where I was going and why. I wanted her to be proud of me, as I knew she was. She whispered back that although she had not known me for very long, she and my mother had often spoke of the next generation in their bloodline, both of them knowing that the child of my mother would be a girl and always suspecting that she would be born to do great things.

That evening we all dressed up, making a special effort with our appearance, and we went out as a group to one of the royal restaurants that was protected by the queen herself. We were the only ones in there, and we gathered with all of our new friends and acquaintances. The queen and Lorchen even managed to pop in, although from her much cooled, less indulgent reaction towards him, I wondered whether she had been told about his less-than-warm reaction to me at the meeting. We all took some time and posed for various photographs for the media, and then we shut the doors.

Janet, Sebastian, and Georgina were not going on with us. Janet informed me that she would like to go back and look in on her shops within the European Territories near to the castle. She promised us that she would visit the emperor and empress in person to update them on our progress. She had also been busy collecting the latest cold-weather suits, not so much for the vampires but for me and Heather, who was now becoming a little bit more excited about the new development and stage of our journey. Lisa and Nick were going to be travelling with Janet and her party, assuring us that the material they had gathered while in the Irish Territories would keep the population going for quite a while—hopefully freeing us a little more.

So after many good-byes, our party—which now included all of the bodyguards, Rachael, and Heather—finally separated from the others. I wasn't the only one who shed some tears when we finally left. The queen herself came to the cottages to say her good-byes, standing with her arm around a very quiet, sad-looking Mia.

We travelled swiftly to the airport and boarded our plane. Heather and I sat close together, trying to comfort each other as the realisation that we had really left Mia behind filled us with a heaviness that I don't think we could have prepared ourselves for. David and Cassius stayed near to the both us but did not intrude, knowing that we needed the time to adjust. The flight was a lengthy one; both Heather and I fell asleep, although Heather remained more restless than I did. I suspect she was not as comfortable on the plane as I was. We were awakened when the night was at its darkest. All anyone could see were groups of green trees in a white wilderness. We touched down at an airport that seemed to be the only thing for miles and miles in the middle of that white wilderness.

Theo lifted me from my seat and covered me with a blanket while Heather put on her animal skin coat and said that she wanted to walk. She stood up and adjusted herself, shaking off the obvious discomfort she had experienced during the journey and looking very much like a proud Forest Dweller, a representative of her people, knowing she was in a region that was unfamiliar and definitely more Theo's domain.

I was glad of Theo's decision, as I still felt exhausted; for me, an emotional sleep was never a satisfying sleep. I felt dishevelled and hungry, and not at all like a representative of anything. I was hoping that there wouldn't be any fuss or anyone from the media, but that wasn't to be; there were photographers and media representatives waiting. I groaned when I saw them and received a disapproving look from Rachael. As soon as we saw them, Theo placed me on my feet and Rachael provided me with a long fur coat with a large hood which covered most of my face.

As always, I was held by David, who walked slightly ahead of me with Cassius leading the way. Theo walked directly behind me and Alex and James placed themselves on either side of him. Rachael walked with a protective arm around Heather. Although I heard the photographers calling my name, I didn't even look up. Instead I concentrated on where my feet were going and on the backs of David's legs.

I was taken completely by surprise when the probe sliced at my mind. I almost stumbled and let go of David's hand. I knew that my barriers had protected me, but I had a feeling that the being that was trying to reach my mind knew where I was and how to reach me. No probe had managed to slice so deeply since my encounter with the twins and their sister.

As soon as it happened, I sent a thought to my bodyguards that I had sensed a threat and everyone, including Theo, who had developed his own way of sensing me, pulled together and closed ranks as they put Heather into the protected inner circle close to me. I did not let them know how serious it had been. David had become aware at the same time as the others. I couldn't help that, but I played it down well, pleading that I was tired and it had taken me by surprise. The Adwar who was in charge of the airport met us as we walked through the doors and were ushered into a secluded room. We didn't enquire what his name was and he didn't offer it. He appeared relaxed and unaware of any type of threat, which was reassuring.

None of our group sat down or relaxed, nor did any of the others question me further about what was happening; they all knew better. I deliberately kept David thinking that I was tired, irritable, and just a little wary. The only one who understood that something more sinister may have occurred was Rachael, who seemed particularly on edge, looking at me constantly, trying to communicate her understanding without letting the others know.

I felt vulnerable waiting in the airport. The building felt tainted, and I just wanted to leave and go to the resort. At least I didn't have long to wait, though. Daniel had sent us one of his chalet managers; I vaguely remembered his face and remembered that he had been with Daniel when I had first visited the resort.

We followed the young Adwar guide down a series of private corridors out of the airport. As we reached the final door, I could already feel the cold fresh air and wanted nothing more than to rush outside to get free of the staleness of the airport, but before we left the building the Adwar guide handed us all protective glasses, explaining that during the hours of daylight the snow could become blindingly bright.

We all gathered our warm coats around us. I pulled my hood up and forward as far as it would go, my head retreating into its warm fur-lined folds. Rachael produced a thick woollen scarf and wrapped it over most of my face, anchoring my hood into place. I took some gloves from her and placed them on my hands. Soon, in the shelter of the building all wrapped up, I could feel myself beginning to become uncomfortably hot.

As we stepped outside, I was momentarily stunned. The Adwar guide was right. Although the sun had not yet reached its full brightness, there was nothing around to cast shadows over the brilliant white snow, which seemed to stretch on forever. In the far distance there were a few trees, but the stretch of snow was a vast no-man's-land.

As I stepped forward, new things awaited us all. To the left of the building there were a number of sleds harnessed to what I knew to be snow wolves. I had only ever heard or read of such animals; to many in the Inner Districts, these animals were no more than legends. They were huge, majestic pure silver-white wolves. Their fur was long and shaggy, and small flakes of snow glistened like dew throughout their coats. Their coats held no hint of greyness, making a perfect camouflage against the whiteness of the snow. Their bodies were large and very muscular; I had read that they could pull a sled weighed down with many times more than their own body weight. The colours of their eyes varied, but all of them were pale and striking. There was no hint of any kind of infusion in any of them. They were pure, as nature intended, and though they were surrounded by vampires, there was no hint of fear in their eyes. None of them wore muzzles, just small harnesses stretched around their bodies for pulling the sleds. Their muzzles were long and their teeth large and sharp; they could easily have snapped me in half without any effort, but strangely I felt no threat from them.

However, I noticed that the vampires with me were unusually wary of the wolves, most of them steering well clear of the wolves' heads—all except Theo, who seemed to want to go and stroke one of them. He moved slowly forward until the wolf he was approaching started to growl a warning at him. The warning wasn't a particularly frightening one, but it was the type of warning that let Theo know that he obviously smelled more of vampire than of Mountain Dweller.

As soon as our bags were loaded onto some sleds, the Adwar gestured us slowly forward. Approaching the nearest sled, I deliberately walked as close to the wolves as possible, curious to see how they would react to me as a human.

Although I heard the rumble of warning from one of the wolves, I didn't feel as if I was being threatened in any way. I sensed that the animal was simply being wary of me, perhaps because he had probably dealt with very few human beings and didn't know if I was a threat to him. I stopped when I became level with his pale blue eye. As I looked into his eyes, I saw a creature that was purely natural, aware and fiercely protective of his planet, and with knowledge that probably had been passed down to him. There was patience in his eyes, and compassion. As we stood staring at each other, the wolf lowered his head slightly. I decided that even though I would have loved to reach out and touch his beautiful deep fur, I would not just in case one of my companions decided to become overly protective.

We arranged ourselves on the giant sleds. David sat close beside me and Theo sat behind us. As soon as we had strapped ourselves in and covered ourselves with the blankets provided, the wolves seemed to sense we were ready and moved off at a steady pace. I thought the Adwar would be coming with us, but he simply shouted instructions to the wolves as they moved away.

Chapter 39

The journey through the mountains was beautiful and the scenery was just as I had imagined it; there were parts that brought back memories that were both good and bad. One of the things I remembered was how quiet everything was. There was always noise where I had come from, whether it was from the castle itself or its many inhabitants.

The huge white snow wolves pulled the sleds silently and effortlessly forward, maintaining a comfortable and steady pace. Although there were no clear paths through the snow, the wolves ran on and on without guidance. We saw no other animals or beings while we travelled. The scenery was peaceful, yet it was serene in a way different from how the Irish Territories had been. Its whiteness looked pure and untainted, and its silence remained surprisingly warm and welcoming.

The goggles I wore made my eyes hot. They were quite uncomfortable and made it a little difficult to see clearly, although I could still appreciate the beauty of my surroundings. After a few moments, purely out of curiosity, I closed my eyes and removed the goggles. At first I kept my eyes almost closed, squinting against the snow's brightness. However, gradually I managed to open them fully, and though my sight wasn't perfect, it was good enough to gaze about me with my eyes unshielded. I nestled back into the warmth of my covers and let my mind wander, smiling to myself for most of the journey, content to know that I could physically adapt to this environment if I needed to.

It felt good knowing that we were moving forward and getting closer to our inevitable goal, but it was also difficult not knowing if the threat I had felt earlier had anything to do with our apparent progress or if it was simply just another challenge from some other unknown vampire. Although I didn't want to dwell on it, I couldn't help myself. There was something about the experience at the airport that bothered me. A niggling voice in the back of my mind told me I should remember and that I had felt that particular probe or something similar somewhere before; the darkness within was already stirring, readying itself to emerge and protect me. In order not to let the feelings of doubt and fear usurp my feelings of enjoyment, I practiced what I had learned in the temple: I let my mind find its own peace and cleared it of any worrying thoughts.

The air in the mountains was fresh and cold. The mountains in the distance were vast peaks of whiteness, broken only by the occasional solitary tree. The journey continued smoothly for a few hours, but because we were travelling in the early morning, we had to stop to cover the vampires before the sun rose to its peak. I pulled my scarf higher so that only my eyes remained unprotected against the morning sun and positioned myself so that I could continue to study my surroundings.

I felt David go rigid and still beside me. I knew that he was catching up on some much needed rest and getting ready for the excitement of another chapter in our adventure. The sled started to slow and the sun had again passed it zenith when I felt David stir. He remained covered while he adjusted to his surroundings, and then I could feel the stiffness slowly leave his body.

I am not sure how I recognised the mountains as we approached, but I did and felt exhilarated as soon as I saw them. Another feeling of being in the right place at the right moment settled on me as I gripped David's cool, slowly softening hand. When he emerged I gestured and pointed to the mountains where I had first learned to ski.

We took a little while longer travelling round the base of the mountain before I caught sight of the clusters of chalets. They were nestled on the side of one of the distant mountains, almost in a valley, and were protected from the worst of the weather. It took us most of that morning to reach the resort and, as I suspected, Daniel was already there waiting to greet us all. As we approached I was relieved that there was no fuss, no big group there to meet us, only Daniel waiting patiently for our approach, smiling and as eager for the sleds to finally stop as we were.

As soon as we had stopped, a chalet master came forward to help us while others brought bowls of food and water for the wolves. Once I had been unwrapped and could move, the chalet master having come forward and peeled off all the layers of blankets, I went to greet Daniel, being careful as I picked my way through the deep snow, which was hard and slippery despite its soft appearance.

The greetings shared between us were warm, and as I approached Daniel he held his arms open. When I reached him I nestled myself within them. It was good to see him; he was exactly the same as I remembered him, although I thought he was a little taller and a little more muscular than I remembered. It seemed that all of us had grown up in more ways than one since we had last been here. His hair was just as red as I remembered it, even redder perhaps in the morning light, and his green eyes still sparkled with the promise of fun.

"Daniel, it is so good to see you. You are looking fine. You seem to have grown a little," I said, laughing and suddenly reluctant to release him and let him go.

"As it is you, Princess, and indeed all of you. You seem to have been on a few adventures yourself. I follow the media and have watched as avidly as all the other beings since you have grown," he said, laughing before turning towards the others who were approaching us.

"Some of you I am acquainted with, and some I have yet to become acquainted with, but it remains unsaid that all of you are welcome," he said, still hugging me close to his side with one arm as he shook the hands of David and then Theo, who had also risen from their sleds. They both greeted him with genuine smiles, although I did see that both of them noticed that Daniel had not released me; perhaps neither had forgotten our first encounter either.

Once it appeared that everyone was present, Daniel used his mobile phone to summon other members of his staff. Almost as soon as he had finished speaking, beings started to appear from inside the chalets.

"I wanted to greet my friends alone, without the fuss of others milling about us," he explained as he gave me one final hug. I didn't want to leave his embrace; I felt as if our distance had been too great for too long. I just wanted to stay near him, but I knew I had to get some of my belongings and turned towards David.

"Tell me, I have heard a rumour that you have embarked on a hunt for a missing Sky Dweller. Do you think you will find one in my mountains?" Daniel said, laughing sceptically.

"I don't know what you have heard. However, there are always rumours, many of which are simply untrue. They appear to follow us wherever we travel," I interrupted him after seeing a look of impatience flick across David's face. "I felt that I needed to get away from castles and traditions for a while. I am here to see you, and that is the only reason I am here." I hated deceiving him, but his question made me feel a little uncomfortable. I thought we had been discreet. Over David's shoulder, I could see Rachael also frowning at Daniel's comment.

Luckily, there was a lot of luggage and further distractions that allowed us to turn away and allow our host no more questions at that moment. The next few hours, until after the evening meal, were spent with settling into our various chalets.

We basically separated in the same way we had in the Irish Territories. The chalets were very close together, so we formed our usual little community. The chalets could house up to six adults at a time, so it was easy to sort ourselves out and there was plenty of room for all of us.

As soon as I was unpacked and able, I put on my warm snowsuit and, without a word to the others, went to collect Rachael and Heather from their chalet. When I got to their chalet, I realised that Alex and James had followed me, as they always did, though neither of them had made any effort to change from their travelling clothes.

Theo answered the door to their chalet when I knocked. When I went inside it appeared that Rachael had anticipated my first activity and had dressed herself and Heather appropriately. When Alex realised what I intended to do, he questioned me about my intentions and then my ability. Theo simply laughed, telling them that it would be a pleasure to allow them to protect me during this trip. I waited reluctantly while they went to get the necessary equipment to enable them to join me.

When David arrived and Theo told him what was happening, they both shared another laugh, which, if I am honest, I found more than a little irritating. Rachael saw my growing discomfort and displeasure and took me outside to help me with my skis. I had to concede that it was a little difficult to start off with because I had forgotten just how slippery everything was.

Rachael helped me to maintain a certain amount of dignity in front of Theo and David. She also appeared to find Theo's laughter, which seemed to be getting louder, just as annoying as I had David's.

"Stay on your feet and I will help you to move off. You will be fine. Once you have started, they will not have time to laugh," she whispered with a cheeky wink.

"Okay" was all I could manage as I finally was able to get my feet into the right position. I had placed myself on a path that looked totally clear of obstacles and we were standing on a relatively steep slope, but it looked manageable so I whispered to Rachael that I was ready. When Rachael gave me that first gentle nudge, it was all I needed to start moving. As I gathered momentum, my memory came back of my first visit to the mountain and, with my enhanced vision and the memories of what I had learned to do during my first visit, I realised that I was probably better at this than any of them realised.

I was halfway down the mountain before I sent the thought to Alex and James to calm down and to join me on the slope. I added that I was fine but that they should be quick. I did not know for certain why, but I began to feel a little bit uneasy alone out there on the mountain with no one to protect me. Usually I welcomed the peace, but out there at that moment, I felt as if I was being watched. I was not skilled enough to take my eyes off my path to take a look around. Although I was a far better skier in the sense that I could actually see obstacles before I hit them, at the speed I had reached by then, my senses did nothing to help me figure out how to stop. My sense of uneasiness was growing the farther away I got from my friends and David, and my pace was increasing.

Rachael, help me. I do not think that I can stop. I sent the thought, trying not to panic or to cause any of my protectors to suddenly overreact.

My usually clear vision was becoming cloudy with panic, and I was beginning to lose the clear path I had mapped out for myself. I barely missed a tree stump and managed to graze my arm on a branch. I could see that I was running out of mountain and I did not know what to do. I had actually resigned myself to getting hurt when I felt a huge arm come out of nowhere and lift me out of my skis.

It was Theo. He slowed us down enough for us to avoid hitting the wire fence that marked out the perimeter of the resort. I had been panicking so much that I hadn't even heard his approach. When I could finally breathe again, I realised I should have known that Theo would not have allowed me to hurt myself; he always seemed to be the first one at my side. When we finally managed to stop, I threw my arms round his massive neck and burst into tears. "I am so sorry," I whimpered.

"That was foolish, Princess," he said as he held me against his huge chest. The worse thing of all was that I could hear the disapproval in his voice.

"I am sorry. I was just showing off!" I cried again.

"All is well. You are with me now and you are safe," he said in his usual gently unemotional way.

"There is something wrong here, Theo. I do not know what it is, but I felt it and it frightened me. I feel as if something bad knows that we are here and was out there somewhere watching us," I said, sobbing again into his shoulder.

"What is it? Can't you tell?" he asked, suddenly serious. He held me at arm's length and made me look at him. When I continued to cry, he held me close to his body again, his arms tightening protectively around me.

"It's okay," he murmured. "I have not forgotten my oath."

I didn't get to say anything further in response because Rachael arrived minutes later, followed closely by Alex and James.

"She says that she feels a threat here," Theo told them as he held me close again. "Go and see if you can find anything," he said, looking at Alex and James and without releasing me. At his words, I felt them slither away on their skis.

"Let's get her back to her chalet," said Rachael. "She is cold and has obviously been frightened."

"As you wish, but I will take her myself." With those final words Theo lifted me off my feet and cradled me against his unusually warm body.

"Before we go back, do not mention this to David. He seems a little tense here for some reason, and if he feels I have been threatened, he will tear this place apart. I will not have that done to Daniel or his resort," I managed to say from behind Theo's shoulder. "I want you to agree and say it now, because I will deny anything other than that I gave myself a fright skiing too fast," I continued. As I spoke I also communicated my wish to Alex and James. They returned within seconds, and I didn't have to look at them to sense the looks of irritation that must have passed between them.

"It will be as you wish," said Theo in a voice that I knew he used deliberately to threaten the others. Without anyone saying anything else, Theo started to carry me up the mountain while the others followed. When we neared the chalet, David came out, concerned when he saw Theo with me in his arms.

"What happened? Is she hurt?" he asked as he reached for me.

Theo put me gently on my feet, steadying me as David approached.

"She got a little too enthusiastic with her skiing again," said Rachael, coming to stand beside Theo.

David laughed a little as he held me close to him and kissed my head. "You must have done enough for one day. Let's get you changed, and perhaps we can spend a little time introducing ourselves to and reacquainting ourselves with our host. After all, he was the first person you ever kissed," he said with an unreadable smile.

"No, he wasn't. You were the first person. He probably would have been, but I found out that before we even met at the dance, Theo threatened him so he wouldn't touch me," I said honestly, knowing that David would find it amusing—and suddenly I was glad that the subject had changed.

I sent the thought *Not a word* to the others as I turned with David and walked towards our chalet. Once inside the warm, bright chalet, David dimmed all of the lights. I felt exhausted, and it took very little persuading on David's part to get me to remove my clothes and lie down beside him for a rest.

I was drifting towards a deep sleep when his phone rang and I felt him leave my side. I did wonder whom he was speaking to and where he was going, but I was too tired to question him.

Chapter 40

When I woke up some hours later, it took a moment for me to realise where I was and why I was there. The blinds were still closed, but I could still see the brightness of the sun, so I guessed it was probably still sometime during the day.

I woke up feeling really good. I finally felt properly rested. My joints were a little stiff and the graze on my arm still remained a little painful, but it felt good to stretch and yawn. I lay there for a few moments, warm and content nestled in the fur blankets of my bed, until nature called and I felt an urgent need to get up.

I got up and opened the blinds. The view that I saw was breathtaking. The whiteness of the snow on the mountains in the distance was spectacular, tinged with orange and yellows, the colours reflecting the sun as it started its descent behind them. Nothing, nothing at all, seemed to have disturbed the perfect white blanket that stretched out in front of my window. There were clouds in the distance, but they were too far away to be a threat to my vision of perfection.

I turned back into my room and stood still for a moment, feeling a little uneasy again, not really understanding why things seemed different. It took a while for me to notice the silence; strangely, I couldn't hear anything, not a single voice outside of my room even when I concentrated. Although it was too quiet, I could not sense any danger, so more out of curiosity than fear I quickly had a shower and put on a pair of soft trousers, a soft warm jumper, and fur-lined boots. I placed my hair up in a neat ponytail and ventured cautiously outside, feeling the need to move as quietly as possible, not willing to break the wall of silence that surrounded me.

The communal area where my friends usually gathered was empty, but I had a feeling that it would be. I stopped and concentrated for a second, and although I could sense Rachael nearby, I couldn't sense anyone else. I started walking tentatively forward, trying not to make any noise.

"Nice of you to make an appearance," Rachael said softly. Her voice startled me, and I stood still for a moment as I scanned the room for her. I finally saw her as she leaned forward in a chair at the far end of the room. She was placing an enormous book on the table beside her.

She rose from her seat and walked towards me with a strange, secretive but kind look on her face. She was smartly dressed. It had been a while since I had seen her in a dress, and she looked stunning. Her dress was floor-length and the customary crimson in colour, but it was free-flowing and floated around her, very unlike the clinging suits and dresses that she normally wore.

"Well, now that you are awake I suppose we should think about preparing you so that you can join me and the others," she said with a very strange look on her face. I stood where I was, unsure of what was going on. I knew that Rachael would never hurt me, but her demeanor was peculiar. The last time she had acted in such a detached manner was when she had been my teacher back at the Enclosure.

"Rachael, what do you mean? Where is David? Where are all the others, and what am I to join them for?" I asked.

Without answering me, she suddenly appeared to become more like herself. She bustled towards me. Without actually answering me, she turned me back towards the bedroom and started telling me what clothes I should wear. After a few more moments of watching her bustle around my bedroom in silence, she started to speak. "I must apologise, child. I was careless in that I could not sense your awakening. You were left in my care and I became distracted with the book I was studying. You caught me with my mind elsewhere. I, like you, am practising. I am trying to broaden my mind in such a way that I can communicate with more than one of those who are farther afield. As you know yourself, thoughts that are sent farther usually can only reach one being at a time. I sense that some of us may need to grow stronger in order for us to meet an impending challenge. But enough about what I was doing. I think it would be better for us both if we were to concentrate on what you should be doing."

I stood there a little while longer, still unsure of what it was she actually wanted me to do.

"Child, if you do not want us both to be in trouble with your beloved, I suggest you disrobe and bathe yourself. Hurry, now, or we will be late," she said, finally putting down the clothes in her hand and turning to face me.

I started to move when I saw the look on her face. I knew she would not tolerate any arguments or questions, even though she knew I didn't really understand what was going on. Even though I had already had a shower, I did not tell her so. I simply ran a bath and did as I was told. I cleansed myself quickly, my curiosity making me hurry. I dried myself and pulled on the dress that Rachael had chosen.

As usual, wherever I went a full-length mirror seemed to follow, and as I looked into the mirror again I was surprised at how much like a vampire I looked. I thought about the changes I had seen in Mia, and I was beginning to think that perhaps, like her, the more time I spent with them the more like them I was becoming. I dismissed the thought, though, as soon as it entered my head, knowing that as long as I had free will, I would never quite be a vampire.

My dress was similar to Rachael's, though it clung to the length of my body more. My hair, like Rachael's, was left loose around my shoulders but kept away from my face by a black diamond tiara.

"Rachael, what is it you are hiding from me? Won't you tell me now that I have been dressed to your satisfaction?" I asked sweetly, hoping she would relent and tell me what was happening.

"Come, Liberty, if you stop asking questions and follow me, I will show you exactly what I am hiding from you," she said, smiling and taking my hand. Everything felt slightly strange— the way she had invoked memories of the way she had been with me as a child and again now as she held my hand as though to lead me safely somewhere. Something was wrong. I could feel my inner darkness stir as if it could sense my uneasiness. Together we left my chalet, but before we had taken more than a few steps forward, Rachael stopped and took a charcoal grey silk scarf from around her waist.

"There is a surprise for you at the place where we are going, so I have been told to cover your eyes, Liberty. Although I find all of these practises a little silly, I have been given a set of instructions by your beloved and was told to follow them, so I am therefore duty bound."

Knowing better than to argue with her and still a little unsure of what she had in mind, and still worried about the whereabouts of all the others, I simply sighed and turned my back to her, allowing her to place the scarf over my eyes. I placed myself in her hands and in total darkness. I tried to relax as she guided me gently but firmly, lifting me slightly so that my feet slid over any protruding obstacles; I felt like I was gliding on skis.

It wasn't long before we stopped. "Take a step forward, Liberty," said Rachael softly. "And another . . . And another . . . Now stand still. Do not move until you are given further instructions to do so," Rachael said seriously.

I stood where she told me to and waited. I still could not hear a thing. The silence remained eerie and unnatural. After a few moments I felt Rachael move behind me to remove the blindfold. When it was gone I opened my eyes slowly, and in front of me were most of the beings on the planet that I loved, all of them smiling happily at me.

As David came forward he said simply, "Happy birthday, darling. Today is the day in your life span that you officially pass from childhood to adulthood." I had actually forgotten it was my birthday! With Mia's Commitment Ceremony and all that had happened recently, I had lost track of the days. I was certain the preparations for this day had not begun before I had left the Irish Territories, yet Mia must have had a hand in those preparations.

As David took my hand and I stepped forward with him, my friends parted and showed me a large stack of gifts. Someone somewhere started to clap and sing "Happy Birthday." I felt as if I would burst with happiness; they had all tried so hard and I felt such love towards all of them. They had decorated one of the chalets with banners of congratulations and had acquired what appeared to be every balloon on the planet.

There were tables of various foods, and along the walls were strings of tiny bright lights and a cleared space for dancing beside the gifts. Another milestone had passed (although it was nearly missed by me), and I was now an adult among my own kind. My friends and loved ones went silent after the song, and every one of them bowed to me as they had done when I had committed myself to David.

I looked at them, feeling their love, and spent the rest of that evening being loved by them. It was the most magical thing I had experienced in a long time. I opened a few of the smaller gifts: a beautifully framed picture of my grandmother from Malachi and Bryna which brought tears to my eyes; some more perfume from the emperor and empress, which I was especially happy about since I wore it constantly and was almost out of it; some delicately woven Celtic-designed hand jewellery from Mia; and the smallest one of a pile of many from David, a beautiful jewel-encrusted box. On the top of the box there was a picture that showed a young girl standing with a woman, both of them with flowing golden hair and delicate features. Although it was a carving, I knew that David had meant it to resemble me standing with my mother.

They were the only small and easily carried gifts among the pile, so I agreed to have the others sent back to the castle, where they would be kept safe and unopened until my return.

That night was magical for all of us. After I had some food, we danced until my feet hurt. I must add that Theo's contribution to the dancing was the funniest of all; I had never seen him look so uncomfortable, even with the quiet encouragement that Rachael had to constantly give him. In the meantime, Daniel and I managed to finally get a proper dance.

When I was too tired to dance anymore, I chatted and laughed with David and the others, each of them having a story to tell. Some were funny, some were sad, but all the stories they told involved me in one way or another. It was a good way to usher in a new chapter of my existence, reminiscing about the events that had led me to the place I was at that moment—an unusual journey by any being's standards.

I felt as if I did not want the sun to rise, bringing with it the morning and finally ending the perfect night. When it did I fell asleep in David's arms, content and safe, all of my earlier misgivings firmly dispelled.

Chapter 41

T he next few days were wonderfully simple because we all spent time relaxing and catching up with Daniel. Daniel was in particularly good spirits because his father had only just recently given him the resort. His father had many businesses in the area, and because Daniel had been practically raised there, it seemed to be a logical decision.

There were times after we arrived when I felt a little uncomfortable. I noticed David watched me constantly when I was in the same room as Daniel. Daniel reassured David over and over that although he still loved me as a friend, he had another female in his life who held all his attention. I was curious, but when I tried to question him on the matter he simply smiled secretively.

He told us that his father had obtained the rank of Hiltian and had become favoured by the American ruling family. From the way the conversations I overheard went, apparently Daniel and his family were now being treated well because of his obvious friendship with David and me. He told us, quite pleased, that his father had put in a request for him to obtain the rank of Nedas.

One afternoon, when we were all together, Rachael politely asked Daniel about his mother. Daniel explained that he had never known his mother and that his father would not discuss her, so no more was ever said on the subject. All he had ever been told was that his mother had been expecting him when she had been captured and brought to one of his father's Enclosures. Daniel did not know whether she was alive or dead, and given his reluctance to talk about her, we didn't pursue the subject a second time.

I had met King Dylan and Queen Claudia a couple of times at vampire functions. Like Queen Sinead, they were traditionalists, but I sensed that they were reserved in their opinion of me. I was never sure that they actually liked me or whether they simply tolerated me because I was David's partner. While our visit was supposed to be low-key, I understood that at some point we would have to spend some time with the king and queen at their palace; it would have been considered very rude of us not to. It was difficult for any of our group to be enthusiastic about that visit, and when we finally decided to go, we agreed that Heather and I would be constantly watched and protected.

Although it had been only a few years since I had visited the chalets, they appeared to have remained very much unchanged. It was comforting because although that holiday would always remind me of my first but terribly close encounter with David, it had also been one of the best holidays I had ever had. I had learned to ski and had met Daniel, who had for one night made me feel beautiful and special. Those memories were still so very clear, and at times when I looked at Daniel I could not stop from smiling, even when he caught me looking and smiled quizzically in return.

Alex and James had to settle for the chalet next to ours since David insisted that during that visit we should have a chalet for ourselves. There were times when we were resting together that he asked me to describe the feeling of love. For a vampire to try to understand the concept of love was very difficult, but he suddenly had the urge to try.

Daniel had appointed each of the chalets its own chalet master. Each chalet master was given instructions to make sure our stay was a comfortable and enjoyable one. Our chalet master was an Adwar named Joseph who had the strange ability to appear instantly when we needed him.

At first it was a novelty because it seemed as if no sooner had one of us spoken his name than he would appear, but that soon wore off. David did not seem that bothered by him and his ability to appear silently, but he startled me a few times with his immediate appearances. For a reason that I could not quite put my finger on, I wondered if it was Joseph whom I had felt watching me on that first day.

Daniel also gave us the use of his personal office, where David and I took the time to check in and catch up on any news from the castle. David spoke to his appointed personal assistant every morning, and fortunately everything appeared to have remained as quiet as we expected. The only real news was that now the emperor and empress had handed some of the royal duties over to David and his assistants. The empress had been hosting various banquets especially for the queens while the emperor and the others kings had been hunting. It appeared that she no longer felt the need to be constantly at Macarius's side; they both had begun to spend time just being themselves. I really stopped listening after I heard that the emperor had been hunting and left David's side to go and join the others. I had once almost been forced to be part of a hunting party, and I still experienced nightmares because of it.

We all practised a lot of skiing during those early days. At first everyone was wary of Heather because she was a beginner and had never done it before, but fortunately she was like every other Dweller I had encountered, extremely well-coordinated, and skiing quickly became her new passion. In fact, she and Rachael often became quite competitive with each other, and they frequently challenged each other to friendly races and competitions. Although they politely invited me to join them in racing, I always declined.

I noticed that Heather was quickly earning the respect of the others; she had a strength within her that began to grow with her confidence day by day. When I think about that time, I believe that at first they considered her to be in need of as much protection as they thought I was since she was constantly supervised.

I am glad to recall that she often challenged their theory; she was quick agile and strong. Cassius was obviously proud of her, and his eyes shone with excitement, pride, and love every time she did something that surprised him. She was equally smitten with him and spent more and more time trying to ease some of her ingrained resentment of vampires.

Things were changing very fast within our group, and in the quietness of the mountain resort each one of us appeared to grow.

My companions all began to open up and release themselves from the restraints of their infused characters and to experience the world of feeling. I was proud of each one of our group as they experienced small glimpses of emotions within themselves that had probably lain dormant for centuries.

As they began to experience the first inklings of feelings, they also began to open their eyes to the planet and for the first time stop and look at things that they found unusual or that intrigued them, often finding a beauty in the things they saw. Of course, it was hard for them to manage the changes at first, and quite often they would need the same solitude that I had always requested.

David appeared to struggle with the feelings that he appeared to be experiencing. There were times that he would just sit with the shell, continuously caressing its smooth outer surface while staring out over the endless pristine white snow to the mountains beyond. At first I tried to sit with him to share those moments, but he never invited me or made me feel welcome so I stopped; if he wanted to spend time alone, I would let him. Sometimes he would come back to the group barely speaking to me, his eyes almost accusing me of doing something harmful to him.

It was during those times that I was free to pursue things that I wanted. Heather and I soon formed a close bond as we skied together. It was nice to ski with someone who was just as happy to ski at my pace.

I did not feel any further direct threats during those days, and although I could sense that many of the group were not happy with me, everyone obeyed my request not to mention the probe incident. I believe also that David was none the wiser about the threat since he did seem distracted or preoccupied with something else. The only other changes were that Theo and Rachael seemed to spend a lot more time near David and me. This was strange, as was David's need for me to give him his own time and space.

Poor Theo tried to pretend that it was his new favourite pastime running down the mountain chasing me, especially when Rachael was enjoying herself off chasing Heather. Eventually, after I had spoken to Daniel, he took pity on Theo and tried to locate some skis for him. He did some research and found that there was a company that had started to make them for the larger of the Dwellers, and they would fit Theo, who was quite large even for a Mountain Dweller. Unfortunately, we could not get the skis to us in time, so he had to remain content with running down the snowy mountains, trying to prevent me from doing myself any permanent damage.

Our evenings were spent wrapped in warm fur-lined blankets, going for sled rides in pairs and groups of four exploring the beautiful surroundings. Occasionally Daniel would disappear for the night. We all presumed that it was to visit his female friend, but none of us asked. As a favour to Daniel we all visited his father's new business, which was a restaurant, for a meal. We all posed with Daniel and his father for various photographers. Daniel looked very much like his father, and his father was obviously very proud of his human son.

We had been at the resort undisturbed for those few days when Heather received a telephone call from the Irish Territories. We were all sitting down enjoying breakfast together when the call came on her private mobile. That was the first clue we had; we knew then that it came from someone she trusted.

She went outside to take the call, and even though I had better than normal hearing, she was either too far away or she was speaking too quietly for me to get any hint of the conversation. Although she was a Dweller, it wasn't always possible to tell if she was excited or not, but when she returned her face was flushed and we could tell that she had been told something exciting. When she had finally composed herself, she said simply, "I believe we have suddenly moved closer to the missing Element than we first thought. It appears that the researchers within the Irish Territories had been given a much more recent photo of my mother accompanied by a young child in the region of mountains, which can be found not far from here. I have requested that they fax us a photograph of the area immediately."

With that, the food we were sharing was left, forgotten, as we all made our way quickly to Daniel's office to wait for the photograph. We didn't have long to wait because it was a matter of a moments before Daniel had a copy of the photograph in his hands. "These mountains are near here—I know them well. However, they have families of their own, and all of us may not be welcome," Daniel said, looking at me.

"Why would I not be welcome?" I asked, sitting away from David.

"Mountain Dwellers are the least forgiving of the races. They have long memories and only remember your race's destruction of their beloved wilderness. They are simpler but no less intelligent," explained Daniel. I believe he added the last comment for Theo's benefit.

"Then only some of us will go, and the others will stay here to protect Liberty," Rachael said, with her hand placed lovingly on Theo's huge shoulder.

I knew what she was already thinking. I knew that she understood that the only ones who could go were Theo and Heather, since as Dwellers they would be more likely to be accepted, if not welcomed. I also knew that Theo would not leave me and that the situation would require some very careful handling. I knew that the sighting was too important for him not to do this, but I also knew I had probably created a situation that would cloud his judgment. I had not felt or sensed the threat since the day I had arrived and was even beginning to wonder if I hadn't overreacted.

"I do not think I would be as welcome as you seem to think, Rachael," Heather said, looking in Theo's direction and understanding that he would need a little persuading.

"That's settled. Theo, you will go, and Rachael will go as your intended mate," David said with a perfectly straight face. I was so relieved that he had read the situation perfectly and had done what needed to be done.

"I can't go," Theo almost shouted as he stood abruptly.

"Might I ask why?" asked David, standing to face Theo, equally serious even though Theo towered over him. They stood there facing each other, both knowing that Theo had no real choice.

"Liberty, is it your wish that I leave you here unprotected?" said Theo, never taking his eyes from David's face.

"She does not have a say. I am her Everlasting Life Partner and therefore am entitled to make this decision for her," snapped David.

I was horrified as I watched them. David had never behaved in that way towards Theo, and as I watched I clung to the idea that David was deliberately behaving in that way to take the decision away from both me and Theo. After a few more seconds of tense silence, Rachael stood beside Theo and placed her hand on his arm.

"Well then, I think I should go and pack some belongings since I am apparently going with you as your intended mate." It took a few moments for the words to sink in, and then a look of almost shy embarrassment slowly crept over Theo's face. He looked so adorable that I got up slowly and went over to him. I knew that he was struggling and the decision would ultimately be mine, but I honestly knew then that I had to stand firmly by David as his Life Partner, as he had done when I had needed him to do the same. I also knew that I would have to do the right thing and send Theo away.

"I will be okay. You know I am well protected, and besides, you have told me yourself that you have a sense of me, especially when I need you," I said as I stood in front of him, willing him to understand and to forgive me. "Now you must go help your intended mate pack," I said, smiling happily at him until he smiled back. I could finally see him soften, but only a little bit. I couldn't stop the lump from forming in my throat, though; I felt as if I had betrayed him since he was my protector. It was what he saw as his role among the group, and I knew without question that had I asked him to stay, he would have stayed with me against David's and even Rachael's wishes. He turned without saying another word and walked towards the door, following Rachael quietly.

I took a step away from David and sat by myself. It wasn't David's fault; I knew he had simply done what was necessary for the quest—even I understood that, yet I already felt a little more vulnerable than I should have and couldn't understand why. Rachael and Theo were back within a few minutes, and they were packed and ready to go. I didn't know what Rachael had said to him, but both of them returned seemingly eager to get started. The good-byes were short and businesslike, with both parties promising to stay in constant contact.

We all stood together waiting for the wolves and sleds to arrive, and then they were gone. As soon as they had settled themselves into the sleds, I turned away and went back into the chalet. I didn't trust myself to stay and watch them as they quickly disappeared from view.

It was Heather who came and sat with me. I could feel my emotions beginning to get the better of me, but when I saw the look on David's face, I swallowed them and tried to smile. We stayed together for a little while, but none of us seemed that willing to make small talk. Eventually when David got up, I got up with him and we held hands. His grip was tender, and I knew that whatever tension had been building between us had finally gone.

Chapter 42

We spent the following day doing pretty much what we had been doing every other day; we all got up and had some nourishment, and then just after noon we went out skiing. It wasn't quite the same because without Theo and Rachael it wasn't as exciting.

I missed the sound of Theo thundering through the trees behind me, running beside me or slightly ahead, trying to anticipate which direction I would be taking and to spot any obstacles before they appeared before me. I missed most of all the feeling of safety that I had when he was around. I felt the same way about not having Rachael there, but for a very different reason. I missed her because she constantly had a knack for stopping me from making a fool of myself; she managed to do that sometimes even without saying anything. I also knew that Heather missed her skiing partner. I tried hard to keep up with her without causing myself an injury, but our hearts were not in it. Their departure left a big hole in my heart that none of the others could fill. I felt strangely incomplete without them and uncomfortable, almost as if I had made the wrong decision in letting the pair of them leave me. There were times when I could shake that feeling of unease off, but as soon as I had a moment to myself it came back again, only worse. It was as if my instincts were trying to warn me of something. My unease remained at the very edges of my consciousness.

Daniel, as if sensing my unease, came to us later that first afternoon after Theo and Rachael had left and announced that he would be inviting a very special guest whom we knew well, an old friend of ours, to join us when we took our nightly nourishment together. Even though we all questioned him throughout the rest of the day, trying hard to discover if the visitor might be his mysterious new female friend, Daniel remained quiet and refused to give us any further information, just promising us a surprise.

We all knew that, whoever it was, that it would be someone good, someone whom Daniel trusted to be among us, and that went a little way to distract me, cheer me up, and make me feel better. Daniel also requested that we dress in formal attire for the meal, and with that final comment I was positively intrigued. I thought that perhaps whoever it was might be someone he would commit himself to. I momentarily wondered whether he had arranged for Mia to join us for a little while just to cheer me up. It made sense to me, but I didn't tell any of the others what I was thinking, just in case I was wrong. These were the only two things I could think of to explain the formality of Daniel's request.

The thought of the meal seemed to lift our entire mood and gave us something else to focus on rather than the gap left by Theo and Rachael. We finished skiing earlier than we normally would, all of us eager to get ready for something different, something good, something new and exciting.

I spent what felt like hours with Heather going through our clothes trying to find something that would be considered formal. I had left most of my formalwear back in the Irish Territories with Janet. Janet knew that, because of my connection with Mia, it would probably be a good idea to have a basic wardrobe of clothes kept there for me. I knew she would have all the rest of them packed and sent back to the castle.

After a lot of indecision, I finally opted for a classic vampire look, a look I knew suited me and one that David liked very much. I decided to wear a tight crimson bodice pulled over a sheer black flowing shirt and tight black trousers with crimson lace detail running up the outer sides of my legs. I pulled my hair back dramatically off my face and wore dark makeup to emphasise my distinctly coloured eyes. Heather wore a more traditional Forest Dweller gown of emerald green that flowed and moved with her. She let her hair flow loosely around her shoulders, wearing a burnished metal tiara, intricately woven with crystal jewels, to keep it off her face. She looked every inch a princess. I knew just by looking at her that we really had found the true representative of her race. It finally dawned on me then that Mia was absolutely right: that it was Heather who was meant to go forward with us on our journey to find the scripts and missing Sky Dweller. It probably always had been.

When Cassius saw us he smiled, came forward immediately, and took Heather's hand. David looked wonderfully handsome in a crimson flowing shirt that was so sheer it was almost see-through, the fine gold threads woven throughout it shimmering in the evening light and showing off the ripples of his chest muscles as he moved.

As soon as he came over to me, he planted a huge kiss on my lips and said, "Very nice," obviously appreciating what he saw as I approached. He gave me goose pimples as he always did when he whispered that soft way in my ear. "I think I would like to feel a little tired tonight. Perhaps you should bring me back early," I whispered back, giggling at the effect he had on me. He smiled and nodded in eager agreement, and then he held me close as we waited for all of our friends to gather.

When all the others of the group joined us, they all looked as handsome as always, all attired similarly as royal bodyguards. For the first time since Theo and Rachael had left, everyone had smiles on their faces, and that was good to see.

We didn't have to wait long before one of Daniel's chalet masters came to escort us to the main chalet, which, throughout the afternoon and early evening, had been specially decorated for the occasion. When I saw the chalet I felt a brief shiver of déjà vu because it was decorated in the reds and golds of my family. The chalet reminded me for a brief second of the Arena, the place in which the direction of my life had been decided when I was a child. As I walked forward I felt a sense of unease, but it faded after a moment and I didn't think much more of it; it disappeared so fast that I thought it was merely me spooking myself, and I smiled at my own silliness as I continued forward with David.

When David felt my hesitation, I felt him tense up. Although he had no idea that I had felt a threat on my arrival, we were both conscious that Theo and Rachael were not behind us to protect our backs. I knew he would protect me, but David was also going to be the emperor of the planet one day, and the threat may well have been against him. Although I had better senses than most humans, I was pretty certain that I would not be of much use to him as protection. I managed to throw off these worries, though, for the time being, and with a reassuring smile for David I continued to walk forward towards the chalet with him, his arm protectively placed around my shoulder.

The chalet was bright and welcoming inside, and it appeared that Daniel had gone to a lot of effort for us to enjoy ourselves so I made a promise to enjoy myself. With Daniel's guidance we were seated at two tables placed next to each other, and when we were settled we were all given drinks to start the evening while we waited for the surprise guest.

The drink was sweet and warming, its flavour not unlike the drink that I had tasted at Mia's Commitment celebrations. This time, however, knowing the drink's previous effect on me, I merely sipped it. We sat and chatted among ourselves, and the topic mainly seemed to centre on Theo and Rachael. The conversation was no longer focused on their progress in finding Mother Lillie and Molly but on the fact that Rachael had not argued or protested when being called Theo's intended mate; in fact, neither of them had reacted at all.

The drinks we were served helped us all to relax. They were free-flowing, and before long even the normally quiet James and Alex were chatting and laughing. The mood in the room was happy and laid-back, as if we all had left whatever worries we'd had at the entrance.

I felt free, safe, and loved, wrapped up in the smiles and mood of my friends. Everyone was giggling and making silly comments, but soon my feelings of uneasiness returned. This time they were even stronger than before. My head filled with alarm bells as if someone or something was trying to reach me. I closed my eyes for a second just to clear my mind, and when I opened them again something had changed: the mood in the room had a falseness to it. I didn't feel as if it was all real; the entire atmosphere that surrounded me had changed. It took me a while to understand that the room was glamoured.

Once I realised that their behaviour was wrong, I stopped laughing and tried to concentrate, to clear my head, knowing that there was definitely something wrong. The safeness I had felt slipped away suddenly, and I felt alone and unprotected. I noticed then that Heather had also stopped laughing and was staring at me with an odd expression on her face; I registered fear and confusion in her eyes, seeing that her mood too had drastically changed.

I turned to David, who was laughing with Cassius beside me, hoping to distract him, to try to understand what was happening. When loud classical music started playing outside the chalet and the lights were lowered, Daniel left the table next to ours and we knew that his guest must have finally arrived. There was something different about him as well. He was not laughing as much as the others and seemed to be distracted. As the lights dimmed I felt the mood of anticipation heighten, and then Daniel and his guest stood in silhouette.

As the lights lifted I found myself unable to move. I suddenly felt a huge weight settle on my chest, knocking all the air from my lungs until I couldn't breathe. The feeling was well-known to me; it was the feeling that as a child I had first understood as fear. Daniel's special guest was Miranda, the sister of the royal princes Samuel and George from the British Territories, the twins who had almost succeeded in killing me. I wanted to scream, but I couldn't. I wanted to shout, to warn everyone, but I was helpless. I tried hard to get David's attention, but I couldn't. He seemed suddenly too tired to care about me or anything.

I looked at the other vampires, my protectors, and they all seemed to be in the same state. The only other one who sensed that we were in danger was Heather, and I saw that she knew who had just entered the chalet. Although she was a Dweller and so much more than human, she was well away from her beloved forests, the only place where she could have been strong enough to overcome a vampire. Heather looked to be struggling just as hard as I was, and I saw her turn to say something perhaps to warn Cassius, but Cassius was still laughing hard and definitely not registering that anything was wrong. Time within the chalet started to slow itself down, and my terror continued to build.

I tried to send my thoughts to the others, but their minds were as erratic as their behaviour had been. It was as if their minds had been filled with a dense fog. I felt angry with them and myself, at how stupid and complacent we had become. As my darkness tried to stir within me, I understood that I had begun to rely on others too much, that it had been too long since I had relied on my own strengths to protect myself. I didn't understand how, but I knew that those who would normally protect me had been made vulnerable.

Miranda looked much the same as I remembered her. She was actually still wearing the same gown that she had worn to my Commitment Ceremony. When she saw me, she gave me a wide, menacing smile, and I could almost hear her humming to herself, congratulating herself because she had planned this and knew that I was now unprotected.

It crossed my mind then that perhaps the message regarding the sighting of Mother Earth, Ana, and Molly in the mountains near to the resort was true. Miranda had been a step ahead of us all the time. I understood then that it had been she who had sliced at my mind at the airport, and she had probably watched me when I was out skiing. "This cannot be possible. You were taken away," I said, mostly to myself since there was no point in continuing trying to alert the others.

Apparently Miranda knew what I was muttering. "Yes, and we were given other options, thanks to you," she said, smiling at me with the same poisonous smile that I remembered. "Shall we have some light?" She led a still smiling Daniel into the centre of the room. I don't know whether he sensed a change in the atmosphere within the room, but Daniel's smile faltered as if he too were trying to fight against something he knew to be unnatural. It was painful to watch these beings, my friends and protectors of utter strength, become so powerless, so weak.

As the lights in the chalet grew brighter, I noticed that we were surrounded by black-clad humans. I had seen humans like that before because they ran the Enclosures for the vampires; they were called 'disciples.' When Miranda saw me shrink back against my chair, she laughed quietly to herself.

"You have no idea what favour you have done us, have you, Princess, or the world of resources you have put at our disposal?" she said, now laughing out loud.

As I studied the creature in front of me, I shuddered and looked away, glancing around at the statue-still disciples. It was then that I noticed the most disturbing thing of all: none of them, Miranda or her human escorts, had souls. All of them had eyes that were black and empty, and I understood then that they must have given Elathan their souls freely in order to ensure their survival. The air surrounding me turned cold, and I felt my fear trickle down into my darkness, hoping that it would not release itself now, feeling that I would most certainly die if it did.

I thought of Elathan. Instinctively I placed my hand over the fine mesh bangle that still remained seemingly invisible, and at that moment of clarity, when the danger surrounding me appeared frozen in time, I hated him. I hoped that the bangle held some type of link between us and that he felt my hatred. My darkness within me was stirring, but I knew that without the full awareness and support of the vampires, I would lose. I don't know what I thought was going to happen when Elathan had removed them from the castle that night, but I didn't think I would encounter them ever again. I trusted him and thought he had made me safe.

My thoughts returned to the present as I was pulled to my feet and dragged by a disciple towards Miranda. There was no point in trying to struggle since I was not strong enough to put up any resistance.

"I believe my brothers cannot wait for you to join them again, especially George, who has missed your sweet and strong, but very human, mind," she said as she placed a cold, dead hand on the back of my neck. Heather was the only one who reacted, the only one who had moved to help me, but she was grabbed and hit so hard she was knocked unconscious to the floor by one of the disciples that surrounded us.

"Thank you, Daniel. Why don't you go and join your friends? You have served me well." Daniel moved as if he were her pet, his face once again filled with serene happiness at her words.

"Where is he? Where is your protector now, Princess?" she whispered in my ear as I felt her talons dig into the soft skin of my neck, the pressure painful and piercing my skin.

"I do not doubt him, Miranda, and neither should you. He will come for me, and he will tear this planet apart finding you," I said, believing my words and knowing that I could not give up, knowing that, without exception, all of the beings who knew me would do the same, but especially Theo.

"Touching, but your friends are beginning to awaken to their situation, and while I am confident in my strength and certain my brothers are also growing impatient, I believe the time has come for us to depart." As she said the words, I could see that David and the others were beginning to come round. I could sense them trying to push back at the fog that dulled their minds; their attempts were almost childlike and confused. It was Alex who first appeared to recognise the situation and the danger we all were in as he sat upright. I could see the self-disgust register on his face, and as his mind cleared I sent the thought that he had no time for self-blame, that he had to stay calm, to think, to help me. It took just a few seconds for everyone else to register what had happened and the dangerous situation they were in.

We started to move towards the chalet door. As I reached up to try to lessen the pressure on my neck, the bangle on my arm must have accidentally brushed Miranda's skin. As it did I felt an almost searing heat, and apparently so did Miranda, who quickly pulled her hand away. "What was that!" she hissed at me. I stayed silent.

We stayed by the door while she rubbed at a red patch of skin that had appeared near her hand. It appeared to irritate her, but not enough to stop her.

Chapter 43

A second later I became more aware of what was happening with my vampires. The channels to their minds were finally beginning to clear of the sense-numbing malaise. While I registered what was happening with them, another part of me, perhaps my darkness within, felt something else. I felt as if the bangle on my wrist was trying to perhaps command my attention. There seemed to be a strange life within it, one I had never felt or experienced before. I clamped my hand over it, hoping to prevent its exposure, unsure whether that was what I should do or not. I did not have time to dwell on it further because the beings I loved were almost fully awake and suddenly on their feet, all of them ready and willing to fight again to protect me. I knew that each of them, though, was in incredible danger and feared that their newfound 'emotions' may be clouding their usually cold and analytical judgment. It took a moment for them to understand that the moment for heroic rescues had already passed, that they could not prevent Miranda from damaging me. As the realisation sank in they all became statue still, waiting for someone to make the next move.

The atmospheric silence became eerie within the room. I felt helpless and angry, knowing that the situation was impossible for them. Miranda seemed to anticipate and even enjoy their sudden snap back into reality; she appeared to find their looks of confusion amusing. There was a cruel confidence in her laughter because she knew that she could afford to laugh; she had planned this whole thing very well, knowing that to them I was a prize worth protecting and that it was she who held my life in her cold, dead fingers. She knew she had the upper hand. For every one vampire there seemed many more of the black-uniformed Disciples. It got worse. As the vampires began to move, more of the Disciples seemed to swarm into the room. In the confusion they continued to fill the chalet like a swarm of black poisonous insects, removing the light and making the room's already dark atmosphere even darker with their presence. They brought to the room a claustrophobia that almost took my breath away.

After a few seconds of watching my vampires preparing themselves for attack, Miranda suddenly shouted, "Stop! Or she will die now by my hand. It is your decision to make my lords. Therefore, I suggest you choose wisely what your next actions will be." Her voice resounded throughout the room with the cold cruelty that had been present in her laughter, leaving me with no doubts that she would do exactly what she threatened, even if it meant upsetting her brothers.

I actually took a second to think about her words and almost reacted, thinking that a quick death from her would be infinitely less painful than anything I would experience at the hands of her brothers. Again I cursed Elathan, feeling idiotic because of the blind trust I had placed in him. How could I have trusted a creature that ruled the realms beneath this world? He was the Lord of Darkness and was never meant to be trusted. No sooner had those thoughts entered my mind when I thought I heard his laughter and the whispered words ringing within: *At last you understand. Now be patient, Princess, all is in hand.*

Miranda was still holding me by my neck. She had forgotten the irritation on her skin from my bangle in the excitement. When my beloved protectors did not appear to hear her, instead of addressing them again directly, she tightened her grip hard enough for me to gasp. Everyone seemed to freeze when they heard me. They froze where they were and turned their full attention to Miranda and me.

"Disciples, come to me," she said quietly. The black-clad army began to close ranks, moving closer, smothering us in a claustrophobic wall of darkness. When the final one had joined us, Miranda produced what appeared to be a small, silver-looking ball from one of the folds of her dress and started to throw it up into the air. As the Disciples began to separate to clear a path for us, she made sure the silver ball could be seen, attracting the attention of every vampire in the room. The ball was about the size of a large jewel, and although it did not look as if it would do much damage, I knew that if it were silver then the quantity was enough to kill any vampire, no matter how big or how powerful they were.

Again I felt cold with fear, but this time it was for them, not me. I tried to speak to warn them, to tell them to stop and stay where they were, that they were in danger too, but the pain in my neck made it impossible to think, let alone speak. I noticed after a few seconds that David and the others had all become focused on that ball in the palm of her hand and that all of them appeared to lean back, away from Miranda's now still and outstretched hand.

"You know what this can do. I wonder which one of you will catch this for your beloved little prince?" As she said the words she threw the ball of silver directly at David. Her throw was accurate and too fast for the eye to follow. What happened then I will never forget. I will be haunted by the memory for all of my existence. Daniel threw himself in front of David, and although he was slower than all of the others, he knew he was the only one who could be sacrificed. The lethal ball hit Daniel in the centre of his chest. As the ball entered his body, it must have disintegrated because as Daniel fell to the floor, liquid silver began to ooze from the wound. His breathing became loud and pained. He gave us his life.

As I saw him fall I screamed silently, the pressure of Miranda's fingers preventing me from calling out. The only thought that brushed through my mind was that Daniel, my Daniel, had died because of me. I felt a cloud of depression begin to wash over me and, to make it worse, I heard Miranda laugh. A deep sob escaped from my chest.

As he fell I could see from the look in his eyes that he understood that he was dying, but he still managed to let me know he was sorry, his mouth working hard to form the words as he began to slip away. I looked back at him and tried to communicate the love I felt, and had always felt, for him. I tried to let him know that the fault wasn't his; it was mine. There was nothing to forgive him for.

I stopped moving, trying to calm myself as I started to remove the barriers I had created, not caring then who knew about my secret darkness. Miranda must have sensed me because she squeezed my neck even harder, shaking me until I lost my concentration. Dark spots began to appear in my vision as I started to lose consciousness.

"My brothers warned me that there is more to you, human, but that was not my only weapon. Do you want another demonstration? Are you ready to be responsible for another death?" she whispered in my ear. Knowing that I didn't want any more of my loved ones to die, my barriers began to mould themselves back into place, almost without effort; such was the control I now had over my self-induced restraints.

But Miranda's will and strength were strong, and I fell back into a blackness of despair. I could feel the last remnants of my strength and resolve leave. Finally, the only thing that stopped me from falling to the floor was Miranda's grip on my neck.

I do not know how long I remained unconscious, but slowly the blackness started to recede and I felt my senses return; in a way I wished they hadn't because the first thing I heard clearly was Heather crying for Daniel. I was thankful that one of us was able to kneel with him as he died. (Just as silver didn't dangerously affect me, it didn't affect her or any of the other Dwellers.)

"You have seen what can happen, and now I suggest you all stay exactly where you are. This creature has been invited to a very different meal especially organised by my brothers, and I do not wish to keep them waiting any longer," Miranda said with a sneer as she started to turn towards the door. "Oh, and I am aware that you cherish her, so just in case you decide to follow when my back is turned, I have given each of the ten Disciples standing in front of you a silver ball to throw if you move." As she said the last sentence, she started to laugh again and then picked me off the floor as if I weighed nothing. As we moved swiftly forward, my neck felt as if it was being stretched almost to its breaking point. It was clear she was also trying to provoke my friends to move, to take a fatal step towards us. And then, as we were about to close the door, she turned again, as if she had changed her mind about something.

"I think we will stay a little while longer to hear how precious you really are," Miranda said. She then addressed the others, who still stood in terror. "Each of you in turn will state who you would rather save, your prince or this creature who has caused so much pain among you." As she said the word "prince," she bowed slightly, still showing the future ruler of the planet a modicum of respect. I knew that there could only be one answer that they could give, but I knew it would still be hard to hear them say their choices out loud.

"You do not have to make them do this. I will go with you wherever you want me to now," I said quietly.

"Oh, but I do, just to demonstrate how precious you really are to them. Speak again and I will have you punished," she hissed, still smiling and looking at the others, waiting. The silence in the room seemed to stretch on for a long time.

"Well?" she persisted.

The first one who spoke was Cassius. He simply said, "Prince David." As I said before, I was glad he was David's closest friend and bodyguard. His answer was the only one I expected from him. As I would have anticipated, Alex and James both said the same, "Prince David." I knew that they had been palace guards for centuries before they had become my royal guards.

Then, through her tears and obvious rage, Heather tried to speak up. I knew she was going to say my name, but Miranda snarled at her that she was not worthy of that type of decision. She informed Heather that her 'kind' was barely better than the humans. And then there was silence again. I knew it was only a couple of seconds, but that was enough. Miranda laughed at us all again and turned and pulled me out through the door with her. I understood they had all done and said the right thing. I knew that David had a duty to the planet and the emperor's throne, and that his life was infinitely more important than mine. I wasn't even given the chance to look back at him, but I knew he would try to find me, that he would go back and raise an army and that the emperor would tear the planet apart looking for me.

I felt tears begin to trickle down my cheeks; as Miranda laughed, her stale breath made me want to pull away from her. Although her lips and teeth were precariously close to my ear, I was no longer in fear for myself and my tears were not because of the fate that awaited me. I did not care for myself anymore; I could not even contemplate what she and her brothers had in mind for me, but it didn't matter now. The tears were for poor Daniel, who was still lying barely alive, with his head cradled gently on Heather's lap, and the for the others who were so helpless and angry, no doubt chastising themselves severely for the situation Miranda had so easily manipulated all of us into.

Miranda's grip on me lessened slightly as she dragged me from the chalet, paying no heed to anything that was in the way. Once outside she didn't appear to feel the need to be quite so dramatic with her handling of me and lowered me slightly so I could put my feet on the floor and walk. As the cold air hit me, I finally felt nothing. The tears had stopped and the fear that was beginning to rise was numbing. With a dreadful certainty I knew as I left the others behind that I was alone, again unprotected, in a very dangerous world. I dug my nails. I didn't want to give up, but it was seemingly impossible not to. An ironic thought crossed my mind: *I am only human.*

I didn't even attempt to struggle against my abductors as leather restraints were wound tightly around my wrists and a hessian hood was placed over my head. There was no point in being anything but compliant. I knew that if I struggled or made another sound of pain or protest, it would only give one of them an excuse to inflict more pain on me.

After a few moments more I felt a sharp pain at the crease of my left arm as Miranda whispered to me that she wanted to deliver me in 'reasonably good condition' to her brothers, who were very much looking forward to seeing me again. As she spoke her whispers sounded hollow and her voice seemed to come from farther and farther away. I tried to concentrate, but my head started to feel heavy and with every step forward it became harder and harder to move my feet; they started dragging as I felt myself drifting into a forced sleep. Finally, the light behind my eyes went black as I started to lose consciousness. My knees buckled and I stumbled, but before I could fall, strong arms grabbed me and stopped my body from falling to the ground. I believe I was then placed in a sled and wrapped in furs.

I really can't tell you how long I travelled that way. The heat from the furs was suffocating me and drenching me in sweat.

Although I had no real concept of time, I am certain that we travelled for more than a day and a night. I was surrounded by blackness and had very little concept of what was happening, but I was positive that the sled stopped more than once. Fighting whatever had been injected into my bloodstream, I tried to listen for a clue as to where I was going. I managed to tap into my inner strength and became resolved that I was not ready to give up on anything yet. My growing anger helped; it helped that I felt every emotional and physical pain that occurred as a direct result of Miranda and her twin brothers' intrusion into my previous, and seemingly untroubled and happy, life.

Finally, we stopped again, and even though I could not make out what was happening, I felt the Disciples in my sled leave and others take over guarding me. I heard lots of movements and noises that sounded like grunts, but no words that I could recognise. There was nothing for me to do but wait for whatever fate they had decided for me.

Not long afterwards I felt the sled dip as the Disciples mounted it again, and we started to move once more. I could feel the sled turn sharply as we appeared to change direction and continue at a much faster speed.

I could barely contain my moans as the sled bounced along on some uneven ground. I tried to reposition myself in an effort to minimise the knocks I was receiving from the sides, but every time I tried to force myself into a semi-upright position, I felt a hand roughly push me lower into the sled. To weigh me down further, more covers were piled on top of me and around the sides of the sled, curtailing any further movement. Someone hissed "Be silent" as they pushed me farther down.

I was raw from being battered around the sled. Everything hurt; my hands and feet had gone beyond numbness into a continuous level of excruciating pain, so much so that by the time the sled stopped, I felt it would be a relief for me to be released from this planet. I was very weak and bruised when I was lifted from the sled and dragged into what sounded and smelled like a castle, or at least an old stone building.

I felt every lump in the uneven floor, the pain travelling in waves through my battered feet and up my legs to settle in the pit of my stomach, making me want to vomit. Soon, through the

291

darkness of my hood, I thought that I could envision a room with a slab for a bed and no window. My mind told me that my life had come full circle, and that I was back in some type of Enclosure.

My hands and feet were unbound, and the rush of blood back into them caused another wave of nausea to rush over me. My hood was removed by a being that stood behind me. I presumed it was a Disciple, so I didn't even bother to look. Instead I took an excruciating step forward into what I assumed would be my prison until the brothers arrived. As the door slammed shut behind me, I did the thing that I usually did when I wanted to let go of my emotions: I cried for a long time. I didn't make any noise but just let the tears come.

When it seemed impossible to cry anymore, when I had no more tears, I lay on the concrete floor and fell into a more natural but restless sleep, exhaustion finally overruling my emotion.

Chapter 44

At first my sleep was full of nightmares, my mind recalling the power and pain of George's first intrusion into my head. I had hoped that my mind would bury the memory deep enough for it never to be recalled, but unfortunately that was obviously not the case. I remembered vividly that they had tried unsuccessfully to penetrate my innermost mind before they almost killed me with poison. Although I knew I was now much stronger both mentally and physically and able to withstand the most intrusive probes, those thoughts and nightmares ran through my dreams, gathering an immobilising fear. I finally lost even that and fell into a deep, desperate sleep. When I finally woke up, I was drenched in my own sweat. I felt as if every connecting muscle and sinew that held me together from my head to my feet was deeply bruised and hurt. After a few agonisingly and tenuous stretches, however, nothing felt as if it had been permanently damaged.

I tried to breathe deeply, and despite all of my pain and fear I opened my eyes very slowly, allowing them to adjust to my unfamiliar surroundings; even the dull light caused me to hesitate. I lay there for an unknown quantity of time and stared at the grey stone ceiling, continuing to take deep breaths and trying to focus on the seriousness of my situation and what was probably going to happen.

I believed I was in control of my emotions, although the memories of what had happened when I was last with my friends came flooding back, and with them came a new rush of fear and panic. I lay there for a few more moments, chastising myself for my very predictable weaknesses and trying to draw on examples from my loved ones for inspiration. I managed to get myself to move and pushed myself up into a sitting position, feeling sweat develop on my forehead with the effort. As I sat leaning with my back against the cold wall, I tried to calm myself again. I observed that my clothes were torn and filthy. The disapproval Mia and Rachael would have felt at seeing me in this state made me smile briefly. For some reason little thoughts like these were making me calmer still.

I realised that nothing good comes from panicking. No clear thoughts enter my head when I am panicked, so I regained control of my beating heart, almost forcing it to beat slower and with more strength in my chest. After a few moments my heart slowed and my breathing quieted.

I studied the bruises on my hands and ankles for something else to distract me from my surroundings. I found it mildly interesting that the bruises were varying sizes and colours, ranging from deep purples to angry reds. Even though my hands had been tied together, none of the bruises on either wrist were the same.

After a few more moments I forced myself to look up and scan the room. It was some type of cell. There wasn't even a tap under which I could clean my face and wipe the tiredness from my mind. It was clearly a standard Enclosure accommodation.

There appeared to be no door at first, nothing but just grey walls. I felt my tenuous strength begin to slip; it was as if I had been dropped into a concrete box. I was convinced that no one would come to help me if I called to them, verbally or with my mind. I strained to listen outside of that grey stone room, but there was no noise that I recognised; at least I heard nothing at first. I don't know exactly how long I sat there as the silence surrounded me like a damp, heavy cloak, weighing me down and forcing me to lie down. I closed my eyes, trying to find peace on some level. I cannot tell you how much time passed before I heard a key turn in the door somewhere to the left of me. I sat up slowly, trying hard to concentrate. I realised that the door must have also been made of concrete, which was why I hadn't noticed it at first. I smiled wryly to myself as I realised that unmarked and unhandled doors were a common feature within certain Enclosure buildings.

As the dark gap in the wall widened, I used my legs to push myself upright, leaning against the wall beside the door for support, and waited, knowing that whoever entered would be the deciding factor in my fate.

The concrete room was still in semi-darkness, so I had to focus all my energy to see who was entering my room. I held my breath as the door silently opened wide enough for someone to step through and reveal himself or herself. I tensed myself as the being entered the room. As I expected, it was dressed in all black, a hood partially covering its face. As it took as step towards me, though, I caught a glimpse of its face. I knew then, somewhere deep within myself, that I was being saved!

I felt my knees begin to buckle and my mind suddenly go blank; thoughts of capture and death began to dissolve and change. I understood then that I was no longer the one in a precarious position. But the ordeal had weakened me horribly, and despite the tiny glimmer of hope I had felt when the being entered the door, I felt myself falling again, my strength finally failing me completely. My back began to slide down the rough, cold stone, but before I could touch the hard floor again, I felt some strong, thickly gloved hands catch me and lift me effortlessly into the air. The person who held me smelled of leather and decay, but I clung to the being as if he or she were someone dear.

"Lillith," I managed to say weakly as she held me gently, almost cradling me with her tenderness.

"Yes, Princess," she said softly in response. "You may rest for a while, but only for a short while. I will give you some much needed peace now, without the disturbance of thought, because I want you to be awake and strong for your long awaited visitors. You must face them again, but not as a victim this time. You must face them as an adversary. We have been tracking the movements of some of our kind with curiosity, and Miranda came to our immediate notice the moment she connected with the trinket you wear on your wrist. The actions of her and her brothers have displeased their master. It is his will that things are allowed to develop this way. Although I recognise your torment and would have them eliminated immediately, you need first to remain stronger for a short while longer, Princess, because my master has insisted that you are to be allowed your own role in their demise." Her soft, whispered voice, almost tender, penetrated the fogginess in my head.

"My master also sends you this message: He asks you to consider the request you gave him before your Commitment Ceremony, and he states that within your request you simply wanted the brothers gone. That is what he did exactly—he removed them from your life. You know he will not ask for your forgiveness, but he senses your anger and he asks for your understanding. Surprisingly, it appears that your thoughts and feelings are important to him." I managed a small smile as I detected a little sarcasm within the female's voice, perhaps even a little jealousy. Even though I should have been afraid, I wasn't because I knew that on some level we had connected; the Princess of the World Beneath had decided I was tolerable. It was a title that Lillith had acquired since she had been rescued and nurtured by, and now sat at the right side of, Elathan. As far as I knew, she had no soul and did not wish to have one. She would not have hesitated to kill me if my path had crossed hers in another way or if I had been unprotected, but because of Elathan's curiosity with regard to me, I was safe.

As I felt myself being lowered gently onto the slab of concrete that functioned as a bed, I began to drift off towards sleep. I carefully kept my expression neutral as I suddenly heard the voice of Sarah.

Child, be cautious. She appeared to be warning me of the presence of demons. She sounded upset, and I wanted to comfort her or quieten her. Even in my tired state I tried to tell her that I knew them, that I knew the demons that were near and that everything was going to be all right, but I wasn't sure if she heard me.

I felt Sarah leave after the overwhelmingly disapproving silence that followed my revelation that I knew them and that I was safe now. As I was covered with some blankets, I tried to push the thoughts of her away and concentrate on one voice only, the voice that was in the room with me. I did exactly what the soft whispered voice suggested and allowed myself to finally drift off to sleep again.

I do not remember anything for a while. The sleep I had was absolute because it was black and dream-free, as Lillith had promised me, with no thoughts or voices to disturb me. Though I knew that Lillith had played a part in my sleep, I did not know how nor how much; there had no sedative. It was almost as if my subconscious feared the consequences of disobeying her as much my awake self did. Although my sleep was deep, it wasn't for very long. I tried hard to wake up, and awareness did come, but reluctantly. I felt that I needed more to heal myself before I dealt with anything else on the planet.

When I did finally wake up fully, I was still in a concrete room, but this time I seemed to be lying on something different, something soft, something that made the pains that tormented me throughout my body lessen. I stretched slowly, straightening most of the aches and pains out of my limbs, and looked up to see Lillith standing silently watching me. Her face was a still mask with no real expression, nothing to give me the slightest idea how she felt about rescuing me and about the favour her master appeared to show me.

Her brother, Dominic, was sitting on the floor beside her, his eyes closed and his breathing slow and even. I guessed rightly that it was probably Dominic who had provided the soft blankets for me to lie on, basing my guess on the fact that he was known to be kinder and less poisonous than his sister.

As I moved about slightly, I knew that they were layers of warm fur blankets. I wanted to stay where I was for as long as possible. I tried to keep my eyes closed and pretend for as long as I could that my level of consciousness hadn't changed much, but I knew she was watching me.

"Wake now, Princess. My master would like you to be returned to where you belong as soon as possible. He has told me that he misses you within the castle walls, but if we are to obey all of his requests, it appears that we have much to take care of before we see him again," Lillith said.

As soon as I heard her voice, I gave up trying to pretend and started to open my eyes. I then opened them wide to try and remove all of the dirt and grit that had accumulated since my capture. I sat up slowly and carefully, realising then that hunger pains were actually helping to clear my head.

"What needs to be done?" was all I could manage to ask as my eyes finally adjusted to the unchanging greyness within my room.

Dominic chose to answer. "Before we speak, or rather explain our presence, I can sense that you have many questions, but before my sister and I answer any of them, I suggest that you eat. I hope that what has been gathered is sufficient right now. I have been schooled in all your needs by my master."

As soon as he spoke, I realised that I could suddenly smell freshly cooked meat and forgot everything else. I was ferociously hungry. As soon as Dominic had spoken, a Disciple entered the room carrying a tray that seemed to be overflowing with food of all types, almost as if the person providing the food did not know what I liked and had simply provided me with everything I had ever tasted.

I sat myself up and pushed the blankets away, making room for the tray to be placed by my side. As soon as it was, I started breaking off pieces of bread and meat and putting small pieces of food into my mouth. It was unbelievably delicious, yet my stomach still continued to give me pain. Because of the variety the food was so plain, so different from the toast and jam that I had called my favourite; I had the strangest thoughts then that for a being who was supposed to be free, I had experienced very little freedom.

I appeared to be almost back in a place where my life had been, shaped in readiness for my life outside. How many more times would I have to be brought back to the beginning to learn lessons on how to deal with beings that would see me harmed, the beginning where I was a mere human and someone else's to manipulate.

Lillith broke my train of thought and started to explain some things to me. "This place is also unknown to us, but a loyal subject—who will be rewarded for her observation skills—managed to get a message to the castle after overhearing a whispered conversation at the mountain resort, and here we are. You have been given more than one gift that is recognisable by my master's followers." She smiled at me, but instead of finding her smile comforting, I found it a little frightening.

It took a while for everything to stop spinning and for me to understand that I was safe, but I was glad when they sent the Disciple away with the almost empty tray. As I looked back at Lillith and Dominic, I could not shake the feeling that somehow I was being placed further in Elathan's debt. My thoughts then turned fully towards Elathan and who had found me; some strange part of me was happy, glad that he had done this. I did not know, though, how I felt about the whole adventure, or how everyone whom I held dear would feel about it, but I decided that Elathan would not be a secret anymore. I wanted him to be a part of my life. I knew that he could and would help me understand the darkness that rested deep within me, and that he understood better than any of my family ever would. I needed someone to help me understand.

I knew that Miranda must have seen and recognised the darkness—either that or her brothers had kept her well informed. Otherwise she would not have given me things to make me feel so heavy and my thoughts unclear. It would be dangerous for another being to manipulate me into using my darkness without being able to control it. The thought that the deep darkness within me was something that I did not have to suppress with Elathan made me feel almost relieved.

"Would you mind if I used the bathroom?" I asked politely, steadying myself as I stood up.

"Not at all, Princess, and perhaps you would consider changing into some more appropriate clothing. We are not that different physically, and my master took the liberty of sending us one of the many pairs of soft boots that you appear to have accumulated at the castle." There was no smile on Lillith's face as she commented on the number of soft boots I had at home, just the slightest of frowns. I knew that if we were ever going to know each other on a deeper level, I would have to show her the benefits of having more than one outfit to choose from.

Without a word the silent Disciple came forward again, and although I did not want to be touched by any of them, I found I had to take the offered arm in order to walk. I kept the contact to the minimum.

I managed to use the bathroom, which was the room next to mine. To make myself feel a little better, I splashed icy water on my face, the coldness forcing me to take a few deep breaths in. I tried to make the best of myself as the vampires did; the demons, I now knew, always appeared to be immaculately beautiful.

I changed quickly into clothes that were not dissimilar to Lillith's. With my flimsy party clothes replaced by more practical, warmer leather trousers and a long-sleeved top, I suddenly felt strong again, ready to aid Lillith and her brother in setting the trap.

Lillith had supplied me with a bag full of what appeared to be random makeup and feminine products, which I knew instinctively she had gathered from various females she had encountered. I used what I needed, choosing a natural healthy look that I suppose I could have called my own, neither vampire nor human; it was *my* look. I had in that prison finally found a look that reflected me. I found a small mirror to aid me, and as I studied myself I noticed that the crimson in my eyes appeared darker, denser—almost overtaking the blue.

Chapter 45

When I was returned to the cell, Lillith appeared not to have moved from the position in which I had left her; her back was against the wall and she was staring off into space, casually smiling to herself. It was a while before I realised that when she was motionless, she was more than likely communicating with Elathan and other beings of her kind.

Dominic also appeared to be speaking to himself, as he continued to offer his words of explanation as to what had brought us all to that place. In fact, it seemed as if he hadn't stopped speaking since I had left the room.

"What is going to happen now?" I asked him, trying not to show how frightened I was by his unusual behaviour and Lillith's detachment.

"We have been told to wait here for the arrival of the twins. Obviously, the sister will be keeping us company while we wait," Dominic replied, smiling slowly as if he was enjoying some internal humour. His voice, though, sounded slightly menacing to me.

"But I need to let my loved ones know that I am safe," I said, already beginning to feel as if my ordeal wasn't quite over and there was more danger to come.

"That is not possible just yet, Princess. We cannot open the lines of communication to those on the upper levels of the castle. They would not understand what needs to happen now. My master requests—in fact, he insists—that you remain patient in this matter."

Although I didn't understand, I simply nodded as if I did, knowing that there was nothing I could do even if I wanted to contact them. "Where is Miranda now?" I asked, trying to take my mind off my loved ones.

"We took her shortly after you left the chalet. We had to get close enough to her so that we could shield her thoughts from those of her brothers who are now on their way here, unhappy that she is no longer communicating with them clearly."

"But where is she now? Would I be able to see her?" I persisted. I didn't know why, but I just wanted to see her in a position of helplessness. There was something within me that needed to be satisfied. Lillith, who I knew had been watching me with renewed interest, not unlike the type of interest Rachael had shown me when I had exceeded expectations as a child, smiled knowingly.

When I glanced at her she appeared to have recognition in her eyes, and as I could feel the darkness within stir restlessly, she smiled her approval and again I felt something connect between us.

"Yes, perhaps it is time you face her, although as we venture out into this complex place, I ask you not to be afraid. Do not let your purpose falter because they have put in place many surprises designed to test your sanity as well as your strength," Dominic said, coming forward to offer me a heavy fur-lined cloak. His words made me feel an inner cold that sent fresh shivers down my spine, and I quickly accepted the cloak, which was soft and warm and strangely comforting. It smelled of earth and soil.

As we stepped out into the corridor I stumbled, with only Dominic's strong grip preventing me from falling to my knees. I thought that I was standing in the corridor of my first Enclosure; this one was identical in every way. I had explored my surroundings so thoroughly as a child that I knew every crack and mark that was imprinted in the walls of my corridor.

"Oh no," I said as I leaned on Dominic for support.

"It seems that they wanted to do more than just eliminate you physically, Princess. It seems that they planned to destroy your mind as well. You have grown into something quite unique on this planet, and they intended to strip that from you. Do you still want to follow me, Princess? Nothing of what you are about to see and hear will give you any comfort."

302

"I want to know what is going to happen. I know that I am safe now, and therefore the knowledge, though it may cause me pain, will not harm me." I stepped forward, removing Dominic's support.

"Do you mind if I join you?" Lillith said quietly, still studying me. I still found her interest terrifying. Without a word I stood aside and let her through. I wouldn't have said that she was comfortable around kindness, but she certainly appeared happier now that we were going to investigate the horrors that Miranda had in store for me.

We started walking together slowly down the corridor. After a short while, we stopped outside the door of one of the cells. The door was just a paler shade of grey, its metal dull and rusted in places. With a sense of dread I realised that, like the corridor, the door was an exact replica of the one that had kept my mother and me locked away during my childhood. Dominic pulled a set of keys from his pocket and inserted a key in the door, pushing it slowly open.

"Surprise number one," Lillith murmured quietly under her breath.

I took a deep breath to steady myself and stepped forward with Lillith. I wasn't really prepared for what I saw when I entered the cell because in front of me, lying on a slab, was my mother. She was lying still on her back with her eyes closed. Her hair, though mainly white, still had a hint of the golden colour it had been when she was young.

She looked frail with age. I could see that she was still alive, although my heart ached in my chest as I saw her. My mind knew she was dead; Rachael had witnessed it. Even though I had processed that information, my heart won, and after a few seconds of looking at her I went towards her. Lillith stopped me by placing her hand very gently on my arm.

"It is nothing more than an illusion. Look closely, Princess. You know what it is—you are better than this mind trick. Do not be seduced by it," Lillith said.

Reluctantly I did as she suggested. I stayed where I was and stared at the being that looked like my mother. I realised that the being in front of me had no real substance to it; I let out a small tendril from my mind, but it reached nothing and that confirmed it for me; it was merely a clever illusion, albeit a very good one.

"Now you may go forward," Lillith said after a few seconds, when she was sure I had a better understanding of what I was looking at.

I walked forward, my heart heavy with emotion, I had not seen my mother since I had been taken from the Enclosure and never had a chance to say good-bye. As I moved forward the illusion spoke; it was my mother's voice, and her words stopped me. She accused me of being a bad child, of leaving her. I was glad that I was knew this was an illusion; otherwise, I would not have been able to cope—I would have wished for the brothers at the first obstacle.

I stood at the side of the concrete slab, controlling myself, preventing grief from overwhelming me, and reached my hand out ready to touch something of substance. All the time my heart felt as if it was in conflict with my mind. I still on some level wanted something to be there, but there was nothing. My hand plunged through the illusion and touched the cold slab of concrete. I withdrew my hand quickly, unnerved.

"She is very good, isn't she?" Dominic said, coming to stand beside me. "In truth, I am surprised at their level of talent. It is a shame that they withheld such a talent from the master. He could perhaps have found a use for it. I believe that with the powerful mind control that they can exert, had they continued injecting you with the sedative, you would have seen and believed whatever they showed you. I wonder what they would have used this particular illusion to achieve, however. Unfortunately, without their participation it appears we will never know."

I took a step away from him, not really comfortable with the words he was speaking but at the same time knowing that he wasn't trying to upset me. I turned and walked out of the room, not waiting for Lillith or Dominic and not looking back. After a few more seconds they joined me in the corridor and Dominic shut the cell door.

We continued down the corridor, and after a few twists and turns that appeared to lead into another building, we stopped outside another cell door. "Let me guess," I said. "Surprise number two?"

"Exactly," Lillith said, smiling as if she was anticipating the prospect of another episode of torture for me.

Dominic waited a moment until I gave him the nod that I was ready to witness what was behind the next door. As the door opened I heard moans of pain and I hesitated. I recognised that the person moaning was Rachael. I almost didn't go in, knowing what the twins were obviously going to force me to witness.

"It is not necessary for you to witness this. I myself found this to be perhaps a little extreme, especially as I know Rachael to be a very loyal and obedient subject," Dominic said softly as he stopped and placed himself in the doorway, effectively blocking my view of whatever was happening beyond.

"How do you know Rachael?" I asked him after a while, trying to control the images of her in that cell that had already visited my mind.

Lillith intervened. "When Rachael was removed from her children, you could say Dominic courted her. She was certainly saying the right things, but unfortunately she wasn't quite ready to commit her soul to us. She has always shown a liberal-minded interest in our kind and has been known to share her knowledge, yet she remains detached. Rachael would probably not approve, but I personally think you should witness this event. It may help you to make the decisions that my master hopes you will make." She then placed her hand on my arm and guided me into the room.

I tried to remain emotionless as I surveyed the scenes in front of me. Master Giles was sitting on a chair, a guard standing over him, a gun (no doubt laden with silver bullets) pointed directly at his heart. Rachael was laid out on a table and the twins were leaning over her, instruments of extraction in their hands. I understood then that it wasn't only for me that Rachael had sacrificed one of her eyes; it was to save the life of Master Giles.

I still can't explain why that realisation helped, because at the time when I witnessed what had happened I didn't feel solely responsible for her pain. I would have tried to do the same thing—endure the same pain for someone whom I obviously loved dearly.

I stayed and watched the whole wretched scene. Rachael's resolve grew in strength as her pain increased. I watched until I thought I had seen enough. Then, again without a word, I turned and left the cell, passing Lillith and Dominic without even looking at them, my darkness finally beginning to give me the strength I needed. Once we were all outside, I turned and faced my two companions.

"Is there much more of this?" I asked, my teeth clenched as I tried to control the anger that was growing. "Because I believe I have seen more than enough of these illusions."

"Enough already? Such a shame. I thought you had an usually high inner strength for a human," said Lillith, her voice dripping with sarcasm.

"I simply meant that I do not need to see any more of the torture of my friends to help you. What is it you want from me?" I chose to direct my question at Dominic, knowing that he would try to answer me honestly.

"Come. I think it is better if I show you," he said without looking at me.

We continued to walk down the corridor until we stopped outside another cell door. Without hesitation, Dominic opened the door and let me enter. There was nothing in the room, no furniture, not even a bed, but suspended in the middle of the room, wrapped in a thick black mist, was Miranda, who looked to be asleep.

"Is she all right in there?" I asked, turning again to Dominic.

"I would not say that she is comfortable, Princess, but she is sufficiently cocooned. None of her thoughts can penetrate the shield, and no thoughts can reach her," he said.

"How do her brothers know to come here? How do they know that all is well?" I asked, still staring at the suspended form of Miranda.

"My sister has many talents, and one of those talents is that she can extract and manipulate thoughts from the minds of others. It is said that you can also link your mind to others at will—her ability is just a progression of that. As far as the twins are concerned, their sister remains in constant contact with them, teasing them with snippets of information about your pain."

"I feel as though I have had enough pain this day. I wish to leave this corridor," I said, feeling overwhelmed at all that I had seen.

"It will be as you ask, Princess. I tend to agree with you, that to show you more of the pain they intended would only serve to weaken you, and that was never our intention," Dominic said.

When I didn't speak again, he continued to speak. "My sister and I understand your need to leave this place, and you will soon, but your capture assures us that her brothers are on their way and our master wishes us to bring all of them to him at the castle. Your eyes are now showing more evidence of that resolve," he explained.

"What do you want from me?" I asked, weary.

I had no fear of the beings in front of me. Through my darkness, I realised that although they were demons, neither they nor any of their kind had ever done anything bad to me. I knew that in a way they loved and loathed me with equal measures of fear. At the same time their master showed a distinct interest in me. I knew, too, that Rachael had previously encountered them.

Yet in the world I lived in, it seemed that half of the vampires I met wanted to see me suffer, and even though David was their absolute ruler, they considered him young and impulsive. A lot of the planet's vampires were reluctant to accept any form of change. At that moment and for the first time in my short life, though not for the last, I doubted that David commanded the same amount of respect and fear from his subjects as Elathan did.

"We wish you to stay here sheltered with us because there is a chance that if you move from here, they may sense you. We also need to dull your senses again," Dominic added apologetically.

"Why, why do you need to do that?" I asked, beginning to lose patience with even these beings.

"For the same reason that Miranda had to. You have a wonderful strength within you that is an unknown," Lillith answered for him this time, smiling less menacingly at me, almost with approval.

"We can sense it, and if we can, then they certainly can. Therefore, in order to draw them ever closer, we need you to suppress your senses," Dominic added.

"Will I have to stay in a cell?" I sighed, knowing that they were right. The twins, especially George, would have very little difficulty sensing the changes of strength within my head.

"No, you can sleep in your kind of comfort. The female Disciple will see that nothing happens to you, although personally I find these cells quite simple, quite adequate, perhaps even a little quaint," replied Lillith.

I was about to ask her why when I felt a small sharp pain in my arm, and then drowsiness began to seep into my awareness. I felt Dominic move close to me and gently catch me before I fell, and then all went black. There was a slight awareness of being cradled and carried back along the corridors, and before I passed out of consciousness, I knew I felt safe with Dominic.

Again as I slept I felt more like my own being again, knowing that I was among friends. I allowed my body to rest and heal. I spent a couple of days just concentrating on getting some of my previous strength back. There were times when I relaxed myself completely and tried to gently probe the darkness within. When my darkness began to reawaken, I welcomed it as a friend. I had reached a new understanding of it and what it was capable of. Even though I was given no more medication to help me sleep, Dominic, who appeared to be quite a bit gentler and certainly more patient with me and my human needs than his sister, taught me how to use some of the strength I had within to shut out events and others around me. He taught me these things so that I could find and use my own solace and place of peace.

Before then, I had believed that the inner darkness held no peace, only anger. With patience Dominic helped me to understand that the darkness was and always had been what I wanted to it to be, but up until now I had not understood my own level of control over it.

Even though she appeared to make an effort to be nice and to be patient with me, there was just something about Lillith that still managed to make my mouth dry and my heart race when she came too close. She made me feel as if I was simply something she chose to let live, especially in those early days.

Although I didn't particularly share Miranda's taste in clothes, I admit I did feel infinitely better to have a little variety to choose from. I had discovered a taste for black clothing, although I still don't know whether it was easier to wear black just to have a sense of belonging or safety among the beings who surrounded me or just because that was the colour of the majority of the clothes that were available to me.

Miranda appeared to like tight leather trousers and tighter, almost painfully restrictive, bodices. I continued to wear my soft boots, as my feet and ankles took a while longer to heal than my wrists and hands.

I began to form a routine for mealtimes with the female Disciple, who continued to appear whenever I so much as thought about a need. The only thing that I missed was contact and updates from the outside world, as I had before when I had been a small child. I had no idea what was happening beyond the concrete cells.

Chapter 46

After I spent a few days in those rooms I felt better, stronger. I also began to feel restless again, not feeling comfortable with the enclosed environment; the grey walls were depressing and claustrophobic, no matter how many mirrors or drapes were hung on them. At first when I asked for my freedom to walk out in the fresh air, I was constantly and resolutely refused. Lillith took the time to explain to me that Miranda and her brothers had built this mock Enclosure into the side of a mountain. She went on to further explain that on the surface and from a distance it would have been nearly impossible for anyone who did not have help to find it. She told me that the twins and their sister had been very clever and that they had learned many things since they had decided to agree to Elathan's offer.

It was strange to hear a demon preaching patience to me, but to help, Dominic tried to inform me as much as possible of what was happening in the world outside. I asked him once what was going to happen when the twins arrived, and even though he must have had an idea, he explained that they thought it would be better if nothing was revealed to me. He explained that I was healing and learning self-control and that he wanted nothing, no extra stress or unpleasant thoughts, to inhibit the process. Through listening and self-discovery, and with Dominic's help, I learned that I was strong enough mentally to avoid thinking about the change of circumstance. After a few days with him, I found that I trusted him, as I had the close members of my vampire family. I even trusted him enough to show him the extent of my darkness; he actually smiled at me when I took off some of my restraints. He found it amusing that I didn't allow my darkness to exist without them. Even though I was prepared for an intrusion, I was grateful that Dominic did not even try to enter my head and manipulate that darkness. Instead he told me what he thought I should do, and with that guidance I managed to project what I hoped were the right images.

Although I remained fearful of Lillith, I tried hard not to lean away from her when she stood near me; a respectful relationship grew between us. She and her brother had rescued me, and for that I would always feel a connection with them.

The female Disciple, with whom I had become a little more relaxed as each day passed, also became part of my encapsulated world. I didn't even bother to ask her name, but she was at my side as soon as I requested anything. She had obviously been told to cater to my every need and request. In the past I would have tried to get to know her a little better, but at this time I felt that there was no need.

Through listening to Dominic I learned that David was still very active in his searches for me and a huge reward was being offered for my safe return. With the reward came an amnesty, which was guaranteed by the emperor himself. Mia had returned to the castle to be with her brother and was often seen organising the searches beside him.

Eventually, when I was beginning to feel as if I couldn't stay locked inside that mountain any longer, Dominic informed me that they were expecting the twins that evening and told me that it would be a good idea for me to get some rest. I tried to take his advice but I couldn't. Instead, I tried to calm myself with a warmly scented shower. After the shower I took my time going through the selection of Miranda's clothes. I eventually found an outfit that was similar in style to Lillith's: black trousers with a tight leather vest and knee-high leather boots. I found a type of knife belt among her other belongings with the knives still attached, and even though I had no idea how I would possibly use them — or even if I could — I still felt they helped me look stronger. I tied my hair back from my face and applied some dark eye makeup. When I was ready I told the ever-present female Disciple to take me to where Dominic and his sister were waiting.

Before I could enter the room, Dominic came out and explained to me that they had placed Miranda in the position I should have been in. He also explained that Lillith had used a simple but effective illusion on her so that she resembled me. I remembered that Elathan had done something similar when he wanted to remove the twins after my Commitment Ceremony; it seemed that I was the only thing that would bring them out of hiding. Their obsession with me and my mind made me shiver momentarily. Although I accepted and understood his words, I admit that I still wasn't quite prepared for what I saw when I entered the cell.

As I followed Dominic into the room, the first thing I noticed was the stench—the room actually smelled of fear, the same fear I had smelled before as a child in the Enclosure. In the centre of an empty room, a filthy-looking woman was chained. She had blonde hair and my face. It was still extremely difficult for me to look at her, even though I knew it was an illusion. It was like looking into a mirror that reflected my worst nightmare. The rage in me started to build again, but a look and a cautionary smile from Lillith made me check myself.

As soon as Miranda saw me, she started to struggle. I could see clearly the hatred in her eyes as she looked at me. With the dark mist that had previously surrounded her removed, she appeared much more aware of what was about to happen. I didn't know what they had done to her, but somehow they had gagged her without it being obvious. As she struggled harder, I watched as Lillith approached her and began to remove one of her gloves. As soon as Miranda saw her coming towards her, her struggles became different—rather trying to move forward to reach me, she now seemed to move as far back as possible. I watched as Lillith leaned down and gently touched Miranda on her face. The touch was only for a second, but it was enough to make Miranda shriek and for a dark bruise to appear on her face. Lillith put on her glove and smiled at me again. I felt a shiver travel from the top of my spine to the bottom, but I still managed a smile in return.

Dominic informed us that the twins had arrived. He told the female Disciple to greet them and to convince them that their sister was busy preparing me properly for their arrival. Because I was back in the room, it was easier to pretend that I was captive.

It wasn't long before I could feel George. I nearly collapsed in fear when I felt his excitement, knowing that he intended to cause me pain. I couldn't tell exactly what he intended to do, but if it was making him happy, I knew that it would be painful for me. "Does he know yet that you are here?" I whispered to Dominic, who had moved closer to me.

"Lillith is shielding us all, and therefore he is only seeing what she is allowing him to see. However, he will be able to sense your fear if you allow it to escape your control—it is what those similar to us feed on, not your blood as others do. Now, do not let his strength distract you. I have heard that you were strong enough to resist him during an earlier trial. Focus on that, and remember, you were merely a child back then," he whispered back.

He moved me to the corner that was farthest away from the door, while Lillith said something else to Miranda, who had stopped struggling. Lillith then seemed to blur for a second as her features moulded themselves into the image of Miranda. It wasn't exact, but it was good enough to fool the twins from a distance, at least until they had entered the room.

When everything had been done as it should have been, I heard Dominic softly speaking to himself. I didn't recognise the words because it certainly wasn't the universal language that I was used to; it was an older language that seemed to trickle into my mind. All of my thoughts were concentrated on the image that I wanted George to see, so I didn't have time to ask before I heard footsteps. I felt my stomach tighten as they approached. It was odd because usually one look from Lillith made me pull myself together, but now she looked like Miranda, the being who had tried to kidnap me and would have kept me weak and captive, and who had intimidated me for as long as I had known her. So I looked at Dominic instead, and even though his smile did not have the same impact as it usually did, it was steady enough.

I tried to stay as still as possible, barely breathing, as the female Disciple entered the room. And then the twins were there. They were no more than a few feet away when my control slipped as soon as I saw them. The anger that I thought I had control of exploded out of me, and I found myself taking steps towards them with a knife in each hand before the door had closed behind them.

313

I heard the word "back" and felt as if I had run into a huge wall. I felt myself being thrown backwards as the door was slammed shut behind the twins, cutting them off from whomever they had brought with them for protection. All of the prepared pretence was lifted from the room. I had not exactly helped, but in a way I was glad. I had no patience, and I wanted them to know that they had been found and now they were captured and I was free. I wanted to let them know that this time I would make sure that they died. In the next few moments, things happened very fast. Lillith transformed her features so that she no longer resembled Miranda and she lifted the illusion that made Miranda appear like me.

I was surprised that the twins did not react faster; they seemed to have been taken completely by surprise. Perhaps it was their own arrogance that made them react slowly, and when they saw whom they were in the presence of, they both fell to the floor.

Both of them seemed to ignore the situation and me. Instead they seemed to concentrate solely on Lillith. There was real fear in their eyes as they knelt before her. I took a little time to study them while they were both on the floor no more than a few feet away from me. They were both so beautiful to look at, with the exception of their eyes, which were burning red now as if they were filled with an inner fire. As I studied them, any fear I had of them finally left me and I even managed to feel a little pity for them. I knew that they should have chosen death when they were given the opportunity, and I knew with a certainty that they would be wishing for it soon. Elathan would see to it this time, and if I could stomach it, I would witness the pain of their final hours.

"You are both charged with trying to harm one of our master's favourites. Do either of you dispute the charge?" Lillith asked in a quiet voice that sliced through the silence that had descended. When neither of them answered her, she continued, "It has been decided that you will be taken to him, where he will decide on a more permanent role for you both," she said with a cold calmness in her softly dangerous voice. There was no emotion and no pity, not even disapproval. She spoke as if she was simply delivering a message.

"No!" I said as I moved towards them again. This time it was Lillith who put her hand out towards me. "I want them gone!

Does he not understand that they will not stop trying to destroy me, that as soon as they are given freedom they will try to find me and hurt me again?" I said, my anger making me sound emotional. As soon as her gloved hand touched me in response, I felt as if something was moving under her skin, and the glove felt cold and clammy; it made me want to be sick.

"He has predicted that you would be dissatisfied with this outcome, Princess, and he told me to inform you that he gives you his word that you will join him this time to see them punished. He also told me to inform you that you will not be disappointed by his choices again."

This time I did detect a little disapproval in her voice. It was as if she did not share or understand his need to give me an explanation. I took her at her word, suddenly very eager to step back away from her hand, which was still resting on my arm. I was beginning to feel unwell, and I wasn't sure if it was because of the sight of the twins or her touch.

"What happens now?" I asked as I stepped away. I had to be careful since there were very few spaces I could go; the fact that I didn't want to be near any of them made me very careful with my movements.

"The Disciple will take you back to the place from which you were taken, and we will transport these back to our master, who will probably want to have one or two conversations with them while we await your return to the castle," Lillith said. As she spoke I felt the Disciple behind me put her hand on my shoulder as if to guide me.

"Do not touch me!" I snapped at her. Dominic smiled and Lillith laughed, and even I had to smile—apparently my attitude towards the Disciple pleased them both. I made my way out of the room for the last time, finally feeling free.

Before I had taken too many steps, Lillith called to me from the doorway. "Princess, before you return to your perfect little life, where your destiny appears to have been decided for you centuries ago and everything is moving along so nicely, I would, if I were you, question why everything is so very perfect, because you have no idea how perfect your life will continue to become. . . ."

"Lillith, that is enough! Our master will punish you if he thinks you have influenced her," Dominic said quickly.

"What does she mean, my life is perfect? Do you not know what I have been through?" I asked, turning to face them.

"Yes, we do, but you seem to be able to emerge from each situation stronger than before, perhaps with more resolve each time," she called from behind her brother.

I didn't know what to say to her, so I turned and started to walk again. Her words made me feel a little unnerved. It was not the words exactly, but she had implied that she knew something that I should know. I pushed those thoughts and doubts out of my head and tried to think of what I had to do to get back to the life I'd had.

Chapter 47

I didn't want to stay and listen to anything else. As far as I was concerned, I had done what I had been asked to do and there was nothing else for me to contribute until I returned to my home, the castle.

I didn't turn back again, and as I walked farther away from the cell, I heard some scuffling noises and what sounded like muffled cries of pain. I smiled, hoping that the journey the twins and their sister had going back to the castle would be filled with as much pain and discomfort as they had caused me.

Dominic came back to say good-bye for both himself and his sister, promising me that we would all be together very soon to witness the judgment passed on the twins and their sister. I was surprised that I felt as if I was actually going to miss both Dominic and his sister. I realised as I smiled and said good-bye that I had definitely formed a bond with the pair of them. A fleeting thought crossed my mind: things had worked out well after all, perhaps perfectly.

After Dominic left and I was alone again, I packed just a few necessary belongings and left the rest behind. I just wanted to take as little as possible from that place. I knew that I had my own belongings at the resort, and as the excitement and adrenalin began to leave my body, I realised that I was now going back to the place where Daniel had died. I couldn't think of it any other way now because the most recent events overshadowed all that had happened there before. As I thought about it, I decided that I wanted that resort removed from the landscape, perhaps leaving room for something to remember Daniel with. He had saved David and should be remembered for his bravery.

I knew I needed to dress warmly, but the furs that I found among Miranda's belongings were real and looked like the fur from a snow wolf, so instead I opted to dress in as many layers as I could wear at once, knowing that I would probably encounter one of these creatures outside of the caves, accepting once again my humanity. I was becoming used to forgetting about it when I was with other beings, but as soon I was left on my own, the frailty of the being I once was came flooding back.

The Disciple, although willing to help, was staying well away from me, perhaps knowing that I did not want her help or that I did not want her anywhere near me anymore. She had served a purpose, and now that purpose had also come to an end. When I was ready and had taken what I needed, I simply looked at her until she walked out of the door without even looking back. I followed her and was surprised at how short the walk was to the freedom of outside. Before I finally emerged from the caves, I had to put on some glasses that I had found among Miranda's belongings. The glasses were not the specially made ones that I usually used to protect my overly sensitive eyes, but they did help a little.

I stood still and closed my eyes for a while, hoping that they would adjust because my first glimpse of the mountains that were surrounding me was beautiful. That first breath that I took—the first feeling of the air on my skin—was worth more to me in those first moments than anything or any being on the planet.

The stench of the caves finally began to leave me, and all I smelled out in the pure white wildness of the planet was nature. As I inhaled deeply I smelled the glorious planet as it should be, untainted and uncorrupted by the petty rivalries and jealousies of the beings that dwelled on it. Although the air was cold, I was dressed warmly enough so that didn't bother me at all since the air felt so amazingly fresh on the skin of my face. Although there was no wind, the still air caressed me. It felt like a gentle touch, and it reminded me for just a moment of David—the way his touch made me feel. At the thought of him, I started to pull myself together. I knew that I had much to sort out in my heart and my head, and I could not let myself be distracted. Still, as I stood and breathed in deeply and felt the coolness fill my lungs, I finally knew that I was free again.

I was living again, and although I had not changed physically, I had changed in the way I thought. I had made some decisions, and I was hoping that I was the free child that my friends hoped I was, because I had made some decisions that I didn't think they would like. As I stood there thinking, a sled pulled by four large white snow wolves arrived in front of me. I stood for a moment and studied the animals in front of me. Even though they were hooked up to a sled, I knew by looking at them that they chose to pull it; should they decide not to, I would not be going anywhere. I looked into the eyes of the wolf nearest to me, took off my glasses, and smiled.

I knew what to do. I settled myself among the blankets that were in the sled and covered myself with them, making sure that I left no part of my body exposed to the cold air. Once I appeared settled, the female Disciple climbed onto the front of the sled and shouted at the snow wolves to move. I tried to relax and enjoy the scenery. The world looked wonderful, fresh and new. The only way to describe the feeling I experienced during that particular journey was that I had awakened.

I had never been far from the familiar scenery of the forests, especially unescorted, but out here there wasn't a single forest to be seen, yet I wanted to know this place with its own magical beauty — it was that beauty during that journey that helped me make a decision as to what I wanted or felt I needed to do next with my life. I laughed quietly to myself, at the thought of being here on my own and making my own decisions for the first time in my life without the influence and instruction of others. The thought thrilled me, but it also frightened me at the same time.

Of course, I did not recognise any of the mountains until I saw the chalets of Daniel's resort in the distance. When I saw them I felt the first tinges of doubt and had to swallow hard to dismiss them quickly before I changed my mind and changed my newly formed plans. We travelled for quite a while longer; I guessed that we had been travelling for at least three or four hours. As we got nearer to the resort and the buildings were finally appearing near to the size I remembered, I called "Stop" to the female Disciple.

"I do not want you to go there. I want to enter the resort by myself, and you are definitely not welcome there," I explained briefly as I struggled to remove all of my coverings. When I finally managed to get myself out of the sled, the female Disciple threw me some snowshoes that I had seen others around the resort use to walk on top of the snow; I was already almost knee deep in snow. I should have thanked her, and before Daniel had died I probably would have, but the beings that wore black had been part of most of the pain in my life. I had no fear now of these beings, only hatred. I accepted the shoes without a word and leaned against the sled, balancing myself to put them on. I took the bag of essentials that I had brought from Miranda's room and slung the bag over my shoulder.

As I walked away I heard her say quietly, with respect and more than a little regret, "Be safe, my lady."

I didn't even change my step. I carried on walking in the direction of the chalets. I looked back to see if she was still there, but she was gone. There was nothing but a field of pure white snow; even the marks from the wolves and the sled were gone. I took this as a symbol that another ordeal was over.

I carried on moving forward, making very slow progress. Eventually I could see the chalets moving towards me. I was exhausted by the time I reached the outer edge of the resort. It appeared to be deserted; I should have expected this—after the death of his son, the Hiltian would have closed it.

As I walked slowly forward towards the main chalet which had been Daniel's, the one where he had his office, I felt alone but free. I knew that it was dangerous to be alone. I also knew that among those whom I loved I would be safe again, but I could not remember a time of ever being this free. I stopped walking for a moment and turned slowly, surveying the empty horizon; it held no threat for me. I was surrounded by complete silence. Even when I strained to use my enhanced hearing, I could not hear anything. That silence was only broken when I heard a wolf howl in the distance.

When I got to the front chalet's office, the door was open and it was predictably empty. It looked as though all signs of Daniel had been removed. I don't know what I expected, but I did not expect to see everything gone. I knew that his father still had feelings for him, even though he was a Hiltian vampire, and I also knew then that because of the being his father was and the relationship they had, it was understandable that nothing had been left there. Some papers were scattered on the floor, though, so I picked a few up. I wanted, needed, anything—even a scrap of paper with his writing would have done—to feel the loss of him then and there. I bit my lip to keep in the sobs that I knew were on the verge of erupting from my chest—so much for control.

As I wandered through the chalet, I realised that David would have had all my belongings removed from this place and taken back to the castle, and I knew that there was no point in going to explore any of the chalets. I walked through the empty office not really knowing what to do, where to go from there. All those plans I had made when I was enjoying my ride here deserted me when an emotional lump formed in my throat. I found a space on the floor and sat down, leaning my head against the wall to try to gather my thoughts again in the silence.

I closed my eyes and must have fallen asleep because I was dreaming that I was back at the castle, but this time I was with Elathan and not David. When I heard the voices, there were two of them. I knew that they were not from my dream because they did not make sense. I opened my eyes and stood up quickly, knowing that I should probably hide, but my fear made it difficult to even think of where. As my eyes frantically searched the room, I knew that there was nowhere to go and no time left to move. I took a deep, lingering breath and held it as the door to the office opened. Two humans were in front of me, both chalet masters. They looked as startled as I was when they saw me, and for a few moments all we could do was stare at each other.

"Princess?" one of them said as he took a step farther into the room.

"Princess, is that you? Are you all right?" said the other one.

It took me just a second to adjust, but I must say my first instinct was to hug them; after all, they were humans and so was I. So I stood up straight and looked directly at them, knowing that regardless of all the love and instruction regarding my position I had received from Rachael and Mia, Dominic and Lillith had taught me who I was and who I could grow to be. But I soon gathered myself together and adopted my princess authority. "I am fine, but I need to get a message to my head of security, Theo. I want to speak with him before I speak to anyone else—is that clear? I do not wish you to concern my beloved until I am sure that it is safe for him to collect me personally. Again I ask you, is that clear?" I said, delivering the last three words in the manner that I had heard David use to command those who worked for him in the castle. I just wanted what I needed to be done without question.

I knew that David would probably want to know why I wanted Theo first, but David hadn't rescued me, the one being he had always claimed was the most important thing in his existence. Another being had rescued me, and I now partially understood Lillith's ambiguous comment about my perfect life, which was threading its way through my thoughts. I understood that I was probably being unfair because I knew better than most the restraints David had faced when I became committed to him. But the doubts were there, and although I wasn't totally sure what her words meant, I knew first that I needed time to think for myself, and second that I would be asking some questions of my own when I got back.

"Do you have a telephone?" I asked the chalet master nearest to me. I stood there and waited silently until I was handed the mobile phone. As soon as I had the phone in my hand, I gestured for them to leave the room. I didn't dial the number I knew by heart until they had left the room. I did not speak until I knew they had gone far enough not to overhear the conversation I would be having.

"Theo?" I said quietly.

"Liberty?" said a familiar low, growling voice on the other end of the phone.

"Theo, by all that is holy, I am so glad to hear your voice. But Theo, before we speak I need you to be alone—really alone. I need you to understand that this is not a request, this is an instruction for you, my protector," I said, knowing what bringing up the link between us would mean to him. I had to smile a little as I heard him order the Adwar, who was forever present, out of the security room.

"I will call you back on this phone shortly," was all he said then before the line went dead. As I sat waiting, I just hoped he would not inform anyone. I didn't think he would. The phone rang in my hand after only a few seconds, and I answered it on the second ring.

"Theo, before we say anything else, you must listen to me. You made me a promise once. Did you mean it?"

"What?" he began to interrupt me.

"Please, Theo, just listen to me for a minute. Are you alone?" I asked quietly, knowing that it would do no good to raise my voice. Theo usually listened to me better when he thought I was unharmed and safe. "Theo, I asked you a question—did you mean what you said after I returned to the castle, after I had been poisoned?"

"Yes, I meant what I said, but I cannot seem to keep my oaths to you. I am not good at protecting you. Perhaps you should—"

"Theo, please, I am tired. I have been through a lot and I need you now. I am going to ask you now to protect me above all others. Do you understand what I am asking?" I said, my heart suddenly beating faster.

"Yes," was all he said after a quiet pause.

"I need you to come and get me, but I want you to come alone, completely alone, and I want your oath as a Mountain Dweller, Theo, that you will tell no one of your intentions and of this conversation," I said, knowing that like the Forest Dwellers, the Mountain Dwellers considered their oath to be a sacred bind, and it was never given freely.

"You have my oath, and that is not a question you should have asked." He continued quietly, "Where are you?"

"I am back at the resort. Can you come to me? There are a couple of the masters here, but the place is deserted and I do not know if they have any food. I will ask. I am in Daniel's chalet, and I won't move until you come for me," I said finally.

"I will come for you, my princess," he said, and I knew he meant it.

When the phone went dead, I pulled the chair from behind the desk and tried to settle myself down to wait. I was warm enough but weak with hunger. I dragged myself out of the office and approached the chalet masters again. They seemed to have settled themselves in the next room and were sharing some basic-looking breads and cheeses.

"I have travelled quite a distance and am extremely hungry. Is there any food left in these buildings? I will see to it that you are well rewarded for helping me here," I added as an incentive.

After a moment of looking at each other, the taller of the two gestured for me to sit with them while the other went to retrieve their own provisions, which consisted of dried meats, breads, and water.

I sat and ate the offered food with them, feeling more strength return as my body nourished itself. There was no conversation during the meal, which suited me fine, but the two beings in front of me appeared very uncomfortable in my presence.

After I had eaten enough food to make me feel a little better, I thanked them and promised again that I would remember them for their kindness. Then I made my way into the empty office. I did not know how long I would have to wait for Theo and felt very tired. I made myself as comfortable as possible and closed my eyes, practising the meditation techniques that Dominic had taught me.

Chapter 48

I slept for most of the time that I waited. I wasn't too comfortable, but I was warm and the hunger pains had finally left my stomach. My sleep wasn't particularly deep or restful, and I did worry a little that the chalet masters would alert someone to where I was, but, on the other hand, I reasoned that Theo would not be too long. He would have used all the vehicles at his disposal to reach me in the shortest time possible.

I don't really know how long I waited, but when I awoke again I was once again hungry and still felt exhausted. Time didn't really matter, not during that wait, but I remained continually on edge. It got to the point where if I heard even the slightest movement in the next room, I jumped, alert to every sound.

Towards dawn I was too lightheaded to care anymore, and the only thing that reacted to sound was my heart, its beats increasing. I did not need to worry because when I heard the connecting door between the rooms begin to open softly, there were no other sounds, no voices, just a familiar safe presence that I sensed.

When I did eventually open my eyes, they resisted me for quite a while as I tried to focus on the being in front of me. He was there, trying to squeeze himself through the doorway, his size making him look a little awkward and endearingly clumsy as he hurried to reach me. Before I could even straighten myself properly in the chair, Theo had me in his huge arms, and given the heat from him and the way he smelled, I could not hold back my tears.

"Princess," was all he said, his voice sounding relieved, with a mixture of real love and fear, his 'emotion' for me becoming almost more than he could obviously deal with.

"Theo," I said as I tried to wake myself fully, trying to shake the exhaustion from my thoughts and at the same time sit myself up in his arms so that I could see his face properly.

"Theo, my protector, we haven't got it right yet—this protection thing, I mean. Theo, I am so sorry that I sent you away. I put myself in this position—it wasn't your fault," I stammered as I tried to smile through my pain and tears.

"Princess, I . . ."

"No, Theo, don't you dare say sorry or tell me that you are not good enough—I don't want to hear it. You are my protector and again it was me—I sent you away, which I will never do again, I promise. This is my own fault. It is you who should forgive me. Will you forgive me?" I asked, trying to sound as serious as possible, knowing that I had probably confused him.

I understood Theo well enough to understand that he had almost certainly blamed himself for what had happened, and he had probably come here with intention of telling me that he was no good as my protector and that I should choose another being, but I couldn't. I had the only protector I had ever needed or wanted.

"Forgive you? It is I who should ask for your forgiveness," he said quietly.

"I will only forgive you if you forgive me, then," I said, looking up at his deeply frowning face, feeling so much love and happiness and knowing that I had given him no opportunity to release himself from me. I could still see the insecure, hurt, and guilty expression on his face, so I simply gripped him round the neck and placed my head in a spot I had discovered as a smaller child until I felt him return the closeness of the grip.

When I moved my head again, I saw that he was smiling slightly and I could see that finally his mood was beginning to change. He was happy again that I was back and safe in his arms.

"Did you bring some food with you?" I said, returning his smile, hoping that all would be well enough between us for him to do the things that I knew I would be asking him.

"Yes, Princess, I did, and while you are eating I will notify the others that you and I are both safe," he said, frowning a little at me, as if he still didn't quite understand why I had called him alone.

"Theo, don't, please, at least not yet. I have some thoughts I want to share with you—we can do it while I eat. I have done some thinking and some things have happened which have created some questions within me, and I think I need your help to place myself back where I should be," I said, letting go of his neck and allowing him to place me back on my feet.

He didn't say anything. He did not look happy, but he did not reach for his phone either.

We sat together. He kept me close and warm while I ate. The food, mainly breads, cheeses, and meats that he had purchased on the way, was warm and simple, but it was delicious and filling. Finally, with the food making me braver (before he had come I hadn't decided to tell him everything, just some of what had happened), I decided that he deserved to know the truth—all of it.

As I ate he listened while I told him everything. I told him every little detail from the beginning. I told him about Elathan and how he had been with me at the castle since I had first arrived. I told him how it was Elathan who had made the twins and their sister disappear as a commitment gift. I even told Theo what my alone time had meant more recently, how I felt when I was with him—everything.

Although he held me close as I told him, I felt him tense as I mentioned Elathan and how I felt. I also made it clear that Elathan protected me in his own way and that I intended for him to be part of my life.

I went on to explain about Lillith and Dominic—where I had first met them, how they had rescued me, and finally how Lillith had said some things that made sense to me. I told him that I wanted to spend some time with Elathan when I returned to the castle, even if it was only to understand that what she was saying was wrong and that there was only one true destiny for me.

I reasoned that if I really was this child of freedom that Sarah and the others apparently thought I was, then I needed for the sake of the quest to be free from doubts. I could see that as I was speaking, many conflicting thoughts were going through Theo's head, but apart from the odd frown, his expression told me that he understood most of what I was trying to explain.

When I finished, he stared at me for a long time before finally asking, "What is it you are asking of me, Princess? I understand now that you are going to ask for things other than my protection."

"Nothing, Theo. I am only asking that you protect me. I know I am loved — I know that David loves me and that I love him back with all my heart. I know that I will remain unharmed, but I still remain human and therefore vulnerable. I need to do this thing with Elathan in order for me to understand and embrace my true destiny by the side of the ruler of this planet."

I knew what I was saying sounded contrived, but it was true — it really was how I felt. I did believe deep down that I was the child of freedom; I didn't think so many important beings would be that interested in me if I weren't.

"What is it you want to do, then?" he asked, appearing to become a little impatient with my over-explaining all the time, but I needed him to understand.

"I want to go somewhere with you on our own until I can think about how to deal with this. It will only be temporary, but I want you to stand between those who would want to take me back before I am ready. I need you to protect me above all others, like you promised," I said, suddenly serious and feeling every bit in control as I hoped I looked. Something changed in me as I spoke, something connected, and I knew that these decisions were meant to be made. I truly believed then that this was part of my destiny.

It only took a few seconds for Theo to bow his head slightly and say, "It will be as you wish, Princess, but I will inform David of your choices as soon as we are safe. David is a brother to me. He will always remain that way and I will not see him hurt, nor will I lie to him on your behalf." As soon as he said the words, knowing that he was right, we both smiled and I threw myself back into his arms.

"Oh Theo, I do love you. Of course, I would expect nothing less of you," I said, laughing and feeling as if the weight of an entire world had suddenly been lifted from my chest. I could suddenly breathe again.

"Where will we go?" I asked, feeling more than a little excited now that he had agreed.

"I believe the best place for us to seek solitude from the others would be among the people of the mountains. I know them and they will still know me. My mountains will protect you, and according to research they are very good at hiding those who want to stay hidden," he said as he stood up with me in his arms and walked purposefully towards the door.

"Research, Theo?" I said, looking at him closely.

"As I am the only one of my kind within the castle and I have no real memory of my existence before my time at the castle, Rachael thought it would be a good idea for me spend my time while she was occupied looking into the history of my origins," he said, smiling. At the mention of her name I was going to ask how the search for the missing Element was progressing, but I didn't—that question belonged in another time at another place.

"You have feelings for her, don't you?" I asked, studying his face.

"Like no other," he said, looking down.

"I understand. She is my new mother in this world, and I could not have survived without her. She will be the next person I see, as I know she does not and will not judge me," I said as I placed my hand gently over his. "But I need to rest again now, as I am only human and my stomach is filled with food, and you are both comfortable and warm."

With my words, Theo gently held me against him as my eyelids became heavier, too heavy to stay open.

Chapter 49

Theo and I stayed where we were. We both knew that I was too tired and too weak to move anywhere, and we both knew that the resort would have already been searched thoroughly after what had happened and was probably a safe place for me to rest for a while. Theo was, as ever, vigilant while I slept safe within his arms again, the smell of the earth that seeped through his skin giving me comfort, until I was ready to wake myself. I only opened my eyes when I was sure that I felt fully rested and had regained some of my strength. When he was sure I was fully awake, Theo convinced me that it was important for me to use the facilities in Daniel's chalet to cleanse myself, insisting that I do it even when I assured him that I had had a shower earlier that day.

Theo explained to me that the Mountain Dwellers' sense of smell was very acute and that even to him, who was accustomed to my scent, I smelled strongly of both vampire and demon and that neither smell would be welcomed among his people. He went on to explain that if I wanted his people to accept and protect me, then I needed to smell less of others and more like myself, that they were more likely to feel less threatened if they smelled my humanity; it made me vulnerable and nonthreatening, as it did with all the other beings on the planet. When I asked him what their reaction to his smell would be, he lowered his head and told me quietly that he did not know. My heart sank as I watched the fear behind his eyes. I did not know what to say or how to comfort him, so without further discussion I did what he told me to do and entered the shower. I washed myself thoroughly as he had instructed me, using the soaps that had been left behind. I made sure that I took my time, concentrating on my hair until it smelled of nothing but a clean me.

While I was in the shower, Theo disappeared for a short while, and when he returned he was carrying with him a familiar small bag. When I emerged from the shower, he handed the bag to me. I couldn't quite believe it was my personal bag, and it appeared that no one had even gone through the contents. Inside was my usual spare bag of makeup, my spare brush, and more importantly, hidden in a pocket was the little book I had been compelled to take from the library and had carried with me ever since, still not able to read it in any detail.

"I thought you might like some of your own things. I wasn't sure what to bring. I had no help in choosing," he said almost shyly. He then handed me another bag that appeared to have some of my own clothes inside.

"Thank you," I said as I rummaged through the second bag. These were my own belongings; they even smelled of me, of my perfume, of my scent. It was the best thing that he could have brought. They brought back some more of my own inner strength, and for the first time in a long time, I felt proud to have remained human. From what Theo had said, it would probably save my life over the next part of my journey. Inside the second bag was a pair of very familiar well-worn jeans, and with them there was a warm baggy jumper and a pair of soft fur-lined boots. He couldn't have chosen better for me.

"Theo, thank you, this is just perfect. Are you sure no one helped you? You seem to know me better than you think you do," I said, laughing as I began to pull on the clothes, with Theo turning his back in respect as I dropped the towel I had used to dry myself and had wrapped myself in. I hadn't even dried off the water thoroughly, but I didn't care. The smells of the castle, of my home, reminded me of what I was about to do. I couldn't change the path I had chosen. Even if I wanted to, I knew that all things happened for a reason, and I felt a now familiar pull in the direction I had chosen. It was going to be hard for everyone, not just me, but I knew that this was part of what I had to do, and I truly believed the words I had spoken to Theo. I knew they were right; I knew that I had to explore my doubts in full before I could possibly move forward in the direction that was expected.

As I was getting dressed, I was startled from my thoughts by the sound of Theo's mobile phone ringing. For a second both of us looked startled, both of us knowing that of course someone from the castle would phone him if he could not be found. I shouldn't have been surprised, but at the sound my heart started pounding in my chest and my mouth felt suddenly very dry.

As he removed the phone from his pocket, he showed me the front and I saw that it was Rachael who was ringing. I nearly changed my mind about what I was going to do, about what I was asking him to do. When I saw the look on his face, my resolve nearly crumbled; the look he gave me was questioning my decision again—one more time. But I knew I couldn't talk to Rachael or tell her what I was planning to do, at least not until I was sure that I was safe from anyone who might influence me. I also knew that she would be the next person whom I would tell and that she and Theo would be reunited soon, so I simply stood still, keeping my face expressionless, and watched Theo come to terms with the oath he had given me.

As I watched him, the tone of the phone changed from a ringing to a beeping sound. Without hesitation, Theo began to dismantle his phone, expertly taking it apart until he found the small circle of his blood embedded within its centre which identified the phone as his alone. This he placed under his foot and ground it into the floor.

"Does that mean they can't locate us now? Did that phone call alert them to our position?" I asked, already guessing that it had and understanding the need for us to very quickly put as much distance as possible between the chalets and ourselves.

"Princess, we need to go, now! I don't know if what I have done will slow their progress down or prevent their searchers from finding us quickly, but I do know that they will come here, the last place where my phone was activated. Besides, we need to reach the mountains before the sun has fully set. It is a long time since I have travelled these mountains unaided, and this world of mine also has its own dangers," he said as he quickly scooped me up and wrapped his own coat around me, trapping me in its warmth.

He stopped only to collect the leftover food, and as soon as we left the chalet, Theo started running, setting a steady, fairly fast pace for us as we ran towards the distant mountains. It was good to be out in the open again, especially with one of my own family. The blue of the sky was already deepening with the onset of evening. Theo ran with me effortlessly, ploughing through the deep snow, the raised temperature of his body keeping me warm. It was in his arms that I finally began to relax, and I even managed to close my eyes and rest again as he raced forward. We ran ever forward, following a path that only Theo appeared to know, the landscape devoid of features, the scenery pure white with mountains remaining in the far distance. Theo pushed himself even more as we heard the distant noise of the castle hovercrafts descending on the resort, their noise making me shudder; I knew that I had probably placed Theo in a very dangerous position.

After we heard them, Theo pulled out a very light cloak which was white with grey speckles, almost the equivalent of the Forest Dwellers cloak I had been given to make myself less obvious in my surroundings. As soon as we had put a little more distance between us and the hovercrafts' sound, Theo stopped for a moment and covered us both with it, hiding me completely. Then he looked around, changed our direction, and increased his pace again.

As the rest of the day wore on, we heard no further evidence of a pursuit behind us, the searchers staying at the resort perhaps to resolutely look for clues and further evidence of where we had gone. I knew that the knowledge that Theo had been there and had left with me had already been relayed back to the castle, probably causing equal measures of both relief and confusion among my loved ones.

Finally, the distant mountains drew closer with every step until, just as the sun finally went down and the moon rose, we reached them, and it was then that the howling began. The sound of the wolves was one of the most frightening yet compelling sounds I had ever heard, eerie and haunting, yet almost melodic, and with every new howl a fresh wave of coldness descended over my skin. I could feel the hairs on the back of my neck rising.

"The wolves are our guards. As I listen I know that all will be well, Princess, for they are probably communicating details of your whereabouts. They will not harm someone like you, but they would not thank me for bringing an unwanted visitor into their territory," Theo whispered as he felt me tense at the sound.

Eventually Theo stopped and placed me on my feet against a shallow indent in the mountainside. It wasn't quite a cave, but it was big enough for me to remain hidden from sight. He gave me what was left of the food and told me that I had to stay hidden for my own safety. He could not continue with me; it would be far too dangerous. He promised me when I tried to cling to him that he would be back as soon as he could, and he explained that before we could go farther, he needed to be certain of our welcome. It was excruciating to let him go again. I did not want to be on my own, especially in a place so restrictive, but eventually I did, knowing that I was making it more difficult for the pair of us. I stood and watched as he lined the small indent in the mountain with his coat, placing the smooth inner lining against the rough stone.

"This should create enough warmth," he said, smiling as he reached for my hand.

I stepped forward and leaned in against the soft fur, settling myself, trying to create a comfortable space. I trusted him and his oath to protect me, so when he covered me with his white and grey cloak and then encased me in a wall of snow, I knew not to panic, even though the feeling of claustrophobia threatened my conscious mind. I closed my eyes and took some deep breaths.

I heard him move away from the twilight cave he had created for me and started to use the methods that Dominic had taught me to relax and to shut out all that surrounded me, to reach within myself to find my inner place of peace. I stayed that way, breathing deeply until I became aware of my hunger, and when the pain in my stomach intruded, I fed myself the leftover scraps of food we had taken with us from the resort. I fed myself enough to settle the hunger pains in my stomach, and then I simply relaxed again. I remained there knowing that I was warm and safe, and I realised that I was, in some odd way, happy too.

My world remained silent; nothing disturbed it, and after a period of time, although I could not really tell how long, the twilight world changed. It went from white-yellow with the sun's influence to a white-grey and dark blue when the sun finally set totally. I tried to rest, but with the rising of the moon more wolves seemed to join in the communal conversation. Eventually, out of loneliness and perhaps boredom, I wriggled until I was again comfortable, pulled the edges of the cloak tightly around me, and drifted off to sleep. Although my sleep was deep, I still heard in the recesses of my mind the howls of the wolves and occasionally thought I felt a searching probe; someone was trying to reach out to me to locate me.

As my little world began to lighten again, I woke from my sleep and ate the last few pieces of food. My body ached again, and for a moment I felt disorientated and alone, especially as some of my other needs were making themselves known.

Fortunately, I did not have to wait long before I was released. At first I didn't see anything, but I heard a scraping noise, and after a few more tense moments I finally heard voices. I tensed myself as I saw the shadows above and in front of me, and then finally the layers that covered me and kept me safe appeared to lighten.

I had to close my eyes since the light was too bright, and when the cover was pulled back, two very large and very familiar hands reached forward, found mine, and gently pulled me up and out of the indent.

Chapter 50

Theo reached for my hands and pulled me gently to my feet, steadying me since my legs felt slightly numb from having been in the same position for too long. He smiled at me, and I could see that he had a look of approval on his face, almost as if this had been a small test that I had passed. I knew he had been worried about leaving me in the cave he had created, and deep down I knew that he had probably expected me to panic a little. Maybe he thought I would be in tears when he arrived back, but I was fine. I was relaxed but relieved to see him, so I simply greeted him with a warm, gentle smile. As soon as I was on my feet and steady enough to let go of him and stand alone, Theo silently took a step to one side and another Mountain Dweller stepped forward. This Dweller was not quite as tall as Theo, but he was just as muscular and he still towered over me.

I understood from the looks that passed between them that there was definitely something between them. They knew each other well, although I could not tell if it was because they were perhaps related; I didn't think so at first. The strange Mountain Dweller's colouring was slightly different from Theo's. It was fairer and less grey, but the line of the jaw was the same and the colouring in their eyes was similar. I thought back to Mia and Thomas and guessed that perhaps he could have been a cousin.

This Mountain Dweller had very long fairish hair with silver streaks running through it; whereas Theo reminded me of mountain rocks, this new Dweller reminded me of clay and sand. Even though I didn't know the new Dweller, there was something about him that made me smile. After a while, I recognised that it was almost as if he was part human, like Heather. He was purer than Theo, unchanged by essence, and definitely seemed more in tune with his surroundings; he stopped to listen as the wind changed around us, something that Theo didn't seem to register. He was dressed casually, in jeans and a loose flowing shirt, oblivious to the chill in the mountain air.

"Princess Liberty, this is Craig, and as you might have guessed from the way you have just studied him, he is my cousin and he is also a prince among my people. He is the youngest son of our king," Theo said respectfully, his eyes never leaving his cousin's face.

"I am sorry. Was I staring? I did not mean to be rude," I said, snapping back to reality, dropping my gaze and bowing my head slightly, still smiling.

"Greetings, Princess. Theo has spoken highly of you, although he did not tell me everything, so it is with great curiosity that I have come personally to greet you myself," Craig said. I noticed that his voice was not as deep as Theo's but still deep and growly—like loose gravel being trod underfoot. His accent also sounded strange, as if he was not accustomed to using the universal language.

"Prince Craig," I responded, not really knowing how I felt about him because I could not get a sense of him yet, almost as if he had his own protective barriers in place. But he had a mind similar to Theo's, filled, I could sense, with swirling grey mists of stubbornness.

After a few more moments of silent stillness, I shivered slightly as the coldness of the mountain air finally penetrated my thoughts and brought my mind back to the present. Theo noticed me shivering and picked me up gently, cradling me protectively to his warm body and wrapping me tightly in his warm coat.

"We will follow where you lead, Craig," Theo said. "I have a sense that it is time for us to move again. I know that we have many miles to cover before we are home and safe again. It is no longer safe for us to remain in one place for too long." He gestured for us to move.

Craig stood directly in front of Theo, blocking his path. "Are you sure, cousin? This decision could have far-reaching

337

consequences for all involved, not just you and this girl," he said. Craig was no longer smiling and looked at me intently as he asked Theo the question.

"I am sure," Theo responded simply.

"Theo, what is going on here?" I asked quietly as Craig turned and gathered up the cloak, shaking the snow out of it and moving ahead, away from us.

"Nothing that you need to know or worry about for now, Princess, but I promise I shall speak with you about it later," Theo said quietly, rubbing his face gently against the top of my head and giving a strange look to the back of his cousin.

Although I had previously thought the terrain to be flat, that perception changed a little more with every few steps I took. I realised that there were many hidden levels that were difficult to see until one was almost upon them. Not too long after we had started walking, we came across a fast-moving stream beside some trees; it was there that we made our first stop. The water was crystal clear, allowing me to cleanse and tend to my other needs and Craig to gather some large berries. Although I did not understand the language that Theo and Craig used to communicate with each other, I understood from the tone of their voices and the sadness in Theo's expression that these two beings had once shared a close bond. A strange thought came to me then: I knew that David was capable of love and compassion and was infinitely more flexible than his parents, but seeing Craig and Theo, I thought that perhaps the flexibility had come too late for many of the planet's beings.

Like the wolves, Craig seemed sure of his path even though there was no visible path to follow. We stopped a few times, usually when Theo sensed I needed nourishment or to stretch my aching body. The food I was given was simple but nourishing, simple breads with some of the berries Craig had gathered earlier and plenty of fresh water.

We travelled in silence, with Theo never moving beyond arm's reach from me even when we stopped. I don't know whether he was protecting me or if it was simply because he wanted to keep me close in case I needed warmth. The silence that sometimes grew among us was palpable and slightly uncomfortable; at times we were all lost in our own thoughts. We all knew, I think, that with those first steps forward we were now crossing a previously uncrossed line together. I wasn't certain how much damage I was doing by not returning to the castle straight away, but I knew that my decision was a very dangerous one perhaps for all of us. There were times when I almost gave up and told Theo to take me back to the resort, but I knew instinctively that it would have been the wrong decision.

I often noticed Craig watching me from a distance and saw him move forward occasionally as if to remove me from Theo. There seemed to be nothing but mild curiosity on his face, and I sensed no harm from him. However, whenever he did make any type of move or gesture towards me, Theo turned, moving me away again and tightening his hold on me.

"What is wrong, Theo? Do you think he will hurt me? Are we not safe with him? I don't think he means me any harm, do you?" I asked when I thought I could without Craig hearing.

"He does not know his own strength, Princess. I myself had difficulty holding you when you first came to the castle, but thanks to your persistence I have had plenty of practice. In truth, I am worried how I am going to keep you from harm among my people, because from memory I know that even the children are bigger and more physically powerful than you. My people are naturally curious, and many of them have never ventured beyond the mountain range they were born within. You will certainly be an object of curiosity for them," he explained with a sigh.

"Don't worry, Theo. I seem to have a knack of getting people to be gentle with me," I said, trying to reassure him.

At my words he did smile, but the smile never reached his eyes. I knew he was worried, but there was nothing that could be done. I would have to deal with things the way I always had: one problem (or rather *being*) at a time. I managed to sleep for short periods, continuously lulled by the heat of Theo's body and the steady rhythm of his gait.

As the day turned to evening and then night, we walked farther and farther into the mountains until eventually we came to a stop. When I opened my eyes, I focused properly and saw that we had walked into a valley that remained hidden from sight until one was almost halfway into it. At some point during my naps, we had moved into another mountain range; this one appeared more sheltered. It had trees and the occasional shrub with the same berries that Craig had collected previously. I also heard running water nearby, although I could not tell where the sound had come from.

As we walked farther in, I took more notice of what appeared in front of me and asked Theo to place me on my feet because I had never even imagined I would see anything like it again. We were standing at the top of what looked like a corridor of stone, on either side of which was a mountain, and I could not see anything above those mountains. It was as if they actually touched and supported the yellow ball of the sun that was beginning to lower itself onto the horizon.

On each side of the mountains was a series of caves. Some looked natural and others looked as if they had been created by the Mountain Dwellers who had need of them. The entrances, although they varied in size, were enormous to accommodate the inhabitants.

The caves appeared to be evenly spaced, and many of them were surrounded by glistening streamers of ice and snow. The scene in front of me was exquisite, with the sun shining down the entire length of the corridor and making the frames of the entrances glisten and sparkle; the whole effect was almost surreal. I stood for a moment taking it all in, but the spell was broken quickly because it seemed as though, as soon as we were visible, somewhere not too far from us a wolf howled. From what Theo had told me before, I knew, though, that the wolf was simply announcing our arrival. We waited a while, unmoving until the pitch of the wolf's howl changed and there was an answer from somewhere below us. Beside me, I felt Theo relax a little. "It is safe," he whispered, more to himself than to me or Craig.

"Welcome home, cousin," Craig said with a crooked and mischievous smile. "This should prove to be a very interesting evening."

After a moment's hesitation, Craig led the way forward down the centre of the corridor. I walked after him, with Theo walking closely behind me.

Chapter 51

As Craig walked slowly forward, howls could still be heard in the distance, and at their sound many Mountain Dwellers began to emerge from the caves. They watched our approach with sombre faces; respect for Craig was obvious in their faces. As soon as Craig was among them, they bowed silently to him in greeting, and even the younger ones appeared to know what was expected from them when their prince was among them.

As we continued along the path, I noticed that out of the ornately carved entrance of a particularly large cave, which was set slightly aside from the others, two extremely tall and regal-looking silver-haired Mountain Dwellers, one female and one male, emerged and walked forward to embrace him. I understood from their greeting that they were probably Craig's parents.

I watched Theo's face as the Mountain Dwellers approached. His eyes seemed to search beyond them, looking for someone or something else. I concentrated and followed the line of his sight in the far distance. I thought I saw other Mountain Dwellers, perhaps another pair or maybe more, standing near the entrance of another large cave. My attention was brought back to the Mountain Dwellers standing directly in front of us when Craig stepped aside in order for them to see me better. At the same time, Theo's mind also seemed to come back to where we stood and he gently took my hand and walked me slowly, almost cautiously, forward. I could not tell the age of the beings in front of me, but I knew they were very old; there was a sedate dignity about them that instantly made me warm to them. I knew that yet again I was standing in the presence of some of the planet's ancient royalty and that these were beings that cared about our planet.

Although their eyes were the colour of slate, there was a silver sparkle to them that was entrancing, almost mesmerising; I noticed the white of the surrounding snow reflected in them. When I felt Theo bow I did the same, again bowing only as low as was expected. I was a princess and that had not changed, not even among these ancient beings.

When we all stood again, they exchanged a few words with Theo, words that sounded heavy with emotion. Again Theo glanced beyond them at the cave in the distance. I did not understand the words they were saying, but their tone was gentle and their faces looked kind. Theo gently placed his arm around my shoulder as he responded to them softly. After many words were exchanged and glances directed my way, they eventually stepped aside and we carried on walking forward, moving deeper into the valley of the Mountain Dwellers.

There were many women, a few children, and even fewer men, all of them dressed similarly in light clothes: shorts or trousers and T-shirts for the men and boys and light dresses for the women and girls; Theo looked overdressed compared with his people. The men who did emerge emerged together, and some of them had snow wolves by their side.

When he saw me looking at the wolves and the small group of men, Theo leaned down and whispered in my ear, "These are the community guards. The wolves are our friends, and they choose to stand with us and protect us. Notice we do not tether them to us. The men of the community are noticeably absent because they prefer to hunt than to stay with the women and children."

Theo had been right about the children. Although some of them were very young, they were definitely bigger than I was and looked strong. Immediately I felt quite insignificant among this race of beings. Although they were physically large, it was the weight of their silence that made them appear even larger. With all this in mind, I did feel very small and vulnerable, but not unsafe. It was the silence, though, that made me more nervous, and I found myself clinging to Theo as we walked. Those who had emerged appeared to ignore me at first because after the prince, Craig, their other main focus appeared to be Theo, whom they regarded with a strange mix of curiosity and hostility. I noticed that some of them also looked at him with sadness and compassion, as if they felt sorry for him.

Craig led us to an empty cave at the far end of the valley, slightly away from the other caves, and after gently moving aside some of the overgrown ice crystals, they led me and Theo inside. The cave was huge and had many chambers that became warmer the farther back we ventured. Although the front chamber was natural, some of the other chambers appeared to have been hollowed out by those who had lived there previously.

There were four main chambers in total: the farthest one was obviously for sleeping because it had fur blankets strewn over the floor and it was poorly lit. It had a small pit in the floor that looked as though it contained the glowing embers of a dying fire. As time went on I learned that those embers never died completely; instead they served to both heat and give the sleeping chamber a warm glow. On one of the walls was a plate of ice that had been polished until it was clean enough to serve as a mirror. I went over to it and was surprised to find its surface cold yet wet, as it was continuously melting. By my feet there was a little trough that ran the drips of water away.

The next chamber held a large hole in the floor that was filled with clear mountain water, which appeared to bubble in a continuous fountain. Even before I bent down and felt the temperature of the water, I knew somehow that it would be warm.

The next chamber was a storage chamber that had shelves carved into its walls. These shelves were stocked with huge drinking vessels and plates the size of the top of my bedside table back at the castle. There was also a recessed area that was kept cool by blocks of ice. Inside the ice blocks looked to be large chunks of meat and various fish. On one of the shelves I noticed that someone had kindly left us a supply of some berries and some bread. There was also a large vessel of a substance that resembled blood. When Craig saw Theo looking at it, he told him that the hunters had collected it when they knew that Craig had given Theo his protection. When Theo saw that we had both been left a little food of our own, he thanked Craig again for his thoughtfulness. After I had finished walking through the chambers, I stood near the entrance of the cave. "Thank you," I said as Craig went to walk by me.

He suddenly turned fast, and before either Theo or I could react, Craig had lifted me by my waist and held me in front of him, my eyes on a level with his. Although his grip was strong, he was gentle and I wasn't frightened. "Cousin, she is more fragile than you think," said Theo gently, placing a hand on Craig's arm.

"But not as fragile as *you* think, perhaps," said Craig, smiling at me with that crooked amused smile that I had seen before.

There was something about him, like others that not been infused. I had liked him almost immediately after I met him, so I smiled back. Up close I realised that he smelled of the earth, of the rocks, and of fresh mountain air.

"If you would just release me a little, it would be easier for me to breathe," I said, smiling even wider.

"She is brave for a little one, though I am not too sure that she is as clever as she thinks. I noticed she has connected with the others who are aware of the gift that is our planet and who claim to care for it. There are marks on her to verify this, which makes her interesting and perhaps worth keeping for the time being, nevertheless," Craig said, placing me gently back on the floor of the cave.

Just as he was about to say something else, a young female appeared and her appearance broke off any other comment, except Craig saying, "You may stay here for as long as you need to. I personally left instructions for more food to be brought to you, but in all other matters I will not interfere." With those words Craig left, the atmosphere within the cave becoming cooler again.

As I wandered around the caves more slowly, placing the few possessions from my bags in the various chambers and trying to satisfy my doubts and my strong longing to see my friends again, I could feel the pull of their sadness and their yearning for my safety.

Theo sat himself just inside the entrance, watching me as I moved from chamber to chamber, gently touching some of the surfaces and trying to make some sense of the fact that this cave had suddenly become my temporary new home. And

I must admit, as I breathed in the natural smell of the caves, the need to return home appeared to vanish as I realised that there was a beautiful simplicity about the place that was most compelling.

As I wandered through the caves, I noticed some darker places in the rocks, like the darkness on the outside of the Temple of Thought, and instinctively knew that these were probably corridors of some sort. I wanted to test my theory, but when I placed my hand against the stone and started to push, I suddenly felt as if it would be the wrong thing to do, that the cave perhaps needed its own time to adjust to me. Besides, I had a feeling that I had done enough for one day. Theo sighed wearily as I turned back to him.

"Do you know where these lead to?" I asked.

"No, I am unfamiliar with this cave. It is not one from my infancy," he said, closing his eyes.

"Have you any memories, Theo? Is your life here before you were taken coming back to you?" I persisted.

"I am not sure—maybe. Well, Princess, it does seem that this is going to be our home for a while. What do you think?" Theo looked at me to see how I might respond. As I gently touched his tired face, he opened his eyes and smiled widely at me; relief was clearly on his face.

"Theo, all of this is wonderful, and your people seem to be welcoming. I sense no threat from this place," I said.

"We will be safe here, Princess, I have Craig's word on that. Besides, I agree it appears you are right: beings of all kinds do appear to like you," he said calmly and happily.

"Why, why do you have Craig's word, though? What is it that has been between you? I have seen the looks that you two have exchanged." I waited eagerly for his response.

"That is a long story, perhaps for another time. Let me just say that he needed my protection a long time ago and I gave it freely. You have my oath that I will share the story at another time, but now I need to rest, Princess," he said as he closed his eyes.

"Do you need to drink, too?" I asked, concerned for him and knowing that he had already endured too much for me. As he stilled himself I went and collected a large vial and dragged one of the huge fur blankets into the chamber with me. After he drank from the vial, he closed his eyes and I sat with him, leaning against him. I sat thinking for the rest of that evening and night, since I had slept too much during the day for me to feel sleepy.

I thought about what the next chapter of my life would hold, knowing that whatever happened from those few relaxing moments onward, I would inevitably have to answer for my actions.

Chapter 52

For the first few days I was a little unsure of myself. Since my life had begun at the castle, at every new place I went there was usually a steady stream of important beings. This was not the case among the Mountain Dwellers. Instead, Theo and I decided that neither of us would leave the safety of our cave. We tried to settle ourselves as best we could, and there were long periods of time when neither of us spoke. I had no doubt that Theo had his own thoughts about the decision and the impossible predicament I had placed us both in. I tried my best to make a home for us. I had a little help because over the first few mornings someone discreetly left us a few more necessary things such as brooms, buckets, and blankets. I never saw who left the supplies, and I don't know whether Theo did either. If he had his suspicions, he never said. I felt I would have liked to thank them, but after a while I simply accepted the gifts and put them all to good use. I may have been a princess in the castle, but because of the Enclosure I was no stranger to cleaning. Besides, after the first day I found that by keeping myself busy and doing chores around the cavern's chambers, I did not think too much. I knew there was no going back or running away from the consequences of my actions now.

Although we did not have any visitors, after the first day a few of the younger children came and sat outside our cave, simply staring at us silently, their young faces creased with curiosity. They didn't approach us, and they usually stayed staring at us until an adult came, rounded them up, and moved them away.

At the beginning, I felt uncomfortable with their silent scrutiny and I called to them, wanting, perhaps even needing, to make contact, but not wanting to frighten them. However, as soon as I spoke or made any kind of move towards them, they moved away a little farther and only moved forward again when I went back into our cave. After a while I left them to their curiosity, even running after them occasionally to try to make a game of it with them.

The only other person who remotely acknowledged us was a woman who consistently brought me food every morning and evening on large platters which were almost too heavy for me to carry. In the morning the food consisted of warm breads and biscuits that were rolled in various fruits, and in the evening the food consisted of a meat stew and breads and berries. The food was nourishing and filling, and left me feeling warm and drowsy after each meal. Because there was plenty, almost too much, I managed to build myself a little store of food in my larder, which for a strange reason made me feel more at home, as if I had something to offer an occasional guest.

After that first day I began to store whatever was left over from our meals, knowing that I would have to become a little more self-sufficient if I was going to survive. That night as I lay down, I realised that I ached after the first day of cleaning and polishing the chambers, and that the aches I felt were a good and satisfying thing.

It took me a couple of days to notice that whenever the female Mountain Dweller approached the entrance to our cave, Theo stood to greet her. At first she did not even look at him, but eventually eye contact was made and I realised that there must have been something between them previously. The look that passed between them was one of sadness and loss, maybe even with a touch of longing, or so I imagined. After contact had been made between Theo and the woman, I took it upon myself to be there when she delivered our food each time she approached. I said hello to her and bowed.

Theo warned me not to get to close and explained that it was deemed insulting for any being to enter the shadow range (the area in front of the cave where the shadow never quite disappeared) of a Mountain Dweller without being formally invited, which was why they had an undeserved reputation for being aloof and withdrawn. I did not listen to him since she was my first point of contact among them. After seeing my stubborn reaction to her appearances and knowing that I was getting restless and not willing to hide myself away in the cavern, Theo told me her name was Adolfina and that he was certain that she had known him and had been close to him in the time before he was taken.

Like all of the other Mountain Dwellers that I had seen, Adolfina was tall, regal, and quiet. Like Craig, she seemed to be extremely curious about me, especially after one morning when I had stepped forward, carefully avoiding the shadow she cast, and greeted her with my best reassuring smile. I faltered a little when I heard a groan escape from Theo's lips. He knew with certainty that I was determined to learn as much as possible while I had the opportunity among these beautiful regal beings, which were the least known among the existing Carers. Eventually she addressed Theo, and from her careful reaction and the questions she appeared to ask him, I gathered that the Mountain Dweller community all knew who I really was without really knowing why I had been brought among them.

One morning after I had greeted her in my customary polite way, instead of simply smiling shyly and walking away, Adolfina stayed where she was and held out her huge hand to me, extending an invitation for me to step into her shadow and therefore her personal space. I walked slowly forward and tentatively placed both of my hands into her offered hand. I took another step towards her until I stood within her shadow and she gently touched my hair, which was all gold in contrast to her silver. Without letting go of my hands and speaking very softly to Theo, Adolfina reached down and picked me up. Unlike Craig, she did not hold me at arm's length. Instead she cradled me to her as Theo had done when he had first encountered me.

I shivered slightly as she sniffed at me. When she seemed satisfied, she smiled and very gently placed me back on my feet and left the cave, her face just as kind and indulgent as Theo's had been. There was a smooth coolness to her skin, and I could see myself reflected in the silver of her eyes. She was strangely beautiful and smelled of fresh air and clean earth. Again it was apparent to me that her aroma was not tainted by the coppery smell that mingled with Theo's aroma.

After that day I made more of an effort to live. I adapted to the living arrangements within the cavern well and was almost able to forget the worries of the outside world. When I questioned Theo about how I felt after just a few days, he simply laughed and told me that it was due to the magic of the mountains. Even at night when the wolves communicated and the wind blew, their combination sounded strangely comforting, lulling me into deep, dreamless sleep. The only annoying thing that became an issue and made me slightly uncomfortable was that my poor well-worn jeans had begun to develop holes and my jumper was simply not warm enough for the mountain winds that blew continuously. Although I had the blankets, they were too heavy and too big for me to keep wrapped around me and were not very practical.

After I finally mentioned the problem to Theo, and after another hole had appeared in my jeans, Theo arranged with Adolfina for some clothes to be brought for me; through Theo I understood that they were her daughter's clothes.

Adolfina kindly altered them so that I could wear them. There was a pair of trousers and thick linen shirts, and Adolfina also provided me with a fur-lined coat that she had obviously made from one of the snow wolf blankets.

When she presented me with my new clothes, I stepped up and hugged her. Although she meant the pat on the head to be gentle, the force of it made me dizzy and I almost fell. However, when Theo spoke to her sharply, I hugged her again and defended her. The smile I received in return was dazzling.

Within the community I had no contact with the outside world, but I did know that the searches continued and that these beings had increased the number of lookouts on the mountaintops. I heard the wolf calls regularly during the first couple of days, but thankfully they became a little quieter as things settled.

The children continued to visit our cave, and though they did not venture inside after a few days, they started to smile shyly and wave back at me before the adults arrived and they ran away. When I felt myself relax enough and began to meditate again, I felt those who would sense me searching for me and knew without a doubt that I had to locate them before they came here.

I often felt that I should return, but something made me resist. I knew that this was part of my destiny; I knew that all of us had to wait and be patient, even though I often caught Theo looking at me with a longing faraway look in his eye.

Chapter 53

After that first week we finally had another visitor. He was a tall, serious, and much older-looking Dweller. His hair was snow white and his skin was the colour of the dark granite that was found in the deeper recesses of the caverns. I couldn't sense his age, but at a guess I would have said he was the oldest natural being I had ever encountered. He was dressed in a loose and flowing fur-lined cloak that appeared to give him an air of importance. At his approach Theo stood in front of me as if to shield me, even though there appeared to be no need for Theo's protection since the stranger did not even bother to look in my direction.

The stranger spoke directly to Theo. His words were precise and clipped as if he was quoting from an old script, and when the old Mountain Dweller left, Theo sat down with me and explained gently to me that it had been decided that Theo was to attend a community meeting. The reason he gave was that the community had little to do with the planet outside and they wanted to know what was happening. He added that the planet was showing signs of age and, because of this, the Mountain Dwellers had noticed changes in the mountains.

Knowing that I would be left on my own, slowly and with Theo's help, I began to venture farther from our cave. I didn't go far, just to the boundaries of its shadows. I began to sit and watch the community, smiling or waving at anyone who glanced in my direction.

I enjoyed watching what was going on from afar. It was relaxing and sometimes strange and amusing. I had begun to enjoy the community of the larger-than-life beings as they went about their business. They generally ignored me and most of the adults kept their distance, but there were days when some of them smiled with kindness when they saw me.

It was the younger children who seemed most at ease with my presence. They spent their days playing with each other, and sometimes they were joined by very young snow wolf cubs. One evening when I asked Theo about them, I learned that it was in nursery that many of the lifelong friendships and bonds were made as the cubs and children played together day after day.

One morning I noticed Adolfina sitting watching the young ones intently. I didn't notice any other adults about; she seemed to be the only one who was looking after the young that day. Feeling extra brave, I got up and walked towards her. She saw me and smiled. I felt then the stares of the other women who had moved into sight at the entrances to their caverns and had begun to move towards me. They were only stopped with a sharp reprimand from Adolfina, who continued to smile and beckon me forward.

When I reached her she patted me gently on the shoulder and began calling to the children and the cubs, who all came running at her call. As they came nearer, Adolfina sat down at the last minute and pulled me onto her lap. She kept her arms outstretched in front of us both to protect me from the enthusiastic youngsters. She told the children to sit down and they did. A lone wolf cub who was with them that day did not really understand what was happening and totally ignored her, clambering all over the both of us.

The cub was already big and strong, and it seemed to like me very much. However hard I tried to defend myself, with one lick it had slobbered over most of my face and my hair, much to the amusement of many of the young Dwellers and because of the cub's obvious delight in me. For the first time in what seemed like a long time, I laughed, a real laugh, not just one that I thought was expected. Its effect felt like magic. For just a moment all of my worries, all of my cares, melted away. After a few seconds Adolfina joined me and laughed at the antics of the overly excited cub, which seemed to be laughing itself with its high-pitched yapping.

The little children were all laughing, not really knowing what was going on but thinking it was silly and fun. All of it was so infectious; it was well-known among all ages and across the diversity of all the beings of this planet that laughter—real, honest, joyous laughter—has a unique way of making us forget our differences. Who I was, who they were? It didn't matter. We were all simply together.

Theo, hearing the commotion coming out of our cave after he had returned early from his morning session at the community meeting, came over to where we were and sat down with us, smiling at our outrageously carefree behaviour. But sadly, Theo's arrival broke the spell. The children who sat closest to me immediately shied away from him. When he went to move the cub, who had taken to sitting determinedly in my lap, he met with a growly resistance. At the same time, the poor animal began to dig his claws painfully into my legs until Adofina spoke to it softly in a language that I was still unfamiliar with. Nevertheless, the cub refused to move from my lap. After a while even Adolfina appeared to give up, leaving the cub where it was. She then addressed Theo. "She is safe," she said with a heavy accent.

The subject then changed. "I know I was among the elders at the meeting when it was decided," Theo said.

"May I ask what was decided?" I asked as I watched the thoughtful exchange between them.

"It is good?" Adolfina asked, appearing not to take any notice of me.

"Yes, it is good," Theo responded.

When I looked at Adolfina she smiled, but it was Theo who grinned wider, bowing his head to her as he explained, "Adolfina has been appointed your guardian while you are here. She is a Community Carer and oversees the care of the young. Since she heard of her new task, she has tried to learn a few words of the universal language to make communication between you easier," he said, smiling at her.

"I thought everyone had to be educated in the language anyway," I said pleasantly.

"The emperor appears to want it this way, but this community is far removed from the rest of the planet. These are a simple but proud people who have lived this way for as long as even the eldest being here can recall. There has never been a reason for them to change."

I smiled at his words—they made perfect sense, and it was comforting to know that these Dwellers had placed their own culture before that of their emperor.

Although at times I still felt awkward, that was my breakthrough day within the community. It appeared that the children liked me very much, and the adults seemed to trust the intuition of their children. After that day I spent most of my time in the nursery with Adolfina and the very young. I rose early with Theo and made breakfast for both of us. I would go to join Adolfina, and Theo would use the corridors within the cavern to access the meeting cave and avoid the sunlight.

There were really no objections from anyone, although a few of the mothers did visit the nursery over the first few days to watch my interaction with their young, but once they were satisfied they did not bother Adolfina again. The children were taught to be gentle, and I was taught to have confidence in them. Adolfina continued to try to use words from the language that I knew, and I had Theo teach me some of the language of the community. Other lessons that interested me and that were taught to the younger children were rock reading and mental mapping, in addition to lessons on the significance of the ancient stone corridors. I listened and concentrated hard, and although I did not understand all of the words that were spoken, I grasped their meaning very quickly.

I was also happy to say that the snow cub never left my side. When I tried after the first afternoon to leave the cub, it cried and became very uncooperative until I came back to its side, even though Adolfina tried to comfort it. When I asked her about the cub, after a lot of effort Aldofina explained that it had been left for dead when its mother had been caught and killed in one of the resorts; its mother had only been looking for food. She told me that the cub was a female and was also in need of someone to care for her. I volunteered without hesitation.

I named my cub Starlight because on the first night all I saw were stars and love in her eyes. She was difficult to leave, and for hours into the night I couldn't sleep. All I heard was her yaps and her crying. I knew that she was calling to me, so eventually

I went to her, knowing that I was probably doing something that I shouldn't. I sneaked over to Adolfina's cavern and released her from her tether. I took her back to the cavern I shared with Theo and lay with her, using the warmth of her thick white fur to warm me. She was pure white with a small grey star-shaped mark near her muzzle, and she grew bigger every day.

As soon as I was able the next day, I ventured out of my cave and sat and waited until Adolfina emerged with the children. I spent all day with them again, with the bond between the cub and me deepening with each passing moment. Although she must have been a little concerned and more than a little surprised to see me with the cub, Adolfina did not say anything. She seemed to understand that there was a deep connection. Adolfina then took the time to show me how to feed her huge pieces of meat from my hand, which Starlight took and swallowed without chewing, and then told me to give her fresh water to drink.

I cleaned up after her when she made a mess. I worked hard; I loved the cub and she loved me back. After the first day, with Adolfina's blessing, I took Starlight back to the cave I shared with Theo and told her this was home. There was no howling that night. Theo took a little bit of persuading when I asked if she could stay with me, but I knew he could never resist me when I wanted something.

Sadly, with each day that passed I knew that this new existence would have to end soon, and I prepared myself a little more every day. The only good thing about my return, apart from my reuniting with my beloved and the others whom I missed, was knowing that my return to the castle spelled the death of my most hated enemies so that I might actually be free of them.

I stayed because I reasoned that I wasn't yet strong enough. However, I became more restless as my birthday neared. I knew that when I returned to my home, I would be a human adult and not a child anymore. I missed David, I missed all of my family, and I knew that no matter what happened I would be loved.

I also missed Elathan as much as I missed the others. I had promised myself that there would be no more secrets, and I intended to keep that promise. The decision of the time for my return was taken from my hands when on the fifteenth day after my arrival, Craig returned to our cave and brought with him a mobile phone. Without saying a word he placed it on the floor of our front chamber. Following him into the cave was Theo, who always appeared if an adult other than Adolfina approached me. Starlight growled at the object on the floor and tried to bat it with her paw. "Starlight, come to me," I said, laughing as I tried to move the ever growing wolf cub away.

"Why have you brought me this?" I asked when I finally managed to pick up the mobile phone.

"He thinks you have had long enough to think and clear your thoughts and that it is time for you to take responsibility for that which you are and what you have done," Theo said in response to my question.

"It is time, Princess, because I have a sense that something is about to happen. Although your presence is and always will be welcome here, you do not belong among us. My people also know this. Therefore, their curiosity is growing, and that is not always a good thing. Adolfina also has other duties and cannot always be at your side," Craig said.

"I know. You are right, but I am here for a reason," I said. "Please give me a few more days. If that reason does not become clear to you all, then I will willingly contact my beloved and those whom I know still search continuously for me. I know what I have done in coming here, and I have no wish for your existence here to be interrupted. It is not my intention to bring those who search for me here, so I will go to them. Please, just give me a little while. That is all I ask."

After a few moments Craig said quietly, "It will be as you wish, Princess, but be aware I can only delay the actions of some of the less patient members of my community. I cannot stop the inevitable." At that, he left the cave. My heart sank as I realised that he looked disappointed, but I didn't think his disappointment was directed at me; instead it was a reflection of his own community.

"He is among the few here who argue your case, who still insist that you are welcome. Scouts have returned with disturbing stories, and it appears that David's patience is running out. There have been demands for information as to where you are," Theo said, frowning and watching Craig's back as he walked away.

"Theo, I am sorry, and I can only imagine the danger I have placed the people in this community in, but please trust me. We are meant to be here at this time. I know this, and the feelings within me are becoming stronger," I said in an equally, if not more, serious voice. It was so hard sometimes to explain these things, the things that I sensed with Theo. He was such a simple and uncomplicated being, and I loved him for it, but sometimes I wanted him to understand just a little more of the feelings that shaped some of my decisions. However, I knew that there was nothing more for me to say on the matter, so we both settled down for the evening. My thoughts were sombre as I settled down, with the knowledge that although Theo was a being of few words even among his own kind, he was becoming quieter as the days went on. I knew that was partly because he missed Rachael. I knew I was asking a lot of him . . . again. As I lay down that night, for the first time in the longest time, I thought of my mother and asked her for her guidance before I went to sleep.

Chapter 54

The next day started like any other day, and like every other day I got up and bathed in the warm clear bath in the centre chamber and got ready to join Adolfina in caring for and teaching the younger children. As always, Starlight rose with me and stayed by my side, although she was reluctant to enter the chamber when I immersed myself in water. She tended to growl a little if I flicked water near her, but soon she would have to be cleaned (but not on that day, I reasoned to myself, as my heart and head were still heavy from the serious thoughts of the night before). I was alone in the cave since Theo always rose before me and disappeared for a while.

After that first morning, I didn't ask him where he went, although sometimes he returned with food, other times he returned with nothing; sometimes he seemed happy, while on other days he appeared to be frustrated and sad. Theo apparently had his own destiny among these people.

I busied myself getting ready, taking my time to choose my outfit for the day. After that first morning when Adolfina had adjusted some clothes for me, some of the other women had given Theo some parcels for me. Adolfina helped me to adjust them to my size so I had a little bit of variety, which was nice. After I was clean, dry, and dressed, and after making something to eat for myself and for Starlight, I left our cave. I walked slowly, enjoying the crispness of the morning air and laughing at the antics of Starlight as she tried to investigate every little movement of every little thing that crossed our path, often growling at the

359

sun's glinting reflection and shadows on the path of the mountain corridor.

I was early that morning, but there was still a lot of activity among the Mountain Dwellers. Many of the males were already leaving for the day's hunt. Again, I no longer felt intimidated by their size since I was mostly ignored by the males. I knew the way to Adolfina's cave very well and followed the unseen route that I had mapped out for myself. I was glad that this was a skill that I had learned while sitting among the younger children during some of their lessons. Theo had explained earnestly during one frustrating exercise that among the whiteness of the mountains, it was a skill that would save a being like me.

As soon as I approached Adolfina's cave, I knew that something was different. It wasn't just she who stood waiting for me; Theo and Craig stood with her, all of them with serious looks on their faces as they stood watching my approach. I still didn't hesitate. There was a determination in my step as I continued to walk forward until I was a few feet away. Starlight stopped beside me, growling softly when she noticed Theo.

"Good morning, Adolfina," I said, greeting her in her language but not sure what was happening.

"Good morning, Liberty. We have been waiting for you," she said in turn with a warm smile. Unfortunately, though, that smile did not reach her eyes, and that worried me more than anything else because, up until then, I had never imagined that a Mountain Dweller would display such doubt and emotion.

Because of what I saw on Adolfina's face, my initial thoughts were that David had lost patience and had finally located me and arrived, but then I realised I would have sensed him, and surely I would have heard or noticed something out of the ordinary.

"Come, come inside, do not worry," Adolfina said softly, sensing my worry and holding out her hand reassuringly. As always, I trusted her so I walked forward and placed my hand in hers, glad to do so, as my legs had begun to falter. Starlight walked with me, keeping her body pressed close to my legs as if she also knew that something was wrong or was perhaps going to happen. As I gently placed my hand on her soft head, I smiled because I knew already that even though she was still very young, like Theo she was ready to protect me. We walked into Adolfina's cave. We were together, and that somehow settled me a little. Once inside, I calmly sat on some cushions in the front chamber, with Starlight sitting by my feet.

"There is someone coming who wishes to meet you. She apparently has waited a long time to do this," Craig offered as an explanation for the tension that was beginning to grow. "At least she has told our council that she has waited quite a while for this meeting, but she believes that the time is now, and I believe that this is the event you have been waiting for," Craig continued as he sat with me on a long stretch of rock that served as a seat for Adolfina. His voice was soft and compassionate, and he seemed gentler with me for some reason, as if he finally understood my reason for doing what I did.

Adolfina busied herself getting a bowl of water for Starlight and some juices for the rest of us. I noticed she looked almost afraid and very nervous. I found that curious because I didn't think that these people were afraid of anything, and I almost felt like I should be the one who should offer comfort to these large, stoic beings. When I looked at Theo, his face was blank, and when I tried to understand the thoughts in his head, he gave me a look that told me not to, to simply wait and see.

The silence in the cave was almost deafening. We waited for a while, none of us speaking, the silence dominating our minds until I thought I heard voices. They sounded far away and muffled. I realised that I hadn't heard any commotion outside; the voices instead seemed to come from somewhere near to me. After a moment I realised that Starlight heard them also because she had risen to her feet and appeared torn, obviously wanting to investigate but also wanting to stay and protect me. As the voices got nearer, I realised that I knew at least one of them, so I stood facing the direction that I thought they were coming from, a direction that did not make sense since I ended up staring at a wall situated to the left of me inside Adolfina's cave. Before long the others joined me, both Adolfina and Theo standing close, possibly to protect me.

I watched a patch of stone the size of a door slowly darken on the wall, as if the stone had suddenly been filled with water, and the voices behind it grew nearer. They sounded like they belonged to a woman and a young child. As I waited I found myself suddenly unable to breathe as the wall in front of us shimmered and darkened. It appeared to become less solid, and in the next moment, through it stepped a white-haired lady and a small child with white curly hair and dimples.

As soon as they were clear of the wall, I ran forward without any hesitation and hugged the old lady. I knew her instantly because she had been part of my life when both of my parents had existed, and I felt as if I had been waiting for her to find me all of my life. Behind me, Craig stepped forward gently, placing a hand on my arm, although I was not sure if it was for my protection or for the visitors' protection.

"Be welcome among us," I heard him say over my shoulder. His voice was filled with respect and possibly a little awe.

"Mother Earth," I said simply, choosing to give the old being her proper title, not really knowing how to address her. Even though I knew that she was the only one who could answer the hundreds of questions that had been in my head since the sorceress called Sarah had told me of the prophesy, I controlled myself, knowing that there would be time later for such questions.

"Hello, child. It has indeed been a while since I have held you. I have watched you often from afar and understand that you have had many adventures. Though at times they were hard, they were needed. It is because of them you are strong. I can sense that strength within you." Her voice was filled with a warm love that soothed me and made most of my worries disappear. As she held me I felt free again, myself again. As we studied each other in silence, I realised that she had not changed since I last remembered her. She still had the same wise, wrinkled yet ageless face I remembered from my childhood. She was dressed in practical travelling clothes, with a cowl wrapped around her shoulders.

"Molly, I would like you to meet Liberty. Although you were very young, I suspect that she is still familiar to you. I know that you have the ability to store more memories than most other beings are capable of."

"I do have a sense that I know her, Mother. It is okay. She is as important to me as I believe I am to her," said a voice that was far too serious for such a young-looking being.

"Molly," I said, feeling a little shy. I hesitated as I held my hand out towards her, knowing that the being in front of me was supposed to be the last one of her kind. She was a Sky Dweller, one who tended to the birds in the trees and their nests in the mountains. I knew that she was as much a part of the planet as were the Mountain, Forest, and Ocean Dwellers I had met. She was beautiful; her skin was white, yet she had blushes of red high on her cheeks, and her eyes were the palest blue. They were mesmerising, the irises appearing to swirl with white like the clouds flitting across a crisp blue winter sky.

Molly stepped forward and bowed her head slightly. "Is she the one whom you have spoken often about, Mother? And is she really a princess? I thought she might have been bigger somehow. We have met bigger princesses than she is, although I admit she smells better than most of the other princesses you have introduced me to. She does not appear as sturdy as you have made her out to be."

"I am sturdy enough for this world. Besides, I thought you may have been a little older," I said, smiling gently, desperately wanting to befriend the little girl.

"I only say that because we seem to have been searching for you for most of my life. I am glad that our searching appears to have come to an end."

Molly frowned at me for a moment more, as if making up her mind whether she really did like me. She must have decided in my favour because she suddenly smiled back, and her smile bought sunshine into the cave. At that point Craig stepped forward and bowed to Mother, breaking the spell that seemed to be weaving itself between Molly and me and binding us together as we once had been as small infants.

"Please do not let me interrupt you, but now all of you appear to be in the right place at the right moment. I have a growing need to protect my people, and I believe your betrothed is getting nearer in his impatient searching for you," Craig said finally.

"Yes, of course. I said I would go as soon as whatever had to happen did, and I believe it has. Therefore, I must make contact with David and the ones who search and make arrangements for us to leave," I said. As I spoke the words, I found myself suddenly feeling a little concerned for my host. Even though he was a man of few words, I knew that he had protected me and kept me safe, and now it was time I returned the favour.

Without another word I stepped away from them all. I could have used the mobile phone to speak with David, but I would get no sense of his real response to me. I wanted to know whether I was in trouble and, if I was, how much. I went back to the cave that I shared with Theo; Starlight, as ever, was close by my side. I sat down and tried to clear my mind of all unnecessary thoughts. I tried to breathe deeply and focus as Dominic had taught me and to reach out my thoughts to him, concentrating solely on David. At first I felt nothing, so I tried to expand my search to anyone who was familiar with my way of communicating. At last, I felt a familiar mind recognise and join with my thoughts; I had finally reached Rachael, who had always had a strong link to me.

We shared the joy of finding each other, relishing the familiar connection in contented silence, but after a few moments she started asking me questions, breaking the spell. I told her I would answer her questions when I saw her face to face. I asked after David, and she told me he was at rest.

I made arrangements with her to meet with one of David's search parties at Daniel's resort in two days, knowing that it would take that long for us to reach there on foot. After the contact had been made with Rachael, there was too much for us to do to allow any time for further socialising. As I made preparations to leave my place of sanctuary, Adolfina stood quietly off to one side watching, with Starlight running back and forth between us, seemingly aware that something was about to happen. When we were packed a woman from a neighbouring cavern came forward with a parcel of food.

As I started down the valley, walking ahead of our small group towards the entrance of the community, I realised that Starlight was not running with me. I stopped and turned towards Adolfina. "I can't bring her with me, can I? "I asked as I walked back to the snow cub to run my hands for what was probably the last time through Starlight's thickening fur.

"I don't think it would be wise. These creatures have evolved to live among the mountains," Theo answered for her.

"I will care for her well, and she has a long memory. Space will not break the bond you share," added Adolfina as she sensed my growing sadness.

"I know, it's just . . ." I stopped speaking as I felt an incredible sadness at leaving the simplicity of these beings and their community.

"Ssshhh, child, it is time for us to go." It was Mother who took my hand to give me strength.

"Okay then, now that there is no other reason for us to stay, we will go. Thank you," I said as the tears started to spill down my cheeks, freezing on my face as the wind from the mountains began to reach me.

Adolfina stepped forward and embraced me softly. Then she stepped back and placed her hand gently on Starlight, restraining her from going forward with me. I gently rubbed my face in Starlight's fur, breathing in her damp earthiness. "I will come back. You are mine, and we will be together again. You have my oath."

I had a sense of Molly observing the emotion among us all, without showing any herself, as if she was making a mental note of our behaviour. I watched as Theo stepped forward and gently touched Adolfina's arm, the look between them tender. When I could look no more without my heart breaking, I turned with Mother and started walking on the unseen path that took us towards the 'outside,' where my life would begin again.

Craig walked with us to the edge of the valley, as always a being of few words. He simply nodded his good-byes to us, smiling his warmth in his own way, before turning back in the direction of his home. He handed me a stone that had been moulded and smoothed into the shape of a snowflake, its inner iridescence catching the rays of the sun and projecting little dancing prisms of colour onto the snow at my feet.

"It is beautiful. Thank you," I said as the tears slowly began to trickle unchecked down my cheeks. As I watched his retreating back, I finally started to look forward to going home, but knowing if I ever needed a place to escape, I would be welcome in these mountains.

Chapter 55

We took no guide with us. Although I had learned some skills, it was Molly and Mother Earth who took on the role of guides. We walked in silence for a while, our snowshoes gliding effortlessly over the crisp and clean untouched snow. The trek towards the resort appeared much easier than the trek away had been, and we made good time. The whiteness of the snow-covered mountains was as beautiful and serene as I had remembered it. I tried to take in as much of the scenery as possible, wanting to imprint it in my memory. The snow we walked through was no deeper than our ankles this time, and all of us stayed together, following Mother's direction. We all knew that although the ground looked level, there were places that hid deep holes and cracks that were capable of swallowing beings whole.

In the far distance, as the sun began to set, I heard the first howlings of the snow wolves. Among them I imagined I heard the higher-pitched one of a very young cub. I knew deep down that it was my Starlight; I knew she was calling to me, and it made my heart ache in response. Molly, as if sensing my pain, came up to walk beside me, and after a few steps she slipped her small hand into mine.

"Would you like me to embrace you? Mother tells me it is how you take comfort," she said, her face so serious that eventually I had to smile.

"Thank you, Molly. That would be nice." I held open my arms and she stepped into them. Her embrace had a surprising strength to it; she held me in position even as I prepared to step away from her. Eventually I began to relax and enjoy her embrace. Her strength gave me strength. Her curly hair tickled at my face, and she smelled fresh as only the air of the outside in the wide open expanse could smell—clean and untainted.

"Enough of that, you two, although it is lovely to see we have an appointment to keep and a destiny to follow," said Mother as she separated us.

To save time Theo held open his arms, lifted both me and Molly into them, and continued to walk. As the night drew near and darkness fell, Mother left us, explaining that she had other 'events' to attend to. Molly had found the place in between Theo's neck and shoulder to rest her head and appeared not to notice when Mother left. I was kept awake by my thoughts.

We finally crested a hill and saw the lights of the resort. My heart skipped a beat as I saw the red and gold of the royal crest fluttering on a pole in front of the main chalet. I clutched Theo tighter as he started walking forward towards the light. As soon as we came into view, figures began to appear and I could hear the excitement of our approach in the voices of the guards.

"Theo, put me down," I said softly, wriggling as I tried to straighten my fur coat.

"Are you sure, Liberty?" he said as he placed me gently on my feet.

"And me." Molly came and stood with me, her small hand back in mine again. Together we walked slowly forward, Theo at my other side. At first I could not see anyone whom I recognised. Then he was there, and as always he took my breath away, my beloved.

It was at that point that I let go of Molly's hand and started to run. I didn't stop until I was no more a foot away from him. I did not move and neither did he as we stared at each other, my heart aching as I waited for him to smile, to speak, to do something.

As the others approached, he silently held out his hand and I took it. He pulled me close and held me as he always had. For just a moment we managed to create our own moment, our own space where no other being existed. I knew in that moment that the bond between us still existed and that even though events might test that bond, nothing would break it.

Review Requested:

If you loved this book, would you please provide
a review at Amazon.com?

9 781946 539236